The Fourth Seal: Behold a Pale Horse

A Tale of the Apocalypse and Armageddon By J. R. Reagan

Copyright © 2020 J.R. Reagan
All Rights Reserved

This is a work of fiction. Names, characters, places, and incidents either are the product of the author's imagination or are used fictitiously, and any resemblance to actual persons, living or dead, businesses, companies, events, or locales is entirely coincidental.

No part of this book may be reproduced, or stored in a retrieval system, or transmitted in any form or by any means, electronic, mechanical, photocopying, recording, or otherwise, without express written permission of the author.

Cover Art includes excise from "The Nightmare," Henry Fuseli, 1781.

Dedication: With much thanks to my editors, Janet, Cara, and Alison, without whose support and assistance this book might never have been published.

J.R. Reagan

TABLE OF CONTENTS:
PROLOGUE – ALEXANDRIA 1
CHAPTER-1 – CHAG HASUKKOT, (Festival of Tabernacles)..7
CHAPTER-2 – THE GATHERING OF EAGLES 33
CHAPTER-3 – THE WITCHING HOUR 58
CHAPTER- 4 – MURDER IN MEDICAL 84
CHAPTER-5 – OBELISKS IN THE CITY 106
CHAPTER-6 – EXODUS and POLICE.......................126
CHAPTER- 7 – INTO THE SUEZ 144
CHAPTER-8 – HELP FROM AVARHOUSE.............161
CHAPTER-9 – FLIGHT OF THE SCARECROWS ...183
CHAPTER- 10 – RESPECT HIS WISHES 199
CHAPTER-11 – STRIKING FOR THE SHENANDOAH 217
CHAPTER-12 - OH! TO LIVE LIKE PHARAOH! 237
CHAPTER- 13 – ANOTHER CORPSE 258
CHAPTER-14 – BUREAUCRATS AND THE HUE AND CRY 275
CHAPTER-15 – ENGINES AND WRECKED CONVOYS...297
CHAPTER- 16 - MURDERS IN THE FAN ROOM ...312
CHAPTER-17 – MORE DAMN POWERPOINTS.....331
CHAPTER-18 – WE'RE NOT MONSTERS, WE'RE A DISEASE 350

CHAPTER- 19 – MURDERED SAILORS AND NEW TACTICS 366

CHAPTER-20 – THE NEW SOLDIERS.....................383

CHAPTER-21 – DOING THE ARITHMETIC 402

CHAPTER- 22 – SHOOT THEM IN THE HEAD......420

CHAPTER-23 – AVARHOUSE'S GUN.....................440

CHAPTER-24 – MOTHER, DAUGHTER AND DRONES 459

APPENDIX 1 469

*Poem: On Passing Deadman's Island, Thomas Moore, 1804..479

Revelation 6:7-8 – KJV:

And when he had opened the fourth seal, I heard the voice of the fourth beast say, Come and see. And I looked, and behold a pale horse: and his name that sat on him was Death, and Hell followed with him. And power was given unto them over the fourth part of the earth, to kill with sword, and with hunger, and with death, and with the beasts of the earth.

PROLOGUE – ALEXANDRIA

The house, the house, somewhere inside the house; sparks without fire, smoke without flame; it woke the Captain like an electric shock. He jerked awake and stared out into the darkness. There, at the door, he could see the shimmering outline of a man. The Captain leapt from his bed and moved across the room searching for a weapon. He watched the figure at the door even as he searched. Finally, he found a wall switch and turned on a bedroom light.

He recognized his father at the door—dead these seven years. His father was trying to speak but made no sound. He waved his hands in front of his face like a man trying to clear frost from a window. As soon as the light went on, the figure began to grow fainter and more obscure. In a moment he was gone.

The Captain stared at the place his father had stood. He did not move until his wife stirred sleepily and asked what was wrong. He turned off the light and got back into bed. Gray light sifting through the bedroom windows cast shadows across the room. He looked out into the darkness and pretended to sleep.

J.R. Reagan

Crew of the USS Cyclops
Identified by Name and Rank/Rate:

Alexander - LT, Communications Department Head
Allred ET3 - Sailor Observing Trading on Fantail
Alschbach - Commander, Repair Department Head, Suicide
Arehart - ET2, Missing Day Two
Asper - HM1, Missing Day Two
Beggs - ET1 Missing Day One
Branson - PS3 Defendant Captain's Mast, Drunkenness
Carroll - ET2 Murder, Tool Issue Storeroom 4-49-4-A
Crammer - Lieutenant Commander, Assistant Repair Department Head
George - ENS, Weapons Division officer
Dempsey - ET3 - Defendant Captain's Mast, Fighting
Gottschalk - PS2, Murder, Storeroom 3-10-2-A
Hardwick - MA1
Jett - Ensign, Acting Admin Department Head
Lamb - Lieutenant Commander, Chief Engineer
McKinely - LT, Repair Department, Duty section OOD
Medioldia - GMC, Weapons Department Chief
Merriam, LT, Deck Department, Duty section OOD
Miller - CWO2, Weapons, Radio news junkie
Minch - FN3, Accused of Proselytizing
Mitchell - LN2, Legalman, Missing Day One
Montgomery - Lieutenant Commander, Acting Supply Department Head

Mollencop – Commander, Supply Department Head, Missing Day One
Moore - MM1, Murder, Engineering
Morgan - Commander, Ships Dentist, Missing Day One
Mulvey - MR2, Murder, Medical Spaces
Newton - GM2, Wounded Day Nine
Nowlin - HM2
O'Day - Lieutenant Commander, First Lieutenant
Overton - LT, Communications, Duty section OOD
Owens - CS3, Missing after Drinking Party
Oxford - MA2, Missing Day 13
Patnaude - HT1, Murder, Fan Room
Parks – LS3, Defendant Captain's Mast, Drunkenness
Perry - GM2
Peters - LT, Ship's Doctor
Pope - MR3, Accused of Harassment
Porter - MA2
Potz – Ensign, Administrative Department Head, Missing Day One
Powers - Lieutenant Commander, Weapons Department Head
Straus – SH3, Missing Day Four
Strong – PS3, Supply, Missing after Drinking Party
Unger - CWO2, Repair
Urquhart - PSC, Admin Chief
Vidlund - MM3, Sexual Harassment Complainant
Wise - HT3, Murder, Fan Room
Worley - Commander (XO)/Acting Captain of USS Cyclops

J.R. Reagan

Deck Log - First Day

OPNAV 3100/99 (Rev 7-84) S/N 0107-LF-031-0498		**SHIP'S DECK LOG SHEET**		IF CLASSIFIED STAMP SECURITY MARKING HERE	

USE BLACK INK TO FILL IN THIS LOG

SHIP TYPE	HULL NUMBER	YEAR	MONTH	ZONE	DAY	USS __CYCLOPS__	CLASS	HANDL
D A	AS 09 43	09	8		15	AT / PASSAGE FROM __PORT SAID__ TO _____	E	

POSITION ZONE TIME	POSITION ZONE TIME	POSITION ZONE TIME	LEGEND
0800 L_____, BY ___ A_____, BY ___	1200 L_____, BY ___ A_____, BY ___	2000 L_____, BY ___ A_____, BY ___	1 - CELESTIAL 2 - ELECTRONIC 3 - VISUAL 4 - D R

TIME	ORDER	CSE	SPEED	DEPTH	RECORD OF EVENTS OF THE DAY
1200					ASSUMED THE WATCH. ANCHORED AS BEFORE. WATCH REPORTS CONDITIONS NORMAL. LIEUTENANT D. M. OVERTON, USN
1535					CALL TO GENERAL QUARTERS UNEXPLAINED LOSS OF CAPTAIN AND LARGE NUMBER OF CREW.
16-1800					ASSUMED THE WATCH. ANCHORED AS BEFORE. CREW REMAINS AT GENERAL QUARTERS.* LIEUTENANT D. M. OVERTON, USN
					*SEE ATTACHED MUSTER REPORT FOR CREW MEMBERS IDENTIFIED AS MISSING.

REPORT SYMBOL OPNAV 2100-10	IF CLASSIFIED STAMP REVIEW / DECLASSIFICATION DATE HERE	IF CLASSIFIED STAMP SECURITY MARKING HERE

The Fourth Seal: Behold a Pale Horse

Main Deck - Aft, Quarter Deck

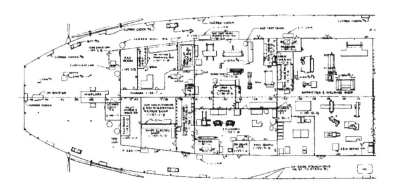

The Chapter of Not Rotting in Khert-neter:

The Osiris Ani saith - O thou who art motionless, O thou who art motionless, O thou whose members are motionless, like unto those of Osiris. Thy members shall not be motionless, they shall not rot, they shall not crumble away, they shall not fall into decay. My members shall be made [permanent] for me as if I were Osiris.

The Papyrus of Ani, (The Egyptian Book of the Dead), 1240 BC, Translated by E.A. Wallis Budge 1914.

CHAPTER-1 – CHAG HASUKKOT, (Festival of Tabernacles)

Monday, Day One: Port Said, Egypt

Lieutenant Irawell watched the small boats traveling to and from his ship. Riding at anchor in Port Said, the USS Cyclops was not due to transit the Suez Canal for another day and, despite the poor weather, the Egyptians were coming out to trade.

As the boats approached the ship, the Lieutenant noticed an Egyptian patrol craft consistently moving to intercept. "I didn't know the Egyptians were providing security."

The Lieutenant spoke to no one in particular, but one of the chiefs responded. "Not security. They're making sure the trading boats are being manned by locals. Any outsiders are being told to sheer off. If you watch close, you can see small gifts to the Egyptian crew are also welcome."

Sure enough, as a small boat began its approach the Egyptian patrol craft drew near. An argument commenced with much waving of hands and arms. The Lieutenant could not hear the argument, but the gestures were unmistakable.

The Cyclops' utility boats provided force protection for the ship from any craft approaching by water. When one of the utility boats began to drift towards the arguing Egyptians, the crew of the small trading boat revved their outboard and took off. The traders in the boats already alongside Cyclops looked up for a moment, and then went back to bargaining with the American sailors standing on the fantail.

A sailing warehouse and repair shop, USS Cyclops provided essential services to the fleet. She was over two football fields in length, 85 feet abeam, and 23,000 long tons. Her main deck, the uppermost complete deck running bow to stern, had five levels above, and six decks below, all ending with the ship's hold and inner hold. She was a great floating leviathan.

Even when she first came out of the yards, Cyclops lacked the power and the elegance of a warship, and with the passage of time, she had grown more infirm. Unreliable engines leaked a variety of fluids. Streaks of red rust colored her gunwales. The nonskid on her decks flaked and peeled with gray psoriasis. In high seas, she waddled and rolled. She had transitioned from ugly stepsister to ancient spinster, an arthritic dowager unrelieved by any sense of irony or humor.

The crew that manned the ship's interior ordinarily had little reason to climb to the higher levels. Their work areas were located so deep within that the inhabitants had developed a morlockian view of sunlight. Too jaded to find a distant view of Port Said of any interest, only trade with the Egyptians brought them up to the fantail. It would be the closest they would be allowed to Egypt or the Egyptians.

Looking down from the ship's quarterdeck, the Lieutenant watched the traders haggling with the sailors along the ship's rails. The Egyptians were not allowed on the ship any more than the Americans were allowed ashore, so agreed exchanges went back and forth in straw baskets tied up with rope and string.

The Egyptians offered a variety of souvenirs. The sailors offered dollars, but the Egyptians seemed little interested in cash, preferring cigarettes or articles of clothing. For a time there was a brisk trade in ball caps embroidered with the ship's name.

The Lieutenant's attention was drawn to one trader with open pustules on his hands and face. He was offering up a small package swathed in bandages. The Lieutenant called down to one of the chiefs on the fantail. "What's that package he's trying to sell?"

The chief leaned over and talked to the traders and then called back a response. "He's selling a mummified cat."

"Not allowed, Chief; don't let that thing aboard. No organics permitted."

As the Lieutenant continued to watch the trading, he could hear a radio playing nearby. He looked over to see two of the ship's warrant officers, Miller and Unger, fooling with a large portable. A voice on the radio warbled up and down. "—tourists were visiting the Cathedral when, allegedly, the preserved remains of the saint opened her eyes. One visitor claims to have captured the moment on video when he was recording a tour of the church. The camera ... body of a little girl, who died over 300-years-ago, suddenly opening her eyes. Millions ... viewed the video since—"

Miller spoke to the Lieutenant as he twisted the radio antenna seeking better reception. "Judge, you definitely don't want them bringing any dead cats aboard. There's been a story in the news that Paris has quarantined all the cats in the city because of some disease."

Unger now spoke up. "I heard a news story this morning that the disease may have crossed species."

As Unger and Miller continued to talk about the cats of Paris, the Lieutenant returned to watching the fantail. A sailor offered a package of dried beef for trade, and the Egyptians became loud and agitated. Soon, cookies, candy bars, chips, packages of jerky, even cans of soup, were being lowered to the trading boats. Brass pyramids, plastic sphinxes, and embroidered scarves were raised to the fantail in exchange.

One of the boats offered up figurines of ancient Egyptian gods. A statue of a woman with the head of a frog excited the bidding; now they offered a bird's head on a man's body; next, a lion's head on a woman's body.

When the Lieutenant saw a bag of grapes go into one of the straw baskets in exchange for a terracotta god, he tried to get the attention of one of the chiefs below. The ship's store did not sell fresh produce. The other foodstuff might have come from private stocks, but no way had a bag of grapes come across the Atlantic in some sailor's locker. The Lieutenant could even see the Hebrew letters marking the bag. Clearly, the grapes came from the supplies taken onboard during the ship's underway replenishment from Israel prior to arrival in Egypt.

As soon as the Lieutenant called out, the sailor responsible knew to disappear. He took his statue and bolted. The Lieutenant called down again. "Who was that man?"

One of the chiefs looked up but just shrugged his shoulders.

Standing behind the Lieutenant, Miller and Unger's struggles with radio reception continued to produce disjointed news stories.

"—study shows that aging might be reversed. We know humans are more complex … lab animals, and there are additional risks with rejuvenation, but … study proves that aging is plastic. Scientists now concede—

"—known for some time that … was possible to turn adult cells back to an earlier state,

"—feared that … could damage organs or even trigger cancer. This discovery, reversing aging, without causing—"

Miller spun his radio antenna like a mystic with a divining rod, and the Lieutenant listened inattentively. Meanwhile, he continued to monitor the trading on the fantail. He noticed a figurine of what looked like a dog's head on a man's body. He called down to one of the traders in the boat. "Hey you! What do you have there?"

In response, the trader held up the figurine of an Egyptian god, half jackal, half-man.

"That's the one I want. How much?"

"You have food?"

"I have dollars."

"No dollars, food."

"I don't have any food to trade, I have dollars."

"You have dried meat?"—holding up a bag of beef jerky.

The Lieutenant called down to the trader. "I don't have jerky. I don't have bread. I don't have soup. I have dollars."

One of the Egyptians on an adjacent boat began to protest. He pointed at the figurine. "Haram! Haram!"

The Lieutenant tried to regain the attention of the first Egyptian. He took some cash from his wallet. He had one of the baskets tossed up to the quarterdeck and he lowered the cash down to the boat.

The Egyptians continued to argue. The first Egyptian took the cash and put the figurine into the basket, but before the basket could be raised to the ship, the second Egyptian reached across, pulled the figurine out of the basket, and threw it into the water.

"You son of a bitch, that was mine."

The first Egyptian looked up at the Lieutenant and shrugged his shoulders. As the boat drifted away, the Lieutenant shouted at the trader, but no one attempted to return his money.

The Lieutenant called out loudly, "Son of a bitch. You rag-headed thief. God damned Arabs."

The Lieutenant quieted only when he realized the sailors and the traders were all looking at him. He almost launched into another tirade but stopped himself. He caught his breath and leaned against the rail nonchalantly.

Miller spoke up as he continued to toy with the radio. "Judge, I don't think Egyptians are necessarily Arabs."

The Lieutenant looked over, preparing to say something, but then changed his mind. He turned back and pretended to watch the trading on the fantail. "I stand corrected, God damned Egyptians then."

The Lieutenant heard one of the Petty Officers tittering nearby.

"God damn it, Allred. You don't think I can't hear you over there."

"Yes sir," came the response, together with more giggling.

Now Miller began to laugh and Unger joined him. Soon, all the men along the rail were laughing. After a time the Lieutenant began to laugh as well.

One of the sailors down on the fantail held up a figurine identical to the one lost to the water. "I got one if you want Lieutenant."

"How much?"

"Just a small mark up, thirty bucks," the sailor responded.

"Keep the damn thing." This started the laughter up again.

As the sailors traded away their private stores, the food that remained became more dear. The Egyptians called out and gestured wildly in an effort to gather in the trade. They offered figurines in greater and greater numbers for any food supplies. Their earlier cheerfulness gave way to desperation.

The Egyptian who had traded for the grapes opened the bag as he waited and began to eat. Suddenly, he spit out a partially chewed grape from his mouth. He examined the other grapes and then dumped the entire bag into the water. He called out to the other Egyptians. One of these now opened a loaf of bread; he bit into a slice of the bread and spit it out. He called out in disgust and then he dumped the bag into the water.

The Egyptians stopped offering up items for trade. Instead, they began to argue among themselves. One of the Egyptians took a small oar and banged on the side of the ship. Other Egyptians examined the ship and sailors with suspicion. One of the Egyptians called out to get the attention of the rest. He pointed in the direction of Port Said. The Egyptians ceased their arguments. They spoke quietly among themselves. A consensus was reached and they cast away the lines tying their boats to the ship without a word to the Americans. The traders revved their engines and headed for shore. The Egyptian patrol craft had already gone. Soon only Cyclops' utility boats remained.

The sailors standing along the rails began to wonder aloud what was happening. The Lieutenant and some of the officers left the quarterdeck and climbed to the helo deck for a better view of the area. They scanned the surrounding water and looked towards Port Said, but they saw no reason for the Egyptian's actions.

A sailor hurried up to the officers. "We've been watching through the 'big eyes.' There's a lot of smoke in Port Said."

Unger produced a pair of binoculars. After looking across the water, he passed the glasses around. Columns of smoke rose from the city. The Lieutenant could hear some of the sailors speculating about bombs or terrorists. They argued about how many bombs it would take to make that much smoke. The Lieutenant ignored them and asked to borrow Unger's binoculars.

The head of the weapons department, Lieutenant Commander Powers, came walking along the deck giving directions to his petty officers. When asked what he was doing, he responded in his usual quiet drawl, "XO wants ready lockers ta be opened an' the 50 calibers loaded." It was clear by the way he spoke that Powers had not bothered to point out to the executive officer, Commander Worley, that the 50 caliber machine guns were already loaded, the gunner's mates standing by.

The Lieutenant posed a question to Powers using the sobriquet "Weps." Like many naval experts, Powers' identity had become intertwined with his job. "What's the Captain say about all this Weps?"

Powers shrugged his shoulders. "Hav'in seen the Captain." A moment later he walked away to continue checking on his guns.

As if in response to the Lieutenant's question, the speakers of the 1MC public address system began to blare, "Captain to the bridge, Captain to the bridge."

The sailors on the helo deck turned to look forward; a moment later they went back to their speculations. Smoke rising from Port Said could now be seen without the aid of binoculars.

The 1MC suddenly came alive with the sound of a boatswain's whistle; instantly followed by, "General quarters, general quarters. All hands man your battle stations. This is not a drill." Immediately the klaxon began to bleat, followed again by the call, "General quarters, general quarters."

Lieutenant Irawell headed for his GQ station, the manpower pool located at the crew's mess on the second deck. He rushed below deck and began to make his way forward. This portion of the ship offered no clear passage. The ship's workshops and working spaces provided only a rough path ahead. Exiting the ship's machine shop, he tried to cross over to the starboard side only to find the way blocked by sailors gathering up equipment at one of the repair lockers. Rather than going athwartships, the Lieutenant tried to go forward on the portside. He bumped against the stream of sailors rushing aft. The sailors said nothing as they hurried along the passageways. The heavy tread of their boondockers echoed throughout the ship as the sailors jogged along linoleum clad decks or slid down steel ladders.

The Lieutenant went past the ship's admin offices, past the ship's store, past the barbershop, past his legal offices, and past the scullery. He eventually arrived on the mess decks only to find Ensign Acedian had beaten him there by many minutes.

Acedian was a short, squat man who always appeared overburdened and long-suffering. Formerly a senior enlisted legalman, he had obtained a commission as a limited duty officer in the Judge Advocate General's Corps. With expertise in office and courtroom management, he should have assumed much of the responsibly for the day-to-day operations of the legal department and the Master-at-Arms force from the Lieutenant. In practice, his uncertain work ethic and doubtful reliability made him as much a hindrance as a help. The Lieutenant found much of his energy taken up with checking on whether tasks, reported as accomplished, had actually, and accurately, been completed.

Acedian greeted the Lieutenant as he arrived. Before the Lieutenant had a chance to respond, another call came over the 1MC. "Captain to the bridge, Captain to the bridge."

On the mess decks, the men and women assigned to the manpower pool formed up in orderly ranks. One of the senior petty officers began taking muster.

The sailors who formed the manpower pool were the Lieutenant's responsibility during GQ. They were personnel recently assigned to the ship and not yet qualified for any particular GQ station. Once qualified and certified they would be assigned to one of the repair lockers, or one of the quick reaction forces. Until then, they would be tasked as needed, including providing stretcher bearers for the adjacent medical aid station.

With the muster taken, the sailors dispersed along the bulkheads waiting for orders. The tables and chairs of the mess decks had been stowed away after lunch, so sitting on the deck or leaning against a bulkhead afforded the only option for comfort.

There should have been about thirty sailors in the manpower pool, but it seemed many were missing, including the legal department's one legalman, LN2 Mitchell. The muster report confirmed it; at least six sailors had not reported. The adjacent aid station was also missing a corpsman and a dental tech.

The yeoman assigned to the aid station stood by waiting for directions, the large headphones and microphone of a sound-powered phone rig balanced on her head and chest. Even in the absence of electricity, the sound-powered phone system could operate; but the equipment was antiquated and awkward to carry. The Lieutenant had the yeoman call around to the other phone talkers scattered about the ship to see if she could gather any news. Her efforts to acquire information proved futile, the other operators being equally ignorant, or not bothering to answer her calls.

Over an hour passed, and no information came down from the bridge. The ship remained quiet but for a faint hum of machinery and the ticks and thumps of a ship at anchor. At some point, the air conditioning and ventilation fans had been shut down, and the air grew warm and unpleasant.

The Lieutenant could hear the sailors talking quietly among themselves as they waited in the darkness.

"I seen him in the workspaces. One minute he was there, the next he was gone."

"Did you see him disappear?"

"No, but there was no way he could have gotten out of the space."

A third sailor chimed in, "I heard a CIVMAR was talking to a couple of guys and he disappeared right in front of them. One minute he was there and the next he was gone."

"Did you see it happen?"

"No," he responded, "but I heard it directly from Chief Urquhart and he was there."

Acedian walked over to the Lieutenant and added to the speculation. "I think this is something big, major terrorism.... Where do you think the Captain went?"

"Never mind the Captain, what happened to LN2 Mitchell?"

"I don't know. I was up in the wardroom when everything went down. I looked into legal as I went by, but there was no sign of her."

After another hour of waiting, fatigued by Acedian's conjectures, the Lieutenant decided to make his way up to the bridge. Five ladders later, he reached the 04 level of the ship. As the Lieutenant stepped onto the bridge, he looked over the gathered watchstanders. He could see immediately that the bridge was not nearly as crowded as it should have been during GQ.

He could hear HM1 Asper, one of the ship's corpsmen, telling the executive officer, Commander Worley, that the ship's dentist had disappeared. Flustered by his cross-examination Asper tried to explain. "Sir, I have no idea how or where he went. Commander Morgan was standing right by me one minute and when I looked up, he was gone. He'd been in medical and now we can't find him."

The Master-at-Arms force's leading petty officer, MA1 Hardwick, waited her turn nearby. The XO turned away from the corpsman and towards Hardwick. "MA1, go look for the Captain again. Search again. Get the entire Master-at-Arms force on this. I want the ship searched from the

Captain's cabin to the ship's bilge. You go find him God damn it."

Hardwick responded. "Sir, we're missing all sorts of people, everywhere on the ship."

The XO leaned towards Hardwick. "Did I ask you that? Get going."

Powers now approached the XO. Before he could even speak, the XO gave him an order. "Weps, get your people on this also. Get back to me as soon as you've got something."

As he stood on the bridge listening to the XO issuing orders, the Lieutenant wondering again about Worley's origins. There was something there, a hint of accent that came out with certain words or American idioms. The Lieutenant could not identify the source of this accent, a slight guttering of words, something German or Russian he suspected.

The XO looked over at the Lieutenant for a moment and then turned away. The Lieutenant followed Hardwick off the bridge. "What's going on?"

"The Master Chief is missing. The Captain's missing. All kinds of people are missing. We're supposed to find him, but we already looked!"

"What do you mean everybody is missing? Where did they go? Are we missing boats?"

Hardwick, normally cheerful and efficient, now sputtered nervously. "Nobody knows. Nobody saw them go. They're just missing. MA2 Oxford says he was standing next to the Master Chief when he just disappeared. One minute he was there talking and the next he was just gone."

As soon as Hardwick finished, she hurried away leaving the Lieutenant standing alone in the passageway. With nothing else to do, the Lieutenant decided to head back down to the mess decks. Just before he reached the second deck the 1MC came on once again, "Secure from general quarters."

The Lieutenant diverted to the legal offices instead of going back to his GQ station. He again found Ensign Acedian had gotten there ahead of him. Acedian called out before he could even enter the space. "The XO wants all department heads to report immediately to his conference room with a muster report."

"Muster report? How are we supposed to do that? Our department is scattered all over this ship." Acedian just shrugged his shoulders.

"Have you figured out yet what happened to LN2 Mitchell? She would never just wander off or hide in berthing."

"I haven't seen her since this morning."

"Do we have a muster for our department?"

"LN2 is missing from legal, and I think the Master-at-Arms force is missing a couple of people."

"I saw MA1 when I was on the bridge. The XO has the Master-at-Arms force out looking for the Captain.... " The Lieutenant paused and shook his head before speaking again. "There's no way this many people could have gotten off the ship.

There's no way. I was up on the quarterdeck all afternoon. There were no launches except for the utility boats. No Egyptian was allowed onboard. There was no way anyone could have come aboard or left the ship without being seen by half the crew."

Acedian's response indicated he was no better informed than the Lieutenant. "When I last saw Master Chief, he was walking along the main deck. He asked whether all of the Master-at-Arms force was out walking the decks. There is no way he would have left the ship without a struggle."

A sudden blast of the boatswain's whistle could be heard over the 1MC followed immediately by the call, "Man overboard, man overboard."

Straightaway a different voice came over the 1MC. "What the fuck are you doing? Who told you to call man overboard?"

"I thought you did. I—"

"What the fuck. I never told you—" The 1MC cutout, and then an instant later the speaker could be heard again. "Secure from man overboard drill. Secure from man overboard drill."

A minute passed and a new call came from the 1MC. "All hands report to quarters for muster and inspection. All hands report to quarters for muster and inspection."

The decks again echoed with the noise of hundreds of sailors hurrying along passageways or going up and down the ship's ladders. As the Lieutenant headed to the XO's conference room, he told Acedian to get a proper muster of everyone in the department. He also jokingly suggested that now would not be a good time to fall overboard. Then he joined the stream of sailors moving through the ship.

When the Lieutenant arrived at the XO's conference room, most of the other department heads were already seated. He first noted the presence of the ship's doctor, Lieutenant Peters, who rarely came to these meetings. The assistant department head for supply, Lieutenant Commander Montgomery, attended rather than his boss. The admin department was also represented by the deputy, Ensign Jett. Commander Alschbach of repair and Lieutenant Alexander for communications sat at the conference table. On the other side of the table sat the First Lieutenant, Lieutenant Commander O'Day. Lieutenant Commander Powers of the weapons department head had decided to sit on the couch across from the entranceway. No one appeared for engineering, nor was any civilian mariner present.

The XO was speaking tersely to Montgomery, "Commander Mollencop is missing?"

"Yes sir, we can't find him."

"And Ensign Potz?" the XO asked.

It was Jett who answered this question, "Yes, sir. She was here this morning and now she's gone."

The XO then turned on Lieutenant Peters, "And you're telling me Doc Morgan disappeared in the middle of a procedure? You're clueless where he went to?"

The XO did not wait for a response. He held a draft message in his hand. He scribbled something and handed it to Lieutenant Alexander. "Get that message out right away." He then turned his attention to Commander Alschbach. "How many are you missing?"

Alschbach did not try to hide his surprise. "We haven't had time to take a proper muster yet!"

"Bullshit. You should know by now." The XO turned on Lieutenant Irawell as he took a seat by Powers. "What about legal?"

"I don't know sir. I'm guessing at least three missing." As soon as he spoke, he heard Powers clucking his tongue in disapproval.

The XO pounced. "What do you mean, 'you guess?' You don't know? A guess is not acceptable. If you don't know you need to find out!"

"Yes sir." He could have responded with an emphatic. "Yes sir! Right away sir!" Now he starred back at the XO and remained silent.

The XO turned his attention to the First Lieutenant, but O'Day preempted him. "This is bullshit. We haven't had time to take a proper muster. You've had us at general quarters all afternoon."

The XO waved his hand dismissively. "Get your departments together and get a proper muster done! Get your reports into admin!"

As the officers left, the Lieutenant cornered Doc Peters in the passageway. "Do we know what happened yet?"

"Don't know. The Captain, the Master Chief, supply, both chaplains, a lot of people missing. God knows how many of the crew are missing."

The Lieutenant made his way down to the legal office on the second deck. On the way, he stopped by the Master-at-Arms office. He found only the duty petty officer, MA2 Porter, present. He gathered that MA1 Hardwick still wandered the ship looking for the Captain.

As the Lieutenant went past the mess decks, he noted several crew members drifting about. It looked like much of the crew had finished with muster, but instead of going to their workspaces, they stood in the passageway sharing in scuttlebutt.

Shortly after the Lieutenant's return to his office, Hardwick arrived. As she stepped into the office her fatigue and anxiousness were obvious.

"I don't know what to do sir! I told the XO we can't find the Captain, but he doesn't want to hear it. When I tried to tell him, he went off again. I've never been talked to that way…. Can you talk to him, sir?"

Now it was Lieutenant's turn to shrug his shoulders. Hardwick left and went back to the search.

The Lieutenant waited in his office for the muster. As he waited, he tried to focus on his usual tasks. He had a variety of papers to get through, including at least one lengthy review of court-martial, but nothing in the paperwork could draw his attention. In the end, he gave up any pretense at working and left the space. He went out on the weather deck hoping to walk off his unease and apprehension. Ashore, smoke from Port Said continued to rise above the city, diffusing the light of the sunset.

The Lieutenant found Miller back out on deck with Unger still working the portable radio. Miller turned various knobs and pointed the radio's antenna in different directions. As the Lieutenant approached he could hear the educated voice of the BBC newsreader fading in and out.

"—attacks that have been reported in Jerusalem. The disappearances reported in Rome and Berlin have now reached—

"—information will be provided when—"

"—the Prime Minister has announced—"

Unger spoke up when he noticed the Lieutenant. "Judge, I heard there were all sorts of Pinnacle and Navy Blue messages flashing from the ships in the Med. It's not just us, hundreds have gone missing."

Miller spoke up as well. "It's not just in the Middle East. Rome has had a major plane crash. Tel Aviv, Rome. At least one over Germany. Planes are just falling out of the sky."

Unger spoke again. "It must be some sort of new weapon, like that neutron bomb."

Miller quickly responded. "Bullshit, nobody has a bomb that makes people disappear. Anyway, this is happening all over. We should have seen something, airplanes, rockets—"

"Not if they were in outer space."

"What do you mean—Aliens?"

"No, space weapons in the space stations, Chinese or Russian maybe."

"Why would the Russians or the Chinese want to make everyone disappear?"

A sudden increase in the radio's volume interrupted the argument. "—news blackout in Egypt. We have confirmed reports that significant numbers of people in Rome are missing. Many of the missing confirmed to be children. Eyewitnesses are reporting that people have simply disappeared while… activities…"

As the signal once again began to fade, all three men leaned in towards the radio to listen. "… of bombings throughout the city have apparently been made in error. Many of the initial accidents…vehicular crashes or unattended equipment."

Unger spoke again. "I told you, some new kind of attack. Not bombs, crashed cars."

Miller turned to the Lieutenant. "That explains the crashing airplanes maybe, pilots disappeared and sucked away."

The BBC newsreader continued his sporadic reporting. "— confirmed reports from Paris.

Thousands are reported missing. …major aircraft crash at the Rome International Airport."

Another voice on the radio interrupted the first new reader. "Reports coming in from Berlin and Paris—"

They waited for the newsreader to continue but heard only silence. Miller started to adjust the antenna again.

Unger offered helpful advice. "I don't think you lost the station. There'd be static if you lost the station. They've gone silent."

Miller seemed to agree. "Just like I said; people are being disappeared right in the sky."

Unger responded. "I wouldn't want to be in an airplane just now."

"It's just like that movie. People are being disappeared."

Unger responded with a question. "You mean the end of the world? The apocalypse? At the end of the world, the good people go, and the bad people are left?"

Miller responded with a question of his own, "Does that mean we're the bad people?"

Unger took the radio and began trying different frequencies.

Miller spoke again. "If it's the rapture, I can understand Chaplain Joe going, but Chaplain Anne was an Episcopalian and not the good kind."

The BBC newsreader came back on over the static, "—Israel, Egypt, and Lebanon," then the signal faded out again.

With the sun going down, the radio signal became even more intermittent. After a time, the Lieutenant decided to go back to his office.

As the Lieutenant made his way aft, he passed several groups of armed men. Even though the XO had secured from general quarters, sailors still moved around on the weather decks carrying rifles and wearing helmets and body armor. The Lieutenant could see that all of the ship's machine guns remained manned. The sailors stood behind the steel shields of the guns as others piled sandbags to either side.

The lights from Port Said shimmered across the water together with drifting smoke. The usual sounds of the city had gone, no engines, no horns, no sirens. As the Lieutenant headed inside the ship the Adhan issued from a distant minaret. He could not make out the words, but the sing-song call to prayer was unmistakable.

The men at the machine guns stopped talking for a moment. Their faces turned towards the minarets. Sailors stood holding the handles of the guns and looked out over the gun sights. The sailors said nothing as the Lieutenant pushed past to make his way into the interior of the ship.

The Lieutenant headed back to his office on the second deck. He tried to log on to his computer in the hope of finding some real news. Every effort to download information resulted in a locked-up computer.

He turned on the ship's closed-circuit television. Even with all the confusion, the ship's entertainment system had channels up and playing. He stopped and listened for a time to a channel playing country-western music. He switched to a second channel playing an old science fiction movie. He cycled through all the channels hoping for a live news feed but found none. He spoke to himself. "Damn DTS television failing on top of everything else."

The Lieutenant checked the time and was surprised by the lateness of the hour. He did not feel tired. He decided to head up to his stateroom anyway, hit his rack, and get some sleep. After he lay down, it seemed like only a few minutes had passed when his phone began to ring. It was MA1 Hardwick. She struggled to stay calm as she told him about the first of the killings.

Daniel 12:1-2 – KJV:

And at that time shall Michael stand up, the great prince which standeth for the children of thy people: and there shall be a time of trouble, such as never was since there was a nation even to that same time: and at that time thy people shall be delivered, every one that shall be found written in the book.

And many of them that sleep in the dust of the earth shall awake, some to everlasting life, and some to shame and everlasting contempt.

CHAPTER-2 – THE GATHERING OF EAGLES

Monday, Day One: Alexandria, Virginia

Captain Pride awoke to the sound of the radio blasting a news story across the room. "—famous recurring miracle, the blood of San Gennaro, martyred in the third century, typically turns liquid three times a year. The legend states that the failure of the blood to liquefy signals war, famine, disease, or disaster."

The Captain turned away from the bedroom windows and the streaming sunlight. He listened to the sound of his wife, Anna, getting out of bed.

She went to the clock and turned down the volume on the radio-alarm. The newsreader continued at a more civilized volume. "The relic failed to liquefy in September 1939, when World War Two broke out; in 1973, during a cholera outbreak; and in 1980, a year of earthquake. The abbot is urging the faithful to pray."

Anna turned the radio off and turned towards her husband. "Did you fool with the alarm last night?"

He responded with a groggy denial.

She said nothing more as she headed into the bathroom. In a moment he could hear the shower start up.

He looked at the clock and saw that the time was nearly 0700. Normally, they would be up by 0600.

He considered Anna's question again and then questioned himself. "Did I change the alarm at some point?" Followed by a second question, "What time did I fall asleep?"

He had been sitting in the darkness trying to remain awake. If he had stolen an hour of extra sleep, he felt no better rested for it. He replayed in his mind the experience of the night before. Nightmares were a rare thing for him. Never had a nightmare been so vivid.

In a few minutes the shower turned off, and Anna came out of the bathroom drying herself with a towel. She started her morning routine every day like a race. Shower, make-up, wardrobe, each step and motion executed with precision. She could be finished and ready for the day before he even sat up in bed.

He stood up and hurriedly began his routine. He started by going to the sink and brushing his teeth. He picked up his razor and began to shave. As he shaved, he turned his head adjusting his view. The steam from Anna's shower had clouded the mirror beyond usability.

Anna stepped back into the bathroom for a moment. He reached playfully for her as she passed by, but she quickly and easily danced beyond his reach. He took a moment to admire her figure as she went about her routine. After twenty-five years of marriage, and three children, she was still trim and athletic.

He now went for his shower. The hot water began to erase the fatigue that burdened him. He got out of the shower and began to towel off. As he stepped out of the bathroom he called out to Anna. "I had the strangest dream—" He stopped mid-sentence.

Anna sat on the edge of the bed intently watching television dressed only in her slip. He watched as she flipped to a different channel. The newsreaders on the television interviewed one another breathlessly.

First Newsreader: "—a terrorist attack?"

Second Newsreader: "It appears some sort of attack in Jerusalem. The city is at a standstill. There are calls for emergency services throughout the city. A number of fires have been set. We are waiting for an official announcement."

As the newsreaders looked down at their papers, the channel switched to a video feed of people running on the street and smoke rising in columns. The on-screen image began to bounce about as the cameraman took off running. It was unclear whether he was running to or from a disturbance. People could be heard on the video shouting in a language the Captain did not recognize.

Over the sound of the television, the Captain called over to Anna. "What's going on?"

"I don't know," she responded. "There's news about attacks in Jerusalem."

The Captain finished toweling off and began to put on his uniform. Anna continued to flip through television channels. After a few more minutes she turned off the set and finished dressing; then she headed downstairs to start breakfast. She spoke as she left the room. "You have to be crazy to live in Jerusalem. There's always war around the corner in that place."

By the time the Captain joined Anna in the kitchen, she already had the coffee brewing. The kitchen television was on and excited newsreaders carried on in the background as she went about the business of preparing breakfast.

"—no official announcements, but we are getting reports that the Israeli defense forces are being mobilized." As the newsreader finished, the video cut from the studio to the image of a burning aircraft.

A second newsreader began to speak. "This now in, at least one passenger airliner has crashed at Tel Aviv International Airport." The image panned across the wreckage of a large aircraft, broken up and burning. "We are waiting for reports on casualties." The view expanded to show firetrucks racing towards the wreckage. People could be seen trying to escape the smoke and flames. The newsreader continued. "We do not yet know the cause of the crash."

The Captain watched the television, mesmerized. Anna pushed away her breakfast and left the kitchen. She returned a minute later with her car keys. She asked him a question about dinner. He absent-mindedly agreed to her suggestion as he continued to watch television reports about fires in Jerusalem.

Anna kissed him on the cheek and headed for the door. "I'm going to be late getting to school if I don't hurry," she announced as she rushed from the house. When next he looked up she was gone.

By the time he grabbed his car keys, the Captain was well and truly late for work. The extra time taken to watch the news would cost him dearly with the rush hour traffic. Driving in the city was always bad, but a few minutes delay in start time could make the difference between a forty-minute commute and an hour and forty-minutes.

He turned on the radio as soon as he got into his car. By the time he approached the Navy Yard, the subject of the reports had changed to Egypt. The newsreaders competed to see who could demonstrate the most restrained excitement as they talked over each other.

"—have an initial report from Cairo—"

Interrupted by "—are waiting for additional information about—"

Followed by "—an aircraft has crashed at da Vinci?" This was followed by audible gasps.

For a moment, the Captain thought he had lost the station; the newsreaders no longer spoke into their microphones. After a minute the Captain switched off the radio.

The uneven stop and go movements of the cars on the highway fully engaged the Captain's attention. He resisted the urge to change lanes knowing any gain would be temporary. Eventually, a break in the traffic allowed him to make up some lost time as he drove the last few miles to the Navy Yard.

The Captain looked at his watch as he parked his car in his reserved space. The trip into work had taken well over an hour.

As he came into the office, he could hear the television in the conference room. "—now have reports that at least two aircraft have collided at da Vinci International—" He strained to hear the rest, but too many others were speaking. When he entered the conference room, he saw three of his lieutenants and two of his legalmen crowded around the television. The lieutenants busily talked over one another.

As soon as one of his officers saw the Captain he cried out, "Attention on deck!"

The Captain acknowledged the show of respect with a nod of his head. He thought it important to cultivate a certain gravitas. A tall, imposing man anyway, the Captain went to great lengths to make sure that life behind a desk did not erode him physically. He enjoyed competition whether at work or play. When necessary, he could lean into another man's personal space and be quite intimidating.

"Two planes collided?" His voice was sterner than he intended.

"Yes sir, in Rome sir."

"Do they know yet what's going on?"

"No sir!"

The Captain wanted to tell his lieutenants to get back to work, but he knew that would be pointless. Instead, he turned and made his way to his inner office. As soon as he sat down, he booted up his computer.

First, he logged on and checked his email for any unusual orders or instructions, but found nothing. Second, he checked the "Early Bird" to see if the Pentagon had collected key stories about the morning's events, but all the highlighted stories seemed routine.

The Captain turned on his office television and began to check the news reports. The first channel had a story about traffic; the next about the weather. He switched to one of the European channels. Usually, this channel had translators or English subtitles accompanying their stories. Today that nicety had been forgotten.

The reporter spoke rapidly in Italian, but with enough imagery that the Captain could follow the gist of the report. The video showed a driverless car traveling at high speed before leaving the road and crashing into some nearby shops. The Captain wondered aloud, "How can that thing go without a foot on the gas pedal?"

The next video showed an apartment complex burning like a roman candle. A reporter was talking rapidly in Italian and passionately gesturing with his hands.

The Captain began to channel surf hoping to find an English speaker. He came to a German news program. The reader had a heavy accent as he reported in English about a group of children suddenly gone missing. The video showed a school building, empty, except for a few shocked teachers left behind. The report provided sparse details beyond references to Stuttgart.

The Captain switched back to the major US news channels. Now they too were covering events in Europe. The newsreaders remained focused on disappearing pilots and drivers throughout major European cities. They showed a video of a plane losing control on the runway, crossing over to a second runway, and narrowly avoiding collision with another plane. He watched several videos of cars piling up on the highways.

One of the video feeds switched to a school in France. Even without translation, he understood that the French schoolchildren, like the German children before them, had gone missing. Men and women rushed to the school. Women wept and cried out demanding answers from policemen in brightly colored vests. Some of the policemen carried submachine guns. The video switched to a group of reporters rushing to interview an elderly woman in a business suit surrounded by more men and women crying and shouting and pointing.

The Captain reached for his desk phone to call Anna. He dialed and waited. When the line failed to connect, he hung up and tried again. When the call again failed to connect, he turned to his cell phone. The phone indicated dialing, but the call never completed. The phone never rang through. He tried a second time with the same result.

The Captain returned to watching television. One of the European news feeds was playing but this time with commentary worthy of translation. The newsreader read from papers on her desk, accompanied by a dubbed English voice. "— schools and a number of teachers have disappeared with their students. Some teachers have evidently been evacuated with their students to a place of safety."

The Captain switched to a channel broadcasting from London. The British newsreader sounded prepared. The planes sat on the runways, the buses parked, the tube stations closed. One of the reporters pedantically explained that unattended equipment led to accidents and fires.

The Captain switched again and found a station broadcasting from Dublin. This newsreader had the same calm demeanor as the British, but his accent was incomprehensible. Instead of crashes and fires, the Irish newsreader showed a map on an easel and pointed to various locations to illustrate the progress of events, east to west.

Listening to the Irish newsreader made the Captain think of his mother's mother. His Nana had a strong Irish brogue, further complicated by a mouth full of ill-fitting dentures. This made it hard to understand her speech, not that she relied on words if a leather belt was handy. He could hear her voice in his head, tough, all business. "Wet air you go'en to two 'bout tis?"

He spoke out loud as if to answer, "Don't know Nan. I just don't know."

The Captain began to use his computer to search for information closer to home. The internet had slowed to a crawl and it was impossible to get any page to properly load. Images and videos only locked-up the machine. If there were emergencies in Iceland or Canada or the US, he could not tell.

The Captain picked up his phone to call his family. He did not know what to say but felt obligated to suggest something: maybe find a bomb shelter or a deep cellar. First, he again tried Anna. When that call failed to connect, he called each of his daughters, Mary and Martha. They were away at college, and like all college students, wed to their cell phones, but he had no more success reaching them then he had Anna. Whether using the office line or his cell phone, either the calls did not connect or he got the message, "All circuits are busy. Please try again later."

He wondered if there was some kind of electronic interference, or maybe it was simply everybody in the world trying to call everyone else. Part of him wondered if it might be the government.

The Captain left his private office and went back to the main spaces. He listened to the chatter as he walked down the passageway. He could hear the anxiety in some voices. Other voices sounded angry. The Captain realized that only the military remained in the office. The civilians had gone.

The Captain walked into the office of his executive officer, Commander Invidia. Invidia was watching his television so intently he did not notice the Captain's approach. Looking up to see him standing by the desk caused Invidia to shoot up from his chair.

The contrasts between Invidia and the Captain could not have been starker. The Captain was tall where Invidia was slight. Instead of the Captain's coffee-colored skin, Invidia had tight pink skin as smooth and hairless as a baby's bottom. The Captain was gregarious, where Invidia was perpetually nervous.

The Captain began by asking about the missing staffers. "What happened to the civilians? Did they suddenly disappear?"

Invidia had no real explanation. "They didn't disappear. They just got up and left."

"Did you give them permission to leave?"

Invidia's expression turned pained as he responded. "They got their things and left."

Not for the first time did the Captain wish for a more capable executive officer. He would have said something more, but for the interruption of a television newsreader. "This just in, the President has ordered all planes flying in United States airspace to land immediately."

A moment later a message in large red letters began to repeatedly flash on Invidia's computer screen: "All non-essential Military and Federal workers are ordered to return to their homes until further notice. If unable to return home, personnel should shelter in place until further notice."

The Captain and Invidia stepped out into the passageway to be joined by several officers and enlisted personnel. As the message continued to flash across all of the computers in the office, the Captain ordered everyone in sight to head home; the office was closed.

The enlisted personnel and junior officers cleared the office quickly. The Captain reluctantly remained when he saw Invidia go back to his desk. Only when Invidia announced his departure did the Captain reply, "I'll be leaving soon as well, and I'll lock up."

The Captain checked his computer for emails or messages, or anything else official. Other than the emergency message concerning early release, there was nothing. As he left the office, he set the alarm, turned out the lights, and locked the doors.

By the time the Captain left the Navy Yard the traffic had snarled. At every intersection, the drivers took turns blocking oncoming cars. When the Captain approached the onramp for the interstate, another driver rolled forward and blocked the intersection. The Captain had reached his limit. He rolled down his car window and unleashed a stream of invective disputing the parentage and sexual proclivities of the driver blocking the grid.

The second driver did not look at the Captain but did respond with a rude hand gesture.

The Captain reached for his door handle but stopped himself. He had always had a bad temper, and it took an effort for him to control his emotions. He reminded himself that he was an educated man and that his conduct should reflect it; besides, Anna would never approve.

After an hour more of sitting in traffic listening to redundant radio chatter, the newsreaders suddenly announced the President would speak to the nation. A few minutes later the man's voice could be heard over the snapping and clicking of dozens of still cameras.

The President began by declaring a state of emergency. There was great danger, its nature not yet fully understood. The county was not under direct attack, at least not by any human element, but until events were better-understood precautions must be taken. He instructed everyone to get to their homes and get undercover. He announced that there would be a national curfew at dusk. As soon as practical, emergency personnel, first responders, National Guard, and essential military forces were ordered to report to their duty stations. By executive order, gas stations, grocery stores, and all public places would be immediately closed. Stores would reopen as soon as the emergency passed. The President urged people to remain calm. If any looting took place the military and the police were authorized to use deadly force. If hoarding took place, a system of rationing would be established.

He closed with. "God bless us all, and God bless the United States."

The Captain wondered about going back to the Navy Yard. He worked in an office providing legal services – criminal defense, landlord-tenant, wills, powers of attorney, and such. Surely, the Captain and his staff were not "emergency personnel" or "first responders," or "essential military."

He wondered too what "as soon as practical" meant, today, tomorrow, next week? Was it before or after whatever was happening happened? The Captain decided the President's order could not possibly apply to him; besides, with traffic deadlocked, getting back to work would be no easier than getting home.

The Captain wondered about the traffic jam. He suspected the cause to be drivers abandoning their cars and striking out on foot. The Captain considered whether he should abandon his car and head for cover. He began to wish he had stayed in the Navy Yard. He could have gone down to one of the old fallout shelters.

He put these thoughts aside and tried to reach Anna again by cell phone. "All circuits are busy. Please remain off the line. Cell phone usage restricted to emergency services only." When he could not reach his wife, he tried calling his daughters with the same results; "All circuits are busy."

The Captain sat in the stop-go, stop-go, traffic, and listened to the radio. The newsreaders interviewed themselves and talked about emergency measures. Sometime around three o'clock, the reporting stopped. After a moment of dead air time, the newsreaders started again. In their voices, he could hear fear competing with excitement.

"The anomaly has reached the eastern seaboard. There are numerous reports of citizens disappearing. The Government is urging all persons to stay in their homes. You are urged not to leave your home. You are urged not to operate heavy equipment. Emergency shelters are being prepared. I repeat, the Government is urging all Americans to shelter in place until the emergency is over."

He looked out his car window towards the surrounding drivers. He could see many of them looking around as well. Some of the nearby drivers got out of their cars, turned around and around in place, and then got back into their cars.

The Captain turned off his radio and turned off his car engine. Other drivers nearby did the same. A heavy blanket smothered everything with silence; the car horns stopped honking, the car engines went silent, the roads quieted. It was midnight in the afternoon, a city suddenly at rest.

The Captain waited.

After a minute, a car horn began to blare. Other cars took up the honking. The engines of the cars around the Captain were once again running, their drivers once again maneuvering for position.

The Captain felt sure that the "anomaly" must have passed, but he had not seen anyone disappear. The Captain turned on his car engine and rejoined the retreat.

The traffic went back to the same stop and start movement as before. Every so often a car would crawl up on the shoulder of the road, or out on the median to snake past an abandoned car. He could see abandoned cars in both the north and southbound lanes. At least one car had crossed the center line and rolled into oncoming traffic. Many of the stalled drivers vented their anger by blasting their horns. The Captain doubted the drivers of all these cars could have suddenly disappeared. "Bastards walked away from the traffic jam," he decided.

The Captain heard a new sound, the sound of sirens. A few minutes later a police car appeared driving along the shoulder of the road and blasting its siren. After the cop car went by, several cars headed for the shoulder to follow. Before these drivers had made much progress, a fire truck, together with an ambulance appeared. When the fire truck arrived the fireman behind the wheel honked his horn and blasted his siren. The lane jumpers stubbornly remained in place. The fireman responded by inching his truck forward until the bumper pressed up against the car ahead. The firemen then used his truck to push the car off the road. The Captain watched a second car pushed aside. There was no need to push aside a third. The lane jumpers quickly found sufficient space to allow a path for the emergency vehicles, and just as quickly jumped back to the shoulder to follow the firetruck clearing the way ahead.

As the Captain sat in traffic, he could see columns of smoke off in the distance. He could smell smoke in the air. Wisps of smoke drifted down onto the highway like fog. The traffic ignored it and continued to drag along—stopping, starting, stopping, starting.

After several hours, his patience exhausted, the Captain gave up on the direct route home. He exited the interstate and backtracked into the city hoping to find another way across the river.

The city roads were in worse shape than the interstate. Any accidents or abandoned cars posed significant difficulties because of the narrow roads. At one point the Captain got out of his car to help some men push an abandoned car aside. The doors of the car had been left locked, so one of the men smashed a window to gain entry. The keys had been taken from the ignition and the locked steering column proved immovable. They could push the car, but only so far. With the road partially clear, the men headed back to their own cars.

One of the men spoke up as he left. "Whoever owned it didn't disappear; they just walked away."

"A good thing, I guess," responded the second man angrily.

The further the Captain went into the city, the more difficult the drive. He cursed his stupidity for turning away from the highway. It took another three hours to get back to where he started. After several more hours, he eventually crossed the river, but much further north and west than he wanted.

The traffic on the Virginia side was just as snarled as in the city. He began a series of turns and detours to try and get home. He reacted to each traffic stop by trying to find an alternative route. He traveled over a series of back roads with which he had only minimal familiarity.

At one point, two cars ahead of him collided for a minor fender bender. The drivers got out to examine their cars blocking the one-lane going south. Traffic went from a snail's pace to a standstill. The driver of a pickup truck stuck behind the accident began to lean on his horn. When the drivers involved in the accident ignored him, he eased his pickup truck forward into the bumper of the car in front. He revved his engine and began to push. At this moment the two drivers began to yell and shout, but the truck driver ignored them and continued to push his way ahead. The first car pushed into the second and both cars began sliding along the road, their tires leaving behind black skid marks.

As the pickup truck revved and pushed, one of the drivers produced a pistol. He waved it at the truck driver, who ducked down into his cab. The Captain too ducked down. The pickup truck driver quickly did a U-turn into oncoming traffic, narrowly avoiding a collision as he headed back the way he came. After a few more minutes of argument, the two drivers involved in the accident got back into their cars and started up again. A few hundred yards later, all had returned to their prior positions and the same stop, start, stop, start, drive along the road.

The Captain looked over at his glove department wishing he still had his pistol.

That morning, the Captain had driven into work with about half a tank of gas. Normally this would have been more than enough for his trip to work and return home. As he watched the needle on his gas gauge steadily decline, he kept a lookout for an open gas station. He passed several stations marked as closed. He pulled off at a station with all of its lights on, only to find the place abandoned. He tried to fill up his tank anyway, only to find the automatic pumps would not take his credit card. Back on the road, he exited at a second station when he saw a long line of cars lined up out to the street. After pulling over, he discovered this station, like the others, was closed. The orderly lines of cars snaking back from the pumps had all been abandoned.

He abandoned his car when it ran out of gas and sputtered to a stop on a two-lane road. He tried repeatedly to restart the engine as the traffic backed up behind him. In due course, a couple of men got out of their vehicles and helped him push his car aside. There was no shoulder at this portion of the road, but there was a deep ditch hidden in the grass. His right front tire sank into the ditch as they rolled the car forward. He could see it would take a tow truck to get it out again. The left rear bumper of the car jutted out onto the road but left just enough room for traffic to get around.

Walking home for the Captain became something of a release. His legs and back had been cramping from the hours of stop and go driving. At times, he walked faster than the cars crawling along the road. He also did not miss the radio. He felt more relaxed away from the barrage of speculation and panic the radio had been serving up all day.

As he walked into town, the Captain saw that most businesses had closed, even the bars. People hurried along the sidewalks looking like fugitives. Despite the President's curfew, other people stood about on street corners talking among themselves. As he passed, they looked at his uniform as he if he should know something, but no one bothered him directly.

He passed by several car accidents as he walked. In one instance, two cars had come together in an intersection. The damage to the cars and the debris on the road indicated they had collided at high speed. In the second and third instances, cars had left the road, and driven into parked cars. One of the cars had knocked over a street lamp. In all instances, the drivers had not bothered to remain with their wrecked vehicles.

Finally, the Captain arrived home, a three-story townhouse on the waterfront, across from a small marina. Reflectively, he looked up and down the street for Anna's car, but he did not see it. Empty cars were parked along the road with no living persons in sight. The neighboring condos, stores, and restaurants that lined the riverfront were all dark.

He went into his house and called out, but no one answered. He turned on the lights and checked the rooms. Nothing was in disarray, but

Anna's purse and work bag were gone. He went to the answering machine. It held only one message, a call from a telemarketer the day before.

With a growing sense of alarm, the Captain again tried calling Anna on his cell phone, and once again the phone failed to connect. He then tried calling on the landline. He could hear the phone ringing, but the result was the same.

The Captain tried to call his daughters at their colleges. He made numerous attempts to get through, all failures. On one try he got the "all circuits are busy," message. He eventually sent out text messages on his cell phone, but he could not tell if the messages went through.

He sat down at his computer to check for email messages. The computer could not sync his account. He prepared a quick email to send to his wife and daughters, but the account cycled endlessly. He thought it doubtful that the message went out.

The Captain went back outside and again looked up and down the street for Anna's car. As he stood outside his home, he could see a light on in the house of his immediate neighbors, the Delaneys. He began to walk towards their house and then stopped. He had only a nodding acquaintance with his neighbors. Anna had been friendly with them, but he had been indifferent.

He spoke to himself aloud, "She's probably still at work." This made the most sense. She would never leave her students alone at school. In all of the chaos, quite likely, she was "sheltering in place" waiting on missing parents.

He considered whether he should walk to Anna's job. The school was miles away and it would take hours to get there, and who knew what the police might do with the curfew. If she was driving while he was walking, she would likely go past him in the dark. This last decided him. It would be better to wait.

He went back into his house and again tried to reach Anna by phone. Once again the call failed.

He turned on the television. The commentators talked anxiously about the disappearances across the United States. There were few reports about Europe now. This changed when the commentators began to discuss rioting in Paris.

First Commentator: "Incredible. This is the first such report we've had."

Second Commentator: "Mass hysteria now taking hold in Europe. People are panicked. We should expect these sorts of reports. The world is ending as far as many of these people are concerned. We should expect reports linked to every myth of apocalypse or Armageddon."

Third Commentator: "We need to remind people that we have a de-facto news blackout right now. We cannot sort out the facts from the chaff. These reports are right now … unsubstantiated."

First Commentator: "I think you're right."

Second Commentator: "I feel compelled to emphasize that these reports are unsubstantiated. Still, people must remain in their homes...."

The Captain was reconsidering whether to go and knock on his neighbor's door when the power went out. After a moment it came back on with a hiss and a ping. He looked out the window. The street lights were on, but every house on the street was dark.

The Captain stepped back outside. He sat at the top of the landing leading into his home. He kept watching the road looking for Anna. After a time, his head began nodding forward as he fought to stay awake.

The Captain went back into his house. He sat down in an easy chair. He watched the television hoping it would help to keep him awake. In the town, in the distance, he could hear what sounded like gunshots, a faint "Pop, pop," echoing along the waterfront. A moment later he heard the sound again, "Pop, pop, pop." He muted the sound of the television set and listened carefully, but the town had quieted, even the noise from the occasional passing car had stopped.

It was a long time since the Captain had felt so tired. He let his eyes close. He intended to rest only for a moment.

He was fast asleep when the television began to show the images of monsters.

J.R. Reagan

Flight from Memphis, Tennessee

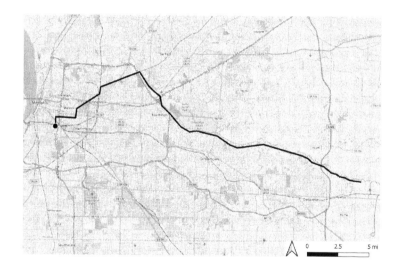

Entitled, The Night Journey; Revealed At Mecca:

We well know with what design they hearken, when they hearken unto thee, and when they privately discourse together: when the ungodly say, Ye follow no other than a madman.

Behold! what epithets they bestow on thee. But they are deceived; neither can they find any just occasion to reproach thee.

They also say, After we shall have become bones and dust, shall we surely be raised a new creature?

Answer, Be ye stones, or iron, or some creature more improbable in your opinions to be raised to life.

But they will say, Who shall restore us to life?

Answer, He who created you the first time: and they will wag their heads at thee, saying, When shall this be? Answer, Peradventure it is nigh.

On that day shall GOD call you forth from your sepulchres, and ye shall obey, with celebration of his praise; and ye shall think that ye tarried but a little while.

The Koran, Chapter XVII, The Night Journey; Translated by George Sales, 1734.

CHAPTER-3 – THE WITCHING HOUR

Tuesday, Ante Meridiem: Memphis, Tennessee

The General fought against the earth. He shifted the soil here; he punched his hand there. He kicked and pushed. He dug and twisted. When he could not break free he began to panic. Soon he would run out of air; soon he would suffocate, but the earth did not choke him. He continued to push and dig and worm his way out. His muscles did not tire. His lungs did not gasp.

He wondered how long had he been buried? How long had he been trying to free himself? He did not know. He had no sense of time. He had no sense of even up or down.

He had nearly given up when he felt and heard others digging around him. He found new confidence and started again to struggle. He pushed his hands up and began to break free. As the General pushed his way up out of the earth others pulled at him. For a moment he resisted, but then he realized they were helping to pull him to the surface.

When the General emerged from the earth, he knew he should be breathless, but he felt no discomfort. He did not breathe the air so much as taste it. He spit the dirt from his mouth, but more than dirt. He spit teeth out into his hand. He examined the false teeth there in his palm. He reached a long dirty finger into his mouth. He gingerly began to exam his gums. He had teeth again! He bit down and ground his teeth as a test. There was no pain. He had strong, healthy teeth!

He began to shake the dirt from his hair. The dirt fell away, but so did clumps of hair. He reached up and touched his face and beard. Dirt and tufts of facial hair dropped away. His face and his fingertips had little sensation. His nose and his lips were a ruin.

He looked down at his body. His chest was thin and wasted. He examined his hands and arms. His fingers were narrow and elongated, the nails black, thick, curved, and sharp, more like the claws of a bear than the hands of a man. His skin was stretched tight as a scar. The color of his flesh was as black as any colored man's, dry as old leather.

He looked down at his clothes. Fragments of cloth were dropping to the ground. The sleeves of his jacket were covered with braid, once gold, now black. The heavy braid was the only thing keeping the remnants of his coat from falling away. He recognized the remains of his uniform, one he had not worn for many years. He was without trousers or boots. He tried to cover himself with the dirty silk sash he wore around his waist.

He was a carnival mummy wrapped in rags. He was dirty and almost naked, physically unrecognizable, but there was something else; he was strong. He could feel it. It had been a long time since he had felt so strong.

The General stood and shook the dirt from his head. He brushed the dirt from his face. He cleared the dirt from his eyes and looked up at the stars. The sky was filled with bright, bright, stars, and he was free of darkness.

Suddenly the General felt pain burning into his gut. Hunger and thirst threatened to double him over. He had never been so hungry, so thirsty. He nearly fell to the ground, and then just as suddenly, the pain abated.

Two figures stood beside him. He realized they were the ones who had helped pull him from the earth. They hissed and croaked. "General! General!"

All around him the General could see other movements. He watched as men rose out of the earth, not men, the ruins of men. Their thin bodies were little more than bones. Their eyes were black, swollen, and bulbous. There was no white left in their eyes. Their skin was black, encrusted with dirt and tufts of dirty hair. Their lips and gums were so shrunken that their teeth jutted from their jaws like those of wolves.

The General remembered Andersonville and the camps. He thought of those prisoners, living skeletons, with their hollow eye sockets.

Those around him were covered in dirty rags. He could tell from the rags that some had been men and some had been women. Some of them were naked. Any hint of gender had been stripped away with the shrinking of their flesh. They were sexless aggregates of dirty black skin glued onto bone. They were not men—scarecrows!

The General tried to speak, but instead of forming words he heard only clicking and hissing sounds. His voice lacked volume and projection. Every sentence ended in a collection of sputters and pops. He was without breath. His lungs would not fill and empty on their own.

It was night, dark, moonless, but the General could see as clear as day. He looked out across the field. A stone, other stones of uniform shape, row upon row of rough-cut square gray stones; he could see acres of them. The orderly rows of small squares gave way to larger monuments, obelisks, carved angels, stone vaults. Some of the vaults were as large as log cabins. The stones were engraved with names and dates, some with accomplishments, some with poem or psalm. He could see that the stones were old and worn, yet the dates inscribed were years beyond any day he had known!

In most places, the earth around the markers remained undisturbed, but in the places where the scarecrows had forced their way to the surface, the graves were open and torn. As more scarecrows emerged from the earth they announced their presence with warbles or croaks or a kind of scream. The General could not make out words or speech. Most of the scarecrows stood or sat by their stones in confusion.

The General examined the stone against which he leaned. He ran a long, black, dirt-encrusted finger along the deep engraving of the marker. He concentrated and sucked air into his lungs; only then could he speak. "Lies, lies ... lies." He uttered his protest with a voice little more than a hiss and a mouth full of dust.

He lay on the ground and called down into the earth from which he escaped. "Mary ... Mary ...." His voice came out as little more than a whisper. He tried to call out louder. "Mary Ann.... Mary Ann." He forced the sound from his body, the volume moderately improved. He pressed his ear to the ground and listened. He forced air into his lungs and called out as forcefully as he could. "Mary Ann! Mary Ann!" He pressed the side of his face to the ground. He listened but could hear nothing. He sunk the long black fingers of his hands into the earth; he could feel no vibration or movement.

He looked again at his marker, the stone inscribed with a beginning and an end. Next to his, he could see Mary's name carved in the stone but with a final date nearly two decades after his. He remembered the many good things they had shared, and then their poverty after the war. He had left her with nothing.

The General remembered illness, each breath a labor. His family had been with him, but gradually they faded from sight. Every thought became a concentration, one more breath. The light contracted around him, and he sunk into darkness as a swimmer sinks into a depthless sea. Then he was alone. Bright light burned him and blinded him. He sought relief below the still surface, only to find a coldness and darkness worse than any burning light; a place inhabited by the others.

He rejected, for a moment, the notion that he had truly died. He considered that they had buried him alive. He considered the possibility that his mind was punishing him with a nightmare born of fever.

The stones and the scarecrows refuted him. He could hear their grunts and groans. He could hear their warbles and whistles as they attempted to speak. They were all castaways washed up on a dark beach each anchored to a stone by an invisible cable. They had been awakened by a trumpet call all had heard, but none had understood.

The General leaned against his stone marker. One of the scarecrows who had helped him now returned and pressed its ear to the ground. After a brief moment, the scarecrow looked up at him. It spoke slowly, quietly, every few words punctuated with a breathless pause. "No one else.... No one else."

The General made a conscious effort to suck in a lungful of air before he spoke. "Where am aah...? Who're yah?"

The scarecrow did not respond but moved on to the next place of digging. The General watched as they pulled another scarecrow from the earth.

The General called out but with a voice not his own. The sounds came out as grunts and hoots rather than speech. One of them caught at his arm and hissed and croaked. "General! General!" Other scarecrows began to gather around him.

The General looked beyond the graveyard and beyond the walls. Everywhere he could see lights. It was a city of a hundred thousand torches, a hundred thousand lanterns, a hundred thousand campfires. Lights hung from posts along the roads. Lights sped back and forth along causeways and bridges. Lights filled the windows of a thousand houses. Beyond the houses, towers of glass and light cascaded across the horizon and climbed into the sky. It was a city made of light. He had to shield his face from the glare of the lights. The lights burned his eyes.

New sounds accompanied the lights. He could hear the sound of engines chasing back and forth outside of the graveyard; the sound of engines that crossed bridges and sped along roads. Masked by the sound of the engines he could hear other sounds, sounds he recognized. He listened to the sounds of battle, gunshots, and screams.

The pain came again unexpectedly, a gnawing worm of hunger and thirst. He felt a body blow to his gut, sudden and vicious.

The General put aside the pain. He put aside his confusion. He put aside the visions and the memories. He pushed away from his stone.

He left the cemetery and stepped out onto a road. The road was solid and black. It was hard as stone, but with a surface smooth and cobble free. The Romans would have envied such a road. He could see other roads crisscrossing in orderly lines.

Homes as far as the eye could see stood along the roads; most had bright lights shining out into the night.

Alongside the roads, carriages and engines of strange design sat idle. Some of the engines had been abandoned, blocking the roads. In the distance, red lights, and white lights marked other engines moving rapidly in all directions at incredible speed; the engines were as busy as ants.

As the General walked, not once did he hear or see a horse. The city lacked the smell of horses. The black roads were free of dung.

The General walked quickly, the fatigue and exhaustion of remembrance gone. Whatever the nature of this new body, he felt strong, and then the hunger struck at him again. He waited for the spasm to pass. He began to walk again.

He felt the need to pick up his pace, but in many places, he discovered the bright lights made it difficult to see. Light posts bordered all the roads, more than possible, far more than needed.

He came to an open area, not a cemetery, but a park. The General crossed into the park to find grass neatly cut, paths well marked, tree-lined.

He climbed a small hill in the park and looked out over the city. He marveled at the tall buildings and the obvious wealth. Along the edge of the city, he could see railroad tracks. He had never seen such railroad tracks, one track right next to another, four and six lines running parallel.

He looked out over the roads and railways trying to gain his bearings. At one point he spoke out loud. "By God! ... They've bridged the river!" Not far from the bridge he could make out an oddly shaped building. "They've built ... a pyramid!"

His speech was disjointed, a smear of sound. He spoke aloud, practicing. "They've built a bridge.... They've built ... a pyramid." He concentrated on his breathing and on pronouncing each syllable. The voice was not his; it was barely intelligible.

He looked out over the city. Nothing looked familiar. He recognized nothing. Everywhere he could see trees, but nowhere could he see forest. He could see only houses, no farms, no fields. Every new thing made him pause. He would have liked to walk into the city and have all of the new things explained. The twist in his gut hinted that this was impossible.

One of the scarecrows following the General spoke. "Where going? What ... are yah ... looking at?"

The General said nothing.

"Can yah ... see anythin'?"

Now the General responded. "Yes, wonderful things!"

The General watched one of the engines with blue and red and white lights roll towards the park. The engine ran on wheels, but without tracks. A terrible shrieking whistle announced the engine's approach. Bright lights from the engine flooded the park making it difficult to see.

The engine stopped, the shrieking sound stopped, but the lights continue to burn bright. They bathed the entire area in red and blue flashes of light. White beams, brighter than any limelight, swept back and forth burning halos into the night.

The General stood and watched as two men got out of the engine. He could see that these were not just men. They wore uniforms. They were soldiers, soldiers in blue. The soldiers said nothing. They raised their arms. Flames shot from their hands. They shot at those walking in the park and along the roads.

Scarecrows ran and scattered. One of the scarecrows next to the General went down from a gunshot. A moment later he was up and running. The General ran with him. The engine with the blue and red and white lights pursued.

The General had never run so fast. He did not gasp or struggle for breath. He felt no fatigue. He could run as swiftly as a horse, but the engine ran faster. It came rushing down the road, striking running scarecrows and tossing them into the air. White lights shined from the front of the engine blinding the General. He could not see where to escape.

The wounded scarecrow running with the General fell behind. When the engine struck him he went flying into space. The General felt sure he would be next. He could hear the engine at his heels and feel the vibrations on the road as it chased him like a living thing.

Just as he felt he must surely go down beneath the wheels of the engine, the machine came to a screeching stop. After a pause, the engine began to run in reverse. The General could hear the sounds of the engine running over and crushing those it had knocked down a moment before. When he realized the engine was not going to run him down, the General felt compelled to turn and watch. The engine with the blue and red and white lights came to a stop. The soldiers left the engine and stepped out onto the road.

The engine had struck any number of scarecrows in the initial pursuit, but only three were so badly broken they could not get up and run. A soldier, bathed in bright white light, walked over to a broken scarecrow. He stood over the scarecrow and shot it in the head. The remaining scarecrows dragged themselves along the road. They mewed and moaned unintelligibly. The soldier walked up to the other two scarecrows and shot each in turn.

The General could see that people in nearby houses had stepped out to their porches to watch. When the soldiers looked in the General's direction, he prepared to run only to realize, instead of watching him, they were listening to voices coming out of the coach of their engine. The General had seen only the two soldiers, but he heard other voices, loud and shrill.

The soldiers got back into the engine. Instead of continuing their pursuit, they turned and headed back towards the city.

The General returned to walking on the road but then began to run. The road felt good beneath his feet. He could run without breath or pause. As long as there were no bright lights, he could see as clearly as if it was day.

As he ran, engines continued to go up and down the roads nearby. The lights and noises of the engines were impossible to mistake. Whenever he heard an engine approach, the General ran for cover. Twice engines came along the road and stopped. The men inside did not exit the engines; instead, they fired guns out of the engine's windows. The men fired randomly in different directions as they drove. The General wondered whether the men could see. He wondered if they aimed their weapons before firing. These men wore no uniforms. They were not soldiers.

The General heard gunfire up ahead. In the distance, he could see an engine caught in a ditch, entangled in brush. Two men stood by the engine and fired rifles in all directions. Great gobs of flame shot from their rifles and lighted their faces. The rifles, repeaters of some sort, were a wonder. The men fired into the dark, never stopping to reload.

Scarecrows hovered around the men and the wreck. The scarecrows crouched down, just beyond the circle of light provided by the engine.

One of the men suddenly threw down his gun, leaped from the ditch, and ran like a deer.

Several of the scarecrows took off in pursuit; they brought him down as easily as hounds hunting a rabbit. The scarecrows tore at him with their nails and teeth. The young man began to screech and scream. Without even thinking about it the General hurried forward. He stopped himself a few feet from the struggle. Soon a dozen scarecrows had hold of the young man tearing him to pieces.

The General could smell the blood in the air. His gut twisted with hunger. Saliva flooded his mouth. He ground his new teeth, teeth that wanted badly to be used. The General turned and tried to move away; he struggled as if bound by strong cables. He bowed down his head as if resisting a storm and finally pushed away.

The older man continued to stand by the engine. He fought holding his rifle by the barrel and using the stock as a club. He looked left and right, forward and back. It was clear he could hear, but he could not see the scarecrows that circled him.

The screams of the young man had stopped. More scarecrows ran up to join those who had pulled the young man to the ground. This, in turn, set off the scarecrows around the older man. They darted in and out trying to pull him down while avoiding blows from his club. Suddenly, the old man bolted in the opposite direction from where the young man lay dying. As he ran, he struck at those who pursued him, but they brought him down like a pack of wolves. The older man began to scream. The General could see the scarecrows as they bit and tore. The General's gut twisted with hunger.

The General forced himself to walk over to the broken engine. He concentrated on examining the remains. He could see the thing had crashed with force sufficient to bend steel. He marveled at the thick rubber-covered wheels. He could see shining fragments scattered all about, the glass housing the different lanterns having shattered. He walked around, examining the thing from all angles, impervious to the broken glass.

No mere piece of machinery, his examination revealed a coach of wonderful luxury. The exterior was made of enameled metal, the interior of upholstered divans. He sat down in one of the cushioned chairs and enjoyed the extravagance. He marveled at the finish of the metal. He ran his hands over the wheel and switches and gauges. Glass windows went all around the carriage shielding the passenger compartment. Other materials he did not recognize, they were smooth and forgiving to the touch. He spoke aloud, "Wonderful ... wonderful things."

Examining the coach, he expected to feel heat and find some evidence of fire, but the wreckage of the carriage felt cool to the touch. Once, many years ago, the General had been present for the destruction of a steamboat. The engine had exploded and members of the crew had screamed as they burned. The General continued with his examination now, until the screaming of the dying man nearby stopped.

Other scarecrows joined the General at the crash site. As he and some of the others examined the wreckage, a man in a nearby house came out onto his porch. Without saying a word the man raised a gun to his shoulder and began to fire. The man fired one shot, then another, then another, then another, a rapid-fire shotgun. Glass windows on the engine shattered. A scarecrow fell to the ground but then, just as quickly, got up and ran.

The General ducked down behind the wreckage of the engine hoping that the carriage would be sufficient to stop the blasts from the repeating shotgun. As the man stopped to reload his weapon, a scarecrow leaped up onto the back of the porch. It leaped like a lion, but not quite fast enough. The man made it back into his house and slammed the door. The scarecrow pursued and tried to force its way into the house. Other scarecrows ran up onto the porch and joined the first.

The scarecrows would have soon forced the door, but the man on the other side began to fire his shotgun again. Solid slugs punched holes through the door letting out streams of light. A slug hit one of the scarecrows on the porch and knocked him down, the rest took off running.

The scarecrow who had been shot regained its feet. It stood on the porch cradling a broken arm. The man behind the door reappeared at a lighted window. Light streamed from the window making it painful to look at the figure of the man. He stood like an angel emblazoned with light. He leaned out of the window and pointed his gun at the scarecrow on the porch. He fired burst after burst into the body of the scarecrow. The scarecrow fell to its back as the fire from the shotgun cut it down. The man returned to firing at those near the engine. As he continued to fire out of his window the General ran for the trees. Other scarecrows followed.

As the General ran, he formed a map of the city in his mind. He tried to place the location of the cemetery in relation to the city and the rivers. For a time he headed east along a railroad track. Somewhere up ahead he should find the Wolf River and the forests and swamps that would provide places to hide.

When he reached the river, he went down an earthen bank to the water. He felt no fatigue, but his thirst consumed him. He felt the thirst in his gut like a living thing. It seemed to scratch and dig at his insides.

He hesitated before reaching his hand into the water. He examined the river from different angles. He threw stones at the river's surface. Finally, he leaned down and swiftly scooped water into his hand. His thin, elongated fingers could barely form a cup. He began to drink but then spit the water onto the ground. The water was muddy, and brackish, and wrong. It did nothing for his thirst. In desperation, he tried again. He scooped up a little water in his hand and drank, and again nothing; he gained no relief from his thirst. The thing in his gut twisted in objection.

The General began to walk along the river bank. He followed the river east. He never stopped; he never rested. Always he had the sense that he must keep going; he must be well beyond the city before the sun came up.

He kept off the roads as much as possible; he kept to the woods and forest and the low lying, swampy areas. When the river turned southeast, he continued to follow along the bank, the river to his left, the road off to his right. The iron coaches zoomed back and forth along the road in an endless parade of swiftly passing red and white lights. Only in the forest did he feel safe.

The General continued his escape. He continued his walk-run pattern steadily through the night. Behind him, a parade of scarecrows followed along, sometimes on the road, sometimes taking cover among the trees.

At one point, half a dozen men looked down from an elevated portion of the road. One of the men began to fire a shotgun towards the river. Everywhere, scarecrows dove for cover or ran for the trees. The General did not slow his pace and soon the shooting stopped. If any had been hurt, none showed it. The parade of scarecrows continued to walk and run along the river; they kept to the cover of the wood line; they ran sometimes south and sometimes east.

To the east, the horizon began to suggest the coming of day. Even this hint of dawn blurred the General's vision. He knew, soon, he must find a hiding place, away from the Army and the men shooting from the engines. He needed food and water and clothing. He could feel the burden of his hunger and his thirst and his nakedness.

He came across a path that headed away from the road into the forest. He turned and followed. Soon he could see that the path headed towards a distant house.

The front door of the house was open, but with no one present. He could barely see past the bright light shining inside the house. He shielded his eyes and stepped into the house. He concentrated on each word as he spoke, "Aah mean no 'arm ... Aah need help."

The voice did not sound like his, but the words were at least recognizable. He forced air into his lungs as if he was diving below water. He pushed the words out with his chest, concentrating on each syllable, "Help me please."

There had been a time when he could shout orders on a battlefield, over the roar of cannons, and muskets, and damn any man who claimed not to hear him. Now it seemed as if a child could shout him down. He tried again, "Someone hare? Is someone hare?" He struggled to make his voice louder, clearer. No answer came from inside.

He went into the house. The light inside blinded him. He reached for the lantern, bright light, some heat, but no flame. He picked up the lantern and tried to throw it outside. Instead of the lantern going out the door, it came springing back and struck him. The lantern fell to the ground quenching the light with shattered glass. The General picked up the lantern. It was heavy, a strange design of brass and stone. It carried no oil, no smell of burning. The General turned the lantern this way and that wondering at the design. He carried the lantern as he made his way inside as if it might still light his way.

The house was familiar but wrong. He could smell meat and drink and this led him to the kitchen. Despite the lack of light in this room, he could see clearly. At the sink, he could see a water pump of odd shape. He pulled at the handle, and water sprayed into the sink. He leaned over the sink and began to wash away the dirt from his face and hands.

The General used his hands as a cup and moved a small amount of water to his lips. He had never been so thirsty, but this water was wrong and tasteless. He let it run out of his mouth and down his chin. He forced himself to drink. He splashed more and more water to his mouth and face. He gained no relief from his thirst. He might just as well been moving handfuls of dust into his mouth. He groaned from the pain of his thirst.

Slices of bread had been scattered across the table and on the floor. Even in the dark, the General could see that the bread was impossibly white and perfectly sliced. He picked up a slice. He had never felt bread so soft. He had never seen bread so evenly cut. He took a bite of the bread and tasted foul sawdust. He spit it out as the pain of hunger washed over him.

He looked up when he heard a woman's voice. She was speaking calmly, but he could taste her fear. He looked around the room; across the way, a door, a door into a cellar. He could hear the woman's voice from behind the door, talking,

talking, pleading. In response to the woman's voice, the pain in his gut returned nearly doubling him over again.

As the woman continued to talk, her fear drew the General towards her. It hummed and pulsed with flavor. It smelled like a rich stew of vibrant color.

The woman's pleading grew in volume and desperation. He could hear movement in the cellar. He could not tell how many others were in the cellar with the woman.

There was something else here, a metallic taste in the air. It had the smell of meat and wine. He looked at the floor and saw a dark stain leading from the table to the cellar door. He reached down and touched the stain, sticky and tacky. He put his fingertip to his mouth. He tasted a savory sweetness never imagined. It assailed his tastes and senses. His hunger and thirst redoubled.

The General opened the door to the stairs leading down into the cellar. Scarecrows stood on the stairs blocking the way. At the base of the stairs, he could see a body. So little remained the General could not tell whether the body was that of a man or woman. Scarecrows pulled meat from the arms and legs, and chest, of the corpse. They did not chew so much as suck at the flesh.

On the far side of the cellar, he could see the woman pleading with them; she reasoned with them; she bargained with them. She faced them, her back to the wall. Scarecrows surrounded her on three sides. When they reached for her the woman began to scream.

The General dismissed his hunger and thirst. He ignored the pain in his gut. He began to force his way down the stairs into the cellar.

A scarecrow stood on the stairs, its skin black as night. It wore a green jacket. When the General tried to move past, the scarecrow tried to stop him. The General did not hesitate. He struck the scarecrow with the brass lantern and caved in its skull.

The General fought his way into the cellar. He struck and kicked at the scarecrows blocking his path. At the same moment, the woman tried to break free. The scarecrows tore the nightdress from her body as she fought to reach the stairs; she screamed as she struggled to escape.

The General struck at the scarecrows in front of him. The scarecrows did not defend themselves from the blows. They struggled and twisted, not like men avoiding a fist, but like dogs intent on their quarry. The General sent a scarecrow sprawling with a kick and moved towards the woman. Other scarecrows grabbed her and pulled her to the ground. As the General continued to fight to reach the woman, they pulled him to the ground. Hands pinned down his arms and legs; others trampled him in their effort to reach the woman. He twisted and turned, but could not free himself.

The woman lay on the floor with scarecrows tearing at her back and biting at her neck; scarecrows pulled at her skin; they bit at her arms and legs. Scarecrows at the edge of the melee reached for her; their fingernails scratched and tore jagged bloody paths across her skin. The scarecrows did not spill her blood; they lapped it with serpent-like tongues before it even reached the floor.

The scarecrows did not release the General until the screaming stopped. Those that had pinned him now pushed the General aside as they joined in the feeding. They pushed and struck at each other anxious to gather in a portion of what remained on the cellar floor.

The General stood and forced his way back up the stairs. He retreated to the kitchen; his body howling in protest. The smell of the feast overwhelmed him. Sticky drool leaked from his mouth.

The group of scarecrows that had followed the General through the forest had also followed him into the house. In the kitchen, they too had found the dark stain. Two scarecrows were on their hands and knees lapping at the floor. A third scarecrow noisily dragged its fingernails along the tiles, and then licked its fingertips. The scarecrows looked towards the cellar as the General emerged. They grunted and hissed and moved towards the stairs.

The General left the kitchen and moved outside the house. He could hear the sounds of gunshots. With the gunshots came the sounds of barking of dogs, not just dogs, howling dogs, hounds. The General knew what the hunters and hounds were seeking. He had chased enough fugitives to know.

The General set aside anger and hunger and pain the way a man might set aside an old coat. He understood the hunters would soon reach the house. He knew that he had to find a place to hide in the swamps and the forest before the coming of daylight.

He stopped for a moment to consider his home and his family. He pushed those thoughts aside.

He called to the others, a voice marred by breathlessness and whistles, but still a voice of command. He ran from the house, away from the road, and back towards the river. He moved quickly and with purpose. Many followed.

The Fourth Seal: Behold a Pale Horse

Deck Log - Second Day

OPNAV 3100/99 (Rev 7-84) S/N 0107-LF-031-0498	SHIP'S DECK LOG SHEET	IF CLASSIFIED STAMP SECURITY MARKING HERE

USE BLACK INK TO FILL IN THIS LOG

SHIP TYPE	HULL NUMBER		YEAR	MONTH	ZONE	DAY	USS __CYCLOPS__ AT : PASSAGE FROM __PORT SAID__ TO _____	CLASS	HANDL
D A	AS	00	43	09	B	16	E		

POSITON ZONE TIME	POSITON ZONE TIME	POSITON ZONE TIME	LEGEND
0800 L_____, BY ___ A_____, BY ___	1200 L_____, BY ___ A_____, BY ___	2000 L_____, BY ___ A_____, BY ___	1 - CELESTIAL 2 - ELECTRONIC 3 - VISUAL 4 - D R

TIME	ORDER	CSE	SPEED	DEPTH	RECORD OF EVENTS OF THE DAY
0400					ASSUMED THE WATCH. ANCHORED AS BEFORE. WATCH REPORTS CONDITIONS NORMAL. LIEUTENANT T.J. MCKINLEY, USN
0425					REPORT OF DEATH OF CREW MEMBER* FOUND IN MEDICAL SPACES WITH STAB WOUNDS.
0700					SEARCH OF SHIP FOR HM1 ASPER.
					*CREW MEMBER IDENTIFIED AS MR2 MULVEY

REPORT SYMBOL OPNAV 2100-10	IF CLASSIFIED STAMP REVIEW / DECLASSIFICATION DATE HERE	IF CLASSIFIED STAMP SECURITY MARKING HERE

01 Level - Midships, Medical Department

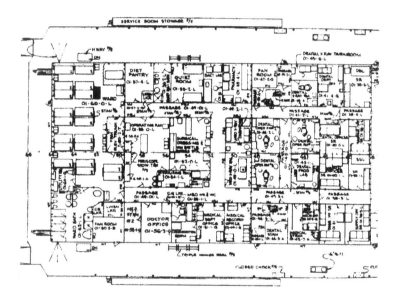

The Fourth Seal: Behold a Pale Horse

The Legend of RA and ISIS:

Isis had the form of a woman, and knew words of power, but she was disgusted with men, and she yearned for the companionship of the gods and the spirits, and she meditated and asked herself whether, supposing she had the knowledge of the Name of Rā, it was not possible to make herself as great as Rā was in heaven and on the earth? Meanwhile Rā appeared in heaven each day upon his throne, but he had become old, and he dribbled at the mouth, and his spittle fell on the ground. One day Isis took some of the spittle and kneaded up dust in it, and made this paste into the form of a serpent with a forked tongue, so that if it struck anyone the person struck would find it impossible to escape death. This figure she placed on the path on which Rā walked as he came into heaven after his daily survey of the Two Lands (i.e. Egypt). Soon after this Rā rose up, and attended by his gods he came into heaven, but as he went along the serpent drove its fangs into him. As soon as he was bitten Rā felt the living fire leaving his body, and he cried out so loudly that his voice reached the uttermost parts of heaven.

The Literature of the Ancient Egyptians, by E. A. Wallis Budge, 1914.

CHAPTER- 4 – MURDER IN MEDICAL

Tuesday, Day Two: Port Said, Egypt

Lieutenant Irawell's day began like no other. He had been well and truly asleep in his rack when his stateroom phone began to ring. He heard MA1 Hardwick on the line. She told him there had been a murder in medical. While waking and still groggy, he asked her to repeat herself.

After a pause, Hardwick spoke again. "The XO wants you right away in medical."

"Okay, I'll be right there. I'm on my way."

The Lieutenant dressed and then splashed some water on his face. The medical and dental spaces were amidships on the 01 level. His stateroom was just forward on the same level. As he hurried down and aft he felt a little annoyed with Hardwick. She could have just as easily have knocked on his stateroom door and briefed him there instead of calling on the phone.

The Lieutenant found Hardwick, MA2 Porter, and MA2 Oxford standing in the passageway. He heard a woman crying in one of the nearby offices. Hardwick did not speak; she stood by the door and signaled for the Lieutenant to enter.

The treatment spaces of the Cyclops were vast. They encompassed nearly a quarter of the ship's 01 level, including offices, dressing stations, and operating rooms. There were a similar number of offices, labs, and treatment spaces for dental. The medical ward had nineteen double racks, sufficient for thirty-eight patients. The area seemed enormous when compared to the cramped working spaces in which most of the crew functioned.

When the Lieutenant entered the ward, the XO, Lieutenant Commander Powers, and Doc Peters were already present. Many of the other medical staff stood around trying to look invisible. The officers talked amongst themselves, some course of action having already been decided.

Ten feet away, in one of the examination rooms, MR2 Mulvey's naked corpse stretched precariously across an exam room table. His throat had been cut. Blood had poured out of the wound, down his chest, and puddled on the deck. Numerous bloody tracks surrounded the body, some made by boots, others by bare feet.

The XO questioned Doc Peters. "Did you check berthing? Do we know where Asper is now?"

"Nobody knows sir. She hasn't been seen since last night."

The XO suddenly turned on Lieutenant Irawell. "You're responsible to get this investigated. Figure it out. Was it murder or suicide? Seal this area off. I want you to contact NCIS. They've got agents assigned to the Carrier Task Force. Also, make sure Admin gets a personnel casualty report out."

"Suicide sir?"

"For all we know, Mulvey came up here, stole a scalpel and cut his own throat. Anything is possible till the experts say different."

"But sir, look at all the tracks in the blood. Someone else was present."

"Maybe Asper tried to save him? We won't know until we find Asper."

The XO turned to Powers without waiting for a response from the Lieutenant. "Weps, you're in charge of finding Asper. I want the ship searched down to the bilges. I want ever workspace, every storage space, every billet, every stateroom, and every fan room searched."

The XO turned back to Peters. "Is it a problem for medical if this space is sealed off?"

"I don't believe so sir."

"Then seal it off. We'll decide what to do next when we hear from NCIS."

As he walked out of the space the XO pointed again at the Lieutenant, "And get the body down to one of the reefers."

Once the XO left, Hardwick acted as if she had been given permission to breathe. She hurriedly began to explain that Mulvey's body had been found in the exam space after the midwatch. HM1 Asper had been working in medical last night and now had disappeared. Her uniform had been found in the exam space. Mulvey's uniform was missing.

"Lots of blood on Asper's uniform," she continued, "but no body. Mulvey's throat's been cut, and it looks like some defensive wounds to his hands as well."

"What was Mulvey doing here in medical?" the Lieutenant asked.

Peters now spoke up. "Nobody has seen Mulvey around here before. As far as I know, Asper was not involved with him."

Hardwick ignored the interruptions. "Murder of passion maybe? Maybe they were secret lovers, or maybe Mulvey showed up to rape her, end of the world and all that."

The Lieutenant continued with his questions, "And nobody knows where Asper is now?"

"She's likely wounded," Hardwick continued. "Maybe she's hiding because she's guilty," she speculated.

"Why take Mulvey's uniform? He has to be twice the size of Asper."

"She would have been covered by blood," Hardwick answered. "Maybe she switched to his because it was clean."

Peters spoke up again. "Look at all that blood. That's at least two different sets of foot prints and a lot of blood."

Hardwick shook her head. "Mulvey's blood. She moved the body to dump him overboard. Maybe she realized he was too big to shift outside."

The Lieutenant got on an office phone and called Acedian's stateroom. When no one answered, he called the legal office. Fortunately, Acedian answered the phone. The Lieutenant directed him to get his camera and report to medical.

While they waited for Acedian, Peters pointed to one of the nearby corpsman. "HM2 Nowlin found him. She walked into medical and no one was here. Then she found Mulvey. She did not see anyone else. She called me as soon as she found him."

The Lieutenant posed a few questions to Nowlin. Although cooperative, she could add nothing beyond the minimum Peters had already volunteered.

Acedian arrived carrying his personal camera, a digital model with a large zoom lens. He began to shoot photos of the murder scene from every angle. Peters and some of the corpsman stood by and watched. After Acedian had run out of angles to photograph, the Lieutenant turned back to Nowlin. "Get a body bag and move the body down to one of supply's reefers."

The corpsman did not immediately move, but looked to Doc Peters. "Do as he says."

Nowlin, two corpsmen, and a dental tech began the process of getting Mulvey into a body bag. They worked carefully, trying to avoid contact with the blood and bodily fluids that covered the corpse. They were not helped by Hardwick's hectoring about disturbing the murder scene.

Mulvey had been a bear of a man. When they lifted the corpse, they discovered he was even heavier then he looked. Porter and Oxford had been standing by watching. The Lieutenant ordered them to jump to and help. They did so, but held the body bag gingerly as they tried to avoid any blood that might have dripped onto the surface.

Once they had removed the body, the Lieutenant asked Hardwick if she had anything they could use to try and find fingerprints.

She had nothing beyond evidence bags. "Anything forensic, NCIS handles it or we send it off ship."

They all donned surgical gloves and began to search through adjacent spaces for any possible evidence. One cabinet contained collections of medical instruments, but nothing that seemed obviously connected to the crime. If one of the scalpels contained in the cabinet was used as a weapon, it had been wiped clean. The Lieutenant noted a container marked "medical waste." He could not bring himself to look inside, but he moved it into the exam space to be locked away for a proper forensics team.

The Lieutenant directed that the exam room be locked up. Hardwick began hanging large swaths of yellow warning tape across the entranceway door.

Once all that could be done had been done to preserve the crime scene, the Lieutenant went below to his office. He drafted several messages about Mulvey's murder and Asper's loss. The messages would need approval before being sent out by the communications department, so he headed up to the XO's office for a signature. Before he left, he sent an email with the same information to the NCIS, Middle East Field Office with a request for help. He hoped the email would find its way to the right person.

When the Lieutenant arrived in the XO's office it was empty. Instead of returning to his workspaces, he went up the signals bridge. He took a few minutes to once again examine Port Said through the big eyes. He expected the usual city tumult but saw little movement in the streets. He looked at the office and apartment buildings that clustered along the shore and then climbed to the horizon. He could see no significant activity around the tall buildings. Smoke still rose from within the city, but not as heavily as the day before. Closer to shore, no small boat traffic was evident. Near the waterfront he could see the mosques. He listened for the sing song call to prayer, but the minarets stood silent.

Stepping away from the fixed binoculars, the Lieutenant took a moment to assess the area around him. Out on the weather deck he could see two men standing by one of the fifty-caliber machine guns. They wore helmets and body armor and leaned casually against the ship's rails. One sailor had been smoking. He dropped his cigarette butt on the deck and crushed it out with his boot. The second sailor got the attention of the first and pointed up towards the Lieutenant on the signal bridge. The first sailor reached down and picked up his cigarette butt and tossed it over the side. Both sailors went back to their gun and turned their gaze towards the city.

Behind him, a radio played a news program. "–reports of many violent attacks during the night. There have been reports of violent attacks taking place, not only in urban areas but in rural communities as well. Emergency services throughout the region have responded heroically. Authorities are reporting order restored with security forces augmented as needed." The news then began to provide a time-line on when people first began to disappear. "There are unofficial reports that Beijing and Moscow were among the last capitals impacted. No official communications have been received from the Russian or Chinese governments."

Nearby, two petty officers stood by the signals shelter speculating.

"Terrorists for sure. Some kind of new weapon."

"What kind of weapon can hit the whole world like that?"

"Don't go on again. It's more likely to be aliens then Jesus."

In the background the reporting shifted to a woman's voice. "In addition, a large number of children are reported missing. We are awaiting confirmation, but we have reports that children have gone missing...."

The petty officers continued to argue as the radio played.

"Of course children have gone missing. Half the world's gone missing."

"It's not half the world, only a small percentage of adults. She's saying all of the children have gone missing."

"That's not what she said."

"But that's what she's getting at. I heard an earlier report."

"That's not what she said though. A lot of those earlier reports have been bullshit."

"You go and ask anybody onboard if they've heard from their kids. The answer is no."

"Not true. That's just because communications are down. If that was true, the official word would have come down from big Navy. We'd be the first to know."

"That's bullshit too."

The Lieutenant was tempted to stay out on the signals bridge a little longer and listen to the debate among the petty officers, but the heat of the sun drove him back into the ship. He left the 05 level and drifted down to the 04 level and radio central. The communications duty section was preoccupied with a flood of messages coming in from commands all across the world. They milled about trying to sort and prioritize the message traffic, some routine and some extraordinary.

The Lieutenant finally crossed paths with the communications officer, but just for a moment. Alexander rushed about too busy to stop and talk. When the Lieutenant asked if he had heard anything new, Alexander became non-comital. "Can't say.

Anything official will go to the XO, and I can't release it anyway till he says so."

The Lieutenant now handed Alexander his draft messages to NCIS. "Look, when you see the XO, can you have him chop on these? I've been chasing him around the ship without success." Alexander agreed and added them to his stack before heading down the nearest ladder.

As the Lieutenant turned to leave, one of the petty officers asked point blank if it was true that there had been a murder onboard. The Lieutenant nodded. "We don't know for sure yet. Murder, self-defense, suicide, we don't know yet."

When the Lieutenant left communications he debated whether he should check into legal, or go and get lunch. He opted for food. He had missed breakfast and was starving. He hurried to the wardroom and disappointment. With the current confusion in duty sections a number of cooks and servers had either gone missing or stayed in their racks. Lunch consisted of salad, bread, and cold cuts.

It did not take long for the Lieutenant to finish his sandwich. Several officers in the wardroom had already finished their meals and gone into the lounge. The Lieutenant grabbed a soda and followed.

Miller, Unger, and a few others sat in the lounge watching a news program. The image of a burning building played on the television. Other buildings nearby had their storefronts smashed, glass and broken merchandise scattered about the street. Rushing in and out of the broken storefronts people carried clothing, or electronics, or even furniture. At least two bodies lay prone in the street.

The Lieutenant took a seat next to Unger. "What's happening now?"

"Looks like big time riots in Paris and London. Can't tell about the rest of Europe. The usual looting, but something different, a lot of crazies killing people. Some kind of disease is making people go crazy, maybe some sort of biological weapon."

Miller spoke up, "I can understand the rioting, people are panicking because of the disappearances, but the random killings make no sense."

One of the other officers asked, "This Armageddon then?"

"I think you mean, 'Is this the Rapture?' " Miller responded. "The rapture means all of the good people go to heaven, and the bad people and not so good people are left to fight it out."

Unger turned and spoke to Miller, "I don't think vacuuming up millions of people all at once makes any sense, and it certainly doesn't explain the riots and the killings."

"Sure it does; the evil people have been left behind, and they're now going crazy."

Unger had a speedy retort, "So are we the evil people or the not so good people?"

"I'm in the not so good category myself," Miller responded.

"Not surprised," Unger answered.

As soon as the Lieutenant finished his soda, he left the lounge and made his way back down to his office. As he walked he tried to figure out how to get an NCIS agent onboard. Twice he had to stand aside for sailors rushing along passageways. The sailors were suited up with helmets and body armor; they carried rifles and shotguns. He would have liked to stop them and ask some questions, but in both instances the teams were gone as quickly as they appeared.

The Lieutenant passed the mess decks as he headed to his office. There he could see long lines of men and women lined up to use the ship's "Sailor Phones." He watched one sailor slam down the telephone receiver and get back into line to wait for another turn. He could hear another sailor crying loudly. He noticed a group around a table towards the back of the space. A man rocked violently back and forth, pushing aside any who tried to comfort him. He dropped to the deck and began to helplessly wail and cry. As the Lieutenant walked past to his offices, he could still hear the cries from down the passageway.

When the Lieutenant arrived in legal, Acedian called out anxiously, "Quick, the XO wants you in his office. They've called down for you twice." The Lieutenant audibly inhaled. Then he turned around and headed back the way he came. In a few minutes he was climbing up the same ladders that he had just descended.

When the Lieutenant reached the XO's conference room, most of the other department heads were already present. He arrived just in time to hear the XO make a pronouncement. "We're leaving tomorrow, with or without permission from the Egyptians, with or without a pilot. We're scheduled to go, we're going."

Lieutenant Commander O'Day protested, "You can't just go through the Suez without a pilot. The Egyptians have all sorts of rules, there may be oncoming traffic. There may be shoals. The channel markers might not be right."

The XO responded tersely, "What part didn't you understand? If they don't get us a pilot, we're going without them."

Lieutenant Commander Lamb from engineering now took up the argument. "I'm missing a fourth of my guys. How are we even going to set a proper watch? We didn't sign on for this. My CIVMARs want to go home. They've got family. We should stay in port until replacements can be flown in."

"We're leaving tomorrow morning as scheduled, with or without the Egyptians. Any civilian who doesn't like it can go ashore now. They may not be too friendly on the Port Said side, but if you like, we can put them ashore on the Sinai side. Doubt they'd be any friendlier myself, but your choice."

Several of the officers began to voice their concerns when the XO picked up a sheaf of papers. He held them out to his right side, and shook them ominously. The conference room quieted and he began to speak again.

"In addition to reports on the missing, last night thousands of people were attacked. There are reports of people coming out of cemeteries and attacking. There are other reports of attackers coming from open fields or even homes. I've one report claiming attackers came out of a hospital morgue. Many of the reports insist the attacker are corpses or mummified bodies. Flash traffic now confirms. These attacks are now taking place inside the United States."

As the XO finished speaking, Lamb sucked in his breath. Alexander and O'Day leaned across the conference table as if expecting more. Peters tried to furtively read the message traffic the XO was waving around. Powers looked covertly around the space at the reaction of the other officers. Montgomery looked preoccupied and clueless.

Several officers began to speak at once but deferred when Powers loudly drawled a question. "Is this a disease or virus? Y'all get bit, yah infected an' die?"

"That does not appear to be the case. We have reports that those wounded are not showing signs of infection or insanity. However, we're still required to quarantine any casualties. Current directives have infection as a minimal concern. It does not appear to be spreading. Those wounded don't turn into monsters. Those killed stay dead."

The XO paused and looked around the room before speaking again. "Whether madmen or monsters, people were attacked and killed last night in their homes or on the street. A degree of insanity touched the world, and we were not immune. As you all know, we had a murder onboard. We have one dead and one missing."

Montgomery became suddenly alert. "You're talking zombies!"

The XO ignored him and put down the papers he had been holding onto the desk. Peters surreptitiously began to slide the messages towards himself. The XO continued. "Our immediate concern has to be figuring out what happened last night. We need to find Asper, or evidence that Asper is no longer onboard. We have to also consider that whoever attacked Mulvey might have been a third party, or even an outsider who somehow made it aboard during yesterday's chaos."

Montgomery spoke up again to voice a complaint. "I've been trying to get information, but nothing seems to be coming through. When are routine comms going to be restored?"

Alexander answered. "We're having some problems. I expect the satellites might be temporarily overwhelmed. We're all going to have to be patient and let the electrons simmer down."

The XO continued in an irritated voice, "As I was saying, we may have a killer onboard. He killed MR2 Mulvey and maybe HM1 Asper. Asper is still missing. We need every space onboard searched immediately. We need armed patrols on every deck. The searchers need to be armed."

Many of the officers nodded their heads up and down. Powers leaned over and whispered to the Lieutenant, "Or maybe Asper's the killer."

The XO now turned on Powers. "Weps, the ship needs to be searched, every shop, every storeroom, every fan room, every berthing space, and every head. We need to find Asper and we need to be sure there are no stowaways onboard. We need armed security watches on every deck. If there is a killer onboard, we need to find it and eliminate it."

The XO turned to Alexander. "Try to get the Canal Authority on the radio again and find out what's going on with the pilot. Don't mention anything about possibly having an Egyptian onboard, or anything about killings, or security problems. If they won't respond to your radio call, or they won't get us a pilot, we're going without them."

As the officers began to file out of the conference room, O'Day and Lamb lagged behind and tried to restart the argument about staying in port. The Lieutenant could hear the sound of their voices as he headed down the passageway.

Back in legal, several sailors were waiting for the Lieutenant's return. Several wanted new wills, others wanted powers of attorney. The Lieutenant asked a few questions and then gave each a questionnaire to fill out. He then told them to make appointments and come back once things settled down.

When two additional sailors arrived, the Lieutenant turned to Acedian. "What's going on? These people all want to change their wills. They're assuming they've lost family members and they haven't even talked to anyone back home yet!"

Acedian did not even bother looking up from his computer. "Better safe than sorry I suppose."

"You're not volunteering us for a lot of legal assistance, are you?"

"Not volunteering, but not discouraging."

"For Christ's sake, LN2 Mitchell has gone missing and you're asking for work?"

"It's not that Lieutenant. People are very worried. They want to get things fixed."

The Lieutenant ignored this comment and asked a new question. "Did you get hold of Ensign Jett to make sure Admin got a message out to casualty affairs about Mulvey?"

"I sure did. He told me to join the crowd. They were trying to get over a hundred of these Personnel Casualty Reports to NAVPERS and nobody's responding back home."

"Well keep on it. Get a copy of the message once it goes out." Before the Lieutenant could step back, Hardwick, Porter and Oxford arrived.

"Lieutenant we've been searching the ship all day…. We've found nothing." Hardwick paused for a moment and then continued. "No sign of Asper. She's really not the type to hurt anyone. I think the idea that Mulvey killed himself is kind of silly. I think she was the first victim and they dumped her body over the side."

Porter spoke up, "Maybe Mulvey killed Asper and then killed himself."

Hardwick responded sarcastically, "That makes sense. Mulvey was wandering around the ship naked, and then cut his own throat."

Porter quickly answered, "Mulvey killed Asper and dumped her body over the side. He then threw his own bloody clothes over the side. He returned to the scene of the crime to clean up the evidence and killed himself instead."

Oxford thoughtfully, "I think a killer came aboard and has already left the ship. He made his kills and then made his getaway. Terrorist, gains entry, kills and gets back off ship. He's off celebrating the end of the world with his jihadi friends."

Acedian now joined the conversation. "Not a jihadi, more likely we have a Zombie aboard. The news has been full of stories about dead people rising and attacking. The people disappeared and the Zs showed up attacking the survivors."

Oxford politely, "Sir, we might want to wait before putting that word out. Crazy people sure, infected people sure, anarchist for sure, jihadi for sure, but I haven't seen anyone claim zombie apocalypse yet."

Porter retorted derisively, "Hard to believe in such things, sir. Mulvey was killed with a blade; Zombies use their teeth. How could a zombie get onboard? If it was onboard, why did it leave? Zombies keep attacking until you kill them. No sir. We've got a killer onboard taking advantage of the confusion."

Oxford spoke again, "We've had even more people failing to muster this morning. I know for a fact that ET1 Beggs was here after the 'great disappearance.' I saw him at chow and now he's missing."

Hardwick nodded her head in agreement. "That just confirms my original theory; we've got a killer onboard. The murders of Asper and Mulvey are just the ones we know about."

Hardwick turned to the Lieutenant, "Sir, the XO has ordered an armed patrol on each deck all night. The Weapons department, Lieutenant Commander Powers, he's added us to the watch bill."

It annoyed the Lieutenant that Powers had taken de facto control of the Master-at-Arms force. Pinching the ship's police force might give him a little additional manpower, but it would make maintaining regular discipline onboard impossible. The Lieutenant made a mental note to speak to the XO.

Dinner that night was much like lunch, minimal. Instead of cold cuts, they had hot dogs and hamburgers. The XO sat at the head of one of the wardroom tables. He ate heartily. He finished his meal in less than twenty minutes and got up to leave. The Lieutenant started to ask about Powers and the Master-at-Arms force, but the XO cut him off. "Get back to me as soon as you've got something from NCIS."

After chow, the Lieutenant headed to his stateroom. He lay down in his rack hoping to catch up on his sleep. The effort proved futile. From one of the staterooms nearby he could hear the sound of weeping through the thin bulkhead. He had no desire to investigate and now had no desire to sleep.

The Lieutenant got up from his rack and headed down to the legal office. When he opened the door, there sat Acedian playing on one of the office computers.

"Late for you to be down here isn't it?"

"Beats sitting around in the stateroom with Jett. Those admin types are all humorless accountants and Jett's an especial asshole. I can't stand to be around him."

Although Cyclops currently had many empty staterooms, the XO still insisted that most of the junior officers be bunked two to a stateroom. Acedian resented it, and had yet to find some advantageous work around. The Lieutenant could not complain about his accommodations. Having a stateroom all to himself was an unheard of luxury for Lieutenants on most Navy ships.

The Lieutenant went to his computer. As he waited for the machine to boot up, Acedian spoke again. "I wanted to let you know that Lieutenant Commander Montgomery came by. He has a problem with you. He says you can't store your dead body in his reefers. He really hit the overhead, says it will spoil the food supplies down there."

"Is the body in a body bag?"

"It is."

"Did they put the body in one of the reefers?"

"Last I seen 'em. I believe they did. Montgomery was still pretty angry though."

"Tell him to take it up with the XO."

Genesis 3:1-7 KJV:

Now the serpent was more subtil than any beast of the field which the Lord God had made. And he said unto the woman, Yea, hath God said, Ye shall not eat of every tree of the garden? And the woman said unto the serpent, We may eat of the fruit of the trees of the garden: But of the fruit of the tree which is in the midst of the garden, God hath said, Ye shall not eat of it, neither shall ye touch it, lest ye die. And the serpent said unto the woman, Ye shall not surely die: For God doth know that in the day ye eat thereof, then your eyes shall be opened, and ye shall be as gods, knowing good and evil. And when the woman saw that the tree was good for food, and that it was pleasant to the eyes, and a tree to be desired to make one wise, she took of the fruit thereof, and did eat, and gave also unto her husband with her; and he did eat. And the eyes of them both were opened, and they knew that they were naked; and they sewed fig leaves together, and made themselves aprons.

CHAPTER-5 – OBELISKS IN THE CITY

Tuesday, Day Two: Alexandria, Virginia

He is sitting in a chair in the sand. It is a beautiful sunny day at the beach, but the surf is running high from an offshore storm. There is a young girl on the beach, no more than twelve. She is running to the edge of the surf and back again as each wave breaks and rolls swift and frothy towards the beach. There is a second girl, younger than the first. She too is running back and forth from the breaking waves.

The girls have a toy ball that they throw and chase as the waves toss it back. This time, they throw the ball too far, and it does not come back to the beach. Instead, it spins in the froth of the wave tops, just a few yards away, going up and down as each wave comes by and breaks and falls. The waves do not sweep the ball back to the beach; they move it slowly away from the land.

A boy, youngest of all, volunteers to get the ball. He dives into the water and smoothly swims beneath the breaking waves. He easily reaches the ball and tosses it back towards the beach. He is there, just beyond the breakers. He is not swimming back. His head rises and falls with each wave. He tries to catch a wave back to the beach, but with each breaking wave, he disappears for a moment.

The boy fights his way back to the surface, but always he is just a little further away from the beach, swimming just a little slower.

He tries to rush down to the beach. The faster he runs the further away the shoreline seems. The sand wraps around his feet and legs and binds him. He calls on all the powers of the universe to let him reach the water in time, but the sand does not release him.

Captain Pride sat up in his chair, his right hand jerking out into space. He knew this dream well. He wished it away, but the harder he pushed the more cemented it became in his mind. Eventually, he got up from his chair; he had no hope of going back to sleep.

He stood and looked around the room. The television, the electric clock, and the lights had all stopped working. Only a modest gray light seeped through the window. Now standing in the living room, he realized sleep had taken him unaware while he sat in his chair.

The Captain walked through his house. Upstairs, he noted the covers on the bed undisturbed from the previous morning. He remembered the chaotic start of the day before.

He fetched his phone and began to make calls. He called Anna first, but the call would not go through. The emergency message had not changed. "All circuits busy." He had no greater success when he tried calling his daughters.

The Captain switched to his landline. He often thought about getting rid of the landline service, but Anna insisted they keep it. He felt grateful to have it now. The landline had power, even if the rest of the house did not.

The landline rang for a minute before shutting down. He tried again; this time he got through to his wife's voice-mail. He was so surprised he could think of nothing to say. He left a message that he was at the house. He continued to hold the phone to his ear, saying nothing. After a lengthy pause, he hung up.

The Captain now used the landline to call each of his daughters. The emergency announcement had come back on, "All circuits busy." He tried again and again. The subsequent calls did not even get the emergency message. Finally, he got through to his oldest daughter's voice-mail. He left a message: "Mary, stay put in your dorm. I'll get there soon. If you talk to Martha, tell her I'll be there as soon as I can."

The Captain began making calls to taxi and car services without success. Either his calls failed to go through, or the person on the other end did not bother to pick up.

Reluctantly, the Captain tried calling Avarhouse. He called both his home and his law office. He had no more luck with these calls than the others. In truth he felt relief; he hated owing Avarhouse favors. He had known Avarhouse for many years, and they had once been shipmates, but there was more mercenary than friend in Avarhouse.

The Captain left his house and walked over to knock on his neighbors' door. He waited for a time, and then knocked again. When he heard no answer at the first home, he went on to the second. When still he received no answer, he went home.

The Captain considered his next move. He had left his car some miles away and in the direction opposite from where he wished to travel, but driving to Anna's school would be much quicker than walking.

Across the street from the Captain's home was a marina. A large sailboat was berthed at the end of the dock. In the sailboat, the Captain had a small plastic gas tank that he used for filling an outboard engine when he sailed during the summer.

The Captain walked out on the dock to retrieve the tank. He took a moment to look across the river into the city. From here he could make out the great white dome of the capital. He thought for a moment he could see the obelisk rising above the mall, but dismissed it as likely just a construction crane. He could see no indication of disturbance in the city, no hints of fire or smoke.

The Captain took the gas tank and went back to his house. He drafted a quick note to Anna, which he left on the kitchen table. He looked around the rooms once again, and then headed out the door.

With tank in hand, the Captain walked up the road heading to the nearest gas station. He hoped to hire a tow truck to take him to his car and pull it from the ditch. Alternatively, he would get some gasoline, walk to the car, and get it out of the ditch on his own.

He arrived and found the station closed. Several cars were lined up at the pumps. One of the drivers called out to the Captain. "The guy came by and said they're going to open up soon."

"Do you believe him?"

"Not sure I do, but what choice is there?"

Deciding not to wait, the Captain returned home. He left the gas tank on his front stoop and went inside his house. He searched through various cabinets and closets until he found what he was looking for, a small portable radio. He swapped out some batteries, turned a switch, and heard the familiar sound of an AM station. He left the house and once again began to walk up the street.

As he walked, he worked his way through various radio frequencies trying to find a news channel. He found one station bleating an emergency broadcast message: "All citizens are to shelter in place. Emergency responders and military are to report to their duty stations. All military leave and liberty is canceled without exception."

The Captain moved on to the next station, "—assaults were unprovoked and indiscriminate. The attackers were ill and beyond reason. Authorities insist that claims of rabies, or the use of rabies as a weapon, are untrue."

Before the newsreader finished his briefing, a second voice interrupted. "I saw a man running down a street and jumping onto a man's back, biting him. I was looking out a window and heard the man screaming. The attacker definitely did not look human. It was naked, incredibly thin, longed limbs. The guy attacked was able to fight it off and take off running. Really not human— was not normal in appearance, extraordinarily thin."

A third voice spoke up. "I saw a group of men out last night. A group of men armed with clubs and bats. They told me they had chased one attacker and killed him, but the things were really fast."

The Captain stopped for a moment. He looked up and down the street. It was a beautiful sunny day, but as far as he could tell, he was the only living soul out on the street. The Captain continued briskly, his head swiveling, left and right, forward and back, as he walked.

The first newsreader continued, "Although the authorities state that these are isolated incidents and the community is safe, everyone is being directed to remain in their homes and stay off the streets."

The second newsreader spoke up as soon as the first paused. "We have a story of a wounded man in a wheelchair waiting in an emergency room. The man was bitten in the neck. They couldn't stop the bleeding. They've been locking up the dead, just in case."

The third voice began to speak, "Everyone needs to go to a place of safety."

The second voice would not be distracted. "Listen, this isn't about hysteria, this is about zombies. We have reports of people being shot and still attacking."

The voices on the radio now erupted simultaneously. As they loudly talked over one another, the Captain had difficulty making out individual voices.

He heard one speaker shout out, "Nonsense, it's drugs, PCP."

A different voice called out, "Bull! Did you see the videos? That's no drug!"

The argument continued, "It's a designer drug, like krokodil or PCP."

A voice could be heard interrupting the onscreen talent. "What's crocodile?"

The Captain turned to another station with a newsreader in the middle of an interview. "Doctor could you explain that again, in plain language for our radio audience."

He heard a woman speaking in reply. "I'm holding an ultrasound image. See, no question about it. The baby's gone." The doctor's voice betrayed no emotion as she continued to explain to the audience the proof that the baby had disappeared in utero.

With the doctor was another woman. The newsreader directed a series of questions at the second woman but received only incoherent responses. The woman wept and cried, but the newsreader continued to fire questions at her anyway. He stopped only when the doctor intervened and began to comfort the second woman.

When the station went to commercial the Captain turned the radio off.

As the Captain walked, the silence of the streets was regularly interrupted by sirens. At one point he could hear a siren so near and so loud that he stopped walking. He expected to see an emergency vehicle rush past him. He waited. He looked up and down the empty streets for the source. After a few minutes the noise abated; only then did he begin to walk again.

As the Captain continued, he passed a home with a man sitting on his porch, a cup of coffee in his hand, a rifle across his lap. The Captain thought that most audacious. Normally, if anyone had seen a rifle out in the open, they would have called the cops and this man would have found himself on his way to jail. The man waved as the Captain walked past. He did not know the man, but the Captain waved back. He wished he had his pistols and rifles again. "Maybe at least a shotgun," he decided.

The streets were a disaster. Old Town had always suffered from narrow streets and too many cars. On the best of days, cars would be parked bumper to bumper along both curbs. Now, in addition to the usual congestion, dozens of cars had been abandoned on the road itself. He came to an intersection completely blocked by three cars that had come together with such force that they welded into a single massive lump of steel and plastic. Several cars had rolled forward into parked cars. He passed one place where a car had driven up over the sidewalk and struck a storefront. He stepped out onto the street to move around the wreckage and debris.

The Captain passed the ruins of a clothing store. A plate glass window had been shattered. Huge fragments of glass covered the sidewalk. A naked mannequin lay amongst the shards and daggers of glass. On the sidewalk, and leading back into the store, he could see a trail of discarded clothing.

The store owner worked at the front of his shop trying to board up broken windows with plywood. The Captain could see inside the store. Much of the shelving and merchandise was on the floor. It appeared free sweaters, blouses, and skirts had proven irresistible to the mob.

Very close to this ruin, he passed a pharmacy that had suffered the same fate. Glass windows had been broken with merchandise scattered out to the sidewalk. Surprisingly, he could see no other signs of looting. The remainder of the shops, restaurants, and bars he passed were untouched.

As he walked along, the Captain looked over some of the abandoned cars. He stopped to take a closer look at one car. He could see keys dangling from the steering column. He considered 'borrowing' the car. Driving he could reach Anna's school in minutes instead of walking for hours. He rejected the temptation; the condition of the roads did not justify the risks.

After a time, the Captain returned to playing with the portable radio. For the most part, the newsreaders recycled the same stories he had already heard. Occasionally they had an interview. "I was on the bus see, and like I looked up, and half the people in the bus were gone. The bus was cruising down the road without a driver. One of the passengers jumped up or I would have been killed."

There was a story about a plane that had continued to fly even after jet fighters had scrambled and tried to force it to land. The military reported it had crashed into a Tennessee mountainside and that burning wreckage had been scattered for a mile or more. The newsreader speculated that the plane must have been on autopilot.

A studio newsreader chimed in, "I bet the military shot the plane down. There's more here than we're being told."

The first newsreader went to the next story without pause. "In Jerusalem, there have been numerous reports of people attacked and killed at random. Authorities have described these attacks as unprovoked and heinous. The Israeli defense forces have been mobilized. The American embassy has issued orders for all Americans to shelter-in-place. No official word yet on evacuations."

The Captain changed to a radio station talking about Europe. A British newsreader described random attacks on the streets and in people's homes. The newsreader had a clipped educated accent that added gravity to his report. "A curfew has been announced for London and Paris. A curfew has been announced for all of Germany.

People are being ordered to remain in their homes from dusk to dawn." The newsreader listed a series of rules and regulations to deal with the current emergency. The Captain switched stations again.

The Captain tried to switch back to one of the previous news stations. He came to a newsreader interviewing an expert on terrorists. He could hear the relief in the newsreader's voice as the unidentified expert reassured him these "—were a series of lone-wolf terrorist attacks orchestrated by anarchists taking advantage of the initial confusion. The attacks thus far have been disorganized as a result."

Another voice cut in with a great deal of impatience, "Sir, that explains nothing about the missing children."

The expert did not miss a beat and repeated his main theme. "The spontaneous nature of the attacks indicates the work of lone-wolves, unplanned and unorganized. The attackers were taking advantage of the mass disappearance that took place earlier in the day. The authorities now have things well in hand. Investigation will soon reveal—"

The Captain continued to walk up the street wishing again that he had a weapon. He began to check the piles of rubbish he passed. He saw nothing with which to defend himself, not a stick, not a pipe, not a brick. At one point he picked up a wine bottle but immediately put it down again after handling something slimy around the neck of the thing.

Closer to the center of town he could see more people out moving about. Now and then, he caught someone peeking at him through a window.

Any time a car approached, he would step off the curb and hold his thumb out. He had never hitchhiked in his entire life. He hoped that one of the drivers might give him a ride, particularly because he was walking in uniform. The cars went slowly by, weaving around any wrecked or abandoned cars; the drivers did not give the Captain a second look.

Only one police car drove past as he walked. It came by blasting its siren as if this would be enough to clear the road. The Captain thought that the policeman might order him to get off the street, but he too went by without a second look. Shortly after the police car went by the Captain heard gunshots. A few minutes after that, a helicopter flew slowly back and forth over the neighborhood.

The Captain continued to listen to the radio. On this channel the newsreader could not contain his excitement as he talked about the night's events. "—reports of long lines of refugees fleeing Paris and Berlin. Although authorities claim to have restored order in both cities, large numbers of people are fleeing. The mass exodus that started during the morning hours further aggravated blocked and congested roadways. Many have been forced to flee on foot carrying with them their most precious possessions. Authorities continue to urge—"

Another voice chimed in, "Folks, the reports of attacks taking place in the cities are not confirmed."

"I heard there were at least two attacks in Leesburg and one in Frederick."

"But not confirmed." This last said with exasperation. "We don't have nearly the same problem as Europe."

"Maybe, but everyone I know is hiding out in their homes."

"But not confirmed. There are cops on every corner."

The newsreaders began to argue about the nature of the attacks. One commentator insisted state-sponsored terrorists were behind the day's events. "This is a massive, organized attack, a bio-weapon. Something far beyond the capability of any ordinary terrorist group."

The station shifted to a story about a local hospital. A reporter interviewed a wounded man brought in for treatment. "This naked creep was just standing there. I went up to him to see if he was okay. He was high on drugs. As soon as I touched him he bites me right on the arm. He almost tore my arm off. I hit him and kicked him, and he wouldn't let go."

A deep tenor voice in the background chimed in, "Definitely PCP." Other voices interrupted. After a moment the interviews resumed.

The Captain could hear the voice of a young woman. She spoke calmly and the other voices quieted. "This, like mummy, was laying on the ground. He's skin, like all scaly, leather-like skin. On the ground, I went up to look at him. He bit me. He, he bit me on the ankle, so I can't walk. He scratched me. He tried to bite my throat.... Am I going to die?"

One of the commentators in the studio, clearly alarmed, tried getting the attention of the reporter in the hospital. "Leave the hospital immediately. It is not safe there. You must leave the hospital immediately." Now the other studio commentators began to speak over the first commentator. Any explanation of why the reporter had to leave the hospital disappeared in the confusion of voices.

When the babble seemed like it would not end, the Captain turned to the next radio frequency. This station only had one reporter taking telephone interviews. Several callers talked about attacks during the night. One verged on hysteria. "My husband saw the attack! The crazy was running through the street naked! He killed this cop for no reason, knifed him right in the throat, and then ran down the street!" Several more persons called in to talk about attacks during the night. After a time the interviews became as redundant and repetitive as the earlier news.

The Captain once again switched frequencies. He found a few stations broadcasting in foreign languages. He found a station playing popular music and he listened for a few minutes. As he changed the channel he commented out loud, "How appropriate for the end of the world."

He thought he had cycled through all the channels when he discovered another news station. Here the radio newsreaders interviewed each other in fairly calm voices.

First newsreader: "Last night was total confusion. A significant number of people have been affected by this disorder—"

Second newsreader: "You should have seen the hospital last night. Hundreds of wounded people brought in. Blood supplies were in short supply; Cops with guns drawn were bringing people into the hospital; Doctors are unsure whether the insanity is contagious."

First newsreader: "Any risk that these bites are infectious? That they're the source of the disease?"

Second newsreader: "Definite problem with infection, but no zombies popping up if that's what you mean. Many people have died of wounds though."

First newsreader: "Do they know what's causing it?"

Second newsreader: "Best guess seems to be some sort of nerve agent; maybe a biologic that makes people crazy, like super rabies. It spread too fast to be a virus."

Third voice, a woman's voice: "Let's not speculate. Things have calmed down. The police and Army have largely restored order."

The Captain stopped walking and once again began to look around for a weapon. He located some broken bottles and a couple of wooden pallets leaning up against a wall, but nothing useful as a club or spear.

One of the radio newsreaders suddenly became solemn. "The president is going to address the Nation.... We're expecting the President of the United States shortly to make an announcement about the current crisis."

Chatter on the news station died down as they waited for the President's speech. One of the newsreaders tried to fill the dead air. "The press corps is standing by. We do not have an advance copy of the President's speech, but we believe it will include the cancelation of all military leave and mobilization of the reserves. We are anticipating the President will arrive at the podium at any moment...."

One of the other newsreaders chimed in, "This has not happened since Pearl Harbor." This was followed by a lengthy pause.

Another newsreader spoke up. "We do know that all military leave has been canceled and that orders will soon be going out to mobilize the National Guard. We do know people are being asked not to engage in unnecessary travel and to not make phone calls unless it is an emergency.... We are standing by for the President."

The newsreaders continued to engage in innocuous commentary as they waited for the President's important speech; the Captain, however, decided not to wait. He had arrived at Anna's school.

When he approached the school, he could see the teacher's parking lot half full of empty cars. He walked around and through the parking lot. He could not see Anna's car anywhere.

The front doors to the school were locked, but a side door had been wedged open. He walked up to the main office, but no one was present. He stopped and listened but heard no sounds.

The Captain walked slowly away from the office. The corridors allowed little light to bleed in from the outside. He suspected the building's electricity had been turned off. When he reached the end of the corridor he again stopped and listened. The place seemed abandoned.

The Captain walked back to his wife's classroom. Here, everything seemed in order. He looked across a room of miniature desks and chairs, all grouped in a circle. He noticed backpacks hanging from the chairs. Crayons and colored papers covered the desks.

The Captain went over to a large desk with an adult's chair. He began to open up the drawers to the desk. He thought, "This is where she would keep her purse," but he did not know for sure. The drawers to the desk held only papers and supplies.

He looked around the room. On a back table, he could see a large, navy blue, practical kind of purse. He went over and examined it. The purse had been turned over, its contents spilled out on the table. He could find neither wallet nor keys.

The Captain went over to his wife's desk and sat in her chair. He could see wires and cords around the chair, computer connections, but no computer. He looked around the room again. In one corner he could see a hook on the wall. A red coat hung from the hook.

The Captain sat and stared at the red coat. Anna was always careful about dressing appropriately before going outside. The Captain never needed to ask about the weather, he just needed to see which coat she had selected in the morning. When the fall turned to winter there would be other coats, heavier, longer, some almost reaching the ground. All of her coats were in shades of red.

The Captain knew that if he searched the other classrooms, he would likely find other abandoned purses. Some would contain keys to cars in the parking lot. He almost got up to look but decided against it. Although he would not to take one of the abandoned cars, he still could use a baseball bat, or perhaps some spare batteries for his radio. With the power off in the school, every room, dark and gloomy, resisted search. In the end, he left the way he came.

As he stepped outside he began once again to fool with his radio. A story about missing children and missing teachers made him pause and listen for a moment, and then he started back on the long walk home.

Entitled, Al Araf; Revealed At Mecca:

God said unto him, Get thee hence, despised, and driven far away: verily whoever of them shall follow thee, I will surely fill hell with you all:

but as for thee, O Adam, dwell thou and thy wife in paradise; and eat of the fruit thereof wherever ye will; but approach not this tree, lest ye become of the number of the unjust.

And Satan suggested to them both, that he would discover unto them their nakedness, which was hidden from them; and he said, Your LORD hath not forbidden you this tree, for any other reason but lest ye should become angels, or lest ye become immortal. And he sware unto them, saying, Verily I am one of those who counsel you aright.

And he caused them to fall through deceit. And when they had tasted of the tree, their nakedness appeared unto them; and they began to join together the leaves of paradise, to cover themselves. And their LORD called to them, saying, Did I not forbid you this tree: and did I not say unto you, Verily Satan is your declared enemy?

They answered, O LORD, we have dealt unjustly with our own souls; and if thou forgive us not, and be not merciful unto us, we shall surely be of those who perish.

God said, Get ye down, the one of you an enemy unto the other; and ye shall have a dwelling-place upon the earth, and a provision for a season.

He said, Therein shall ye live, and therein shall ye die, and from thence shall ye be taken forth at the resurrection.

The Koran, Chapter VII Entitled, Al Araf; translated by George Sales, 1734.

CHAPTER-6 – EXODUS and POLICE

Tuesday, Day Two: Near LaFayette Station, Tennessee

The General tried to continue the retreat even as the sun began to rise. The need to flee the city was irresistible, but the blinding light of day was impossible to face. Still, for a time, he persisted. To stay near the city meant death, something worse than death.

As he fled, he tried to keep to the woods. The trees and thick underbrush provided some protection, but even the minimal light filtering through the trees had forced him to shield his eyes with his hands. To leave the shade of the trees meant pain. The direct sunlight blinded him, more than blinded him; it felt like a hot iron searing into his brain. Too many open spaces and too much light made his skin itch and his head ache. The sun bordered the forest with a wall of light.

The scarecrows following the General stumbled through the trees and brush in the early, blinding daylight. At times they bunched up, at other times they became spread out. The walk-run of their retreat became more difficult to maintain as the sun rose higher in the sky. Only the sounds of engines on the road and random gunfire kept the scarecrows moving forward.

When they passed a sign by the road, the General remembered another retreat. "Skirmish at LaFayette Station." He remembered that fight on the Memphis and Charleston railroad; how he and his men had forced their way across the bridge against Sherman's soldiers.

The General took the arm of a scarecrow following close and showed him the sign. As the scarecrow looked over the writing the General spoke. "Sherman, Hurlbut ... they chased us." He paused and drew in breath. He remembered to concentrate on each word as he spoke. He paused for a moment and then began to push out the words. "The River flooded.... We could not cross." A pause again, a breath, a deep breath followed by another flurry of words, "They burned the bridges.... " A pause and breath, "We attacked ... most without muskets." A pause, a breath, "But we drove 'em." A pause, a breath, "Aah got an Army an' Hurlbut lost his job."

The General began to laugh at his joke but immediately stopped. The sound could not be the sound of his laughter. He had always had a deep resonate laugh. This new laughter sounded like the cackling of an old woman. Even his nakedness did not mortify him as much as the sound of this cackling.

He returned to the march, but in the end, it became too much. They were forced to stop and look for shelter. The General found a dark patch well away from the road and sat down at the base of a tree. Here he waited in the shadows.

The General did not know how many scarecrows had followed him. They had been herded into the forest by the daylight, by the hunters, by the dogs, by the roving engines. The scarecrows stopped when he stopped. They pointed at him and spoke among themselves, their speech punctuated with whistles and grunts.

The General sat in his hiding place. He hid from the hunters and he hid from the sunlight. He waited for the night to come again. He waited patiently. Only the return of night would allow the General and his scarecrows to move freely.

As the General waited in the forest for the sun to set, he sought calm. All around him scarecrows lay in the shadows tossing and turning restlessly. The General knew he needed to sleep, but the effort brought only anxiety.

When he closed his eyes and let his mind rest, he found himself back in the true darkness, cold and drifting. The others, those that lived in the darkness, waited for him, insatiable as leeches. If ever the General fell asleep he soon jerked awake swinging his arms out in defense; then he would look about and remember that he waited in the woods for the day to end.

As he sat beneath the tree, the General examined his long, fleshless fingers. His fingernails were like arrowheads caked in dirt. His uniform, what was left of it, was caked in dirt. His legs and feet were covered in dirt and dust. His toenails were sharp, black, pointed, and dirt-encrusted.

The General longed to be clean. He left the tree and approached a nearby stream, a clear shallow place alongside some rocks. He examined the pool from this and that angle. Finally, he lay down in the water. Even in the twilight of the forest, he could see the dirt swirl away.

The water was cool, but not unpleasant, especially when compared to the cold of the dark place from which he had escaped. Thinking of that dark prison led him to other thoughts, of sinking, of drowning, of the hated ones who waited below the surface. He got up out of the stream with a start.

He felt as thirsty and as hungry as he had ever been. The ability to find rations, no matter how scarce, was the mark of a true soldier, but he was thirsty and hungry.

He reached down to the stream and cupped his hand. He brought water to his mouth. He gagged and spit it out. He reached down to the green things that grew around him. He tried chewing on grass, on herbs, on leaves, on moss, but the spasm in his gut only became worse.

When his thoughts turned to other food and drink, he thought of the screaming woman. His stomach cramped and twisted with demands. He felt a constant ache, a worm crawling backwards and forwards in his gut. At one point he lifted the raged remains of his coat to see if a living parasite might be moving in his flesh, but he could see nothing. The pain remained with him in the day as it had in the night, neither weaker nor stronger.

He felt tired and lay down in the shadows of the trees. He closed his eyes and tried again to sleep.

The ability to sleep, no matter what the condition, was the mark of a true soldier, but now he knew it as a place of nightmares. In the past, he could always sleep, anytime, anywhere, but now he could only drowse fitfully. Whenever he seemed on the verge of real sleep, he would snap awake as if falling from a cliff. Sleep was a cold, thick, dark ocean, populated by the damned waiting to pull him under.

In the distance, he heard gunshots and dogs. He could hear the sound of the hunters, now close, and now far. His mind turned to thoughts of escape. The river went east and southeast. There had been great forests to the east, not like the country around the city. These forests around him had diminished, too many roads, too many houses, too many farms. He visualized the old maps and considered time and distance. Uncertainty washed over him. He needed a map and a compass. He needed them badly.

Suddenly, overhead, engines appeared in the sky. Machines crisscrossed back and forth leaving white lines of steam like the hand of God tracing out the law. There would be nowhere to hide from such machines. He looked up to the sky his mouth agape. He pointed at the flying engines and cried out.

One of the Scarecrows nearby spoke up harshly. "Don't worry, they're not ... 'bout us."

Another voice answered. "The hell with them … and the cops ... and troopers….. Whence we're away, we'll be safe." The answering voice had a rasping sound. It lacked the mellowness of a southern voice.

The harsh voice again. "You're not an Admiral… are you? I've seen Admirals with less braid." The General looked over to see the talking scarecrow pointing at the remnants of his uniform.

The Sailor appeared as thin and ragged as the rest, but his face seemed less black, flushed, almost feverish. He spoke clearly compared to the General's croak. His clothes were moldy and ragged, but with a bloody stain across the remains of a white shirt. The General could smell the iron tang about him.

"Yah bloody," the General accused.

"I reckon. One of those feckers…. Tried to send me back down to hell." The Sailor's voice remained unapologetic.

The General wanted to shout at the Sailor, but he could not increase the volume of his voice. He stopped mid-speech to force air into his lungs. "Yah attacked the woman in the house!"

"I bit a man." The Sailor gave a thoughtful pause. "He did scream like a girl though."

The General picked up a stick but did not advance on the Sailor. "What are yah, an animal?" He paused to draw in breath. "How could yah do this?"

"It was him or me." The Sailor paused and then continued, "We're devils. We're in hell."

The General concentrated on forcing air into his lungs. The voice was not his, but it grew louder, "Yah fool—Aah'm not a devil…. Yah rabid dog—a plague of rabid dogs."

"We have rabies?" The Sailor considered this for a moment but then shook his head. "We're dead and in hell. Instead of them eating us, we're eating them."

Across the way, another speaker, croaking. "Aah saw yah, the graveyard." There was an audible sucking in of breath. "General. I saw yah. Aah was with yah … in the Army."

The Sailor continued, "We're in hell. Kill or be killed."

The Old Soldier spoke again, "After the war, when aah was old…. There was a big tomb, big statue."

The General now with hesitancy, "When aah awoke, aah was alone…. A simple marker, mah name only."

The Sailor again, "I remember that statue, you on a horse."

Another voice, a mix of Yankee twang and heavy stutter spoke up. "I used to g-g-go there." The Yankee punctuated his sentence with a loud drawn-out "ah" sound and then continued. "C-c-city d-d-decided, ah, no more d-d-dead rebels."

The Old Soldier spoke, "We'uns tain't in hell." A pause and a breath, "This'n Tennessee."

The Sailor again, "You looked a lot better up on that horse."

A fifth voice, clear and distinct, a voice of reason. "God would not condemn us so." The voice took in a breath and then continued, "We have been given a second chance." Again a pause and breath, "Even on the day of judgment."

The Sailor again, "Reverend, I'd say strange way to summon the angels." He gestured towards the city. "Pistols and rifles! Pistols and rifles!" The words came out in a rushed staccato.

The Old Soldier answered, "Last trump.... Aah say."

As the scarecrows debated, the General listened to the barking of the dogs. The hunters had returned and were coming closer. On the fringes of the wood, he could see movement. He could hear voices. The hunters were mere specks in the distance, but he could hear them talking as if they were only a few feet away. He could hear them moving through the brush. He could hear the hunters cursing the dogs, but the dogs would go no further into the wood. They remained at the fringes, barking and whining in turn. The dogs had the scent, but not the desire for the hunt.

The General stood and pointed towards the approaching hunters. He turned and hurried deeper into the woods. He looked behind to see dozens of scarecrows following him. They walked quickly but with stealth.

Suddenly a gunshot echoed through the wood and all began to run. The brush and the tree branches pulled at the rags of the scarecrows, but no cut or scratch impeded them. They ran, calling out with raspy voices, but none paused. The underbrush pulled at them, the sunlight blinded them, but they put distance between themselves and the hunters. Despite the speed of the run, none were breathless. Despite cuts and scratches from the underbrush, none complained; none bled.

The scarecrows continued to move away from the sounds of the hunters and the dogs in their clumsy fashion. The General hoped the hunters might give up the pursuit rather than chase them through the woods and swampy ground, but he still could hear shooting in the distance.

Just as the General thought they must pull free of the hunters, he smelled smoke. As he moved forward he could see fire and smoke ahead.

The General paused only for a moment. If they stopped, the fire would force them back towards the hunters. He ran and leaped through the flames into a field of light. He had left the shelter of the forest and moved through an open field, a field of long grass that burned all around him. The smoke and the fire and the sunlight blinded him.

Off to his left, blue and red and white lights flashed. He could hear the engines and the men with the engines. He could hear gunshots. He felt a bullet strike him and drive him to the ground.

The General lay on the ground surrounded by patches of burning grass. Scarecrows ran past him through the field and flames. The open area consisted of only a narrow break in the woods, but many stumbled, lost and confused in the smoke and fire and sunlight.

The General crept forward trying to keep his head down as the bullets sang through the burning grass. He could not decide which direction to flee. He remembered going uphill before the ambush, so he tried working his way uphill now.

He did not mind the swirling smoke of the fire. The smoke shaded his eyes and brought no discomfort to his lungs. The smoldering grass fascinated him. He pinched some of the embers in his hand. He could smell the slight odor of burning, but it did not hurt. It felt like he wore thick gauntlets protecting his slender fingers.

Ahead scarecrows called out. Some uttered little screams, others warbled, some howled.

The General heard the voice of the Sailor. "This way! This way!" Unlike the others, the Sailor called out with confidence, clear and certain.

The General got up and ran towards the sound of the Sailor's voice. As he ran he could see figures of men to his left. A scarecrow crossed his path running in the direction of the soldiers. The scarecrow's flight ended with a shotgun blast.

In moments the General escaped the burning grass and made it back to the woods. Behind him, he could hear the shooting growing in intensity. More scarecrows ran the gauntlet.

Deeper in the woods the Sailor tried to rally the scarecrows He managed to lead a few scarecrows down towards the men and the engines.

The Sailor called out to the scarecrows to throw stones and sticks at the soldiers.

The General stopped and examined his body. He looked for the bullet that had knocked him down. He had to take off his coat to find it, a hole in his left side, through the ribs, and into the lung. When he sucked in breath to speak, he could feel air dribbling out, but no blood. He could see a black sticky matter around the edges of the wound, but no blood. It hurt only when he poked his finger into it.

The General knew a great deal about gunshots. How many men had he shot? How many times had he been shot?

The Old Soldier came up to rest beside the General. "Y'all hurt?"

The General considered a moment before responding. "Aah was hit by a ball at Shiloh…. Now aah been shot through the lung…. Aah should be killed, but it does not trouble me."

The Old Soldier was not surprised. "No pain… 'cause not men." The Old Soldier waved his hands towards the gathering scarecrows. "Locusts! Locusts!"

The General walked deeper into the woods. When he looked about him he could see several hundred scarecrows following him in stumbling retreat. The sounds of the hunters, the hounds, and the gunfire, decreased with the decrease in daylight. He hoped the enemy would break off pursuit once night came. He hoped, without the light of day, the enemy would be reluctant to press any attack.

To be chased through the night and day and never allowed to sleep would have been disastrous for any normal body of troops, but none had difficulty keeping up, or even running when needed. The pursuit by the enemy had temporarily cured them of straggling or wandering off. The hunters drove them together into a tight pack, like dogs driving sheep.

Despite his wound and lack of sleep, the General continued walking without pause. He badly wanted to sleep but had no desire to close his eyes. Nor did he see any evidence of any of the scarecrows being tired enough or fatigued enough to leave the march. Slowly the sun went down allowing them to move without the blinding light.

The General tried to keep directly to the east and head for the safety of the mountains, but the river began to turn to the south. As much as he wished to keep to the safety of the woods and swampy areas alongside the river, he was forced to find a place and cross.

The scarecrows that followed looked neither left nor right as they crossed the bridge. Away from the river they rapidly advanced. Much of the ground they covered was open country. As they moved along black paths that smelled of oil and tar, all were anxious to find the security of a new forest, a new hiding place. All were afraid of the hunters and the busy little engines that controlled the roadways.

The General continued to lead, but these roads lacked the feel of the earthen paths so familiar to him. Dense patches of scrub and brush had replaced the farms. Farms and buildings of extraordinary design had replaced the forests. At last, they came to a railroad right of way and they marched east without fear of being chased.

Late into the night, a train approached. Clackety clack clack it sounded as the train rolled down the tracks. The cars were many and massive, but the engine was truly amazing. Instead of spewing great black clouds of smoke as it moved along the tracks, it sped forward as if feeding on air; it pulled unhindered dozens and dozens of train cars trailing in its wake.

The train took many minutes to pass. Clackety clack clack, it rolled on, uninterested in the crowd of scarecrows that huddled in the scrub on both sides of the right of way. The busy little engines that ran up and down the roads were mere mosquitoes compared to the leviathan that ran down the railroad tracks. The train rolled forward as imperiously as if the hand of God himself pushed it.

The General could see that the trains had grown colossal, just like the cities, but there was one thing that confused him, "Why the paint an' drawings?" he asked. "New and strange designs?"

The Sailor answered him, "Not designs, graffiti. Feking vandals. Nothing by design."

They eventually reached an area of forests and lakes, crisscrossed with roads. Near the roads, the hunters waited. As soon as the scarecrows emerged from the trees and began to cross an open road the hunters aimed and fired; they fired as rapidly as machines. Bullets filled the air like swarms of angry bees.

Scarecrows ran in all directions. Others dove to the earth and crawled through the brush like animals. Some remained frozen in place. They hooted and hissed and screamed in panic like the thing of nightmares.

The General lay on the ground. He felt the wound to his side and fought against a sense of panic. He needed to get across the open field and gain to the cover of the trees to escape, but the hunters fired without pause at any who moved.

Finally, the voice of reason, "If we speak to them, they will understand." A thoughtful pause, "We are not a danger to them, now. We are … God-fearing."

The Sailor spoke up, "Reverend, you're an idiot.… It's kill and be killed."

The General interjected, "Maybe if yah trash… hadn't bitten people."

He meant to say this in the voice of command, but it came out barely above a whisper. The impossibly rapid gunfire of the soldier's repeaters punctuated their conversation.

The Reverend called out to the Sailor. "Your shirt for a flag of truce. I'll parley."

"Use your own bloody shirt."

Reluctantly, the Reverend tore off a portion of his shirt. It was indeed bloody. The stain smelt as sweet as if it had been soaked in perfume.

The Reverend walked towards the hunters. They could hear him call out in a raspy voice. "We want to surrender."

The General moved towards the Reverend, "The hell yah say," but there was no need to stop him. As soon as the Reverend went out to meet the hunters, dozens of rifles and shotguns began to fire. The General could hear the Reverend call out as the bullets struck him down.

The General and those around him took the opportunity to run. They ran deep into the darkness of the forest. Those who had followed the General since the city did not lag far behind. They kept up with the General as he ran through woods in stumbling retreat.

It would be three days before the General saw the Reverend again.

Deck Log – Third Day

SHIP'S DECK LOG SHEET

OPNAV 3100/99 (Rev 7-84)
S/N 0107-LF-031-0498

USE BLACK INK TO FILL IN THIS LOG

SHIP TYPE	HULL NUMBER	YEAR	MONTH	ZONE	DAY
AS	00	43	09	B	17

USS __CYCLOPS__
AT / PASSAGE FROM __NORFOLK VA__
TO __MUSCAT, OMAN__

POSITION	ZONE	TIME	POSITION	ZONE	TIME	POSITION	ZONE	TIME	LEGEND
0800			1200			2000			1 – CELESTIAL
L_____, BY ___			L_____, BY ___			L_____, BY ___			2 – ELECTRONIC
A_____, BY ___			A_____, BY ___			A_____, BY ___			3 – VISUAL
									4 – D R

TIME	ORDER	CSE	SPEED	DEPTH	RECORD OF EVENTS OF THE DAY
0800					ASSUMED THE WATCH. MOORED AS BEFORE. LIEUTENANT R.S. MERRIAM, USN
					MUSTER THE CREW ON STATION, ET2 AREHART REPORTED MISSING
0910					RECEIVED FUEL, WATER AND DRAFT REPORT.
0930					STATIONED THE SPECIAL SEA DETAIL.
0950					EXECUTIVE OFFICER AND NAVIGATOR ON THE BRIDGE.
0952					STEERING SHIFTED TO BRIDGE.
0955					COMPLETED ALL PREPARATIONS FOR GETTING UNDERWAY.
1000					ANCHOR HEAVED AND SHIP PROCEEDED INTO THE CANAL.

REPORT SYMBOL
OPNAV 2100-10

01 Level - Forward, Wardroom

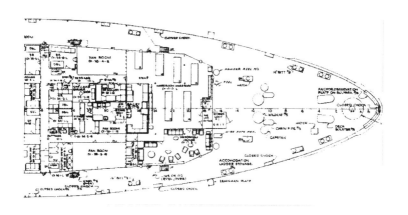

Litany:

Those who dwell in the heights and those who dwell in the depths worship thee. Thoth and the goddess Maāt have laid down thy course for thee daily for ever. Thine Enemy the Serpent hath been cast into the fire, the fiend hath fallen down into it headlong. His arms have been bound in chains, and Rā hath hacked off his legs; the Mesu Betshet shall never more rise up.

The Literature of the Ancient Egyptians, by E. A. Wallis Budge, 1914.

CHAPTER- 7 – INTO THE SUEZ

Wednesday, Day Three: Suez Canal, Egypt

It seemed to Lieutenant Irawell that he had only just fallen asleep when it was time to get up again. He could feel the vibrations of the ship's engines humming through the steel decks. It produced an optimistic sensation, a sense of the ship coming awake, happy to be underway again.

The Lieutenant left his stateroom and headed up to the wardroom. He desperately wanted some coffee. He poured a cup, but before he could sit down to breakfast, he was drawn into the adjacent lounge area.

Warrant Officer Unger held the television remote flipping through channels. He hit a button on the remote and a montage of crashed cars, burning buildings, and at least one burning aircraft appeared on the television. As the images played in the background a newsreader gave his report. "—cascade event swept across every major city in the world. People disappeared in the thousands. There has been no explanation. Government bulletins have provided little—"

The view suddenly switched as Unger pressed a button on the remote. Now a different newsreader appeared, speaking excitedly, "We have unconfirmed reports that the assassins of the King of Saudi Arabia included his own security team. There is no word on whether the killers have been arrested. Meanwhile, royalist forces are fighting to regain control of the Masjid al-Haram in Mecca, as well as the television and radio stations. The insurgents claim to be led by the Mahdi and called on all Muslims to obey him. We have unconfirmed reports that Saudi Special Forces, sent to liberate the mosque, may have joined the insurgents. In related news, the Grand Ayatollah of Iran has issued a press release ridiculing this 'Saudi Mahdi' as an American-influenced leftist, and claims that the attack on the Masjid al-Haram is the work of criminal American imperialism and international Zionism."

The camera switched to a new video showing a large crowd demonstrating in front of a wall and gate. Beyond the gate, the American flag flew over a nondescript building. Men in camouflage uniforms huddled behind sandbagged positions in the courtyard. The demonstrators screamed and shouted and burned flags at the wall's gate.

The newsreader provided explanation. "Large demonstrations are taking place around the United States embassy in Riyadh. Senior military officers have been appearing on Saudi television and radio demanding the immediate expulsion of all foreign military and intelligence assets. Additionally, they are demanding that all non-Muslims immediately leave the Kingdom. These military officers claim they represent the new interim government of–"

Unger switched channels again to a station with two newsreaders arguing. "There must be other explanations for the attacks. I mean, for example, dehydration can lead to seizures and brain damage. Some sort of virus—"

The second newsreader held up some papers and interrupted dramatically. "We've reports of mass murder and rioting in virtually every major city. Your explanation is we suffered some sort of instantaneous global pandemic?"

As the Lieutenant sat in the lounge drinking coffee and watching television, he heard the sound of giant sledgehammers striking against anvils. It was the sound of the ship's anchor being raised, each enormous link of chain clattering into the ship as it came aboard.

The Lieutenant reconsidered his plan of staying in the wardroom and getting some breakfast; instead, he hurried up to the bridge. On the way, he passed two armed sailors keeping watch in the passageway.

When the Lieutenant arrived, he could see the Sea and Anchor detail preparing the ship for departure. The Lieutenant had never been part of the detail, and he had no reason for being on the bridge beyond his desire to see the last of Port Said. He watched with interest as the sailors hurried about in preparation for the transit.

There in the Captain's chair sat the XO. He examined message traffic as sailors hurried about the bridge. After a moment he looked up at the men and women around him. The sailors went quiet and waited. Finally, the XO told the Officer of the Deck to get underway.

Now the Sea and Anchor detail truly began their work. The OOD gave the helmsmen his course and speed. The Helmsman repeated back the order along with a chopped, "Aye Aye." The ship's telegraph rang, ahead 1/3. The navigator began to call out his landmarks and compass points.

One of the ship's signalmen tried to raise the canal authority. "Port Said, Port Said, this is USS Cyclops, over." There was no response. "Port Said, Port Said, this is USS Cyclops calling about the status of our Pilot, over." Again there was no response. The radio receiver returned only static.

The Lieutenant listened intently as the crew of some of the merchant ships began chatting on the radio. They too sought instructions from the port. He could hear voices talking about a Navy ship heading towards the canal; they could only have been talking about the Cyclops. Now more voices could be heard on the radio talking about transiting, with or without a pilot, with or without Egyptian approval. Several captains indicated that they intended to get underway as well.

As the Lieutenant watched the sailors at work on the bridge, the XO called over. "Do you have anything new yet about the killing?"

"I was told this morning they found some boots near the centerline crane sir, but no sign of Asper or any stowaways."

"That's rich, 'stowaways.' " The XO dismissed the Lieutenant with a wave of his hand.

The Lieutenant was not the only observer on the bridge trying to keep from underfoot. The XO must have noticed the crowding as well. After speaking to the Lieutenant, he called out to the OOD, "Clear the bridge of tourists."

Most of the spectators obediently headed below, but the Lieutenant went up to the signal bridge. One of the members of the Sea and Anchor detail checked navigational markers on the big eyes. Several signalers stood by looking towards the city.

In Port Said, the Lieutenant could see little in the way of activity. The smell of smoke still hung in the air, but he could see no fires. No cars moved along the roads. No small boats moved near the quays. The only sign of life came from the minarets. He could make out the call to prayer even over the sound of the ship's engines.

Soon the Cyclops headed for the canal, and the buildings of Port Said began to grow small. In the Cyclops' wake, several great merchant ships began to follow.

The Lieutenant walked about the ship enjoying the beauty of the morning. Sometimes he would stop and lean against the ship's rails. Cool breezes flowed over the deck as gray dawn gave way to bright morning. In a day they would be through the Suez and heading for the Red Sea. It felt good to be underway.

All of the ship's machine guns remained manned, and he could hear the gunners talking quietly among themselves, wondering if the Egyptians would take some action or make some protest, but all remained quiet ashore. If the Egyptians cared about the ship's movement, they showed no sign of it.

Along the shores of the Suez, steeply piled dunes rose well above the water. Here and there, a few buildings and a few roads could be seen. No people or vehicles were in sight.

In the background, the Lieutenant could hear the BBC playing. The Lieutenant could not make out the words, but he recognized a British accent. He turned to find Miller holding his radio and continuing his search for the perfect signal. The voices on the radio faded in and out with each fluctuation in reception.

After a time Miller began to speak. "When I first seen Suez, I was a youngster then. Going through, you could see all the wreckage from the different wars. The Israelis and the Egyptians had already fought two or three wars along here by then. There were burned-out tanks and wrecked bunkers and forts. It was like the battles had just happened, not all cleaned up like now."

As he spoke Miller continued to make adjustments to the radio. The BBC news station played loud and clear.

"—a night of chaos and rioting, calm is once again settling over the great cities of Europe. Reports of murders, shootings, lootings, and fires have swept across Europe, more violent than any seen since the Second World War. Everywhere emergency services have been stretched to their maximum limits. In Germany, France, and Britain, martial law has been declared, but military forces have been taken by surprise. Fires have erupted in every major city, unchecked by available firefighters. Police and Military forces have everywhere been obliged to employ deadly force in the face of violent rampages. Only the coming of daylight has restored order."

The newsreader paused for a moment and the Lieutenant thought they had lost the signal once again when the broadcast continued.

"—today taking place in Brussels to discuss emergency economic measures and in The Hague to discuss security issues. Britain, France, the Netherlands, and Germany have invoked NATO provisions calling for collective self-defense. Italy and Turkey are expected to follow. "

As the BBC newsreader went on with his report the Lieutenant became impatient. "Doesn't sound like they figured out what happened, does it?"

"Not yet, but the Brits at least seem to know what it's not."

"How so?" responded the Lieutenant.

"Well, they know it's not the zombie apocalypse; these things talk and think and apparently can use knives and guns; and they know it's not God because even if there was a God, he would be more sensible then this."

"Do you think this is some kind of weapon?" the Lieutenant asked.

"I don't see it. Assuming you had something that could make people go lunatic, how would it happen everywhere at once. Even then, how do you explain all the missing people?"

"Maybe they're not missing. Some of them are in the streets going crazy, some are in their homes sick, some are in their basements dead."

The Warrant Officer just shrugged his shoulders in reply.

In the background, the newsreader continued his litany of doom. "—Portions of Paris have become no-go zones. Hand-to-hand fighting has been reported in some apartment buildings. Refugees have fled the city to the countryside. In London security teams are going from house to house to make certain—dangerous—custody—"

As the signal again faded, Miller returned to making adjustments to the radio antenna. He moved to the other side of the ship and then back again. He began to work the frequency dial. He raised a channel and new voices could be heard. These voices had a slight British accent, but they were not BBC.

First voice: "...Hitler in Berlin ...? Not possible, whatever was left of Hitler went to Moscow."

Second Voice: "No news from Moscow or Beijing. You know that Lenin and Mao were both under glass. If those two start moving around again, I reckon they'll shoot them, or make them the Premier."

There were few things to see as they traveled. At one point they passed a guard tower rising over the canal. Near the tower, a collection of military buildings could be seen. Further along, they passed some sort of housing compound. Occasionally people could be seen on the banks or driving vehicles along the roads.

By late afternoon they approached Ismailia. On the Egyptian side, two outsized memorials could be seen. One was a large dual-obelisk-type structure standing above shrouded figures. Not far away there was a second monument, a giant AK-47 muzzle and bayonet rising from the sand.

The Lieutenant had not moved during Miller's radio ministrations. He remained on deck leaning against the ship's rails. He could feel the sun reddening and burning his skin, but he did not leave. Miller spent the afternoon outside along with the Lieutenant, but he finally gave up on the radio. This he had turned off and left sitting on the deck.

Unger eventually came out and joined them. He asked a question as he approached. "Judge, you been able to check on your family?"

The Lieutenant had no close family. He had a sister and a brother. Only with his sister did he have any sort of regular contact, and that did not exceed more than one phone call a month. He answered the question with a shake of his head.

"You know, I was married once," Miller chuckled to himself recalling some private joke. "Can't say I'm worried about her now though."

Unger ignored him and pursued his earlier train of thought. "I've been hardly able to talk to my daughter for years. Not interested in my advice. My son is a great kid though." Unger paused for a moment and then began to reminisce. "In the old days, you couldn't call home when underway. No email. We went months without a phone call, only letters. Now, if everything is at an end and some new civilization starts, history will say civilization really ended about 1990. That's when people stopped writing letters. Nothing else will be left. Some letters, maybe some books, but even books are no longer on paper."

The Lieutenant would have happily spent the day lounging on the deck with the cool breezes flowing over him, listening to Miller and Unger, but Acedian appeared. He came walking by carrying a cup of coffee. He found a spot at the ship's rail and looked over at the Lieutenant. He told him, almost absently mindedly, that the XO was looking for him. The Lieutenant said nothing in response. He turned on his heel and left. He went up the nearest ladder to the XO's offices on the 02 level. There was a message on the door directing all department heads to the Captain's Conference room on the 03 level. By the time the Lieutenant arrived the meeting was already in full swing.

The XO sat at the head of the Captain's conference table with most of the other department heads gathered around. The Lieutenant grabbed a chair and tried to join them surreptitiously.

Commander Alschbach was talking about email. "Lots of crew worried about missing family members. One of my petty officers had to be sedated during the night."

"She's now in medical," Doc Peters volunteered.

Alschbach responded with surprise. "God, she's in medical with the murder victim?"

The Lieutenant spoke up in defense, "No sir. The body's in the chill storage, down in supply."

Lieutenant Commander Montgomery glared at the Lieutenant. "You can't leave dead bodies there you know. We can't have dead bodies in with the food storage."

The Lieutenant had a ready response, "We need to keep him on ice until a helo can come and get him and transport him to one of the mortuary units."

"Regs don't allow for bodies to be stored with food," Montgomery complained.

"NAVMEDCOM instructions say bodies are to be mechanically refrigerated until transported. We can do something different if the XO says. I'm only doing what I've been told to do."

The two officers looked to the XO for resolution, but he ignored them. Instead, he looked around at the assembled officers and began to speak as if they had only just arrived. "We're down to three duty sections and even that's a problem. You need to shake the tree and get everyone who's qualified on the roster. If they are not qualified, get them qualified. We need to supplement the engineering watches especially. Everyone can expect to pick up some extra duties."

Lieutenant Commander Lamb interrupted. "We don't need to do this. We can steam back to Naples to pick up replacements. We'll be in safe harbor while this all gets sorted out."

Alschbach joined his protest. "There's also a base in Djibouti. Once we near Djibouti we can divert and wait for replacements. We can let folks who need to leave fly out."

The XO replied with some heat, "There are no ready replacements. This is Navy-wide. We are not going to delay. We are going to complete the mission. We've got plenty of manpower to see us through, more than most." The XO paused and looked around the conference table for any dissent. "I want you, all your officers, all your chiefs and LPOs to get on top of any problems. We don't have complete information. Don't let people panic. Don't let people speculate. If anybody starts talking end of the world, you shut them down."

That night, dinner in the Wardroom consisted of a buffet of dry rice, nebulous meat, and glutinous boiled vegetables. The Lieutenant sat down with his salad to join the other officers at table. Some additional enlisted men had been detailed to take their turn at "mess crank." The sailors hovered about while civilian staff kept the serving trays filled with food.

The XO sat at the head of the table talking to Alschbach and Alexander. The Lieutenant could only hear portions of their conversation but could make out there were problems with the ship's communications.

After Alexander left, the XO turned on the Lieutenant while holding the draft radio message the Lieutenant had given to Alexander for processing. "What the fuck is wrong with you. You want to send in the clear a radio message that we had a murder onboard, maybe two. That maybe we have a zombie onboard?"

The Lieutenant was taken aback, "Sir, with the urgency, I didn't realize that was a problem. You said to contact NCIS immediately."

"Immediate was when you needed to find Asper, but you missed that chance." The XO thrust the radio message into the Lieutenant's hands. "Don't you have email? Don't you have other ways to get this done without telling the world we might have a murderer onboard?"

The Lieutenant replied with irritation, "Sir, I did send an email, but I've had no response, not even a read receipt. I'm not sure how well email is working, and I didn't say anything to anyone about zombies."

"Don't wait on NCIS. Nobody can spare manpower right now. Assume that to be the case. Do your own investigation. Don't try to pawn it off on NCIS with your bullshit messages."

The Lieutenant looked down at his draft. He could see various scribbles and annotations in green ink. As he considered his response, the XO snapped his fingers to regain his attention.

"Lieutenant, review it later on your own time. Listen, we've another missing sailor since yesterday. Petty Officer Arehart, definite depression case. Could be suicide. Repair will give you the details. Get on it."

"Get on it, sir?"

The XO acted exasperated. "Figure it out. Is she still on the ship? Did she jump overboard? Did she commit suicide? Is she just hiding somewhere?"

"Sir, if she jumped overboard, we have to try and find her. There are all sorts of regs—"

"When I said jumped overboard, I meant desertion in Port Said. If she jumped, she did it last night. She could easily have swam ashore and hidden in the city."

"Sir, you said suicide."

The XO made no effort to hide his annoyance. "I'm talking about somewhere onboard. She went into some storage space or hiding space and harmed herself. That's why she can't be found. She was definitely depressed 'cause her kids may be dead. We need to create records of all this, line of duty, and so forth, JAGMAN. You've heard of JAGMAN investigations haven't you?"

"Of course I've heard of JAGMAN investigations. I usually review them, I don't generate them. That's usually done by someone in the department in question."

The Lieutenant turned towards Alschbach and the repair officer began to speak. "Petty Officer

Arehart has been very distraught. She has been unable to contact her husband or children—"

The Lieutenant turned away to look back at the XO. "Surely, repair and medical are better equipped to figure this out. Sir, I've got underway CIC watches, department head duties, as well as running legal. The Master-at-Arms are scattered all over the ship. For all intents and purposes, I only have Ensign Acedian still working for me."

"Do you understand what I just told you to do?"

"Yes sir."

The XO thumped the table as he continued. "There's no sticking NCIS or somebody else with this. You figure out what's going on and generate the paperwork. I want this done by the book, the JAGMAN book that is." The XO chuckled to himself. In a moment he turned back to Alschbach. "See, he can help you with this."

Alschbach just shook his head and responded quietly, "We shouldn't have left port."

After chow, the Lieutenant went back out on the weather deck. Now, late in the day with the sun going down, the outside air felt almost refreshing. Passing through the Great Bitter Lake the Lieutenant could see numerous ships at anchor waiting their turn to travel through the canal.

Acedian came back out on deck and joined the Lieutenant as he stood by the ship's rails. The two of them watched the land flow by until Acedian unexpectedly asked a question. "Lieutenant, you still interested in getting one of the Egyptian god statues for a souvenir?"

The Lieutenant deliberated before answering. "How did you hear about that?"

"Lieutenant, everybody heard about that. People think it's pretty funny when you lose your temper."

"I didn't see you on the fantail."

"Don't have one myself, but I can get one."

"What are you talking about?"

"Friend needs some legal paperwork looked over. Favor for a favor."

"I don't do favors for gifts, and I better not hear about you doing those kinds of favors."

Acedian quickly backpedaled, "Nothing like that. They offered and I said I'd ask. It's not really a big deal."

The Lieutenant would have liked to remain on the weather deck to enjoy the cool of the evening, but Acedian's presence irritated him. He went inside and headed for his stateroom. Soon they would be through the canal and the ship's regular underway routine would resume. The Lieutenant would once again be standing watch, starting with the one he most loathed, the midwatch. He thought about a quick nap before midnight but he was too keyed up to sleep.

Genesis 3:9-19 KJV:

And the Lord God called unto Adam, and said unto him, Where art thou? And he said, I heard thy voice in the garden, and I was afraid, because I was naked; and I hid myself. And he said, Who told thee that thou wast naked? Hast thou eaten of the tree, whereof I commanded thee that thou shouldest not eat? And the man said, The woman whom thou gavest to be with me, she gave me of the tree, and I did eat. And the Lord God said unto the woman, What is this that thou hast done? And the woman said, The serpent beguiled me, and I did eat. And the Lord God said unto the serpent, Because thou hast done this, thou art cursed above all cattle, and above every beast of the field; upon thy belly shalt thou go, and dust shalt thou eat all the days of thy life: And I will put enmity between thee and the woman, and between thy seed and her seed; it shall bruise thy head, and thou shalt bruise his heel. Unto the woman he said, I will greatly multiply thy sorrow and thy conception; in sorrow thou shalt bring forth children; and thy desire shall be to thy husband, and he shall rule over thee. And unto Adam he said, Because thou hast hearkened unto the voice of thy wife, and hast eaten of the tree, of which I commanded thee, saying, Thou shalt not eat of it: cursed is the ground for thy sake; in sorrow shalt thou eat of it all the days of thy life; Thorns also and thistles shall it bring forth to thee; and thou shalt eat the herb of the field; In the sweat of thy face shalt thou eat bread, till thou return unto the ground; for out of it wast thou taken: for dust thou art, and unto dust shalt thou return.

CHAPTER-8 – HELP FROM AVARHOUSE

Wednesday, Day Three: Anacostia, Maryland

He knows he is dreaming, but the dream is impossible to escape.

He is a boy again, back in his parent's house, back in his old room. It is nighttime. He is in his bed calling for his father. Something is moving beneath his bed. His father comes into the room exasperated. His father glances beneath the bed and tells him nothing is there. His father tells him to stop the foolishness and to go to sleep.

He lies in his bed as his father turns off the lights and leaves the room. He tries to sleep, but there again is the noise of movement, of scratching. He runs to get his father, but his father tells him to get to bed. His father will not return.

Back in his room, he forces himself to look under the bed; nothing is there. He turns off the light, proud of himself for facing his fear. Before he can fall asleep, he hears the noise again, a scratching, mewing sound, but now the noise is coming from across the room.

He leaps from his bed, grabs a chair, and jams it under the door handle of the closet. He gets back into bed and waits. Something is in the closet. It turns the handle of the closet door. It tries to push open the door. The chair, jammed beneath the door handle, begins to slip across the carpet.

Captain Pride woke with a start when the radio-alarm went off. He felt grateful to discover the power on in the house again and grateful to abandon a restless sleep. He got up from his chair and began to get ready to leave his house.

As he walked home yesterday, he had tried to get help with his car at multiple gas stations. All had been closed. This morning, he decided, he would try again.

As if the speaker on the radio read his mind, he heard an announcement, "For all of you folks who have left your car because of the traffic jams, you need to get your cars off the road into a proper parking space. The President is issuing an executive order to allow for salvage rights on abandoned vehicles—"

This caught his attention immediately. He had no idea where to find Anna's car. The notion that his car and Anna's car could be seized as abandoned property caused him to curse out loud.

The radio continued with various news stories as he went to find his phone. "—is announcing a largely quiet night here in the city. This compares favorably with many major European cities. There have been periods of unrest reported in Berlin, Paris, and London. Authorities are disputing that these are anything other than ordinary riots brought about by the initial panic.

Reports of attacks by persons allegedly deceased have been greatly exaggerated. With the coming of day, law and order has been restored. Mohammed James, Mayor of London, has congratulated the police on their efforts. He also dismissed as ridiculous the claims that police have been given 'shoot on sight' orders. The policy of limiting weapons use to specially trained, authorized firearms officers remains unchanged. He also continues to deny that certain parts of the city have been declared 'no-go zones' and—"

The Captain turned the radio off as he once again tried to reach Anna by phone. This time the phone rang three or four times before the line went dead. He tried a second time and got the "all circuits busy" message. Next, he tried calling his children's cell phones. The results were the same as before.

He noted again the low power warning on his cell phone. For some reason, the battery was only intermittently charging. He plugged the charger back in and left the phone on the table in disgust.

He switched to the landline and tried calling the police with no greater success than before. He tried calling his office at the Navy Yard. This call did not go through and only resulted in the "All circuits busy" message.

Using his computer the Captain tried looking up phone numbers or email contacts for nearby hospitals. He could not get the machine to properly log in to the internet. The slow service caused him to try a reboot, but it made no difference. Service remained lethargic.

He started to rummage around in the closets hoping to find a traditional printed phone book. He could not remember the last time he had looked at one. He knew before he started that such relics had gone to the dump long ago, but he looked anyway, not surprised when he found nothing.

Before he stepped outside he left another note for Anna. Then he left his house and headed for the nearest gas station. He carried in his hand the plastic gas tank taken from the boat. As he walked he noted the faint odor of smoke in the air. He looked around but could see no indications of fire. He listened for the sounds of sirens but heard none. He spoke aloud as he walked. "People disappear, fires result."

When he arrived at the gas station he could see a line of cars waiting at the station pumps. The line stretched down the street, only a single gas pump working. One of the garage mechanics agreed to drive the tow truck and help get his car out of the ditch, but he would not promise to sell any gas.

"Why the hell not?"

"The President's new rules. Even number license plates today, odd numbers tomorrow. Also, I'm limiting my customers to five gallons anyway, until I get resupplied."

The Captain offered up a credit card for the cost of hiring the tow truck.

"Credit machines not working. Got to be paid in cash."

"This is all I've got. I've got no cash. Surely, you can write a credit slip out by hand and submit it to the bank that way?"

The mechanic thought about it for a minute. "Okay, I'll take credit, but you'll have to agree to a surcharge. That's for use of credit and for mileage on the tow."

When the Captain climbed into the tow truck, he saw a pistol in the mechanic's waistband. The mechanic must have noticed; while driving up the road, he offered a suggestion. "Strange things have been happening around here. You would be smart to have a means to defend yourself."

"You're not worried about the cops finding that on you?"

"More worried about the zombies than I am about the cops."

The Captain said nothing in response but he wished he still had his pistols and rifles.

As they drove the Captain could see that the roads remained a jumble of abandoned cars, but at least the wreckers were out towing them away. In some places, emergency vehicles had cleared a path by pushing cars up onto the sidewalks.

He could see more people out on the street today heading to work or running errands. He suspected others were engaged simply in sightseeing. They passed several groups standing out on the sidewalks talking.

It took very little time to reach the place where the Captain had abandoned his car. They drove to the spot without making a single detour. When the Captain saw his car, however, he felt new frustration. The car had been vandalized. It was pushed completely off the road and into the ditch. It had been pushed with such force that the right front tire was bent over into the ground. The front of the car was partially submerged in mud and muck, the taillights, windshield, and driver's side window were smashed.

The mechanic got out and looked at the car. He got down and examined it underneath. "Axle's broken."

The Captain bit back the sarcasm and kept it polite. "See if you can get it back to your station."

The mechanic hooked up the car and attempted to drag the car out, but on the narrow road, he could not gain any traction. After several tries, the car broke free from the muck and the driver managed to drag it back up on the road. By the time they towed the car back to the gas station, it was late morning.

The mechanic offered to have the car fixed at his garage, but he could not say when they would start, or how long it would take, or how much it would cost. The Captain told him to leave it alone until he had an insurance adjuster look at it.

The Captain walked home. He hoped that Anna might have returned, but found no sign of her. When he walked into the house he could see the emergency broadcast signal playing across the television screen. When he turned the volume up, he heard a solid tone, followed by an announcement. "—responders are to report to their place of employment. All military personnel are to report to their duty stations. All military leave and liberty is canceled.

"The curfew ordered by the President remains in effect. Citizens are required to be in their homes after sunset. Only essential personnel, first responders, or members of the military on duty, are permitted outside of their homes after dark. Again all leave and liberty for military personnel is canceled."

The emergency broadcast repeated with few further details. The Captain tried different channels hoping to hear some real news, but without success. He did learn that the subway and buses were running on a holiday schedule.

The Captain again thought about going into work. Despite the emergency broadcast notice, he decided he would go to Mary and Martha and bring his daughters home. For this, he would need a car.

He knew Avarhouse would loan him a car.

If anyone had asked, the Captain would not have referred to Avarhouse as a friend. They had served together as lieutenants, but even on active duty, there had been a degree of separation. Avarhouse always specialized in playing the angles. On at least two occasions he had been the subject of an investigation. The first time, he was suspected of fraternizing with an extremely attractive petty officer. The second occasion concerned suspicions of steering business to a local law firm. It turned out Avarhouse had been moonlighting with the firm, and without permission. A timely resignation saved Lieutenant Commander Isaac Avarhouse, and the Navy, any further embarrassment.

As a civilian attorney Avarhouse thrived. His specialty was flamboyance. He loved to call attention to himself, pastel-colored suits, gold rings on every finger, bowties of extraordinary patterns. Outside of the courtroom, he dressed like a drunken rodeo clown; but in court, it was all pinstripes and sobriety. Avarhouse enjoyed exploring the limits of veracity. Judges and prosecutors hated him, juries forgave him, criminals embraced him.

Avarhouse liked to boast that he earned more in a month in private practice than he had earned in a year as a naval officer. In addition to a successful law practice, he liked to speculate in real-estate. Success in these endeavors had resulted in two small office buildings in the city, as well as a farm, and an apple orchard in the country

In addition to real estate holdings, Avarhouse acquired a large sailboat. The Captain's home included a deeded boat slip that had remained empty long after the house had been purchased. Avarhouse, as usual, saw the opportunity for a deal, and so a bargain had been struck. Avarhouse had a free place to keep his boat, and the Captain had free use of a 38-foot sailboat he otherwise would never have been able to touch.

On several occasions, Avarhouse had invited the Captain to leave military service and join him in private practice. He even offered to give the Captain the sailboat as a sort of signing bonus. The Captain always told Avarhouse that he enjoyed his work with the Navy too much. In truth, although he sometimes envied Avarhouse, he always expected Avarhouse would come to the bad end he so diligently pursued. Also, the fact that Anna disliked Avarhouse, and made little effort to hide it, would have made a business relationship impossible.

The Captain knew he could rely on Avarhouse when it came to borrowing a car. He also knew that if anyone could provide him useful information, it would be Avarhouse. When he could not reach Avarhouse by phone he started out for his office on foot. Finding Avarhouse seemed like his last chance of securing a car.

When he arrived, he feared the building might be empty and the trip wasted, but he found Avarhouse in an alleyway unloading boxes. When the Captain asked to borrow a car, Avarhouse declared he was happy to help, provided the Captain helped him first. Avarhouse wanted to go to the Navy Yard.

"Isaac, what possible reason can you have to go to the Navy Yard?"

Avarhouse acted as if the answer was obvious, "I want boxes of MREs; I want ammunition; I need some camping gear too. The exchange will have everything I need."

Avarhouse's explanation made the Captain uneasy. "You know you can't shop at the Exchanges."

"Yes, but you can."

The Captain's frustration became obvious, "Look, I just want to get on the road to get to Martha and Mary."

"To get there and back, you'll need gas. You can't count on the stations right now."

"Can I borrow some extra gasoline from you?"

"No, but you can borrow some extra gas cans."

When Avarhouse moved towards his car, the Captain asked to drive. Avarhouse gave him the keys without comment. On their drive into the city, the Captain took a very indirect route. Avarhouse became curious enough to sit up and look around, but not curious enough to ask any questions. Several times the Captain stopped and carefully looked over cars abandoned along the street. When they reached Anna's school, the Captain slowly drove around the parking lot. Avarhouse did not ask about Anna, and the Captain did not volunteer.

The trip into the city today was unlike any the Captain had experienced before. There was none of the usual traffic congestion; instead abandoned or wrecked cars created new kinds of bottle-necks. Their progress might have been faster except for the number of tow trucks and police moving about. The cops cleared the travel lanes by pushing some cars to the shoulder of the road and having other cars towed away. As the Captain and Avarhouse snaked around these moving roadblocks one or two cops looked up, but they could see the Captain in his uniform and took no further interest.

On the slow drive into the city, the Captain began to talk about his inability to reach Anna or the kids by phone. For once Avarhouse seemed genuinely sympathetic. Avarhouse himself had no family to speak of, just two ex-wives. When Avarhouse stated he had not heard from his wives the Captain spoke up. "Maybe they're among the disappeared?"

"Maybe I should be that lucky."

By the time they arrived at the gate to the Navy Yard, it was late afternoon. A line of cars waited to enter, delayed by zealous inspectors. Civilian guards looked under every car with a mirror. They opened every trunk. They checked various compartments and ran background checks on some of the drivers.

The Captain got out of the car when the guards began their search. One pointed to the many empty jerry cans. "What are those for?"

"Just looking for a chance to fill up," the Captain replied cheerfully. "I travel a lot and can't risk running out of gas." This seemed to satisfy the gate guard.

When they finally arrived, the Captain felt obligated to check in with his office. "I'll be only a few minutes. I'll help you get what you need and we can go."

Avarhouse squirmed impatiently. "Just so long as we get going on time. I don't know how long the exchange will be open."

The Captain responded as he headed inside, "You don't know if the exchange is open at all. Just wait for me."

When the Captain entered his spaces, he was surprised to find several Lieutenants standing in the passageway engaged in debate. They stopped their argument and came loosely to attention as he approached. "Afternoon sir."

The Captain greeted them briefly but did not stop to talk. He headed towards his inner office intending to make a quick check for any messages. One of the officers called out to him as he passed, "Sir, it's the apocalypse, isn't it? The rapture, judgment day."

Ordinarily, the Captain would have handled such a comment more tactfully. Instead, he yelled at the officers. "Get the hell back to work. I don't want to hear any more about the 'rapture,' or any religious speculation. Now get back to your offices."

The Captain never swore at his Lieutenants. He preferred to think of himself as a mentor. He realized then how tired he was. He rationalized that they deserved it with this talk about the "rapture."

The Captain had to pass Invidia's office on route to his own. He stopped and looked in to find Invidia sitting at his desk watching television.

Invidia began to speak as the Captain stepped through his door. "This reporter is interviewing a couple who claim they were abducted by zombies. Same people are always claiming alien abduction, or bigfoot, or whatever. I can't believe that this is what it takes to get on television."

The Captain ignored the commentary and began to pose questions. "Where is everybody? Have we received any instructions?"

Invidia kept watching the television set as he answered. "The Admiral came by looking for you. All sorts of things are happening. All officers and men are being mustered for security assignments."

This first surprised the Captain. The Admiral never came by unannounced to the office. Having an Admiral looking, and not finding, was not a good thing. He knew also that Invidia lacked the ability to finesse such a situation, but the Captain did not miss a beat. "What do you mean security assignments?"

"Grocery stores, gas stations, power plants, government buildings. Everything's to be guarded. Everyone who's small arms qualified could end up being temporarily assigned to the Army, even staff officers."

"Are we missing people?"

Invidia took a moment and looked around his desk. Finding a piece of paper, he picked it up and handed it to the Captain. "We were supposed to have an emergency muster, but we're having trouble with the phones. This is what I've got so far."

The Captain looked over the muster report and began to decipher Invidia's handwritten annotations. The Captain could see two officers, three enlisted, and three civilian workers listed as missing. Several other names had notations with question marks. One name was annotated "UA?"

"What's this about Gula?" the Captain asked.

"The others are missing. Gula decided he needed to take some time off."

"What did you tell him?"

"I told him no. Get into the office immediately. He still stayed home yesterday and took his time today."

The Captain thought for a moment about having Gula charged with unauthorized absence. His absence the day before would have made such a charge awkward. He decided against it but considered an alternative. "Gula's out in the passageway arguing about the rapture. You need to get his attention. No talking religion in the office. Make it a formal counseling chit."

Invidia nodded his head as the Captain went on to his next question. "Did you send out any runners to confirm the missing?"

Invidia just looked at him quizzically.

The Captain continued. "You've got a government sedan and officers and men sitting around talking about the rapture. Did you think about sending people out?"

"The roads are pretty messed up. It's hard to get around."

"The cops have been clearing the roads. There are plenty of back roads."

The Captain found Invidia's lack of initiative annoying. He liked to find barriers to action. The Captain had spoken to him several times about this deficiency and it was reflected in his fitness reports. It was unlikely the Commander would ever make Captain.

"I want a verified list of everyone who's missing, including family members. If you can't get them on the phone, send out a runner. If the runners find them, and it turns out they just don't want to go to work write them up."

The Captain turned to walk away but then stopped. "Something else, make sure you get control over the gossiping in the passageways. Remind them of the regs. I don't want any complaints that someone's proselytizing. I don't want any complaints about religion."

The Captain went to his office and checked for phone messages. He also tried logging on to his computer. The connection here was no better than his machine at home so he gave up and logged off. Although impatient to leave the office, he knew he had better touch base with the Admiral, at least by phone. This call went through immediately. When he learned the Admiral was not in her office, he asked only that she be told that he had called in follow up on her visit to the RLSO.

The Captain stopped by Invidia's office once last time as he left. "Hold everyone here until the end of working hours. Check to see if any additional instructions are sent out. Assuming liberty is not denied, explain to everyone they are subject to immediate recall. Understood?"

"Yes sir." Invidia sounded anything but cheerful.

"XO, I'm on the road and may be late getting in tomorrow. I'm making a quick run to the Shenandoah to get my daughters from school. I will be back the next day at the latest."

"If the Admiral comes looking for you again?" Invidia asked.

"If the Admiral contacts you, you will let the Admiral know my situation."

"I'll let her know," Invidia answered, "But she may not like it."

The Captain merely shrugged his shoulders. Invidia was a man without family. The Admiral was a woman without family. It would be useless to explain.

When he got back to the car Avarhouse was waiting. "Sorry for the delay, Isaac."

"I almost gave you up," replied Avarhouse.

As the Captain started the engine he spoke again. "We can go to the exchange now."

Avarhouse replied nonchalantly. "Already been, the Yard exchange that is. They've got nothing I need. But we go right past Bolling on the way back. I'd like to check there."

Bolling Force Air Base was only a few minutes' drive across the Anacostia River from the Navy Yard. The NCO's on guard at the gate wore camouflage fatigues and carried carbines. One of the guards took the Captain's and Avarhouse's identification and looked at them briefly. He gave the cards back and waved them through the gate. He did not salute.

At the Base Exchange, Avarhouse went in with the Captain. As soon as they entered Avarhouse grabbed a cart and began to load up on camping gear and shooting supplies. He went up to the weapons counter and asked how many boxes of nine-millimeter ammo he could purchase.

The clerk looked up at the Captain. "You know sir, civilians aren't allowed to shop here."

"I know that. He's merely with me to help carry. How much nine-millimeter can I get?"

The clerk fetched one box of fifty rounds. The Captain went to take it from him. The clerk stopped him. "Got to fill out the paperwork first."

"Just for ammo?"

"Yes sir. I also need to make a copy of your ID card."

The Captain looked at the forms the clerk had given him. In addition to a great deal of personal information, he needed a background check, a firearms registration number, and had to assert the ammo was needed for training. Avarhouse tried to get his attention, holding up a card of some type. The Captain turned back to the clerk. "A background check for ammo?"

"Not to worry. It just takes a few minutes. You can finish with your shopping while I run it."

The Captain hesitated with the forms. "Before I start filling this out, how much is the ammo."

The clerk quoted a fair price but then added. "That doesn't include taxes though. The taxes are as much as the ammo."

"Since when does the Exchange charge tax?"

"There are taxes on ammo. That's the law."

The Captain's questions had been a play for time. He decided he was not going to falsify government documents for Avarhouse and walked away from the counter.

Before they left the base, they pulled into the Base Exchange gas station. There were no lines here. Avarhouse filled up the car's gas tank and then began to fill the extra gas cans he had brought with him. The station attendant came outside but went back in when he saw the Captain.

Avarhouse had four gas cans of five gallons each. "Two for you and two for me. This should about get you back home if you have trouble finding an open station tomorrow." When they drove away from the station the car stunk of gasoline.

On the way home Avarhouse complained about the ammo. "Nine-millimeter is scarce as hen's teeth right now."

"Isaac, what do you need that for? You're not licensed."

He replied cryptically, "So you say, but I say there's more than one way to skin that cat."

When the Captain finally dropped Avarhouse back at his offices, it was growing dark. His gratitude to Avarhouse for loaning him the car had diminished with the frustration of hours wasted driving back and forth to the city and shopping at the exchange.

The Captain felt tired and hungry. He had not eaten a real meal for two days. He had little sleep the night before. He considered the state of the highways and risks of the curfew. Caution won out. Instead of driving immediately to the Shenandoah, he decided to drive home.

When he entered the house he could sense the emptiness. He could see no evidence anyone had been there since he left. No one had disturbed his note. The cup of coffee left on the table two days before remained.

He tried calling Anna. The phone repeatedly rang but she did not pick up, nor did the call go to voice-mail. When he called a second time the phone again repeatedly rang and again refused to connect to voice-mail. He did not try a third time.

He tried use his computer to search for hospital phone numbers but had no more success now than he had in the morning. The computer web pages cycled and failed to load.

When he became frustrated with the computer, he called the police non-emergency number. If someone had been transported to a hospital after an accident or assault surely the police would know. The first call he made rang busy. The second call went to a generic emergency message that advised people to shelter in place.

He called each of his daughter's cell phones in turn. The phones rang but did not connect. He expected to be put through to voice-mail but the phones only rang. He again considered driving straight to their universities but decided on prudence, rest now and wait until morning to travel.

He made himself comfortable in his easy chair. He expected to fall asleep in minutes but found he could only toss and turn. He thought about Anna. He thought about his children and whether they too might be among the missing. It did not matter, tomorrow he would travel south.

Candle Wood Lakes past Davis Bridge heading towards Cornith

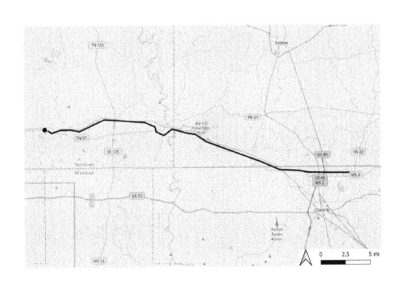

Entitled, Al Araf; Revealed At Mecca:

O children of Adam, we have sent down unto you apparel, to conceal your nakedness, and fair garments; but the clothing of piety is better. This is one of the signs of God; that peradventure ye may consider.

O children of Adam, let not Satan seduce you, as he expelled your parents out of paradise, by stripping them of their clothing, that he might show them their nakedness: verily he seeth you, both he and his companions, whereas ye see not them. We have appointed the devils to be patrons of those who believe not.

The Koran, Chapter VII Entitled, Al Araf; translated by George Sales, 1734.

CHAPTER-9 – FLIGHT OF THE SCARECROWS

Wednesday, Day Three: Near Davis Bridge Battlefield, Tennessee

As the General waited in the forest, he examined the bullet wound to his side. It did not cause him discomfort, more annoying than painful. Black treacly matter gathered around the edges, sticky and stringy. It did not smell like fresh blood, instead, it had an odor of rotten eggs. The wound showed no signs of scabbing or scarring as a proper wound should, but he could sense a kind of healing—not healing, binding.

When the sun went down the General began to walk. The scarecrows joined him a few at a time until hundreds followed.

Sometimes the scarecrows bunched up and walked as a group; sometimes their numbers stretched out along woodland paths. Sometimes they travel along the railroad right away, other times through open fields. They walked through the woods as long as they could. In many places, they were forced to cross shallow streams or creeks. Some would not enter the water and were forced to seek another way around. Near any major town they were forced to the north or south.

The General was anxious to gain the safety of the Tennessee River and the dense cover it was sure to offer. Whenever possible, he and the scarecrows hurried along the railroad or eastbound roads, quick to flee whenever one of the engines appeared. The scarecrows constantly turned their heads left and right as they walked. Every obstruction up ahead, every turn in the path, offered the possibility of exposure and ambush.

They came to a road and a collection of signs identifying different highways that led north, south, east, or west. Other signs spoke of battles and skirmishes or great houses long since gone to ruin. The General stood and read the signs. He stood and looked out over the roads and the water for a long time.

Only the Old Soldier showed the same interest in the signs as the General. "Davis Bridge and Van Dorn.... Aah remember."

The General nodded. "Van Dorn thought ... he could handle cavalry ... as good as me. But Hurlbut and Ord handled him roughly."

It was the Old Soldier's turn to nod. "Poor Van Dorn.... the terror of ugly husbands everywhere ... till one caught 'em."

This rejoinder caused the General to laugh, only for the sound of his laughter to shock him into silence.

The General and the Old Soldier rejoined the march.

They approached a settlement only to find a roadblock made up of engines, and fencing, and other debris. The roadblock was manned by farmers. This required the General to find another path to the east. Here the Old Soldier proved invaluable. He understood what the General desired, and he had a better sense of the roads. The forest provided alternative pathways and refuge. Safety led always to the east.

They came to another roadblock manned not by farmers, but by soldiers. There were three or four of them dressed in blue, armed with their black rifles. The engines of the soldiers blocked the road with blinding red, blue, and white lights.

The General stopped and took cover. The Old Soldier volunteered to find a way around. As the General waited the Sailor came up to investigate the reason for the delay. The General pointed to the roadblock and the armed men.

"Not soldiers, cops," the Sailor explained. When the General did not react he spoke again. "You know, sheriffs and deputies."

"You mean ... coppers."

"That's right," the Sailor responded, his tone somewhat derisive.

It irritated the General that the Sailor had knowledge he lacked. It irritated the General even more that the Sailor could speak so smoothly. The General had to suck in a lung full of air with every sentence. When he spoke a whistling sound came out of the hole in his chest.

In the past, over six feet tall, strongly built, handsome in face and figure, the General imposed his will by mere physical presence. Now his body was a ruin, partially naked, partially clad in rags; he felt ridiculous. The facial expressions of the scarecrows never changed, but their tendency to avoid, and their slowness to obey, convinced him they looked on him with contempt.

At one point, an engine came by on the road manned, not by farmers, or soldiers or coppers, but by six scarecrows squeezed into the engine coach. The General just pointed at them.

"Where they going?" he asked the Sailor.

"Going hunting I think."

The engine stopped just beyond the roadblock. The General could see the scarecrows inside debating. Finally, the engine turned and sped off in the direction from which it came.

The General badly wanted to find a working engine and speed down the road. With a few working engines, they would fly faster than any cavalry. They could strike with impunity anywhere, at any time, with such machines. "We must get there furst with the most."

The Sailor counseled against it. "Remember the planes. Better keep to the woods."

In the end, the General, and the scarecrows, stayed in the woods. The Old Soldier found a path around the roadblock, and they continued in their flight.

The march lacked discipline, the scarecrows constantly breaking for cover. They straggled, but not from fatigue. As they went past one isolated place the Sailor, the Yankee, and some of the scarecrows fell out and moved towards a house. Whatever happened next, the General did not wish to see. He hurried ahead.

Further up the road, they came to another isolated house. As the General continued to walk to the east, he heard rapid-fire gunshots. Kirk-kirk-kirk-kirk, kirk-kirk-kirk. The sound of rifles echoed through the woods; he counted the number of rifle shots with amazement. The rifle could fire more rapidly than any repeater he had ever known.

These sounds were followed by the "Pop, pop, pop, pop, pop, pop, pop, pop," of a pistol. The pistol fired rapidly and without pause. The deeper sound of the rifle started again as soon as the pistol fire stopped firing.

One or two scarecrows ran past the General at speed. The General suspected that whoever fired the rifles now fired at an enemy in retreat. Confirmation of the General's suspicion came when he saw three scarecrows hurrying up the road, the arms of one scarecrow draped over the shoulders of the other two as they dragged and carried it along. The General stopped to watch them go past. The disabled scarecrow had black skin, shrunken so tightly to his bones it could almost have been painted on. He could see a clear depression in its skull where a portion of its head had been caved in. It wore a green jacket.

The General continued to walk, sometimes on forest tracks, sometimes on the road. Frequently he would hear the sound of the racing engines. He would leap or run to a place of safety and then watch in fascination as the engines went past. He expected the passengers to stop and fire weapons as they had done when he fled the city, but they did not. They flew down the road scattering unwary scarecrows and taking no more interest than they would a herd of running deer.

A few miles further ahead, the General found an abandoned engine. The engine hummed and thrummed as it sat on the road, its doors open. Bright lights made it hard to approach, but the General forced himself forward. He examined the engine. If there had been a fight, he could see no sign of it. The engine had no bullet holes in it; whoever had been riding in it had simply fled.

The General lingered at the engine for some time. He sat down in the operator's seat. He turned the wheel left and right. When he pressed the pedals on the floor the engine thrummed and coughed. He looked at the various handles around the wheel. He found a metal switch at the side of the wheel. He turned it forward and the engine began to make a grinding noise. He released the metal switch. He called out to passing scarecrows asking if one of them knew how to operate the engine.

One of the scarecrows, shielding its eyes from the glare of the lights, joined the General. "I can … drive." It moved the General to the next seat and got behind the wheel. It closed the open door. It reached down between the seats and moved a lever. It pressed its feet to peddles on the floor.

The engine accelerated with tremendous speed. The General called out with a yell and a howl—"Wa-woo-woohoo, wa-woo-woohoo, yee—haw."

The General yelled so loudly and unexpectedly that the scarecrow at the wheel missed a turn and took the engine into a ditch. The engine came to a halt as sudden as it had leapt ahead. Thrown violently forward, the General struck his head into the glass shield and a spider web of lines appeared in the glass. The engine continued to thrum, but no longer moved.

The General spoke as he checked his head for damage, "Aah think yah killed me."

The other scarecrow suddenly threw the door open and fled. The General called after it, but it was no use. No others volunteered to drive, and the General abandoned the engine to continue the march on foot. He returned to walking the forest paths, never straight. He and his many scarecrows continued through the night.

The General next saw the Sailor and Yankee when he sought protection from the coming sunlight. The Sailor carried a pistol and a shotgun. They both smelled of fresh blood. Following close on their heels came a cadre of a dozen scarecrows. They hovered around the Sailor as he sat down. The electric tang of the blood drew them around the Sailor like a bottle of cheap booze draws a collection of drunks.

"Who have yah killed?" the General rasped. The smell of the blood made the worm in his gut twist and squirm. The General bent forward in anticipation of the pain. As he spoke he covered the hole in his chest to keep the wound from making any sound.

The Sailor handed the pistol to the General. "One of those crackers got too close. I wasn't the only one who got him."

The Sailor spoke with increased fluidity. His movements too had grown fluid, graceful, compared to the scarecrows. The skin of his face and hands seemed fuller, less stretched. It irritated the General that the Sailor could produce some facial expressions. His own expression remained unchanging, his face bound by an inflexible leather mask.

The General examined the pistol. It was a weapon like nothing he had ever seen.

The Sailor took the pistol back. "You operate it like this." He pulled back the slide and a cartridge came springing out of the weapon.

"The bullets are loaded into a magazine, and that slides up into the handle. The gas from the bullet causes the slide to go back and forth and load a new round."

He gave the pistol back to the General. The General pulled the slide back ejecting another bullet to the ground. The Sailor picked up the bullet and showed him how to load it back into the magazine.

The General enjoyed the feel of the pistol in his hand. "Much lighter ... more compact ... than Navy Colt. Wonderful weapon.... Wonderful."

The Sailor signaled for the Yankee to come over. At first, the Yankee seemed reluctant to approach. The stains to his rags were obvious as he drew near.

The Sailor took him by the arm and forced him to come close. "Don't worry, he won't bite. Tell him what you told me."

"We need, ah, oxidizer, ah, ammonium nitrate, ah, p-p-potassium nitrate, ah, will do. Oxidizer and a f-f-fuel," the Yankee began.

The General had trouble understanding him, not only because of the accent, not only because of the unfamiliar words, but because his speech was as slurred as a drunk's. He drew out every word with an annoying 'ah' as a kind of punctuation.

"That's the key, ah, Afghan'stan, ah, IEDs from, ah, ammonium nit'ate, ah, f-f-fer'liza, ah, or gun shops, ah, r-r-reactive targets. Ammonium nit'ate, ah, powder, or mix. Super sto', ah, find f-f-fer'liza, ah, cold packs, ah, s-s-stump remover, ah, diesel, suga' even. Maybe fa'm supply, ah, lots of f-f-fer'liza."

The General looked at the Yankee bomb maker and said nothing. He could not make out half the ingredients being recited, but he understood the concept of mixing up explosives well enough.

The Sailor spoke again. "Can we set it off? Electric charge or some kind of fuse?"

"ANFO, c-c-can do," the Yankee responded.

The Sailor nodded his head up and down enthusiastically. The General said nothing.

In the distance, the General could hear sirens as engines drew near and then passed. He got up and moved through the brush towards the road. He tried to shield his eyes so that he could see out onto the road, but the light remained too bright. He went back into the shade of the forest, but not to his resting spot. Instead, he went searching for the wounded scarecrow. He found him still with his friends.

As the General approached he drew the pistol given to him by the Sailor. The scarecrows with Green Jacket looked up and immediately moved away. Green Jacket looked up at him but said nothing. He tried to move away but could only push himself along the ground.

The General stepped on the leg of Green Jacket. The scarecrow made no sound but became more frantic as he struggled to crawl away. The General leaned over and examined Green Jacket. He had a hole in the center of his back, just below the shoulders. The General could see the small entrance wound at the scarecrow's back and the large exit wound through the chest, a hole as big as his fist. The General put his finger into the wound. He could feel the severed the spine. The scarecrow's torn leather skin oozed stuff the color and consistency of black tar. It smelled of sulphur.

Green Jacket could read the General's mind. "Don't hurt.... Can walk."

"Yah cannot walk," the General replied. He spoke slowly enunciating each syllable. He covered his own wound as he spoke. "Can you sit up?"

"Don't hurt."

The General pointed his pistol at the scarecrow's head. "Yah no-good ... ta me ... like this."

The wounded figure began to rock back and forth. He writhed about on the ground. He called out to the General, "Please, no ... don't ... no cause." His speech sounded as if he had a mouth full of mush.

The General pointed his pistol at the wounded scarecrow's head and repeated his statement. "Yah no-good ta me, like this."

He pulled the trigger, but the weapon did not fire. The General pulled the hammer of the pistol back with his thumb. He aimed and pulled the trigger again. Still, nothing happened. The wounded scarecrow continued to try and roll away.

"Please ... Please ... Don't ... send back!" The wounded scarecrow continued to rock his body back and forth. He struck his head against the ground and pushed with the back of his head and neck trying to move away.

The General continued to calmly examine the pistol. He repositioned himself to shoot the wounded scarecrow. Again he aimed and again the weapon failed to fire.

One of the wounded scarecrow's friends intervened. He pointed to a slight armature on the side of the weapon. "Goes down ... see red ... you're dead."

The General looked at the pistol and then pushed the little lever back and forth. By now the begging of the wounded scarecrow had become a kind of keening and weeping. "Please don't! Don't send back!"

A crowd gathered around the place where the General examined the pistol while still standing on Green Jacket's leg.

"Yah no-good ta me ... like this."

The General pulled the trigger.

The action of the pistol surprised him. Fire burst from the muzzle and the slide slammed back and forth in one swift motion as it loaded the next bullet. A little smoke rose out of the hole in the scarecrow's head, but virtually no smoke from the pistol. There was no spattering of blood or brains.

The General looked down at the pistol. "By God—Wonderful." He leaned forward and fired a second bullet into the scarecrow's head. He continued to stand over the scarecrow looking for any further movement.

After a time, one of the scarecrow's former companions spoke up. "Safety General ... if done."

The General looked down at the pistol and pushed the little lever back over the red dot. "By God! Wonderful weapon.... Wonderful!"

The General returned to where he had left the Sailor and Yankee. He pointed at his pistol and the shotgun. "Need more guns."

The Sailor responded, "I think I know where we can get those. I know exactly where we need to go."

Deck Log - Fourth Day

| OPNAV 3100/99 (Rev 7-84) | SHIP'S DECK LOG SHEET | IF CLASSIFIED STAMP |
| S/N 0107-LF-031-0498 | | SECURITY MARKING HERE |

USE BLACK INK TO FILL IN THIS LOG

SHIP TYPE	HULL NUMBER	YEAR	MONTH	ZONE	DAY	USS __CYCLOPS__	CLASS	HANDL
AS	09	43	09	B	18	AE-/ PASSAGE FROM __NORFOLK VA__		
					F	TO __MUSCAT, OMAN__		

POSITION	ZONE	TIME	POSITION	ZONE	TIME	POSITION	ZONE	TIME	LEGEND
0800			1200			2000			1 – CELESTIAL
L 29.268237		BY	L 26.909657		BY	L		BY	2 – ELECTRONIC
A 32.735679		BY	A 34.364974		BY	A		BY	3 – VISUAL
									4 – D R

TIME	ORDER	CSE	SPEED	DEPTH	RECORD OF EVENTS OF THE DAY
08-1200					ASSUMED THE WATCH. STEAMING AS BEFORE. LIEUTENANT T.J. MCKINLEY, USN
					MUSTER THE CREW ON STATION, SH3 STRAUS MISSING.
1200					ASSUMED THE WATCH. STEAMING AS BEFORE. WATCH REPORTS CONDITIONS NORMAL. LIEUTENANT D. M. OVERTON, USN
16-1800					ASSUMED THE WATCH. STEAMING AS BEFORE. WATCH REPORTS CONDITIONS NORMAL. LIEUTENANT R.S. MERRIAM, USN
1840					REPORT OF GUNSHOT LEVEL TWO STATEROOM 02-34-2-L. CDR ALSCHBACH- GUNSHOT, POSSIBLE SELF INFLICTED.

| REPORT SYMBOL | IF CLASSIFIED STAMP REVIEW / DECLASSIFICATION DATE HERE | IF CLASSIFIED STAMP |
| OPNAV 2100-10 | | SECURITY MARKING HERE |

02 Level - Forward, Executive Officer Suite and Senior Officer Staterooms

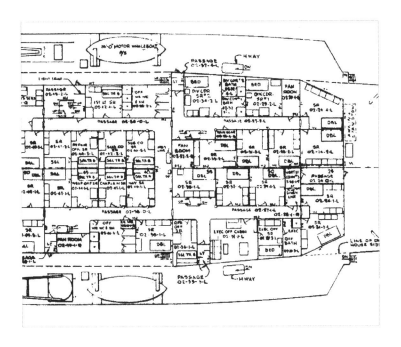

The Legend of the Wanderings of Isis:

I am Isis. I escaped from the dwelling wherein my brother Set placed me. Thoth, the great god, the Prince of Truth in heaven and on earth, said unto me: "Come, O goddess Isis [hearken thou], it is a good thing to hearken, for he who is guided by another liveth. Hide thyself with thy child, and these things shall happen unto him. His body shall grow and flourish, and strength of every kind shall be in him. He shall sit upon his father's throne, he shall avenge him, and he shall hold the exalted position of 'Governor of the Two Lands.' " I left the house of Set in the evening, and there accompanied me Seven Scorpions, that were to travel with me, and sting with their stings on my behalf.

The Literature of the Ancient Egyptians, by E. A. Wallis Budge, 1914.

CHAPTER- 10 – RESPECT HIS WISHES

Thursday, Day Four: Gulf of Suez

Lieutenant Irawell looked forward to finishing the midwatch in the Combat Information Center, CIC. He wanted nothing more than to hit his rack and to get some sleep. Now that they were underway again, he would have to adjust to the new three duty section watch, four hours on, eight hours off, with the dog watch split for shift rotation. During his eight hours "off," the Lieutenant would have to find time for sleep, for meals, and for all of his regular duties.

Crossing the Atlantic and through the Mediterranean, the crew had been in five sections; "four and sixes," which meant standing watch less than once per twenty-four-hours. With the disappearances, the continuation of five duty sections became impossible.

The civilian mariners, sailors employed by Military Sealift Command, ran most of the ship's basic functions, including navigation, deck, ship logistics, and engineering. They had been hard hit by the disappearances. Now the Navy, outnumbering the CIVMARs two to one, would be compelled to make up for these losses as well as their own. On a ship already perpetually undermanned, everyone would have to find time to take on additional tasks and responsibilities.

Even before the disappearances, the Lieutenant had made some inquiries about being relieved of his underway watches. None of the other department heads stood underway watch. To add insult to injury, Acedian stood only in port watch as OOD on the quarterdeck. Despite the Lieutenant's constant urging, Acedian never seemed to get qualified for anything underway. He knew it would be impossible to get off the watch bill now. Still, the Lieutenant supposed he should be grateful; some departments had only enough qualified watchstanders for two duty sections.

As the ship moved steadily towards the Red Sea, the Lieutenant sat in the darkened space of CIC. The watch had been uneventful and the hours passed slowly. Periodically he glanced over at the radar. The sweep went round and round, but nothing threatened to cross their path. On the radio he could hear some background chatter in a language he did not understand, but nothing with which he had to concern himself.

The Lieutenant had expected the area beyond the Suez to be teaming with activity. Keeping track of the other surface ships, the "skunks," should have been sufficiently challenging to keep him awake, but things had slowed. The traffic coming in and out of the canal had abated.

The Lieutenant's senior petty officer of the watch was MM1 Moore. Petty Officer Moore was an easy-going man with the girth of Santa Claus and a temperament to match. Whatever happened on watch, he never grew alarmed or excited. Moore could always be counted on for a joke or a story in the long hours when staying awake remained the principal burden.

Moore had been in the Navy for as long as the Lieutenant had years, and tonight he was in a mood to ruminate. "I remember when, in a ship this size, we would have had twenty watchstanders up here. There would have been a man on every station, not some computer. There would have been ten people in CIC, with at least that many out on the bridge. Every station would be manned and a written record of every decision."

He pointed to an empty corner. "There would have been somebody behind the status boards writing everything, and writing it backwards to boot. They would have kept track of every contact. There would have been someone on the plot tracker, yards and yards of paper. Nothing was chanced."

Moore lapsed into silence. The other watchstanders concentrated on their tasks, speaking only when necessary. Finally, the Lieutenant had enough of the silence and walked out onto the bridge.

The CIC on Cyclops interacted with the bridge watch when radio communications required it, or if some skunk wandered in too close. Tonight the bridge watch was also unusually quiet with none of the easy banter he had come to expect. The CIVMARs were completely uninterested in his presence. They scanned the darkness with their binoculars looking for shadows. They took frequent looks at the radar repeater. The silence, heat, and darkness were oppressive.

For a time the Lieutenant stood on one of the bridge wings and let the apparent wind wash over him. The ship moved forward through the sea, the bow rising and falling as rhythmically as a beating heart. Surging waves of bioluminescence lighted the way with cascading froths of blue and green.

The Lieutenant stepped back onto the bridge on his way to returning to CIC. As he stepped in, he brushed the Captain's chair on the portside. "Enjoying the evening Lieutenant?"

He jumped when he heard the voice came from the chair. In his preoccupation with looking out over the ocean, he had not realized that the XO had come to the bridge. He certainly was not expecting him to be in the Captain's chair. He quickly gathered his wits. "Yes sir, beautiful out there sir."

"Do you know where we are now Lieutenant?"

"Not far from Suez sir."

"Off to the portside Lieutenant."

"Sinai Peninsula sir."

"We are not far from Mount Sinai Lieutenant. Do you know the significance of Mount Sinai?"

The Lieutenant hesitated to answer, doubtful that the XO had any real interest in quizzing him. The XO took a moment before continuing to speak. "Soon we'll enter the Red Sea and go by Mecca and Medina. We'll pass out of the Red Sea, into the Gulf of Aden, up through the Gulf of Oman and into the Persian Gulf."

"You mean the Iranian Gulf sir?"

"I mean the Persian Gulf. Do you know what lies in the Persian Gulf?" The Lieutenant shook his head still too suspicious to offer any guesses.

"The ruins of Eden Lieutenant. Once we get near the Straits of Hormuz, they'll send us word and arrange an escort. We are expected there, east of Eden."

The Lieutenant listened to Worley speaking but said nothing in response. He heard again that indeterminate accent pronounced with the word "Eden." The Lieutenant tried to place its origins noting it lacked the music of a romance language or the rhythm of the Celtic.

After a moment the XO continued, "Do you know what's east of Eden Lieutenant? ... No, of course not."

After watch, the Lieutenant headed down to his stateroom for a short nap. When he awoke, he felt as tired as when he lay down. He would have much preferred to stay in his rack rather than attend the morning department head meeting.

When he got to the XO's office the place was empty. He waited for a time, thinking that the XO must have just stepped out. After standing around sluggishly for fifteen minutes, he realized he was in the wrong place. He hurried up to the 03 level and the Captain's conference room.

He arrived in time to hear the XO browbeating Montgomery. "Do we know that for sure? Do we know that for sure? Don't spread stories until we know. We've got enough on our plate."

"Sir, no one has seen him since yesterday."

"Get back to me when you know for sure."

Powers now turned to Montgomery, "Don't worry. We've got this."

Across the Captain's conference table, large diagrams of every deck of the ship were spread out with every detail marked. The Lieutenant recognized the diagrams from damage control central on the main deck.

"Security teams will maintain paa-trols throughout the ship. All hands not directly involved in communications, engineering, or navigation, will be given train-en and assigned a duty section fo-wah patrol an' security. Every sailor on security watch will be issued a shotgun or a pistol."

Powers pointed to the different diagrams speaking slowly as he continued. "The security watch will be set on every deck an' ma'ntained until the killer is found. Every military member will contribute fo-wah hours of active patrolling. Thaar be at least fo-wah armed sailors paa-trollen' every deck every minute of the day."

As Powers finished, the Lieutenant could not stop looking at the diagrams. He could see only a convoluted maze. Few places on the ship offered unobstructed views of the workspaces or passageways. Every deck was broken up into numerous compartments, storage areas, fan rooms, access points, ladders, escape trunks. The design of the various decks made it impossible for small patrols to see each other, or to directly communicate. Patrols, forward and aft, sounded feasible until you looked at the diagrams.

Alschbach objected as soon as the weapons officer finished. "Even if the patrols were four times that number, there are nearly a thousand spaces on this ship where people can disappear or be made to disappear. There are thirteen decks, never mind the ship's hold and hull. The crew has already been significantly reduced by … the loss event. This plan isn't workable."

Lamb could barely contain himself as he too dissented. "In engineering, we need more help, not less. The CIVMARs are already outside of their contract."

The XO answered calmly, "Nobody's talking about the civilians being on security."

This did not quiet the engineer. "We should be arming everybody. We should allow everyone to defend themselves. They want to protect themselves like anybody else. They deserve guns if they're going to be on watch down in engineering."

The weapons officer did not wait for the XO before replying, "Aah'm not going ta be arming a bunch of civilians, especially when yah not contributing ta security."

Doc Peters now spoke up. "Medical and dental personal aren't going to provide security, are we? This would be very unusual."

Before he could be answered, Montgomery spoke again. "My people in supply are crucial to food preparation and galley operations, and most of them are civilians anyway."

Alschbach ignored Montgomery and continued his protest. "If you insist on this, I hope you understand that my nuclear guys are already fully engaged."

Lamb interrupted vehemently, "Weapons has plenty of manpower and this is their party. They can't expect everyone else to take this on. If security can't be guaranteed, we need to divert to a safe port and get what we need. Empty the ship and bring in some German shepherds. Bring in a SEAL team and really hunt them down."

The XO answered just as vehemently, "Lieutenant Commander Powers and his people have been running patrols twenty-four-seven since Port Said. The gunner's mates have also been manning the ship's defensive weapons. They have also been standing watch in the weapons storage areas, including the torpedoes and missiles. They can't be expected to do this on their own. We have enough manpower to get this done."

Alschbach loudly raised his voice, "We need to divert."

The XO responded just as forcefully, "We're not diverting. We have our orders. We're needed in the Iranian Gulf. We're going to accomplish our mission."

Alschbach could not contain himself, "Those orders were issued before the God damn world came to an end. How do we know if those orders are still valid?"

"We will obey our orders unless or until they are superseded!"

Alschbach continued to argue, "How do we even know? When was the last time we got any message directed to this ship?"

"We get messages every hour."

"I don't mean broadcasts, or Navy-wide messages, or some generic OSHA crap. When did this ship—when did USS Cyclops hear from anybody?"

The XO did not immediately respond. Alexander dutifully looked away.

After a pause, the XO spoke again, calmly. "We will obey our orders until when and if they are superseded. We are not diverting. Is that clear?" Here the XO looked not only at Alschbach but at the other officers seated around the table. Powers alone acknowledged the statement by nodding his head slowly up and down.

When the Lieutenant left the meeting, he had no idea what his duties would be regarding security. Looking over the roster, he saw his name and Acedian's assigned as part of the security force for second deck. At least some consideration, he thought. Hopefully, with legal located on second deck, he and Acedian could work in the office and wait to be called only if necessary.

Montgomery intercepted the Lieutenant as he started to make his way down to his office. "You can't continue to store dead bodies in my reefers, God damn it. I won't have it."

"Commander, I'm doing what the XO told me to do."

Before Montgomery could blast him again, Powers moved to intercept. "Lieutenant, Aah've got a job and y'all just the man fo-wah it." As Powers led him away, explaining why his help was needed, the Lieutenant's sense of gratitude began to evaporate. He also realized it would be futile to argue.

In the afternoon the Lieutenant went back up to the conference spaces looking for the XO. He found him sitting behind the Captain's desk.

"Sir, we were scheduled for XOI. Do you want to reschedule?"

"What do you got?"

"We have one fight and two drunks. We also have one matter concerning proselytizing, and sexually suggestive remarks."

The last comment caused the XO to sit up. "Proselytizing and sexually suggestive?"

"Not exactly. It seems Petty Officer Minch was carrying on and saying God was judging us, the world was going to end, everyone needed to read the bible and so forth. Petty Officer Pope said, if the world was ending, he hoped he could have sex at least one more time. I'm paraphrasing."

The XO waved his hand dismissively, "I'm not interested in your social justice crap. We'll deal with the drunks and the fights. We won't do XOI. We'll go right to Captain's Mast."

"Are you sure sir? The sexually suggestive comment was made in front of Petty Officer Vidlund. She's the one who made the hostile workplace complaint last year."

The XO reaffirmed his decision by staring silently at the Lieutenant.

"One thing more sir. I need the Master-at-Arms to finish putting together their reports. They normally complete the forms and give the defendants their rights and so forth."

"The Master-at-Arms force needs to help with ship's security. You and Acedian can finish up the reports and set things up for mast."

"Yes sir. One final question if I may sir. To hold Captain's Mast you have to be assigned to certain duties. I understand you are acting Captain, but is there anything official in that regard?"

"We'll have Captain's Mast and I'll worry about any procedural problems."

After meeting with the XO, the Lieutenant went back down to legal. On his way, he passed by the mess decks.

Most of the crew had lined up for chow, but the usual efficient process of getting hundreds of people fed three times a day, four including mid-rats, had broken down. Food had not been prepared, and many of the usual cooks and servers were missing.

Whatever else might be said about the Cyclops, her crew ate well. Steak, fried shrimp, hamburgers, cold cuts, fresh vegetables and fruit, all were part of their regular diet. The officers did not eat quite as well as the crew. Navy tradition required the officers to pay for their mess, and the officers tended to go cheap; many preferred to put their subsistence allowance into the bank. The chiefs also paid for their mess but were required to contribute all of their subsistence allowance. As a result, they ate the best of all. A wise officer tended to treat his chiefs well, not only because they were subject matter experts, but because an invitation to the chiefs' mess for a good meal was much appreciated.

When the Lieutenant reached legal he found Acedian sitting at a computer trying to surf the internet. When he asked about the disciplinary packages for Captain's Mast Acedian began to make excuses. "Sir, I was told that Captain's Mast would not take place."

"Wrong guess, we're skipping XOI, but Captain's Mast is going to happen. I want the paperwork finished before you head up to chow."

Acedian protested so vociferously the Lieutenant gave in and agreed to split the work. Acedian happily passed the Lieutenant one of the complaints. As soon as he opened the package he could see only minimal work had been completed. Significantly, he needed to meet with the accused sailor to make sure he understood the nature of the charges and his limited rights as defendant. He also needed to arrange for any necessary witnesses. He called down to the Master-at-Arms force and caught MA2 Oxford. The Master-at-Arms might not now belong to the Lieutenant, but they were still going to round up anyone needed for mast.

Satisfied he had done what he could, for the time being, the Lieutenant headed up to the wardroom. When he arrived most of the ship's officers, including Acadian, were already eating dinner. The Lieutenant noted the XO once again seated at the head of the main table. The Lieutenant thought it interesting that the XO had taken over the Captain's offices, but had not taken over the Captain's galley.

As the Lieutenant looked about for a place to sit, he could hear the XO again arguing with Montgomery.

As the Lieutenant sat down he could hear the exasperation in Montgomery's voice. "Nobody has seen Straus since last night. If he was still onboard the search teams would have found him."

The XO responded as he bit into his sandwich. "He's been talking suicide. Suicide seems most likely. Maybe he learned his kids are gone."

"Sir, we don't know that, but even if Straus jumped, we need to call man overboard and get a search started."

The XO was emphatic in his refusal. "We're not heading back towards Egypt. That would endanger the ship and jeopardize the mission." He began to forcefully tap the table. "Nothing has changed. They ordered 'with all deliberate speed.' Do you think our circumstances changed that? We may be needed more than ever. We may be needed to gather in refugees. I'm not going to jeopardize the mission trying to do the impossible."

"Straus might still be alive! If he went overboard, he might even now be in the water. He might have made it to the shoreline. He might have been picked up. The regs require us to look!"

XO turned his attention to Lieutenant Alexander. "Cut off email traffic and the satellite phone. From now on, nobody sends or receives a message without going through Comms. Until we get to the Gulf, I don't want any bad news that we can't do anything about."

Montgomery persisted, "We can't go on without looking for him. Straus is smart. He'd know how to set up a float to keep alive."

XO responded tersely, "If he jumped from the ship to commit suicide, fuck it. We'll respect his wishes."

The XO now turned to the Lieutenant. "You hear all that. Straus might have jumped or he might still be onboard. Wouldn't be the first time someone went UA from quarters and hid out onboard. Get your MAs to search the hold, search the storage spaces, search the berthing spaces. See if you can find out what happened to him. If he's on the ship and chose to miss quarters I want to know. Don't use the 1MC to call for him. This is routine. I don't want any more panic."

After the XO left the wardroom, Lamb called over to the Lieutenant. "That proves it's the rapture; the chaplains are gone, but the lawyers are left behind."

The Lieutenant gave a quick response. "Seems to me, not too many engineers got taken."

"I guess the devil likes his gates built strong."

"And his contracts iron clad."

The engineer's tone turned suddenly serious. "Listen, I wanted to check on something with you. The CIVMARs onboard, they're now working port and starboard shifts, and that was never part of their contract. Can they make the XO divert to the nearest base until we can bring on replacements?"

"Unless MSC gets involved, I think the XO has the final word."

"Okay, but the CIVMARs, they're not subject to the UCMJ, right?"

"What do you mean?"

"Civilians can't be court-martialed."

"You mean civilians embarked on a warship?"

"That's right, just because of their jobs, doesn't mean they can be court-martialed."

"Generally no, but Federal law allows for the application of military law in some circumstances. Contingency operations count, but there are some questions remaining concerning the constitutionality of applying military law to civilians in the same manner as the military."

"Look, let's cut to the chase. Can the XO make the civilians stay on the job if they don't want to?"

"I don't know. Maybe, maybe not."

The chief engineer responded with a sarcastic, "Thanks for the help." As he began to walk away he turned and paused. "That damned Jew will be the ruin of us all."

After chow, the Lieutenant went to his stateroom. He thought about watching some television, but he badly needed a nap. He had the evening watch; afterward, he would be able to get a full night's sleep, but he worried he might not be able to stay awake until then. He was just about to get into his rack when he was summoned by the XO to Commander Alschbach's stateroom.

Climbing up to the 02 level he hurried along the passageway. Hardwick and Oxford waited for him outside the stateroom.

When he entered the space, he found Alschbach sitting in a chair at his desk a large pistol in his hand. Blood and brains had been sprayed across the desk and over the far bulkhead.

Genesis 4:3-8 KJV:

And in process of time it came to pass, that Cain brought of the fruit of the ground an offering unto the Lord. And Abel, he also brought of the firstlings of his flock and of the fat thereof. And the Lord had respect unto Abel and to his offering: But unto Cain and to his offering he had not respect. And Cain was very wroth, and his countenance fell. And the Lord said unto Cain, Why art thou wroth? and why is thy countenance fallen? If thou doest well, shalt thou not be accepted? and if thou doest not well, sin lieth at the door. And unto thee shall be his desire, and thou shalt rule over him. And Cain talked with Abel his brother: and it came to pass, when they were in the field, that Cain rose up against Abel his brother, and slew him.

CHAPTER-11 – STRIKING FOR THE SHENANDOAH

Thursday, Day Four: Manassas, Virginia

Some disturbance, some sound or movement, causes him to look around the room. He gets up from his chair. There is the scent of perfume, his wife's perfume. He begins to search the house going from room to room. He calls out for Anna. He searches and finds nothing. He searches and finds nothing. He searches and finds nothing. Always there is the scent of perfume. It is just ahead of him. He calls out and no one answers. He cannot force himself awake.

Captain Pride awoke tired and disoriented. Rather than trying to go back to sleep, he began to walk through his house. He called out his wife's name as he went from room to room. In the end, the Captain dismissed the dream; the power of suggestion precipitated perhaps by some spilled perfume playing on his subconscious mind.

He remembered an incident many years before. Towards the end of her life, his Nana had purchased a house at the Cape, a beautiful Victorian, all brick and slate. The previous owner had died in the house and all of the contents had been included with the sale. When his Nan had enquired of the late owner's surviving son what he wished to do with his mother's personal effects, he suggested they send it all to the dump. Rather than take his advice, his Nan had taken the late owner's keepsakes, her knickknacks, her photo albums and letters, boxed them up, and trundled them to the house attic.

Then a young man, the Captain, together with an uncle, had helped his Nan move into the house. She was delighted with the place but had one complaint. She claimed to have seen the image of a woman moving through the house; she claimed she could smell the ghost's perfume when it moved about at night.

After hearing about the ghost, he could not resist playing a joke on his uncle. Late one night he went to his uncle's bedroom and sprayed some old perfume he had found beneath the door. He had scratched at the door until he felt sure his uncle was awake. He then silently went back to his room pleased with his joke. Later, asleep in his bed, something caused him to come awake. When he looked around the darkened room he saw nothing, but he noted the strong smell of perfume.

The next morning, neither he nor his uncle boasted about any successful practical jokes, but both mentioned having smelled perfume during the night. That decided his Nan. At her expense, she mailed the boxes of personal effects to the son's address. "Send 'em to Hawaii. She kin haunt 'im for a while."

With the first hint of light coming through the bedroom windows the Captain headed downstairs. He tried once again to phone Anna and

Mary and Martha, each in turn. This time he did not get the "All circuits are busy" message, but neither did he connect. The phone rang without any indication the system still worked properly. Finally, he reached Mary's voice-mail. He began to leave a message but stopped. He did not know what to say about Anna. Just before the phone cut him off, he told her to stay put because he was driving to her school and would be there as soon as he could. He was not sure if the message went through and subsequent efforts to call again went unanswered.

Instead of making further efforts by phone, he logged onto his computer and his email. He composed a message explaining about their mom. Midway through, he struck his draft and began again. In the end, he sent a message with just the basic facts and concluded by telling them to keep safe and not take any chances. He would see them soon.

The Captain badly wanted to head out and bring his daughters home, but before he left he had more phone calls to make. He began by calling the hospitals near his home. Sometimes the call went through, more often it did not. He got through to one operator who quickly told him there was no record of Anna being admitted. The Captain had doubts that any staffer could be that efficient.

Next, the Captain called the police. These calls surprising went through in an almost normal fashion. After the phone rang for a time a staffer picked up and gave a well-rehearsed response: "If there had been a police report filed involving an injured citizen, police would have called the next of kin. If you have not received such a message it was because no such report has been filed."

The Captain made a call to Anna's school, but if school employees had any information he would never know. The call went straight to voicemail which informed him that the system was full and not taking any further messages.

While the Captain made his phone calls, he let the television play in the background. The emergency broadcasts had ceased and standard programing had resumed.

One news story caught his attention. A reporter and cameraman had trapped a figure against a garden wall. It held its hands up in front of his face trying to shield its eyes from the television lights. As the figure ducked its head forward and back, the Captain could see that its eyes consisted of enormous black pupils devoid of any surrounding white. The fingernails of its hands formed elongated claws. As the reporter peppered it with questions, the figure kept repeating, "Go home, home…. Go home." To every question, the same response, "Go home."

As it backed away the reporter continued to pursue. "Who are you? Why are you here? What do you want?" As he asked his questions, the reporter pushed the microphone at the thing's face clearly hoping for some response beyond "Go home."

Finally, it had enough. It stopped backing away, grabbed the reporter's hand and bit deeply into the wrist. There was a spray of blood. The cameraman dropped everything and ran. The screenshot became one of moving feet and swirling grass. Shrill screaming could be heard off-camera until the news feed was cut. The Captain did not wait to learn the condition of the reporter. He turned off the television and finished with his phone calls.

Having accomplished nothing at home, the Captain began the drive to the Shenandoah Valley. Normally this would have been a drive of a few hours on the interstate, but now he constantly slowed down to maneuver around wrecked and abandoned cars. The Captain saw a number of cars heading east, but none heading west.

Police activity to clear the roads had not yet reached this far along the highway, and the Captain was constantly slowing and being forced to change lanes around abandoned or wrecked cars. He came to a place where the interstate was completely blocked. Some accident up ahead had stopped the traffic and those caught in the jam, rather than detouring or turning around, had simply walked away. The road west was blocked with vehicles as far as the eye could see.

The Captain drove the car up onto the shoulder of the highway. He drove slowly, making his way to the next exit. In a few places, he felt sure he would tear the paint off Avarhouse's car or knock off the side mirror. He managed to just squeeze by the abandoned cars.

The Captain took the next off-ramp and began to drive southwest. He was not overly familiar with the back roads having been accustomed to passing through the area on the interstate. These roads were relatively clear. Cars had been pushed onto the shoulder of the road, enough to slow him, but not enough to stop him.

Leaving the interstate, the Captain turned on his GPS to help guide him on the back roads. A woman's voice with a crisp British accent instructed him to "Make a U-turn."

As he neared the next town, he had to pass through a roadblock. Some state troopers, together with some locals, had placed jersey walls in the road. Every civilian carried a shotgun. The policemen had rifles and pistols.

The Captain slowly drove through the zigzagging barriers that composed the roadblock. A policeman looked down through his window, saw the uniform, gave a salute, and waved him through.

On the other side of the town, he reached a second roadblock. Here the policeman stopped the car and asked where he was headed. The policeman then gave him a series of instructions, about what towns or roads to avoid. Just before waving him on, the policeman asked if he had any weapons in his car. The Captain responded forcefully that he did not.

"Well in that case," said the policeman, "Don't stop for anybody. Don't stop no matter what."

The Captain listened to the radio as he drove. The newsreaders were discussing the new executive order but clearly did not understand it. Their comments seemed calculated to just cause more confusion. The Captain listened for information on gasoline rationing, but they never came to that part of the order. In disgust, he switched to another channel. Here a commentator proclaimed how the "zombie crisis" could be brought to a swift conclusion.

"All that's needed is a bounty for zombie ears. You give good money for the ears of the dead and this will be over in no time."

"What about the shortage of rifles, and training? If you put a bounty on ears, how do you know they'll even be zombie ears?" his fellow commentator asked. "You will be sending out thousands of amateurs with a license to kill. Let the Army do it."

A third commentator chimed in with his opinion. "The Army is already overstretched. Most of the Army's overseas. There's a real problem getting good rifles. The Army has some surplus, but most of the confiscations were crushed or melted down. The politicians can make promises, but it will take time for them to make rifles and ammo."

The Captain grew tired of the commentators; he tried finding a music station. He tried several stations, but the music playing was incomprehensible. After a few of these attempts, he went back to the news channels. He came to a station interviewing phone callers.

First caller: "Last night I saw zombies. There was a group of them in the woods."

Newsreader: "How do you know they were zombies?"

First caller: "They looked like naked mummies. All skin and bones, but they were eating someone. Well, I shot at them. They didn't seem to care. They started walking towards me and didn't even care ... had a shotgun."

Second Caller: "I saw two of them crossing my yard. I set my dogs on them."

Newsreader: "What happened then?"

Second Caller: "Nothing. The dogs wouldn't go near them. They barked their heads off. Even when the zombies ran, the dogs wouldn't chase them."

Third Caller: "I don't believe the so-called 'zombies' are dead. If the dead were rising Paris and Rome would be swarming with them. They've got tens of thousands of bodies beneath every city in their catacombs. Their catacombs seem to be completely safe."

Newsreader: "Well those skeletons are disarticulated. Do you think that could be the reason?"

Third Caller: "I don't know about that. Seems to me bones is bones."

Before the next caller could speak, the station interrupted for breaking news:

First newsreader: "This just in, the Russian news service is broadcasting that the attacks in Russia are being committed by monsters returned from the dead. People are being directed to stay indoors. If attacked, the victim should try to destroy the head of the monster."

Second newsreader: "You've got to be shitting me. The Russians are just now discovering they've got zombies?"

First newsreader: "Ah— sorry folk, Jim's just excited. We know we're not supposed to use that word. We're sorry, please don't write in."

Second newsreader: "I'm sorry! I'm sorry! But do we know that this story's legitimate and not just some God damn hacker."

First newsreader sotto voice: "Can't say that either."

Second newsreader: "I'm sorry, I'm sorry, you're right."

The Captain switched stations. Here the newsreader was interviewing an expert who reeked of cheerful condescension. As the expert explained his theories, the newsreader made some effort to hide his lack of comprehension of how "string theory," and the "multiverse," might be relevant. Ultimately, the interviewer capitulated. "Doctor, I have to confess. I don't know what you're talking about."

The expert's tone changed. "Imagine it thus: two soap bubbles are in the air. The bubbles come into contact; they interact; they move one through the other. To the casual observer, after they separate, the bubbles appear unchanged, but they are not unchanged. The interaction, no matter how slight, will have changed them.

"We are assuming our universe is the same as it has always been, but it is not. There have been changes we have not fully observed, have not fully measured, and do not yet fully understand. The disappearances of some, and the possible resurrection of others, might be the least of the changes that have taken place."

The Captain spoke aloud in his car, "What total bullshit."

As the commentators on the radio argued, the Captain reached Warrenton. He debated whether to go around the town or through it, but hunger won out. He decided to stop for a few minutes and get something to eat. As he crested a hill, he saw a television truck with its long antenna post extended up through the vehicle. Further ahead two police cars blocked the road.

The policemen hunkered down behind their cars holding rifles. One of the policemen signaled for the Captain to stop. Then he waved and signaled for the Captain to turn around and drive back the way he came.

The Captain did a quick U-turn and headed back down the hill. At its base, he could see a small group of people. The Captain had been relying on GPS to guide him but it had been useless since the interstate, constantly commanding him to "Make a U-turn." Before he became further lost, he decided that it should get some directions, if not to the Shenandoah Valley, at least the best place to buy a map.

When he stopped the car an attractive woman in a business suit waved at him. She came hurrying over carrying a microphone. He rolled down his window. The Captain could hear a police scanner playing in the background.

"Do you live around here?" she asked eagerly.

Before he could answer, her cameraman called over with excitement in his voice. "The Chief's not just killing prisoners; he and his wife are eating them."

The Reporter turned her attention back to the cameraman. "I thought the wife was dead?"

"Not dead, just missing," responded the cameraman.

Another man in the van called over. "Looks like they found her."

The cameraman held a headphone to his ear. "They're about to launch the assault against the jail."

The Captain sat in his car and listened. He heard gunshots. Instead of the spectators scattering, more people came out to watch. As the crowd continued to grow, the Captain decided to continue driving.

A mere ten miles from town the highway was hopelessly blocked. Five wrecked cars sat on the road obstructing it from shoulder to shoulder. No policemen could be seen. No effort had been made to clear the wrecks.

The median consisted of a wide-open grassy area with a ditch down the middle. The Captain had to backtrack several miles before he found a place to turn around. The northbound lanes were worse than the south, and he was forced frequently onto the shoulder. When he came to the scene of yet another accident, he returned to the southbound lanes. He soon found another road and began to look for a detour to take him south or west.

After driving for a half-hour, he came to a roadblock composed of four pickup trucks parked in a zig-zag pattern across the lanes and the shoulder of the road. One police officer stood at the roadblock; he carried a rifle only loosely pointed at the ground. He would not approach the Captain's car but signaled for him to turn the car around.

The Captain got out of the car and called over to the officer. "Look, the roads are blocked up there. I'm just trying to go Southbound."

The Trooper ducked down and aimed his rifle at the Captain. "I told you to go back the way you came. Nobody's coming through here." The trooper's voice was angry and impatient. The Captain put his hands up. He got back in his car without speaking, turned around, and left.

The Captain knew there must be an alternate route but his GPS insisted on sabotage. Every time he drove down a side road, his British guide ordered him to make a series of concentric turns that took him back to the road he had just left. The woman on the GPS sounded as exasperated as he felt. He began cursing the voice of the GPS and its educated English accent.

His Nan did not like English people. He now understood why. He suspected one of his children had fooled with the GPS settings; either Mary because she could never resist fooling with all things electronic, or Martha because she could not resist playing with his mind.

Of his two daughters, Mary was most like her mother. She was courageous and determined but tending to sudden weepiness when responding to a hurt friend or a missing puppy. Otherwise, she was of even temperament, goal-driven, and a rule follower.

Mary called her mother almost every day. Genuine friends, they discussed everything. She made calls to him less frequently, more from duty than affection.

Martha, on the other hand, was very much his clone. She was less interested in following rules. She was skillful in the art of operating on the edge without falling over the precipice. She did not shy away from arguments or confrontations, but if she did grow angry, it was like a summer storm, fierce and soon gone.

Martha generally called only when she had something to talk about. Independent and confident, she was impatient on the phone. Her calls were task-oriented. Martha made small talk only when she was in the mood.

Physically too, his daughters had chosen sides. His oldest resembled her mom, slight, with creamy skin and dark, wavy, auburn hair. His youngest most reflected him, tall, with coffee-colored skin, and black, tangled, unruly hair. Only in their eyes were they both different from their parents. His wife's eyes were green and his were brown. His daughters both had bright blue eyes, Viking eyes.

Once, when he was a child, he asked his father's mother if she was a negro. She answered, with a sudden Cajun accent, that she was not a negro, but a Moor. Her people had once ruled Spain and nearly conquered France. On hearing this, his grandfather had laughed, and claimed that he was not a Yankee but a Viking. His people had once conquered France, and England, and Ireland, and Russia, and Italy, and a few others. Many years later, he learned that his grandfather and his grandmother had married at a time when the marriage of Moors and Vikings was not permitted.

The Captain's grandfather came from a long line, not only of Vikings but of rebels. His ancestors had been among the first Marylanders. The family had grown wealthy through shipbuilding. Lacking the strong southern sympathies of many of their neighbors, the family moved north during the Civil War. Among the Boston Brahmins, they were much too Catholic to be welcomed. Additionally, the streak of rebelliousness continued to run strong. This culminated in his great-grandfather running off with the family's Irish maid. His grandfather liked to hint that the resulting disinheritance led to certain financial embarrassments, but he said this with a wink and a nod. Everyone understood that the wealth of the Pride family had vanished well before his great-grandfather's elopement.

The Captain's grandfather had bright blue eyes that glinted when amused. The Captain knew this to be the source of the blue in Mary and

Martha's eyes. The Captain's dark skin and wild hair came from his "Moorish" grandmother, if not by way of Spain, at least by way of Louisiana. He had bequeathed these traits to Martha, together with his Viking and Moorish temperament.

The Captain had never encouraged Martha in her pursuit of a military education. He had, on occasion, been obliged to weather some storms in his career, and it concerned him that Martha's temperament, so similar to his, might make a military career undesirable.

He remembered coming home one day to find her in a state of defeat. She told him that she had been rejected by the academy. She told him the news in a matter of fact way, but he could see that she had been crying. It had been a long time since he had seen any evidence of her crying. It had been a long time since she had failed at anything.

He had hoped that she would give up on attending any military academies and set her sights instead on one of the Virginia universities. If she still desired a military career, she could join one of the ROTC programs, but she had no interest. Instead, she chose the Military Institute.

The Captain still hoped, considering the unpleasant reputation of the Institute in its treatment of freshmen "Rats," that she would change her mind and transfer to one of the other state schools; instead, she had thrived. She excelled in academics, sports, and any military duty. Always competitive, Martha seemed determined to be the best. As she progressed in school, she became more capable, but also more alone. She developed a certain grimness that had not been present when she first went away. She offered no stories of camaraderie, or hijinks, no stories of successes, or failures. No amount of prodding would get her to say anything negative about the Institute, but neither did she speak positively about it.

As the Captain continued to find his way to the valley, he made a series of turns always trying to head south or west. Whenever he came to what looked like a main road, he would take it, hoping it would lead him to a better road. He cursed the ancient Virginians' apparent inability to lay down roads in straight lines. His British GPS friend, meanwhile, remained fascinated with circular detours. After countless turns, he had burned a great deal of gas but made no forward progress.

It was dusk and he had wasted hours driving in no particular direction. The Captain wanted nothing more than to find a place to stop, empty his bladder, and get a drink. Appallingly, he recognized the area through which he now drove. He was in the vicinity of a national park, a Civil War battlefield, one of the many that dotted the region. His series of detours and turns had taken him back nearly too where he started.

Despite his disappointment, he decided to make the best of it. He knew there was a visitor center nearby. He would make a rest stop and be on his way. He hoped it would be open; if not, he would have to find a private place in the woods to relieve his bladder.

The visitor's center was not particularly large. It sat a short distance from the road surrounded by open fields and trees. Scattered around the fields were a few cannons, historic markers, and memorials. As he drove up, he could see three cars out in the parking lot. He could see no one outside the building. He hoped his luck was turning when he walked up to the center and found the doors unlocked.

He entered the building but no one was in the reception area. He hurried into the restroom. A few minutes later, he returned to the entranceway. He noticed debris scattered about, the remnants of a meal. Some of the food lay along a counter and some on the floor. A can of soda sat on the counter; he could see moisture condensing on its outer surface. The Captain stopped and listened. He had a sense that the place was empty. He called out but heard no response.

He briefly explored the building. He located a small book store and a souvenir shop near the front. Off the main entrance, glass cases filled exhibit rooms. The cases held muskets and pistols and swords. There were artifacts from the battle and mementos of the war. Except for the evidence of a disturbance at the receptionist's desk, everything looked to be in order. He almost called out again but thought better of it. He stopped and listened for sounds. The building remained silent; he heard nothing.

He stood and thought and considered. The cars sat in the parking lot; the doors stood open; the center seemed to be in order, but he could find no sign of activity. There was no hint of where the people might have gone. There were other rooms and spaces he could explore. He opened one door to a storage area. He opened another to steps leading down to a darkened cellar. He stood at the top of the steps and listened; he heard nothing. After a few minutes more of listening, he quietly left the building and got back into his car.

Not far from the visitor center stood a crossroads. He knew that one road would take him back to Alexandria. He realized that driving about on back roads and finding his way to the Shenandoah would be impossible in the dark. He could be home in little more than an hour if he headed home now. If he waited to try another day the roads south might well be cleared. With a little luck, tomorrow, he might not have to contend with the roadblocks and crashes. If nothing else, he could get a good map and follow the back roads.

As he debated at the cross-roads, he noticed shapes moving in the shadows of the trees. If he looked straight ahead, he saw nothing; but if he turned away, there was something just at the periphery of his vision.

He did not wait to find out what might be hiding in the trees. The Captain left the visitor's center and drove towards home. After the waste of a day and many gallons of gas, he made good time.

He entered his house and the blinking light on the answering machine caught his eye. He immediately checked and found a message from his daughter Mary: "Mom … Dad … things got weird here for a time, but I'm safe. They're talking about canceling classes, but we're sorting it out. Are you and Mom safe? I spoke to Martha and she's fine. Please call me back when you can. I love you." Then the message ended.

Next, he heard a series of hang-up calls without messages. He heard Martha's voice: "Mom? Dad …? Mom? Dad …?" After a pause, the line went dead.

When the Captain heard his children's voices, he felt like a swimmer who has gone too deep and is struggling back to the surface unable to breathe. He had to sit down to catch his breath. He felt fought out, exhausted, but relieved.

For a long time, the Captain stood by the answering machine. After a while, he began to speak. "Your mom is gone, and I can't find her." He paused and walked to the window. "Your Mom is gone. I went to the school. Her car was gone, but I think her purse was still there. I'm not sure; her wallet and phone were missing." He began to pace back and forth across the room, repeating the same explanations with slight variations. "Your mom is gone…. Your mom did not come back from school…. I've tried the hospitals and police. Your mom is one of the missing." After a time he stopped and took out his cell phone, but then he began practicing again. It was a long time before he dialed the phone.

Entitled, The Table; Revealed At Medina:

Relate unto them also the history of the two sons of Adam, with truth. When they offered their offering, and it was accepted from one of them, and was not accepted from the other, Cain said to his brother, I will certainly kill thee. Abel answered, GOD only accepteth the offering of the pious;

if thou stretchest forth thy hand against me, to slay me, I will not stretch forth my hand against thee, to slay thee; for I fear GOD, the LORD of all creatures.

I choose that thou shouldest bear my iniquity and thine own iniquity; and that thou become a companion of hell fire; for that is the reward of the unjust.

But his soul suffered him to slay his brother, and he slew him; wherefore he became of the number of those who perish.

And GOD sent a raven, which scratched the earth, to show him how he should hide the shame of his brother, and he said, Woe is me! am I unable to be like this raven, that I may hide my brother's shame?

The Koran, Chapter V, The Table; translated by George Sales, 1734.

CHAPTER-12 - OH! TO LIVE LIKE PHARAOH!

Thursday, Day Four: South of Pickwick Landing, Tennessee River

The General and his scarecrows moved quickly. Whenever the road diverged away from the forest, some of the scarecrows insisted on taking the easy path. The General ignored them and kept to the slower but safer route through the brush and scrub. He balked at this unaccustomed restraint. He cherished speed and decisiveness, but this new world required caution. Now and then he would hear the sirens and sometimes even see the pulsing of blue and red lights. The lights flashed by at great speed, hurrying to locations unknown. The General listened for gunfire but heard nothing.

The Sailor urged him to hurry. He pointed into the distance, "Up ahead, on the highway, there's a store. We'll get guns there. Plenty of supplies there."

The Old Soldier found the General as the river forced them to turn south. "They'ns air taken us ta Luka."

"Aah remember…. Rosecrans advanced against Price … and Ord did nothing. The Yankees should have destroyed Price ... but he combined with Van Dorn.... All wasted at Corinth."

The General wanted to keep to the river, but the bright lights drove him away. There were too many roads, too many houses, too many lights. At every intersection he found himself hesitating.

He came to a road leading past a nearby house. The house had bright lights shining across the field. Something about the house disturbed him. Contrary to his nature he resisted going ahead.

Some scarecrows grew impatient and went forward despite the General. As they approached the house a sudden burst of gunfire cut them down. The General and the scarecrows near him dove to the ground. Others retreated into the woods. The General waited for the gunfire to begin again, but when he looked up he saw half a dozen farmers running down the road.

There was no additional shooting. Two scarecrows had been hit, but if the wounds had been severe, they hid any incapacity.

The Sailor ran back to the General's position. "They run off. We can catch them pretty easy. They smell like blood."

The General dismissed the notion of chasing armed men, at least until they had more weapons of their own. The scarecrows continued the march.

After several hours of walking, they came to a great warehouse surrounded by a black, empty field. The field was huge, covered with the black tar of the roads and crisscrossed with thick white lines.

Several engines stood abandoned among the white lines. None of the engines appeared to be running. No people could be seen moving about the area.

"No cop cars anyway," the Sailor volunteered.

The General could make out a sign identifying the warehouse as a "super store," but the lights were so bright he could not look at the place without shielding his eyes.

He turned to talk to the Sailor, "What place is this?" But the Sailor was already making his way across the black road surface. He watched the Sailor moving towards the building, bent over as if walking into a dust storm, his eyes covered against the light. The Sailor made his way to the side of the building. The lights did not shine as brightly there, and the Sailor soon disappeared around the back of the building.

The General heard a shotgun blast; a second blast quickly followed the first. With the second blast, the lights on the warehouse went out.

The General and the scarecrows advanced across the black roadway to the front of the warehouse. The entranceway was composed of huge glass doors. One of the scarecrows tried to push through the doors, but without success. One of the others picked up a rock and hurled it against the glass. The rock bounced off and almost hit the General.

The Sailor returned from the back of the building. He went directly to one of the engines. He smashed a window with the stock of his shotgun and leaned inside. Other scarecrows came up and joined the Sailor. They began to push the engine, the Sailor hanging partly inside through the broken window. He yelled for the General to get out of the way as the engine rolled forward.

The engine collided with the great glass doors and shattered them. Fragments of glass flew everywhere and covered the entranceway leading into the warehouse. Now the scarecrows rushed inside.

The General had never been to such a place. There were shelves of merchandise as far as the eyes could see. There were limitless amounts of clothing. There were stacks of tools and furniture. Adjacent rows held infinite boxes of cakes and candies. Nearby he could see glass jars marked with images of pears and apples and oranges; they looked like fruits gathered in Eden.

Near the center of the warehouse, steel and glass cabinets, the kind a museum might have, held all manner of things. The General could not resist. It took him a moment to figure out how to open the cabinet doors, but once opened a wave of icy air washed over him.

He found all manner of wonderful objects. There were foods carefully packaged in slick, cold, frozen bags. On the outside of the bags were pictures of peas and carrots. Nearby were packages of strawberries and blueberries. There were paper boxes with all manner of vegetables. There were packages of meat and sausage. All the things inside the glass cases were frozen solid.

The General took out a box that looked like a marvelous mixture of fruit and cream. He opened the box. The contents did not look like the picture; still, he could see the cream and the collection of bright mixed berries. He poked at the frozen contents with his finger. He smelled the stuff inside. The mixture was frozen, but it smelled spoiled. He took a small portion and tasted, but found the substance revolting. He tried another box with the same result. He tried another package marked with images of strawberries. The fruit in this package was also frozen solid, but the fruit smelled rank. He forced himself to take a bite of the frozen berries. If anything had been in his stomach, he would have surely vomited.

The General noted other scarecrows systematically going through the glass cabinets of frozen foods. The General watched one scarecrow open a package, taste the contents, and then throw all to the ground. As soon as it tasted and discarded one package, it would open an identical package only to discard the contents of that one as well. From the look of the floor, other scarecrows enjoyed the frozen food about as much as the General.

The Sailor came up beside him pushing a small cart. From the cart he took some clothing and gave it to the General, "You'll want this."

The clothing was the strangest sort the General had ever seen. The Sailor gave him a shirt and coat and trousers, all swirls of different colors. The clothing felt and smelled like new, but consisted of an outrageous mixture of browns, and blues, and greens, and even some reds. The General looked at the odd pattern of colors with distaste. It reminded him of the patchwork quilts some of the field hands adopted for pants and coats.

"You'll want this for sure," the Sailor said continued. "Camouflage. It keeps the cops from seeing you. Get your own boots."

Now the Sailor pushed a new item into the General's hand, black spectacles, glasses, of a sort he had never seen. The Sailor wore a pair and the spectacles covered his eyes and wrapped halfway around his head. It looked like a black blindfold but smooth and cool to the touch.

"If we get enough sunglasses, we'll be able to move in daylight," the Sailor explained.

The General let his rags drop to the ground. He made no effort to cover himself. He looked down at the wreck of his body. Impossibly lean, black leathery skin pulled up tight against the bone. He had little flesh to his arms or legs, but he felt strong. He put on the clothes the Sailor had brought him and felt good clean cloth. He expected the fabric to itch, but it did not. He began to tighten the belts and strings that helped fit the clothing.

He had no boots or shoes to cover his feet. He had walked so many miles and so swiftly, he knew he no longer needed such things, but he went to look anyway. Civilized men must wear boots, even if their clothes were as gaudy as a field hand's.

The General saw a place across the store with shoes on display. He began to walk in that direction, passing all manner of boxes and screens that he did not recognize. Before he reached the shoes, he came across a different sort of gold mine.

Books, rows and rows of books, and here among the books an atlas. He immediately pulled it from the shelf and began to fan the pages looking for maps. The atlas laid out the states and cities, forests and rivers; best of all it showed the major highways.

Near the atlas, he found picture books. These contained extraordinary photographs of people and scenery. Many of them contained guidance for travelers visiting splendid places. He recognized the obvious improvements in the science of photography, but he felt disappointed by the washed-out colors.

A few rows over, the General could hear glass breaking and scarecrows shouting. The Sailor tried to get the General's attention, "I need help. Can't expect me to carry all this."

The General looked at him quizzically, and the Sailor waved his hand and began to point. "Fertilizer, stump remover, diesel, propane if it's handy. We'll also need some steel drums and reloading supplies. A lot to carry. No trucks on these roads. Too many cops."

"What all fo-wah?"

"Bombs," the Sailor said eagerly, "Booby traps."

The Yankee joined the Sailor and spoke up with enthusiasm, "Bombs! Ah-ah-IEDs!"

The Sailor nodded his head vigorously in agreement. "We'll need a big battery," he said, before hurrying off with the Yankee.

The Old Soldier hissed and whispered at the General, "They'ns made ... land torpedoes." He gathered breath and spoke again, "Don't trust 'em."

The General grabbed some nearby scarecrows and ordered them with words and gestures to help the Sailor and the Yankee gather up supplies. When one of the scarecrows looked at the General feigning incomprehension, the General struck it to the ground. The others had no further difficulty understanding the General's meaning.

As the General moved through the store, he passed a group of scarecrows trying on shirts, and pants and jackets. He thought the styles strange; the cloth too. Much of it was ordinary cotton or canvas, but some seemed incredibly rich, smooth as silk. It offended him to see this wealth thrown to the floor to join the dirty rags discarded by the scarecrows.

The General tried to concentrate on his search for boots but was easily distracted. Every shelf he passed held items of fascination. There were objects and tools the purpose of which he could only guess. He could not believe that a store holding unlimited supplies could exist; he could not conceive that such a store would exist far out in the country well away from the major cities.

As he moved into a different section of the store, he saw a group of scarecrows that had once been women. He could tell they had been women, not from their physical appearance, but by the clothes they were trying. These included all manner of undergarments of doubtful utility. The appearance of the female scarecrows, without clothes, was only marginally different from that of the males. Their heads held only wisps of hair. Their breasts were shrunken or non-existent. The curve of their hips had gone, shriveled away like so much dried beef. Even their manner of laughing and joking little differed from that of the other scarecrows. The rich soprano of their speech in life had degraded to a low tenor of grunting and hissing and hooting.

  One of the scarecrows noticed the General watching. It looked up at him and tried to force a smile across its face. Despite its efforts, only a shrunken rictus appeared in substitution for the facial expression. As it struggled to form a smile, black shrunken skin pulled back highlighting white, elongated, feral teeth.

  The General walked over to a section of store holding shoes. Some of the female scarecrows had already discovered this area. Three of them picked out shoes, tossing to the floor those they found unsatisfactory. These scarecrows wore colorful dresses that reached only to their knees. They had wrapped scarves around their heads. Most curious of all, they wore spiked high heels. The ridiculous shoes refused to properly stay on their feet as they practiced walking. The overall effect was less than pleasing. The shoes accentuated their long skinny legs, their knobby knees, and their exposed skin; skin as black as any field hand's.

There were hundreds and hundreds of shoes, all manner of shoes. Even in the semi-darkness of the store, he could make out the intricacies of design. He had hoped to find a pair of plain leather boots, something to protect his feet and ankles; something to keep his new trousers out of the mud; something to remind the scarecrows of his significance. A general could not be expected to walk around barefoot like an ill-supplied private soldier, or worse, an ignorant field hand.

After looking and looking, he could only find a kind of canvas-covered boot. Rivets had been cut through the canvas and they had soles made of an unknown material molded in the strangest of patterns. These boots had never met leather, and would never hold a shine.

He tried on a pair but found his fleshless feet and elongated toes were not well suited. He tried on a second pair that fit the length of his foot but were too wide for comfort. The boots were heavy on his feet and uncomfortably hot. The long laces and endless eyelets were bothersome to tie up. He put on multiple pairs of socks but felt the boots slip out of balance.

In the end, he discarded the boots and found some rubbery moccasins to wear. He liked the springy sole, and the lightweight cloth and leather. The moccasins had better traction and a better fit, even if they lacked the dignity of a proper boot.

With his new clothes and new shoes, he returned to wandering through the store. He carried his new atlas under his arm. Eventually, he came to an area more exciting than all the rest; this section of the store held guns and ammunition.

The cabinets holding the guns had been broken open, their glass panels smashed. The broken glass crunched under his feet as he walked. Several scarecrows examined a variety of weapons. One of the scarecrows had found a set of keys, apparently only after the worse damage had been done. The keys remained useful for removing locks on the triggers of the rifles.

The General thought about his needs, perhaps a second pistol, more ammunition, maps, a compass; it seemed like everything imaginable could be found here, everything except a proper sword. He did find, however, a large silver Bowie knife encased by a new leather scabbard. It was not a sword, but it would have to do. He spoke aloud as he picked it up, "Oh to live like Pharaoh!"

The General looked out over the warehouse. More and more of the store's goods lay scattered about on the floor. Clothes, furniture, bottles, cans, broken bottles, foodstuffs, all manner of things had been examined and then discarded.

Suddenly a gunshot. The General stepped around the corner. Two scarecrows had been arguing over a rifle. One of the Scarecrows now lay on the floor, a bullet through its eye, its brains, and fragments of skull smeared across adjacent shelves. As soon as the other scarecrow looked up and saw the General, it dropped the rifle and ran.

The General looked down at the dead scarecrow. He nudged it with his foot. The skull was shattered but lacked a flow of blood, just the same black treacly matter he had seen before. It leaked rather than pulsed from the skull onto the floor. He noticed again the smell of rotten eggs instead of the smell of fresh clean blood.

The brain itself did not look like it ever belonged to a man. The General had seen enough broken skulls to know. The color seemed wrong, too much black and gray. It lacked the vibrancy that should have been present with any living man having his head shot off.

The General bent down and touched the dead scarecrow's chest at the place where the heart should be. He felt a faint pulse. The General placed his hand over his heart. He compared his pulse with the pulse of the dying scarecrow. Both went on with a slight but steady beat. As the heart continued to beat, the black treacle continued to drip steadily onto the floor. The General waited for the heart to stop; he waited for the lungs to shudder one last gasp. He knelt by the body, his hand on the chest, and waited. Nothing changed. The scarecrow was dead but its body did not know it.

The General picked up the abandoned rifle. He began to work the bolt back and forth. He had a box of bullets and looked at the butt plate of the repeater to see where the bullets went; then he realized the bullets were intended to be stacked inside the rifle. He had a certain expertise with the old Federal Carbines and a professional's appreciation of the improvements. The bolt went forward and back, loading each bullet and ejecting each in turn.

"Wonderful.... Wonderful."

As the General marveled at the bolt action rifle, the Sailor rushed over. He carried a knapsack loaded with goods.

"General! We've got cops."

As soon as he spoke rifle shots came from the front of the store, "Tat-tat-tattoo.... Tat-tat-tattoo." The gunfire was immediately joined by the sounds of another rifle firing at the opposite side of the store, "Tat-tat-tat, tat-tat-tat .... Tat-tat-tat." Other rifles joined in, the sound of individual gunshots subsumed in the fusillade of fire. The rifles fired more rapidly than the General could believe. The sustained and furious gunfire took on the sound of tearing of cloth. Objects on shelves flew into the air. Glass shattered as bullets ripped through the store. Bullets flew through the store in all directions, front and back, left and right.

As the shooting started, scarecrows fell or dropped to the ground. Those on the ground crawled for cover. Those still on their feet ran towards the nearest exit. Scarecrows ran for the front doors; some headed to side exits where rows of plants and flowers offered hope of concealment. A spray of gunshots met any who went near a door or an opening.

Over the sounds of the gunfire, the General could hear scarecrows hooting and grunting. He heard no screaming or cursing.

The General yelled and pointed, "Git ta the back!"

The General and Sailor joined the rush of those running from the gunfire. Going through two large swinging doors, they came out into a storage area. The back wall at the of the storage area consisted of great steel doors. A smaller door adjacent to these led outside.

The Sailor signaled to one of the scarecrows to go out the small door. It proved reluctant until the Sailor pointed his shotgun at it. As soon as the scarecrow pushed open the door more gunfire erupted. "Tat-tat-tat-tat-tattoo," echoed through the store.

The first scarecrow was hit at least once as the bullets entered the room. Others, following the first scarecrow, pulled the door shut and moved back into the storage area. The scarecrow that had been shot regained its feet and stood looking at the Sailor. It seemed to be considering some appropriate remark or gesture. It did not matter; the General was already heading to the other side of the storage area and running for a ladder.

"Get them on the door! Rifles ta the ruff!"

The Sailor took off running. The General signaled for the wounded scarecrow to climb up the ladder heading to the roof. He held out the rifle he had been examining earlier.

The scarecrow hesitated. "Git! Safer thay're," pointing to the roof, "than with me."

Despite the gunshot wound, the scarecrow took the rifle and scaled the ladder as fast as a monkey. After some banging away, it opened the hatch and disappeared out onto the roof.

Inside the main part of the store, the gunfire continued. The initial burst of fire had ended, but then a steady, "Tat-tat-tat.... Tat-tat-tattoo," started again.

The rapid fire of the rifles was being answered by a slower, heavier, return fire from within the store. Each of the different rifles and shotguns sang out as the scarecrows fired back.

The "Crack.... Crack," of a rifle mixed with the "Boom, ka-boom," of a shotgun and even the "Pop, pop, pop" of a pistol, but the scarecrows could not match the rapid and sustained fire of the soldiers.

Three scarecrows arrived at the back storage room carrying rifles and shotguns. The General sent them up the roof but told them to keep low and not to fire until ordered. He also told them to send down a report on what they could see.

The first scarecrow came down. His new clothes were stained with the black treacly blood, but he gave a clear, albeit petulant, report using minimal speech and hand gestures.

A dozen shooters were to the front and sides of the store, but there were only two shooters in the back. He pointed and spoke as if looking through the closed door, "An alley and wooden fence... beyond the fence, forest." When asked if the shooters were soldiers or farmers, the scarecrow pointed at the jacket the General wore and thumped his fingers on one of the patches of blue, "Coppers."

The Sailor returned with more scarecrows. The General explained his plan. He wanted two at the doors and two more on the roof. He wanted teams with sledgehammers and axes at the large steel doors.

The Sailor began to divide up the scarecrows. He sent some back into the store to get hammers and axes and waited for their return. Meanwhile, the shooting at the front and side doors never stopped. Some bullets traveled as far back as the storage area and penetrated through the flimsy plaster walls. Scarecrows huddled along the walls looking for cover. At least one was shot in the head and fell to the floor like a broken tree. The General saw the scarecrows on the roof starting to climb back down the ladder.

The General pointed his pistol at them, "Back up! Shoot when aah—"

One scarecrow protested, "Fair play! Won't leave us?"

The General continued to point his pistol, "—tell yah. God damn yah! Git back up!"

The "Tat-tat-tat" of the soldier's rapid-fire rifles seemed to never stop. The answering fire from inside the store began to slow. Now the General only heard the "Boom, ca-boom" of a single shotgun.

Once the Sailor had his teams assembled, he called up the ladder, "You on the roof. Start shooting!"

Above him, the General could hear the "Crack…. Crack," of the scarecrows' rifles, and "Boom, ka-boom," of their shotguns.

As soon as the shooting started from the roof, the enemy responded with an endless "Tat-tat-tat-tat-tat-tat-tat-tat-tat," from their rifles. Bullets, previously coming in from all directions, now seemed directed solely at the roof; the crisscrossing of bullets flying through the store had, for the moment, stopped. Now the General ordered the gathered scarecrows to escape. The great steel doors opened and the scarecrows with the hammers and axes poured out. They made short work of the fence, and now all of the scarecrows began to run for the woods.

Inside the store, some scarecrows still traded fire with the soldiers to the front and side. One of the scarecrows on the roof called down through the hatch, "Two cops by fence—running."

A second scarecrow on the roof began to edge down the ladder and called into the storeroom, "Call retreat?"

"Yes, hurry!" Two scarecrows came down the ladder as fast as firemen on a slippery pole.

The General went back into the store. He called to the Sailor and the Yankee, "Now! Do it now! Retreat!"

As the General gave his orders, he struggled to raise the volume of his voice. He made up for the lack of volume by laying about him with his heavy bowie knife to get nearby scarecrows running for the door. Scarecrows carrying full knapsacks rushed past him towards the back of the store and out towards the woods.

Two scarecrows from the front of the store ran quickly past the General. The "Tat-tat-tat…. Tat-tat-tattoo," of gunfire followed them all of the way out of the building.

The General tried again to shout orders of retreat. He tried to gain the attention of the scarecrows fighting at the side entrance of the warehouse where broken flower pots and plants and flowers now covered the ground. The low volume of his voice frustrated him. He shouted to be heard over the noise of the gunfire, but no response came from the remaining fighters.

The General waited for a moment and then joined the others running for the woods. As he entered the woods, he heard the sounds of sirens and engines and more rifle fire.

When they were well and truly clear of the enemy, the General stopped. The scattered scarecrows began to assemble around him.

After a time the General spoke, "Whip 'em, next time. Whip 'em next time fo-wah sho-wah."

Deck Log - Fifth Day

OPNAV 3100/99 (Rev 7-84)
S/N 0107-LF-031-0498

SHIP'S DECK LOG SHEET

IF CLASSIFIED STAMP SECURITY MARKING HERE

USE BLACK INK TO FILL IN THIS LOG

SHIP TYPE	HULL NUMBER	YEAR	MONTH	ZONE	DAY
D A	AS 09	45	09	B	19 E

USS __CYCLOPS__
AT / PASSAGE FROM __NORFOLK VA__
TO __MUSCAT OMAN__

POSITION	ZONE	TIME	POSITION	ZONE	TIME	POSITION	ZONE	TIME	LEGEND
0800 L_____, BY___ A_____, BY___			1200 L 23.326411, BY___ A 36.597935, BY___			2000 L_____, BY___ A_____, BY___			1 - CELESTIAL 2 - ELECTRONIC 3 - VISUAL 4 - D.R.

TIME	ORDER	CSE	SPEED	DEPTH	RECORD OF EVENTS OF THE DAY
1200					ASSUMED THE WATCH. STEAMING AS BEFORE. WATCH REPORTS CONDITIONS NORMAL. LIEUTENANT R.S. MERRIAM, USN

REPORT SYMBOL OPNAV 2100-10

IF CLASSIFIED STAMP REVIEW / DECLASSIFICATION DATE HERE

IF CLASSIFIED STAMP SECURITY MARKING HERE

04 Level, Bridge and CIC

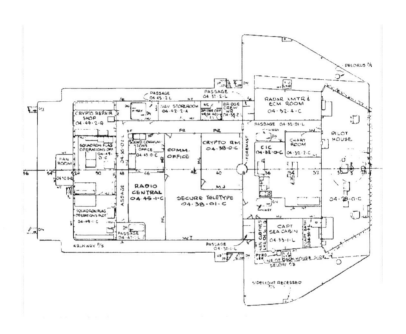

Fairy Tales:

Bata looked under the door of the byre, and saw the feet of his elder brother as he stood behind the door with his dagger in his hand. Then he set down his load upon the ground, and he ran away as fast as he could run, and Anpu followed him grasping his dagger. And Bata cried out to Rā-Harmakhis (the Sun-god) and said. "O my fair Lord, thou art he who judgeth between the wrong and the right." And the god Rā hearkened unto all his words, and he caused a great stream to come into being, and to separate the two brothers, and the water was filled with crocodiles. Now Anpu was on one side of the stream and Bata on the other, and Anpu wrung his hands together in bitter wrath because he could not kill his brother. Then Bata cried out to Anpu on the other bank, saying. "Stay where thou art until daylight, and until the Disk (i.e. the Sun-god) riseth. I will enter into judgment with thee in his presence, for it is he who setteth right what is wrong. I shall never more live with thee, and I shall never again dwell in the place where thou art.

The Literature of the Ancient Egyptians, by E. A. Wallis Budge 1914.

CHAPTER- 13 – ANOTHER CORPSE

Friday, Day Five: The Red Sea, Off Shore Saudi Arabia

Ordinarily, Lieutenant Irawell minded the evening watch least of all. He would be relieved by midnight and have nearly eight hours off. He would not be needed again until the morning department head meeting followed by the forenoon watch.

Tonight his biggest challenge in CIC was staying awake. He had spent the preceding hours collecting evidence and documenting conditions in Alschbach's stateroom. The entire time the XO had hovered over him pointing out any perceived deficiency in his usual inelegant way. He leaned back in his chair and muttered to himself. "Screw the XO, screw this job, and screw this ship." The Lieutenant felt tired of it all.

MM1 Moore sat in an adjacent chair sipping a cup of coffee. He had his feet up, positioned in such a way that he could see the radar repeater at a glance. He must have noticed the Lieutenant nodding off.

"Sir, I know where you can get a cup of coffee if you like."

"Thanks, but no thanks. The last thing I need is a shot of caffeine. As soon as I'm relieved, I'm hitting my rack to get some sleep."

Moore nodded his head in understanding. He took a moment before speaking again. "Sir, they're saying Commander Alschbach's death was a suicide."

The Lieutenant responded monosyllabically, tired of thinking about dead people, but Moore would not let it go.

"I heard it was the XO who found him."

The Lieutenant nodded, "Apparently he heard a gunshot. Alschbach's stateroom is pretty close to the XO's."

"I heard he used an M1911 Colt automatic that he smuggled aboard."

"You've heard a lot it seems."

"Forty-five caliber handgun. A bullet that size must make a pretty big mess."

"A mess, yes, pretty, no," was the Lieutenant's response.

In CIC the watch continued uneventfully. At one point the Lieutenant jerked his head up off his chest, fearful that he might have fallen asleep. He realized that Moore was telling him a story.

"—had been told that the magical ring could be found in a hot spring. The water was as clear as crystal glass. He could see it some sixty feet down glinting on a rock. People warned him not to bring the ring to the surface. If he did, the ring would grant his wish, but something terrible would happen too.

"The water was deeper than it looked. He dove down easily enough. He grabbed the ring and put it on his finger. He began to swim for the surface, but the closer he got the heavier the ring got. He swam for the surface but found himself desperate for air. He began to see things, things from the past, and things from the future.

"The ring was so heavy he began to sink. He tried to shake the ring loose, but he couldn't get it to drop. He was about to drown, but he swam with all of his might. Just as he was going to drown, he made it. At that same moment, the ring slipped from his finger. It dropped away and disappeared back into the spring."

The Lieutenant waited for Petty Officer Moore to continue, but Moore just sat in his chair looking over at the sweep of the radar.

The Lieutenant broke the silence, "And?"

"And what?"

"What's the rest of the story? Did he get his wish? Did he have to pay for the wish?"

"I don't know what he wished for. What does a man wish for who thinks he's about to drown?"

"And what did the wish cost him?"

"I don't know. I'll ask him next time I see him, sir."

"That's not much of a story. A story should have a beginning, a middle, and an end."

"Aye, but I wasn't telling you a story. I was giving you a history."

During the last hour on watch, the Lieutenant felt he was drawing his second wind. He considered the merits of going to his stateroom for sleep or swinging by the wardroom to check on the quality of the midrats. He decided on his rack and sleep. When the Lieutenant's relief appeared, he quickly turned over the watch and immediately went down to his stateroom.

The next morning the Lieutenant awoke grateful for a solid night of uninterrupted sleep. He would have been positively cheerful, except that he had to attend the department head meeting. When he arrived several of the department heads were already present in the conference room. Others filed in behind. Lieutenant Commander Crammer was seated at the conference table arguing with the XO.

Crammer was the assistant department head of repair. He had taken Alschbach's seat at the table. He took no notice of the late arrivals as he tapped on the conference table and spoke. "Sir, we've lost several people to the killer onboard. We need more security."

Powers answered before the XO had a chance, "We only know what we know. We 'ave two killed. Anything mo-wah is speculation. We need fo-wah people to stay in their workspaces or watch standing spaces. We need 'em to stop wandering around like tourists."

The XO now spoke up. "We've got security teams on every deck. We'll find the stowaway. I don't want to hear anybody using the term 'zombie.' "

This failed to satisfy Lamb. "It will be about four days to transit the Red Sea. Before we head into the Gulf of Aden, we can divert to Djibouti, fix security, and let off anybody who wants to leave. They can get a flight home from our base there."

The XO waved his hand dismissively. "I don't want to hear anything more about Djibouti. You're wasting my time rehashing this. We're headed to the gulf as directed."

Lamb responded, "A lot of the CIVMARs want off. Those who want to go home should be allowed to go home."

The XO became impatient, "Negative, we're not going to Djibouti."

Lamb continued to argue. "They're not slaves. Those who want to get off need to be allowed to go home. They're not military. They're not bound by orders."

The XO leaned forward menacingly, "Guess again."

Lamb still would not give up. "Maybe you should talk to your JAG," he persisted. "Civilians are not subject to the UCMJ. They can leave when they want."

The Lieutenant sat up straight as all eyes now turned on him. He began to protest when the XO cut him off. "I don't give a shit what the JAG told you. We'll comply with our orders. We're heading into the gulf. We're not diverting."

Montgomery joined the argument. "Do we know if those orders are still valid? We haven't been told anything since this started."

The XO stood up and signaled the meeting over, "Until we have new orders we will comply with the orders in hand. We will proceed with all deliberate speed. Nothing has changed."

As the Lieutenant exited the conference room he looked around for Lamb, but Lamb had been to first to make his getaway. When he looked back into the conference room, he could see the XO glaring at him. He signaled for the Lieutenant to return by the use of a hand gesture.

The Lieutenant stepped back in expecting to get blasted because of Lamb's dissembling. Instead, the XO began to talk about Alschbach.

"You know I was in my stateroom when I heard the gunshot. I went to Alschbach's stateroom. His door was unlocked." The XO stopped for a moment and looked at the Lieutenant. "You need to write this down; you'll need it for your investigation."

"Sir?"

"Your JAGMAN investigation. It's a suicide dumb-ass, and we need to do a formal investigation. You understand that don't you?"

"Yes sir."

"He's been depressed the whole cruise, recent events have just made things worse. You might have noticed if you'd been paying attention. You also need to figure out where the pistol came from. It wasn't one of ours. We haven't used 1911s in decades. We need to find out if he had a license." The XO now dismissed the Lieutenant away with a wave of his hand. "This is your investigation. Do it by the book. Get a draft report to me as soon as you can."

After the department head meeting, the Lieutenant made his way to the wardroom. He wanted to scrounge some coffee before going back to CIC for the forenoon watch. Talking to himself, he grew angrier and angrier. "Asshole wants me to do more paperwork. World's crashing down around us, and he just wants paperwork. God damn useless bastard." The Lieutenant did not realize how loudly he was voicing his thoughts until he saw a couple of the mess-cranks staring at him.

The Lieutenant chose a donut to go with his coffee and headed into the lounge. He needed to take a few minutes to relax. He sat down and turned on the television for electronic companionship as he ate his donut.

The ship's closed-circuit TV network provided the usual news programs, as well as one or two channels playing some sort of entertainment. In the evenings they had a movie channel. The news stories could be a little perplexing, often playing a day later than the original broadcast back home. Sometimes the stories, through other means, had already become well known to the crew. When the satellite feed for the television failed to sync with other information systems the deja vu effect could be a little confusing.

The Lieutenant turned to a news channel. The video feed showed a reporter standing on a city street at night. His voice sounded British. "—rioters have been dealt with forcefully by security forces." As the reporter spoke into his microphone, two bodies in the background could be seen lying in the street. Policemen wearing bright yellow vests walked nearby. Two policemen held a bound prisoner, as a third spoke rapidly into a radio. A fourth policeman stood with his back to the others. He held a rifle with a flashlight attached. He aimed his rifle and flashlight down the street sweeping it back and forth as he walked. Nothing could be seen beyond the dim cone of light that swept left and right as they retreated.

When the reporter saw the policemen, he rushed towards the prisoner. He called out as he approached, "Who are you? Why are you here? Did you attack these people? Why are you attacking people?" The prisoner did not respond. When the reporter got too close, one of the policemen shoved him away.

The Lieutenant stepped towards the television screen hoping to get a better view. He could see they had bound the prisoner with some sort of rope or wire. It walked awkwardly. Lacking bulk, it looked starved to the point of illness. The prisoner was dressed in rags.

As the reporter hovered nearby shouting his questions, the prisoner twisted and turned trying to shield its face from the cameras. The lights flashed over the prisoner's face, but only for a moment. The Lieutenant could see large black eyes, and lips so shrunken that the teeth protruded like those of a wild animal's.

As the cameraman maneuvered to get his shot, the prisoner weaved its head back and forth still trying to avoid the lights. As it continued to struggle, the prisoner began to howl; the reporter jumped back, suddenly fearful.

The scene switched to the main television studio. The newsreader cut in breathlessly. "This just in, the King of Jordan has been assassinated. There are unconfirmed reports that the King of Jordan has been assassinated by members of his own security team."

His co-anchor looked down at his desk shuffling papers. Finally, he asked a question. "Did we train these people?" There was no response.

The Lieutenant left the wardroom and went back to CIC for the forenoon watch. After four uneventful hours, he left for the legal office intent on catching up with his regular work.

Near the ship's store, a group of sailors was seated on chairs they had pulled into the passageway. They sat outside the space watching television through an open door. An advertisement interrupted the program to announce "American Forces Radio and Television." It looked like any other commercial broadcasting station identifying its brand. After a few odd advertisements, the program returned to playing some sort of game show.

The sailors had two pistols, a rifle, and a shotgun between them. They handled the weapons haphazardly. The Lieutenant had little idea of what this "security watch" was supposed to do, or where the patrols were supposed to go. He had a rudimentary idea the patrols needed to actively check the various work, storage, and berthing spaces located on this deck; but the actual plan to be followed remained a mystery.

The Lieutenant entered his empty office. He was thankful, for once; no one was waiting for him. He turned on his computer and tried surfing through the internet. The connection proved unbearably slow; he assumed the bandwidth was insufficient for everyone trying to use the system. Just as the Lieutenant got a news page to load he heard a knock on the door. A sailor stepped into the office and politely asked the Lieutenant if she could interrupt. "Sir, I need a new power of attorney."

"Well, we can help you with that. Come on in."

The sailor carried a piece of paper. "I received an email from my sister. She said my ex-husband's missing, and she has my kids now." If the Sailor felt distress about her ex-husband, she showed no sign of it.

"How old are your kids?"

"My son David is seven, Jenny's nine."

"You're lucky. There have been a lot of stories about kids going missing, especially young kids."

"I'm lucky, but I have to make arrangements for my kids. I love my sister, but she's not always the most responsible. She says she won't keep the kids unless I give her a power of attorney to take care of them and help with the finances. She needs access to my checking account." The Sailor handed over the copy of the email as she spoke.

"She loves the kids, but she don't know money. She can't take the kids without money. I've been trying to get through to her. I've tried to send her my account information, but I'm not sure email is getting through. She keeps sending the same message over and over again, how I gotta help her. I'm going to send her the power of attorney when the mail leaves the ship."

The Lieutenant looked down at the copy of the email. "How many times has she sent this?"

"Twice a day since this started; the same message every day."

"You don't think that's strange?"

"I just think she's not getting my email. Not surprised, communications are all screwed up right now."

It only took a few minutes to print out a power of attorney and have it signed and notarized. The Lieutenant spoke as he gave the document to the sailor, "Sorry to hear about your husband, but I'm glad your children are okay."

She looked down at the document before speaking. "I feel sad for some of the others, but at least my kids are okay. My sister wouldn't lie about that."

As the Lieutenant finished the power of attorney he walked the sailor out of his inner office only to find PS3 Branson.

Branson had reported as directed and been waiting patiently for the Lieutenant for at least half an hour. In truth, the Lieutenant had forgotten all about Branson and would have left him waiting, but for the earlier interruption. The Lieutenant got down to business and began to review Branson's Article 15 package. Flipping through the file, the details quickly came back to him; Branson and one of his mates had been found drunk in berthing.

As the Lieutenant explained the charges and the defendant's rights, Branson kept trying to interrupt. The Lieutenant lost patience, "Look, I'm not here to question you about what happened. You can tell the XO at Captain's Mast."

"Sir, I don't have any questions. I brewed the bug juice and I'm guilty. That's not what I'm worried about."

"Fine, spill it."

"It wasn't just me and Parks."

"It's no defense that others are guilty and did not get caught."

"Lieutenant, you don't understand. There were four of us. We've been brewing the bug juice for weeks. Me and Parks went down that night to check on it. It was pretty strong. We got really drunk."

"I told you, don't tell me any details, tell the XO."

"But sir, Commander Montgomery already told the XO; that's what I'm trying to tell you. Strong and Owens went down later that night. They went down to get a drink, but they never come back."

After finishing Branson's disciplinary paperwork, the Lieutenant went to find Hardwick. He learned that the disappearance of Strong and Owens was common knowledge. "They're not the only ones sir." Hardwick's tone suggested she thought the Lieutenant somewhat obtuse.

The Lieutenant had the second dog watch at the end of the day and was glad for the excuse to get out of his office. That evening, the watch passed slowly and the Lieutenant tried to ignore a growing sense of apprehension. It was a restlessness stoked by confusion. He knew, that as a result of his participation in the department head meetings, he was better informed than most. Even so, he felt adrift, with no control over events. If he was anxious, how much worse for the ordinary crewmembers onboard Cyclops.

After finishing his watch, the Lieutenant had eight hours off, but instead of going down to his stateroom, he decided to go to the wardroom lounge. Although tired, he was not yet ready for sleep.

The news played on the wardroom's television "—convoy of westerners was prevented from crossing the border. A mob then formed and began to attack those trying to flee."

As the narrator spoke the video showed an attack on a man wearing a dark suit. His attacker wore white flowing robes with a checkered scarf around his head. The man in the robes repeatedly struck the man in the suit with some sort of stick or rod. The man in the suit ineffectually blocked the attack using his right arm. His hand flayed about as he tried to block the blows. It seemed clear his wrist, or maybe his arm, had been broken by an earlier strike. Finally, the man was struck in the face and he fell to the ground. Other men in robes rushed forward and began to kick and stomp on the man. The mob shouted and screamed in Arabic as they attacked.

The camera cut to a second attack. This showed a woman seated on the ground, partially naked. Her clothes had been torn to rags and scattered around her. She tried to cover her breasts with her arms. A teenage boy ran up from behind her and struck her in the head with his closed fist. Her head rocked violently from the blow. The woman looked calmly up at the cameraman. She said nothing. She continued to try to cover her nakedness with her hands and arms. The boy came back and kicked her solidly in the chest.

When the camera angle changed, the Lieutenant could see soldiers or policemen with machine guns. They watched the attacks. They did nothing to help the man or the woman lying on the ground.

"Where is this?"

"Some Saudi city near Bahrain."

As the Lieutenant watched the video, one of the officers in the lounge spoke up. "If we're supposed to go help those people, I'm afraid we may be late."

A second voice replied, "That's assuming we get there at all. I'm more afraid of our zombies than Arabs."

The Lieutenant turned to see Miller and Unger inclining in club chairs in the far corner. He felt obliged to say something. "Surely it shouldn't be too hard to find the killer onboard."

Unger responded first. "Don't know about that Lieutenant. This ship is pretty massive. If you leaned this ship up against the empire state building we'd go halfway up the side. We're as long as the average skyscraper's tall. Add to that ten wide decks honeycombed with spaces, not so easy to find someone who doesn't want to be found."

Miller then spoke up. "Judge, how many men do you think we've got to search with?"

The Lieutenant's only response was the perplexed look on his face.

Miller continued, "Even if they turned the whole crew out, there're just not that many, once you pull the watchstanders."

The Lieutenant began to argue, "Surely, we could get by with just a skeleton watch on the bridge and in engineering."

"Aye, but don't forget weapons and repair. They've their own watches."

Miller must have noticed another quizzical look. "This ship does more than basic repairs for the fleet. There're things onboard that are guarded by armed men twenty-four-seven. Judge, there's a reason they make us wear these things." Here Miller pointed to the radiation counters they all wore on their belts.

Unger joined in, "Not to mention a quarter of the crew have gone missing and it don't look like they're going to be found."

The Lieutenant left the lounge for his stateroom. He was looking forward to some well-deserved sleep. At around 0130 he awoke to urgent knocking at his stateroom door. Answering the door, he found Hardwick standing outside.

"Hardwick, God damn it, don't you ever sleep."

Hardwick ignored his outburst as she provided him details about the murders on the fourth deck.

Genesis 4:9-16 KJV:

And the Lord said unto Cain, Where is Abel thy brother? And he said, I know not: Am I my brother's keeper? And he said, What hast thou done? the voice of thy brother's blood crieth unto me from the ground. And now art thou cursed from the earth, which hath opened her mouth to receive thy brother's blood from thy hand; When thou tillest the ground, it shall not henceforth yield unto thee her strength; a fugitive and a vagabond shalt thou be in the earth. And Cain said unto the Lord, My punishment is greater than I can bear. Behold, thou hast driven me out this day from the face of the earth; and from thy face shall I be hid; and I shall be a fugitive and a vagabond in the earth; and it shall come to pass, that every one that findeth me shall slay me. And the Lord said unto him, Therefore whosoever slayeth Cain, vengeance shall be taken on him sevenfold. And the Lord set a mark upon Cain, lest any finding him should kill him. And Cain went out from the presence of the Lord, and dwelt in the land of Nod, on the east of Eden.

CHAPTER-14 – BUREAUCRATS AND THE HUE AND CRY

Friday, Day Five: Navy Yard

He walks towards the edge. Above him are cliffs, remnants of a mountain torn down by age. All around him are the bleached bones of animals that have fallen from the surrounding cliffs. He is walking in a field of bones that leads to the edge. Dust rises with each step he takes. The heat of the day bears down on him. The heat of the sun burns him. He is covered in fine dust.

There is a figure ahead of him gliding over the dust. The figure has reached the edge of a cliff and turns and waits.

He looks at the figure standing at the edge. He walks forward, but at the last moment, he drops to his hands and knees and crawls, too fearful to stand at the precipice.

He looks below. He can see cliff walls going straight down for hundreds and hundreds of feet. The bottom is a blur. He can see waves striking at the base of the cliff. He can feel them vibrating up through the solid stone of the cliff face. He can feel the wind rising against the stone wall like a river of air. Down below are sea birds. They fly near the water, so far away that they are just black specs circling above the waves. The birds fly in and out of a gray mist thrown up from the crashing waves.

On the far side, opposite the cliff, he sees still water, clear blue water. The water laps gently at a narrow beach of snow-white sand. At the edge of the beach are palm trees. The trees climb up the far hill and are joined by evergreens, not evergreens, ironwood. He knows the place. It is the island; his first posting. He and Anna had been newlyweds here, one of many young couples far from home and thankful for adventure.

He gets up on his knees and then stands at the edge of the cliff. He hovers at the edge. He moves closer and closer, and peers out towards the island. He sees the clear blue of the water, as clear as sky. Now he feels cool wind rising from the sea gently caressing his face. He edges closer and closer still. He is afraid of the great height, but he longs to swim again in the cool clear water.

The figure has reappeared, but now he stands behind. The figure's hand is resting gently on his back. "What do you see?"

"Wonderful things!"

"Step off the edge and let the wind carry you down, like a bird in flight."

Captain Pride awoke in his chair trembling. He turned on the lights of his room. He stood up and began to pace, back and forth, back and forth, door to window. Once he looked out the window and thought he saw movement at an adjacent house. In the darkness, he could make out a figure, a shadow, on the balcony of a neighbor's house. After a minute the figure disappeared. He saw it next down in the alley running as silently as a cat. It had gone so quickly that the Captain wondered if he had really seen it.

The disappearing shadow made the Captain think of the banshees.

Although his maternal grandmother was definitely a woman of the Old Testament, she was fond of stories about ghosts and fairies and the little people. She particularly liked to tell stories about the banshee. The banshee came when she was owed a soul. She had to be given permission to enter a house. If denied, she would skulk and wait in the darkness. Sometimes she howled and wailed until given what was hers.

His Nan claimed to have heard the banshee the night her father died. He was a wastrel of a man and fond of drink. She could not say that she was sorry to see him go, but her mother loved him. When the banshee came, her mother found some means to satisfy her. Here the story would end. His Nan claimed not to know the nature of the bargain, but if pressed further would say, but for the desperation of her mother, her own father would most certainly be in hell.

His paternal grandmother was also partial to the Old Testament but apparently read different chapters. Gentle where his Nan was hard, forgiving where his Nan was cold, she imparted to her sons fear of God, the truth of the scriptures, and the infallibility of the prophets. His father, Eleazar, liked to joke that, but for the quality of Charlton

Heston's acting, Elijah Pride might well have been named Moses.

After a time the Captain turned out the lights and sat back down in his chair. He could feel himself growing drowsy, but whenever he began to drift towards sleep something would disturb him and bring him back awake. Finally, gray light began to seep through the window. Any further possibility of sleep became impossible.

With the break of day, the Captain again thought about driving to the Shenandoah and bringing his daughters home. He knew it to be a foolish idea. He had spoken to them both the night before; to argue further with them about returning home would only cause them to worry about his mental state.

Yesterday, when he got through on the phone, he reached Mary first. Relief and sorrow washed over him in equal parts. He did not appreciate how much he wanted to talk to her until he heard her voice.

"Dad, are you okay?"

"I'm okay dear heart, but I have some bad news."

"About Mom?"

"Yes."

"Your email…."

"But I don't think I talked about your Mom in the email."

"Yes, I know."

He could not think of anything else to say. Mary mournfully filled the silence, but without sobbing or crying, "Martha and I thought that Mom was gone. We couldn't get through to her on her phone, and then when we got your email...."

"I'm sorry dear heart. I didn't know how to tell you both. I tried to get out there to see you, but the roads are jammed up and gas is impossible to come by."

"It's alright Dad. Is everything else okay?"

"Everything here is about as good as can be expected. Are you safe?"

"It's okay now. It was bad when people disappeared. It was worse when the stories about the monsters started. There was a lot of panic. People are scared to go out after dark, but as far as I know, nothing has attacked the dorms, and we've got a lot of volunteers providing security.... Dad, what does it all mean? People are saying that it's the end of the world."

"I don't think the world is ending, but the crazies are certainly dangerous. I don't think they're monsters; they are more likely brain-damaged or diseased. Some sort of virus, or maybe some sort of mass hysteria. One thing's for sure, you must stay away from them. You need to have a safe place, especially after dark."

When he suggested to Mary that she come from school, she demurred, insisting that all was well at school and she did not want to miss class. She promised, if anything changed, she would call right away.

When he had reached Martha, he could hear in her voice that she had been asleep. The phone connection proved poor and it was hard for her to hear him. As he tried to talk to her she kept repeating, "Dad …. Dad …." Finally, he hung up and tried again, "Martha…. Martha …. Can you hear me?" He could hear her voice but she could not hear his. He hung up and immediately called back. The third attempt succeeded. The call went through and Martha answered.

"I'm so glad to hear your voice. I've been trying to reach you for days."

"I've been trying to reach you too. I got through to Mary, but you and Mom have not been answering."

"Martha, I'm sorry, there's no easy way to tell you this."

Before he could say anything more, Martha interrupted. "You're going to tell me something has happened to Mom."

"Yes."

"I knew something was wrong when she never called. I think Mary knew before me."

"Are you safe there Martha? I tried to get through earlier in the week but the roads were jammed up. I can come and get you and bring you home."

Martha seemed scandalized by his suggestion. "Dad, don't worry. I'm safer here than anywhere in the state. You don't need to come and get me."

The Captain resisted an urge to call his daughters again this morning simply to hear their voices. Instead, he began to get ready for work. After showering and dressing he went downstairs to make breakfast. As he worked in the kitchen, he turned on the television news for company.

The newsreader reported on a story that the graveyards were closed because local authorities believed them unsafe. As the newsreader spoke a grainy video played. It showed a vandalized cemetery with holes in the ground and stone markers knocked over. An individual could be seen walking through the graveyard in the twilight. The figure seemed to be wandering around drunkenly. The figure covered its eyes with both hands when the spotlight shined on it. Suddenly the figure started to run, disappearing into the darkness with remarkable speed.

The television switched to a video shot the afternoon before. A reporter interviewed people walking down the street adjacent to the cemetery. He asked each a variation of the same question. "Do you know there have been reports of the dead coming out of this graveyard?"

First Respondent: "If the dead are coming back, the Army needs to go into the cemeteries and clean things up."

Second Respondent: "If people have come back from the dead, we can't just leave them. We need to defend ourselves."

Third Respondent: "The dead, the resurrected? You mean the zombies?"

Fourth Respondent: "We can't leave people trapped in grave vaults or buried alive. We have to open the graves. As long as they are not dangerous, they should be freed. I guess."

The last comment made the Captain consider his family. His parents loved the mountains the way he loved the ocean. They had retired to a little town in Tennessee. Ailments had unexpectedly overtaken his mother. When she died they had buried her on the hill overlooking the town, the forest behind, the mountains above, the river below. She had been his father's best friend, really his only friend. Not long after her death, his time came. The Captain buried him alongside her on the hill above the town. It was a quiet place in the shade of old trees. Some of the memorials went back two hundred years. He could not imagine that place with undead hiding among the gravestones. He could not imagine his parents trapped underground struggling to escape.

He thought about his son and Arlington Cemetery, but this proved too much. The Captain turned off the television. He finished his morning routine and got ready to leave. He should have headed straight into work, but he had one more chore before leaving.

The Captain called his insurance company. He called repeatedly until he got through. In the exchange that followed, the insurance adjuster, in a very pleasant voice, told him they could do nothing until he had the car transported to the insurance company's preferred garage for inspection. The adjuster also warned him there would likely be a problem getting spare parts.

"You're kidding me. Why can't you send an inspector to where the car is located? It's not drivable. I would have to get it towed to your garage."

"I'm sorry Captain. We're really shorthanded. It would take several weeks, maybe longer to get someone to your location."

"How soon can I get this done if I have it towed to you?"

The voice on the phone gave him a date. "That's nearly two weeks. Can't you do better than that?"

"I'm sorry Captain. We're swamped because of the crisis. We're also pretty shorthanded."

"What about my wife's car. I have looked for it everywhere. I believe it's been stolen."

"Where was the car last?"

"My wife drove it to work."

"Where is your wife now sir?"

"My wife is among the missing."

"Captain, there is nothing we can do now. I suggest that you file a police report concerning the possible theft of the car and a missing person's report."

Despite the fact the Captain's would be without a car, he decided to return the car he had borrowed. Avarhouse told him he could keep it as long as he needed, but favors from Avarhouse always brought him a sense of unease. The fact that he could not buy gas for the car decided it. Before heading to Avarhouse's office, he had one more duty to perform.

The trip should have taken less than twenty minutes, with minimal traffic, and lanes sufficiently clear. Still, he made several detours as he considered roads that might have provided alternative routes. He slowed or stopped whenever he approached a car that looked like it might be Anna's.

Arriving at the school, he drove around the parking lot. He could see no sign of Anna's car. He parked and tried to walk into the school. This time all the doors to the building were locked. Looking into the windows he could see no indication anyone was inside the building.

After a slow drive back, the Captain arrived at Avarhouse's office. He knocked on the door but no one responded. He slipped the keys into the mail slot and left the car parked outside of the office.

The Captain walked up to the subway station without incident. The autumn air felt fresh and clean as he walked. Although many people queued up to ride, there were plenty of places to sit down. His train arrived and left on time and getting into work proved fairly easy, even with having to make a switch to the green line.

Riding into the city, he began to feel hopeful that things might get back to normal. His feeling of optimism departed when he walked up to the Navy Yard gate. Across the street, he could see a long line of people waiting at one of the convenience marts. A similar line had formed up at the nearest gas station. Two marines in full battle rattle stood nearby.

When the Captain arrived at the RLSO, he walked quickly towards his inner office. He felt anxious to get to work after the wasted morning. He could not help noticing, however, the unusual quiet of the office.

He went to Invidia's office instead of his. "Where is everybody?"

Invidia passed him an annotated muster report. "Let me start by showing you this."

The Captain scanned the report. One officer, two enlisted, and two civilians had disappeared. Family members had confirmed they had not returned home the day of the event. The status of two other officers, one enlisted and two civilians remained unknown. Phone messages and messengers had been ignored. No family or friends with information could be found.

"Okay, but where is everyone else?"

Invidia paused for a moment before answering. "Everybody else is over at OJAG. They left us the civilians to answer the phones and deal with emergencies."

Invidia did not look at the Captain as he answered his questions. His attention remained fixed on a news story playing on his office television. It concerned a series of murderous attacks committed during the night. He remained mesmerized even as the Captain turned to go. As an afterthought, Invidia called out to him. "Also, the Admiral wants to meet with you at 1500, some sort of emergency conference."

The Captain felt this morning's neutral feelings towards Invidia begin to evaporate. He stepped back into Invidia's office. "Obviously, some sort of emergency," he responded.

Invidia seemed oblivious to the sarcasm. "The Admiral seemed a little put out. She wanted to know why you haven't been at work."

Now Invidia turned and looked up. The Captain could see that Invidia shared the Admiral's curiosity. The Captain considered what to say. He knew Invidia to be a solitary man with few interests outside of work. The Captain did not think he would understand, but he volunteered anyway, "I've been looking for Anna and my daughters."

Invidia feigned surprise, "Are they okay?"

"The girls are okay, but Anna is among the missing."

Invidia seemed to deliberate for a moment. "You know, a lot of the disappeared are still around. They've merely used the confusion as an opportunity to restart their lives."

"Anna isn't the sort who would run away."

"I don't mean Anna, of course, just others who are confused or frightened. There are stories about others who were missing now coming home."

"Anna did not run away in a moment of confusion."

"I don't mean Anna. Just saying there's always hope."

The Captain responded with a simple thank you as he turned and left.

The Captain reached his office, logged on to his computer, and began to check his emails. There were considerably more than usual. Many seemed to be from offices outside of his purview. Entire email chains related to missing personnel, as if people might rematerialize if only enough strangers read their names.

Just before he logged off the email server, he thought better of it. He drafted a quick email to Invidia re-emphasizing the need to remind people about the "free expression" regulations. If any whistleblowers made allegations of proselytizing in the workplace, it would be important to have a record.

He closed his email server and began to search the internet for substantive news. Each web page loaded painfully slow. The fake videos were the worse, but even the regular news sites had started to play them.

One video showed an alleged angel walking along a city street. The angel appeared nearly translucent. She walked along the street as people backed away and pointed. The video showed the angel walking into a bright light and disappearing.

Another video showed a man being beamed up into the sky by a science-fiction-like teleporter. A caption noted that the original video had been viewed over four million times. An identical video included the fakers taking credit for the fake. The posters claimed to be providing a public service by alerting the public to the existence of fake videos, but the screaming headlines were calculated to draw traffic to their site. This video had already been viewed over two million times.

At about 1430, the Captain decided to walk over to the Admiral's office. Invidia looked up as the Captain went down the passageway. He looked like he wanted to say something, but the Captain did not pause. "I'm going to see the Admiral," he said as he walked out of the office.

The offices of the Judge Advocate were on the other side of the Navy Yard and the Captain walked briskly. He understood well enough that today he needed to be early.

When he reached the Admiral's office, one of her aides manned the front desk. The Captain had been introduced to the woman but could not remember her name. Both from his prior meeting, as well as her reputation, he knew he did not like her; he remembered her as obsequious to her superiors, obnoxious to her peers, and abusive to her subordinates.

As if in response to an unspoken query, she volunteered that, because of missing personnel, they were shorthanded.

"Are they among the disappeared?" he asked.

"Deserted more likely."

Ordinarily, the Admiral proved very courteous whenever one of her senior officers visited, but today she kept him waiting. He sat in a chair and watched others go in and out of the office. He listened to phone calls being made, the voices barely audible, shielded by walls and doors. After a time one of the aids volunteered that the Admiral had expected him at 1400, but now had a telephone conference. He would have to wait until the conference concluded.

The Captain was flustered, "I understood the meeting was at 1500."

The aide answered with a slight clucking sound, "I'm sure that's not the case. The Admiral's calendar has you down for 1400."

After nearly an hour, the Admiral called him into her office. She did not bother with any of the usual pleasantries. "Where were you yesterday?"

Admiral Lezuria had the grace and sensuality of a tiger. Her long legs and narrow waist would be the envy of any college girl. Her facial skin, however, was so sun damaged she looked like a fugitive from an Egyptian tomb. Her searing blue eyes dared any to remark on the evident contrast, the youthful body holding up an ancient head. She was a confused portrait of Dorian Gray, in which the face alone revealed age and sin. When the Admiral turned angry, the face made no effort to disguise the fact that truth could be unpleasant.

Rather than give the Admiral a cogent answer the Captain sputtered.

The Admiral immediately fired off another question. "Where have you been? You've been UA for three days."

The Captain was tempted to provide excuses: his car was wrecked, the subway was down, Anna was missing, he could not reach his children, instead he kept silent. The Admiral continued to look at him waiting for him to break the silence. In the end, he became stubborn, "Admiral, I did check in on Wednesday."

"I left word for you to be in my office at 1400."

"I received a message to be here at 1500. I did not receive any earlier messages." He again was tempted to provide a detailed excuse but stopped himself; he kept it simple. "Admiral, I was out of the office yesterday trying to get my family situation sorted."

"Captain, I called your office twice and came by your office twice. I appreciate the personal distress you may be feeling, but others similarly situated, with much less responsibility I might add, managed to make it into work. Your home is just across the river, minutes away. You failed to make the briefing. You failed to appreciate that you, as well as your officers, are crucial to our efforts to restore order."

The Captain could think of nothing else to say. The Admiral continued to stare at him waiting. Finally, he offered up a different response. "Yes, ma'am. My judgment was deficient. It won't happen again, Admiral."

The Admiral became conciliatory. "Elijah, you know that I have always depended on you. In the next few weeks, you and your officers are going to be tasked with new and heavy burdens. I need to know I can count on you. Now, more than ever, we all have to work together as a team."

After the meeting, dejected, the Captain went back to his side of the Navy Yard. He was not used to being lectured or chastised. When he returned to work, he hoped to find the place bustling with activity, but his junior officers were still absent. The Captain walked past Invidia and headed to his office without speaking.

He had reports to generate and plans to make. Instead, he started calling local hospitals. He got through to one hospital's administrative offices, asked his question, and waited. After a moment of silence, the staffer told him that Anna Pride was not a patient. "I suggest you contact the police. They will have a list of emergency transports in the last five days. You can add your wife's name to the list of the missing." The staffer rattled off the message so quickly it was clear she was reciting it from rote. She hung up as soon as she pronounced the last syllable.

Before he could take her advice, the phone rang at his desk. Normally his receptionist would have screened his calls, and she would have told him who was on the phone and why before he was obliged to answer. This call came directly to his desk from one of the area commands. He regretted answering as soon as he picked up the phone. Their legal officer had questions about how to classify missing members of their units. Were they KIA, or MIA, or UA or something else? The Captain only partially paid attention to the questions, still wondering why outside calls were being forwarded directly to his desk. He dodged the question by saying no Navy-wide decision had been made on how to process the missing beyond identifying them as such on muster reports.

As soon as he hung up, his phone rang again. This caller had questions about how to deal with an officer who arrived at work drunk. This call was followed by a third about a service member arrested for shoplifting at the exchange. Calls came in about violence and disrespect and service members refusing to work. As soon as he finished with one call another would start. Finally, he ignored the ringing phone and went to look for Invidia.

He expected to find Invidia in his office, but his computer and lights had been turned off. Invidia was gone and the whole office was empty. The Captain had a moment of panic but then he recognized the lateness of the hour; still, it surprised him that Invidia had headed home without first checking in with him.

The Captain turned off his computer, turned off the office lights, and set the alarm. Before heading home he went by the Navy Exchange mini-mart. He had little food in the house, so he bought some bread, milk, and cold cuts. Unlike the stores outside the gate, there were no lines here.

He carried the groceries with him as he walked home from the subway. Undoubtedly, the bags caught Mrs. Delaney's attention. She came out on the sidewalk and intercepted him just before he entered his house.

She spoke apologetic, "I wouldn't trouble you, but I need to go grocery shopping you see. We don't drive much anymore. I can't leave George now, and I can't reach our medical aide. I was going to go grocery shopping, and his medicine is going to run out, but I need someone to stay with George."

He stopped and turned to face her. "You're Mrs. ..." He had once been introduced to the lady, but it was Anna who kept track of the neighbors and names.

"You know me, Elijah. I'm Amy Delaney. I'm sorry to trouble you. But I can't leave him alone, you see, and drive to the store." As she spoke she came up to the Captain and stood in front of him. Despite a significant difference in height, she looked intently into his eyes as if trying to answer some question about him.

"We've that in common. My car's vandalized and broken down. Tell you what, why don't you let me know what you need, and I'll see what I can do."

She made to follow him and took a step onto his landing. Rather than going into the house, he stopped. He thought if she followed him inside, he would never be rid of her. "Mrs. Delaney, why don't you go home and prepare your list of the groceries, and I'll come by."

She turned on the steps, but instead of walking away, she looked out over the street. She turned her head left and right, back and forth.

"It's alright Mrs. Delaney. No one will bother you. I'll come by and get your list."

Without looking at him or saying another word she went back to her own house. As she walked away it occurred to him that, despite her empathetic eyes, she had failed to ask about Anna.

Margerum to South of Muscle Shoals

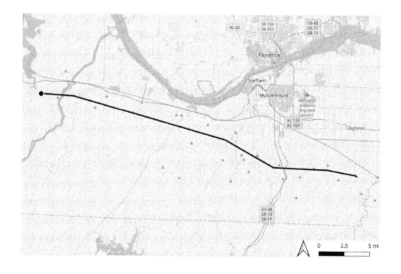

Entitled, Mohammed; Revealed At Medina:

Verily they who turn their backs, after the true direction is made manifest unto them, Satan shall prepare their wickedness for them, and God shall bear with them for a time.

This shall befall them, because they say privately unto those who detest what GOD hath revealed, We will obey you in part of the matter. But GOD knoweth their secrets.

How therefore will it be with them, when the angels shall cause them to die, and shall strike their faces, and their backs?

This shall they suffer, because they follow that which provoketh GOD to wrath, and are averse to what is well pleasing unto him: and he will render their works vain.

Do they in whose hearts is an infirmity imagine that GOD will not bring their malice to light?

If we pleased, we could surely show them unto thee, and thou shouldest know them by their marks; but thou shalt certainly know them by their perverse pronunciation of their words.

The Koran, Chapter XLVII, Mohammed; Revealed At Medina; Translated by George Sales, 1734.

CHAPTER-15 – ENGINES AND WRECKED CONVOYS

Friday, Day Five: South of Colbert Ferry, Mississippi

Once the sun rose in the sky, the General noted the number of engines greatly increased. The General waited for an engine to appear and watched as it disappeared down the road. He marveled at their speed. The General knew that if they could control the engines rushing back and forth, it would change everything.

The Yankee urged him to use the engines. They could take some of the abandoned engines or steal engines from some of the towns or farms they passed. He did his best to argue the point, "Switch to ca's. Wit ca's we would, ah, m-m-most move fast."

The General understood the Yankee's frustration. Those serving him were encumbered with backpacks of chemicals and supplies. One of the Yankee's troopers pushed a wheelbarrow full of red containers; another pulled a cart like a donkey. The Yankee's beasts of burden did not tire. It amazed the General that they could maintain the pace despite the heavy packs. Still, the carts and the barrows constantly snagged in the undergrowth.

Despite their best efforts, the bomb makers found it difficult to keep up.

The Sailor urged caution. He argued at great length about the killing power of airplanes. The Army would react with a fury the General could only imagine. Any caught on the roads by the Army would be easily destroyed. The General suspected that the Sailor and his wolves were perfectly happy moving along on foot and attacking isolated farmhouses at their leisure.

The Sailor's speech remained smooth and languid as he argued his case. The iron twang of blood oozed from him like perfume; it spoke of a success and ruthlessness the Yankee could not match. "Better to stay off the roads. You'll never have more guns than the cops, and even if you could, you'd never get more guns than the Army."

The Yankee responded heatedly. "Not afraid of the A'my, ah, hide ah, fight like injuns. The A'my can't touch us."

"If you start driving down the road, the Army's not going to have any trouble. They'll touch the hell out of you."

The Yankee just shook his head vehemently. "Ca's, ah, if not ca's then t-trucks."

The Sailor responded impassively. "What would happen if airplanes spotted us strung out on the highway? They would blast us back to hell. Eagles against squirrels, with us as the squirrels."

The Yankee continued to pester the General to try one of the abandoned engines. He could sense the General's reluctance and reassured him. "D-d-don't worry ... I know how to d-d-drive. I won't c'ash like that otha fool."

The first engine they tried only made grinding noises. The Yankee spun wheels and turned switches, but it made no difference. The engine remained fixed and unmoving. They were luckier with the second.

The General was just getting comfortable in the passenger seat when the engine took off down the road as fast as any train, but unhindered by tracks. "Yee-haw," he shouted, slapping at his seat as if he was whipping a horse.

The Yankee was as pleased as the General. "We can be in the m-m-mountains in hou's instead of days."

The General turned to face the Yankee as the engine sped down the road, "Where do we git 'nough?"

"Enough what?"

"Fo-wah the rest.... Fo-wah all ta ride?"

"You mean them back thay're?" The Yankee looked over his shoulder as he spoke. "Feck 'em. We don't need 'em once ... we's in the m-m-mountains."

The General took hold of the Yankee's arm. "Go back." When the Yankee did not immediately respond, the General shook his arm forcefully, "Go back!" The Yankee turned the car around. In a few minutes, they had returned to where they started.

Once the sun went down, the General resumed the march. The atlas he acquired in the warehouse showed him the way. It outlined the roads and the towns; it marked the rivers and the woods. He could look at the map and remember famous names, Corinth and Nashville and Franklin and Shiloh and Chattanooga. The General no longer knew the roads, but the maps gave him confidence.

The General watched his parade of scarecrows. They marched without discipline, strung out along the road or among the trees. They moved mechanically, without fatigue, but also without speed—unless threatened. The sound of an engine along a road, or somewhere in the sky, would make them run like rabbits. They would head for the trees or the tall grass. They would fight among themselves for the cover of some hole or roadside ditch.

The flying gunships filled them with terror. They flew in the sky mostly invisible, traceable only by sound. After a time, the gunships would grow bored and leave. When the coast was clear, the scarecrows returned to the march.

They traveled east, the number of scarecrows constantly waxing and waning. Scarecrows would break off in their pursuits, other scarecrows would join. Some of those who joined were the long-dead, carnival mummies, dressed in rags, black skin as tough as leather. They walked with little noise as if they had forgotten how to speak.

Others who joined were the newly dead. They dressed better than the carnival mummies, but how they stank. Fluid drained from open wounds and cracked, mottled skin wept decay. They warbled and gibbered even if no one walked near. The newly dead drew hissing complaints from those scarecrows further advanced in the curing process. The newly dead were a caste of untouchables.

The General thought some of the new arrivals must have been recent kills by his other scarecrows. If so, the recruits showed little in the way of resentment or grievance. The hunger with which they all awoke replaced any prior sense of ethics. Hunger and fear was the basis of their new moral code. The scarecrows seemed to understand that there was no place for them among the living. They joined the parade marching east, always east. There was safety in numbers and safety in the remote woods.

An entirely different type of the dead had gathered around the Sailor. The members of this group moved along the column of marching scarecrows. Many carried rifles in their hands. They had energy to spare. There had a purpose to them missing from the simple scarecrows.

The Sailor's followers took up sticks and branches and moved among the scarecrows. They struck at the scarecrows. They cursed and growled at them. They struck the slowest marchers with the sticks; sometimes they used rifle butts, anything to maintain a speedy march.

The General studied the Sailor's followers. In the first days, they had been like the rest, fearful as beaten dogs. Quickly they had turned into rabid dogs. Now they were as suspicious and hungry as wolves. Whatever came next, they would never again be men. It suited the Sailor and his wolves to be led for a time, but the current situation could not last.

The Sailor came up and caught at the General's sleeve. He pointed to a civilian following to the rear. The corpse had been large in life, and now it was swollen with decay. Its flesh was split, and fluid drained from many wounds. It wore a jacket speckled with many colors, covered by brown and copper-colored stains from its throat to its waist.

The Sailor spoke and pointed. "So you see that fat stinky one there?"

The General looked at the bloated corpse at which the Sailor pointed.

The Sailor spoke again as the thing walked past. "That's the cracker I took the shotgun and pistol from." The Sailor called over, "Hey stinky, do you remember me?"

If the corpse was listening, it gave no indication. It just continued to trudge along with the rest.

Despite the best efforts of the Sailor and his wolves, scarecrows were strung out along the line of march as far as the eye could see. The General could hear the wolves in the distance forcing the slowest to move along. The fastest marchers were well ahead, moving down one hill, into a hollow, and back up towards a parallel ridge.

The General noticed two new scarecrows that would not be rushed. They wore uniforms; one a sickly mix of green and black, the other, a mixture of browns and greens. The new recruits stumbled along drunkenly, disregarding any effort by the wolves to hurry them along. The General noticed their throats were intact and the blood on their uniforms was minimal. The General could see no evidence of violence, no tearing or ripping of their flesh. It was not until they walked past that he could see both had suffered gunshots to the back of the head. The Brown-Green soldier still had twine around a wrist where he had been bound.

The General called the two soldiers to him. He could see that their skin was beginning to crack and their uniforms clung to their bodies from the dripping fluids. The stink forced the General to stand some feet away as he began to question them.

The Green-Black soldier had been the older of the two. He listened carefully to the General's questions and took his time to answer. "From the sky ... they can see everything. Any vehicle... they can destroy from the sky.... No warning."

The Brown-Green soldier interrupted Green-Black with speech clipped and angry. "National Guard Armory—machine guns— rifles—ammo. All we need."

As Brown-Green spit out words, Green-Black looked at him. Despite the soldier's cracked and shrinking skin, the General thought he still could see expressions of frustration and annoyance.

The General turned to the Sailor, "Can yah do this?"

"If they show me the armory, I reckon we can.... If we get some machine guns, the helicopters won't come near. We could move in trucks."

Green-Black just shook his head and pointed to the sky, "Worse things ... than helicopters."

As if summoned, a small engine suddenly flew up over a nearby hill. It hovered just above the trees. It seemed like a toy, a whirligig, humming and singing as it flew about. The General called the Sailor to him, but the Sailor did not know what to call the thing.

Brown-Green spoke up quietly, "A drone."

The General found it unpleasant having the new recruit so close, a walking corpse left out in the sun too long. He stopped the soldier from walking away but did not try to hide his distaste. "Explain.... What do yah mean 'drone?'"

The soldier spoke slowly, concentrating on his speech. "The Army ... use them to spy... deliver bombs."

"You mean ... that toy's a bomb?"

"Maybe."

The Sailor stood and began to shoot into the sky. The noisy engine continued to move back and forth above the adjacent hill unperturbed by the gunfire. Suddenly, it darted towards them and began to hover over their heads. The wolves, scarecrows, and recruits all scattered into the forest. The drone seemed satisfied and moved on.

After the drone left, the scarecrows and wolves that had sheepishly fled began to return. The General hooted and used a tree branch as a whip to get them moving. Soon they were once again heading towards the east. Stragglers continued to find their way out of the woods and a sizable number of scarecrows and wolves once again followed the General.

One of those who followed was the Reverend. The General noticed him at the back of the parade. He was making his way forward weaving in and out of the slower scarecrows and always staying out of reach of the Sailor's wolves. His clothes were torn and ragged.

The General waited for him to approach. He immediately began to look for any signs of bullet wounds, but the Reverend kept his coat cinched closed.

"Were yah shot? … Were yah killed?"

The Reverend shook himself free. "You already know. You know why we're here. You know."

Before the Reverend could move away, the General noticed something else. He grabbed the Reverend and tore open his coat. He could see the blood that stained the entire front of the Reverend's shirt. The worm in the General's gut twisted so fiercely, the General had to step back.

The General offered a question, "Thou shall not kill Reverend?"

The Reverend responded with smooth and fluent speech, "Rules that apply only to men."

Not far behind the Reverend, trying to keep up with the march, came another returned. This one wore a green jacket. Whenever the General came close, it hurried away.

The General could not believe that Green Jacket had returned, but the Sailor confirmed it. The General went up to Green Jacket and grabbed its arm. He examined the wounds to its chest and back. He examined the bullet wound to its head. The skin around the wounds was black and puckered. It resembled the healing of burns more than bullet wounds. Green Jacket's body had knitted together, but its back was twisted; its neck was twisted. Still, the General could sense a new strength, a predatory alertness.

The General held the arm of Green Jacket. "Where did yah go...? Whin aah shot yah? Did yah go back?"

Green Jacket seemed to understand the importance of the question, but could no longer properly form the words. It responded with the slurred speech of a drunkard. "No-god ... to me ... lie this."

When the General asked again, it repeated the same response. No matter how the General phrased the question the response remained the same, "No-god ... to me ... lie this." Finally, Green

Jacket grew impatient. It shook off the General's hand and hurried to catch up with the others.

The question of whether to move using engines was fully settled when they crossed over the parallel ridge and came to the ruins of a convoy. Wrecked engines were burned out and scattered along the roadway. Each of the wrecks held the remains of several bodies. The bodies sat in the engines, black and shrunken with fire. The attack had happened with such speed the occupants had not even opened the doors to seek a chance of escape.

Up ahead other broken engines lay across the road. The General could not tell how many had been with the engines; the bodies had been torn to pieces. Portions of bodies sat in the engines or lay in the road. Fragments of bodies could be seen in the trees above.

The General knew these scarecrows could not have been with them when they raided the warehouse. The bodies of those not burned wore rags.

As they passed the wrecks, a survivor of the air attack could be seen dragging itself into the woods. The General approached taking out his pistol as he did so. The General examined the remains of the scarecrow in front of him. The lower portion of the body had been mangled beyond recognition. The General probed the holes to its chest and back.

The scarecrow must have sensed what was coming. It stopped dragging itself along the ground and propped itself up against a tree and waited. It said nothing. The General raised his pistol and shot it in the head.

The General gathered scarecrows around him. He pointed to the bodies and portions of bodies scattered throughout the wreckage. He began to issue orders, "See if yah kin find the rest of 'em."

They soon returned dragging bodies and carrying pieces of bodies. "This is everything not burnt General."

The General pointed at the remains, "Bury 'em as best yah can, but not ta deep."

As the sun began to rise, the General urged those around him to make haste. They needed to return to the forests and the swamps. They hurried south and east but did not find a place to hide until just before daybreak.

Deck Log - Sixth Day

OPNAV 3100/99 (Rev 7-84) S/N 0107-LF-031-0498	**SHIP'S DECK LOG SHEET** — IF CLASSIFIED STAMP SECURITY MARKING HERE

USE BLACK INK TO FILL IN THIS LOG

SHIP TYPE: O A / AS | HULL NUMBER: 00 / 43 | YEAR: 09 | MONTH: B | ZONE / DAY: 70 | F
USS **CYCLOPS**
AT / PASSAGE FROM **NORFOLK VA**
TO **MUSCAT OMAN**

POSITION	ZONE	TIME	POSITION	ZONE	TIME	POSITION	ZONE	TIME	LEGEND
0800 L ____ , BY __ ; A ____ , BY __			1200 L ____ , BY __ ; A ____ , BY __			2000 L ____ , BY __ ; A ____ , BY __			1 – CELESTIAL 2 – ELECTRONIC 3 – VISUAL 4 – DR

TIME	ORDER	CSE	SPEED	DEPTH	RECORD OF EVENTS OF THE DAY
0000					ASSUMED THE WATCH. STEAMING AS BEFORE. WATCH REPORTS CONDITIONS NORMAL. LIEUTENANT T.J. MCKINLEY, USN
0125					0125 REPORT OF MURDER OF TWO CREW MEMBERS. FOUND IN SPACE 4-80-1-Q WITH THEIR THROATS SLASHED.
0320					0320 ** CREW MEMBERS IDENTIFIED AS WISE AND PATNAUDE

REPORT SYMBOL OPNAV 2100-10 — IF CLASSIFIED STAMP REVIEW / DECLASSIFICATION DATE HERE — IF CLASSIFIED STAMP SECURITY MARKING HERE

Fourth Deck - Aft, Fan Room, Starboard Side

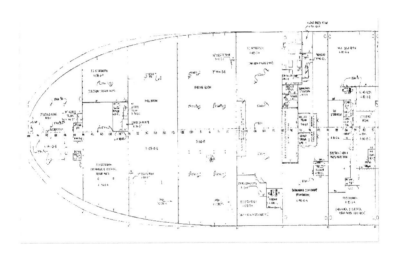

The Book of the Dead, Litany:

Homage to you, O ye gods who dwell in your Hall of Maāti! I know you and I know your names. Let me not fall under your knives, and bring ye not before the god whom ye follow my wickedness, and let not evil come upon me through you. Declare ye me innocent in the presence of Nebertcher, because I have done that which is right in Tamera (Egypt), neither blaspheming God, nor imputing evil (?) to the king in his day. Homage to you, O ye gods, who live in your Hall of Maāti, who have no taint of sin in you, who live upon truth, who feed upon truth before Horus, the dweller in his disk. Deliver me from Baba, who liveth upon the entrails of the mighty ones, on the day of the Great Judgment.

The Literature of the Ancient Egyptians, by E. A. Wallis Budge, 1914.

CHAPTER- 16 - MURDERS IN THE FAN ROOM

Saturday, Day Six: The Red Sea

Lieutenant Irawell climbed down multiple ladders finally arriving at a vestibule on the fourth deck. He stepped out into a passageway followed closely by Hardwick. He could hear people talking. He could see figures going in and out of one of the doors ahead. The XO stood in the passageway talking to Powers and Crammer.

The fan room was a small, hot, narrow space, filled with ductwork and insulation. There was a loud, steady hum from the fans and machinery that partially occupied the space. Entering, he had to crouch down to look around. He noticed numerous sets of bloody shoeprints going in and out of the space. No effort had been made to secure the compartment, and various observers had already gone in to look over the crime scene.

The Lieutenant examined the scene. He could see blankets and pillows beneath the ductwork. Someone had been using the space for a private place to sleep, or for other purposes. When HM2 Nowlin sought to enter, the Lieutenant was forced deeper into the space, still crouched down because of the low overhead. Nowlin found an unbloodied portion of the deck on which to kneel.

She pulled back several blankets revealing the bodies of a man and a woman.

Blood covered the man's face; his cheeks had been slashed open. His front teeth had been knocked out; other teeth hung around his face on fragments of tissue. In addition to the injuries to his face, his throat was slashed. Two of the fingers on his right hand were missing. The raggedness of the wounds indicated the fingers had been torn off rather than cut. A bloody spray marked the kill zone. The blankets around the victim were saturated with blood.

The woman lay in the further corner. She had wounds to her breasts and hands, clean stab and slicing wounds indicative of a knife; but there were other wounds. Portions of her body had been mauled. Her throat was torn so severely her head barely remained attached to her body. Great clots of blood clung to the edges of the wound. The pooling of blood, so evident around the man, was less pronounced as to the woman.

A white t-shirt, well stained with blood, covered the woman's face. Her working uniform lay beside her. The man's clothes and coveralls were missing. No weapons were visible.

When the Lieutenant came out of the fan room the XO was waiting. He pointed at the Lieutenant and said only one thing to him, "Fix this."

The Lieutenant began to give his observations, but the XO turned and walked away. Powers followed close on his heels.

HM2 Nowlin began to speak, "Sir, it's Wise and Patnaude. Somebody from repair found them. What do you want us to do with the bodies sir?"

Before the Lieutenant could say anything, Hardwick spoke up, "Sir, we've already taken photographs and positively identified them."

"Bag them up and take them down to the cold storage. Once the bodies are removed, seal the place up."

Hardwick spoke again, "Lieutenant, do you want us to try and collect any evidence?"

"Photograph everything, remove the bodies, gather up anything at risk of being lost, but leave the rest; get a padlock and lock up the space. Other than removing the bodies, and taking any key evidence, nothing is to be touched." After giving his instructions the Lieutenant turned to leave. "I've got the morning watch in CIC. You know where to find me."

The Lieutenant walking away could hear Hardwick directing one of the other petty officers to go and find a padlock.

The Lieutenant arrived in CIC and found MM1 Moore there ahead of him. Moore posed a question before the Lieutenant even sat down. "Word is Lieutenant there's been two more murders."

"Looks that way."

Moore continued, his tone morose, "When are they going to kill the thing? How hard can this be?"

"No idea MM1. It's proving difficult."

"They going to get some help onboard?"

"Don't know. Don't think so."

For a time Moore lapsed into silence. He sat in his chair twisting his wedding ring. The Lieutenant and Moore had stood many watches together. As he watched Moore, he realized he had never asked about his wife or children. He was not even sure Moore was married, other than he continued to wear a wedding ring. It occurred to the Lieutenant that common politeness required him to ask.

"MM1, do you know about your family yet?"

"I've been trying to reach them. My son's in Colorado; I'm sure he'll be fine. My daughter's back in Norfolk. She's married with two kids of her own. It would kill her if something happened to her kids. My wife never cared for computers. I don't expect emails from her, but I'm hoping for a letter soon. I've tried the shipboard phones, but they're not worth a damn."

The Lieutenant shared a current rumor, "I heard that the XO might be controlling the phones and email because he was afraid of too many people getting bad news all at once."

Moore just shook his head. "I don't think that's it." He took a moment before he continued, "Out here, I always knew there was a bit of a risk. I was happy to take my chances, but I always thought they'd be safe at home...."

The Lieutenant waited for Moore to finish his thought, but he lapsed into silence. It was some minutes before he spoke again. "They're likely going make me stand engineering watches instead of CIC. They're making everyone they can get qualified to take engineering watches."

"Surely there are others that can take a watch."

"We're already shorthanded before this started. Engineering and weapons were already shorthanded. We're carrying all sorts of weapons, radars, maybe nukes; the weapons guys won't tell you, but they sure as hell complain. All I know is there is a lot of dangerous and top-secret stuff onboard, and they got to guard it."

Moore paused again before continuing. "The killers are moving around this ship. They can set fires. They can set fires in areas with explosives, or propellants, or fuels that would blow this ship apart. If they haven't tried to sink us yet, it's only because they don't want to."

"It might only be one killer."

"It's more than one. How many have been killed? How many are missing? People can tell themselves it's just one. I don't think so Lieutenant. It's a lot worse."

The Lieutenant had no response. He sat in his chair and tried to show interest in the radar. After a time Moore began a new conversation.

"Lieutenant, did I ever tell you why I joined the Navy? Had a good job as a garbage man. Union wages those days. One day was picking up trash to dump in the truck. Somebody left a toilet out there. I was young and strong and foolish. I lifted it overhead to toss into the truck. Something had been plugging that thing. It came loose when I hoisted it up and that toilet flushed right into my face. My mouth was open at the time. Joined the Navy the next day."

As the morning watch dragged on the Lieutenant struggled to stay awake. When the watch turned over at 0800, he went to the wardroom hoping for some strong coffee to shock him awake. As he made his way below, he hoped that Acedian had remembered to go to the department head meeting.

In the wardroom, they had French toast and bacon for breakfast. He did not feel like talking to anyone, so instead of joining the other officers at one of the mess tables, he took his meal into the lounge. He began to feel more awake with each bite of his breakfast and each sip of coffee. Before he could finish eating, however, one of the mess attendants came to summon him to the Captain's conference room.

He cursed Acedian as he headed up to the 03 level. "I bet that son of a bitch didn't show up for the meeting."

It was past 0900 when the Lieutenant arrived. The other department heads were gathered around the conference room table in the middle of a discussion.

The XO exclaimed as the Lieutenant entered the space, "Just in time!" He then turned and looked at the other officers as he continued, "Apparently the Master-at-Arms couldn't find their little love nest, but the killer could."

Unsure of the target of the XO's remarks, the Lieutenant made no response as he sat down. The XO recognized the Lieutenant's quizzical expression. "Patnaude and Wise—shacking up in the fan room."

When the Lieutenant still did not respond, the XO waved it aside and returned to the original discussion. "From now on, nobody moves around the ship after taps unless they're on watch. I don't want anyone moving about unless they have a buddy, even if they're only going to the head. No one is to move about this ship unescorted. I want armed patrols set for every passageway. I want armed sentries outside of every berthing area."

The XO turned towards Powers, "Weps, I want roving patrols and search parties throughout the ship. I want all hands to search every space on this ship, again. Every department shares responsibility for setting up guards. In half an hour, we'll have all hands report to their muster stations. I want this sorted out then."

Powers responded in a slightly defensive tone, "Skipper, aah'm missing a lot of mah folks. Aah've only twenty-five folks left in mah department. Aah've barely enough folks ta man the ship's guns an' secure weapons storage, never mind rovin' patrols."

The XO turned to Crammer of repair, "You've got the largest department onboard. You need to provide the manpower, Weps will provide the equipment." The XO glance over to the Lieutenant and then back to Powers, "Your control over the Master-at-Arms should help some."

The Lieutenant said nothing.

As officers began to stand up and head out of the conference room Lamb spoke up. "Hold on, I want to talk about engineering. We need guards or we need everyone on watch in engineering to be armed. If you expect us to continue to work down there everyone needs at least a pistol."

Powers turned from the door, "Aah'm not goen ta give weapons ta civilians. Only military, properly qualified."

Lamb responded vehemently, "That's bullshit and unacceptable."

Powers ignored Lamb and took the Lieutenant's arm as he went past, "Don't forget about the trainin'." Powers had a smile on his face as he provided this gentle reminder. He then went back into the conference room.

The volume of the argument escalated as the Lieutenant went down the passageway. He could hear Lamb's voice followed by snippets of response from Powers or the XO. Descending the nearest ladder, he could hear only the engineer's voice, "Bullshit, bullshit, bullshit. You're endangering us all."

The Lieutenant arrived in legal still irritated about being called away from his breakfast. He doubted that Acedian had attended the morning department head meeting. When he stepped inside and saw Acedian sitting at his desk, he nonchalantly asked, "How did it go this morning?"

"You didn't miss anything. Mostly arguments by O'Day that we need to bring security teams onboard. I swear he gets uglier every time I see him. All that estrogen he's been taking hasn't been doing him any favors."

The Lieutenant angrily slapped his hand on the desk to get Acedian's attention. "Ensign, watch the disrespect, and for now on you will use his preferred pronoun whenever speaking about Lieutenant Commander O'Day!"

Acedian began to sputter, "I was only saying—"

The Lieutenant continued without pause, "I don't care. You of all people should know. You've broken a half dozen articles and directives, everything from disrespect of a superior officer to gender discrimination. You will not make such statements again, even as a joke! Understood!"

"Yes sir!"

Early in the afternoon the Lieutenant left his office and climbed up the nearest ladder. He made his way aft to the midships passageway and then entered the ship's conference and briefing room. Fifty sailors were in the space.

The conference room had been set up as a theatre with rows of old-fashioned fold-down wooden seats. Chief Medioldia of the weapon's department was just finishing his safety training. The Lieutenant took a seat and waited.

The chief held up an M9 pistol as he spoke, "I say again, this is not a fucking toy. Don't point it at anybody you don't want to shoot. If you accidentally point it at me, you better shoot, because I will shove this pistol so far up your ass you'll blow your own brains out the next time you sneeze."

The chief stepped down from the podium and walked past the Lieutenant, "Your turn, sir."

When the sailors saw the Lieutenant they began to call out questions, "Lieutenant is it okay if we take a turn around the deck every hour? That's what other patrols are doing."

"I don't know about that. I'm supposed to be giving training on the use of deadly force."

Another sailor stood up and called out a question, "Lieutenant we're not supposed to tell them hands up, are we?"

The Lieutenant waved his hand as a signal for the sailor to be seated. "Let me put this out first." He placed some papers on the podium and began to read aloud.

"'Standing Orders for Security Watches and Patrols. Security watches and patrols may be assigned at the discretion of the CO. Security watches and patrols are established to increase the physical security of the ship. Sailors assigned to security watches and patrols will be trained and qualified by the department head responsible for the areas to which specific watches and patrols are assigned. Duties of security watches and patrols include but are not limited to the following:

"'Maintaining continuous patrols above decks and below decks; checking classified stowage, including spaces containing classified equipment; being alert for evidence of sabotage, thievery, and fire hazards—' "

As the Lieutenant continued to read, he changed the inflection and volume of his voice at each new section. He could still see the sailors losing interest as he went through the monotonous instruction.

"Hold on now. This next part is really important." The Lieutenant raised his voice slightly and continued to speak, "'Note, when standing an armed watch with a pistol, you must strictly observe the following additional precautions:

"'One, keep the pistol in its holster except when the watch is relieved or circumstances require you to use it. Never engage in horseplay with the pistol; it is a deadly weapon and must always be treated as such. Two, do not surrender the pistol to any unauthorized person. Three, the pistol normally is carried loaded aboard ship with one round in the chamber. Two loaded clips (magazines) are in the pouches attached to the pistol belt. Leave the clips in their pouches. Four, when being relieved, a safe area for unloading a pistol must be established. In a safe area, remove the magazine from the pistol. With the weapon pointed in a safe direction i.e., barrel full of sand, carefully jack the slide to the rear and remove the round from the chamber. Check the chamber, ensuring no rounds are present. Release the slide and let the hammer go home.' "

The Lieutenant lowered his voice and started again, "'Weapons terminology for returning the hammer to the uncocked position. Dry fire the weapon and then engage the safety.' "

"Okay, everybody got that. The guys in the weapons departments will walk you through clearing when you get issued weapons."

A sailor in the back of the space called out, "Lieutenant, does this mean we don't get our own guns?"

"Everybody on watch will have a pistol or a shotgun. A select few will have rifles. You'll switch out when you go on and off watch. We don't have enough guns for everybody. The Captain doesn't want people carrying around guns unless they're on watch."

A second sailor called out, "Sir, does this mean we've got to go down to the weapons spaces to assume the watch?"

"We don't have a means of clearing a weapon on the other decks. You'll have to go below. Okay, this part is the main part."

The Lieutenant raised his voice to emphasize the text, "'Circumstances under which a weapon may be fired. Only the Captain can authorize the use of deadly force. The term deadly force is defined as that force which, if used, has the potential to cause death or serious bodily harm.' "

He paused for a moment and looked around the space, then he continued. "'The pistol or rifle should be used only as a last resort and then only under the following conditions:

"'One, to protect your life or the life of another person where no other means of defense will be effective in the particular situation;

"'Two, when no other effective means is available to prevent the commission of or to prevent the escape of a person known to have committed robbery, murder, rape, arson, or kidnapping;

"'Three, to prevent acts of sabotage, espionage, or other crimes against the government after failure of all other available means of preventing such crime;

"'Four, deadly force against any intruder who is or may be on this ship and is not part of the ship's company has been authorized.' "

A voice in the back, "Does this mean the XO is now the skipper?"

Before the Lieutenant could answer another voice interrupted. "I thought we was suppose' to find and kill the zombies. We're not supposed to arrest the zombies?"

Another voice, "Don't tell me the zombies are rapists too."

Another voice interrupted, "Are we getting rifles?"

"All right, all right. Let me finish. You got to do this by the rules, okay." The Lieutenant paused to look at the sailors around him.

"Okay, Lieutenant Commander Powers and his officers have set up the duty sections. First, does anyone here stand an underway watch?"

One of the petty officers spoke up, "They told me I was supposed to help out in engineering."

Chief Medioldia returned to the podium and turned to the Lieutenant, "I'll take care of the rest of it, sir." The chief turned his back to the Lieutenant and faced the sailors, "Okay, is everyone here weapons qualified?"

Another voice, "Not sure if I am."

"For Christ's sake. You were supposed to be qualified before you reported."

"I took the test, but I didn't get no ribbon."

The Lieutenant spoke up over the increasing volume of questions, "Chief, I'll leave this in your hands."

"Nothing to worry about Lieutenant. We'll get this all fixed up."

When the Lieutenant returned to legal Acedian still sat at his computer surfing the internet. "How did training go?"

"I don't think Gunny Medioldia got the word about the kinder, gentler Navy."

The Lieutenant glanced over at Acedian's computer. "You find a decent newsfeed yet on what's happening in the rest of the world?"

"Not yet. There are food riots in the third world. Paris has declared no-go zones. Looks like Jordan and Syria have armies on the move. The Egyptians are gathering on the canal. Army units may be moving through the Sinai Peninsula. Hamas and the Palestinians are shooting rockets into Israel. The Israelis are blaming Iran."

As the Lieutenant stood by talking to Acedian, he noticed on the desk a small figurine. It had the body of a man and the head of a dog. Its blazing red eyes seemed to watch him carefully.

The Lieutenant stepped back and began to look at the figure from different angles. Always its eyes followed him. "Beads of glass I suppose." He picked up the figurine and examined it closely. It was not the cheap toy he expected. It was a true sculpture made from carefully carved black stone.

The Lieutenant took control of Acedian's computer and started an internet search. Acedian hovered nearby trying to look over the Lieutenant's shoulder. The Lieutenant stopped looking at the computer screen and pointed at the figurine. "Get rid of it."

Acedian was surprised. "What are you talking about? It's my property. I didn't do anything wrong."

"What part didn't you understand? Get rid of it, God damn you."

Acedian reluctantly removed it from view, "Fine, all get rid of it."

In the late afternoon, the Lieutenant went to CIC for the first dog watch. When he arrived, however, the officer he was relieving was in no hurry to leave. Normally, once relieved, any watchstander was impatient to be gone, but today they finally had some excitement.

A schooner traveled across the ship's bow with no one at her wheel. Her sails flapped loosely in the wind as she stalled for a moment. Then the boat turned, her booms swinging randomly as variances in the wind determined her tack.

The XO was on the bridge and he ordered the engines stopped. Soon one of the ship's launches headed over to the schooner to investigate. As the launch set out, the sailboat caught the wind and turned aside as if an invisible hand urged her to flee. Still, it was easy for the powered launch to overtake her.

From the bridge, the Lieutenant could see the sailors from the launch boarding the schooner. They emerged a few minutes later, signaling no one aboard. They left the boat and started back. Soon the launch pulled up alongside Cyclops to be hauled back up to the boat deck.

As the Cyclops drifted with a light wind, the Officer of the Deck turned to the XO to ask for orders. The XO signaled for him to wait.

Powers arrived on the bridge and joined the Lieutenant watching the schooner. With the departure of the launch, she headed west only to change her mind and begin a slow turn to the east. Suddenly the wind caught her at a new angle; she came about violently and starting sailing to the north.

After watching the boat for a time Powers spoke up in his southern accent. "'See yah, beneath yon cloud so dark, fast gliding along, a gloomy bark? Her sails air full, though the wind is still, an' thay're blows not a breath her sails ta fill.

"Oh! what doth that vessel of darkness bear? The silent calm of the grave is thay're, save now and again a death-knell rung, and the flap of the sails, with night-fog hung.' "*

The Lieutenant looked over in surprise. It was a rare day when the weapons officer spoke a full sentence to him, never mind lines of poetry.

Before the Lieutenant could think of a response, the XO called over to the weapons officer. "We've got a vessel adrift nearby. She's a danger to navigation. Sink her."

As soon as the XO gave the command, Powers headed below to join his gunners mates manning the machine guns on the port side.

The sound of the guns opening up was terrific, "Kirk-kirk-kirk-kirk-kirk-kirk." It could be heard throughout the ship. Many sailors made their way up to the weather deck in response to the noise. "Kirk-kirk-kirk-kirk-kirk-kirk.... Kirk-kirk-kirk.... Kirk-kirk-kirk-kirk."

The fifty caliber rounds began to slam into the wooden boat. The bullets splashed in the water all around. Fountains of water carried aloft fragments of wood with each strike.

As the fifty-calibers chewed up the wooden sailing craft, one of the gunner's mates appeared at the rail with a 240 machine gun. The tearing of the light machine gun joined the hammer strikes of the fifty, "Ta-ta-ta-ta-ta-ta-ta-ta.... Ta-ta-ta-ta-ta-ta-ta-ta .... Ta-ta-ta-ta-ta-ta-ta-ta."

Along the ship's rails, the crew laughed and cheered and covered their ears from the noise of the guns, "Kirk-kirk-kirk.... Ta-ta-ta-ta-ta-ta-ta-ta. Kirk-kirk-kirk-kirk-kirk-kirk. Ta-ta-ta-ta-ta-ta-ta-ta" Out on the weather deck, brass casings and black steel rings flew and bounced.

The Weapons officer invited nearby sailors to take a turn firing the guns. "Careful now, three ta five rounds, then pause. We don't want the barrel ta overheat."

More machine gun rounds slammed into the wooden boat. Pieces of the boat shot up towards the sky. Machine gun rounds set fountains of water into the air all around. The bullets skipped across the sea like skimming stones on the surface of a pond. Stubbornly the wooden vessel held on, still sailing. The machine guns along the port side continued to fire, "Kirk-kirk-kirk-kirk-kirk-kirk.... Kirk-kirk-kirk."

The sailboat visibly shook as the guns fired. Wooden planks flew into the air. Mast and rigging fell over and leaned drunkenly into the water.

As the sinking wreck fell astern, all the crew cheered.

Joel 2:2-10 KJV:

A day of darkness and of gloominess, a day of clouds and of thick darkness, as the morning spread upon the mountains: a great people and a strong; there hath not been ever the like, neither shall be any more after it, even to the years of many generations. A fire devoureth before them; and behind them a flame burneth: the land is as the garden of Eden before them, and behind them a desolate wilderness; yea, and nothing shall escape them. The appearance of them is as the appearance of horses; and as horsemen, so shall they run. Like the noise of chariots on the tops of mountains shall they leap, like the noise of a flame of fire that devoureth the stubble, as a strong people set in battle array. Before their face the people shall be much pained: all faces shall gather blackness. They shall run like mighty men; they shall climb the wall like men of war; and they shall march every one on his ways, and they shall not break their ranks: Neither shall one thrust another; they shall walk every one in his path: and when they fall upon the sword, they shall not be wounded. They shall run to and fro in the city; they shall run upon the wall, they shall climb up upon the houses; they shall enter in at the windows like a thief. The earth shall quake before them; the heavens shall tremble: the sun and the moon shall be dark, and the stars shall withdraw their shining.

CHAPTER-17 – MORE DAMN POWERPOINTS

Saturday, Day Six: Navy Yard

He is wedged in a narrow cave, unable to move. He is trapped. His arms are stretched out before him bound by stone on either side. The cave is so narrow he cannot move forward or back. As he tries to free himself, he twists and pushes, but the more he struggles the more tightly wedged he becomes.

He gives up the effort to free himself and takes a moment to rest. Wedged between the rock walls, he listens. He can hear the sounds of the ocean, the great waves strike rhythmically against the stone cliffs nearby. The waves sound through the stone like the beating of a heart. The sounds grow louder as he lays still.

Before him is darkness, but in the darkness are shadows that move and dance across the cave wall. They carry burdens; they carry weapons; they carry children. The shadows perform for him and they whisper among themselves, moving back and forth, back and forth.

Captain Pride awoke remembering his dream well. This was a new habit in the making. Instead of awakening every morning refreshed, his dreams a flickering afterthought; now he wakes every morning weary, nightmares cemented into his mind. He resented his dreams, just as he resented having to go into the city every morning for work. He particularly resented having to go into work on a Saturday. He sat in his kitchen, drank his coffee, listened to the radio, and made no effort to rush.

First newsreader: "Safe havens have been established at the following schools and government buildings…. These buildings are being guarded by the National Guard. National Guard and Police are patrolling streets throughout the region."

Second newsreader: "The rumors that parts of Boston have been abandoned are not true. However, refugee centers have been set up outside of the city."

First newsreader: "I'm a little confused; the safe centers are in the city. People have been asked to go to the safe centers in the city."

Second newsreader: "In Boston, the refugee centers are in the suburbs."

First newsreader: "What about New York?"

Second newsreader: "I can only tell you about Manhattan. There's a curfew there. The bridges are blocked. No entry into the city except for essential services."

First newsreader: "But people can leave the city? What about the infected. What about the reports that the hospitals have been overrun."

Second newsreader: "Official word is that the Army and police have things under control. They have shoot to kill orders to enforce the curfew. Essential services are intact."

The newsreader began to read off a list of buildings and safe locations, none of which the Captain recognized. Every location mentioned was outside of Virginia. It struck the Captain as curious that there was no mention of safe centers being needed around the capital.

The First newsreader continued: "What about those bitten and infected?"

Second newsreader: "There are no reports of anyone being 'infected' as result of bites. There is no indication that the bites are anything other than bites. The bitten are receiving medical treatment. The wounds respond to medical treatment, including antibiotics. The infection is being spread through other means. This is not the zombie apocalypse."

First newsreader: "Then how come the biters don't go down when shot?"

Second newsreader: "They go down if you shoot them. They are just nerve dead. They don't feel pain. That's the difference."

Third newsreader: "Headshots only. And the biters are not just biting, they go full zombie. You've seen the videos. And there have been stories of the dead showing up again."

Second newsreader: "Those stories have been greatly exaggerated."

First newsreader, exasperated: "Every morgue has the same story. Every morgue has had people killed. The dead are rising. If they aren't zombies what are they?"

Second newsreader: "They may have just been wounded, and then gone into a deep coma as a result of their wounds. The infection may be communicated in other ways, not just bites."

Third newsreader: "I thought you said they weren't infected."

Second newsreader: "I meant that some succumb to infection. Those are different cases entirely. Different circumstances, different data, different results. You can't mix cases."

Third newsreader: "We have lost contact with our affiliates in Paris, but the BBC is still broadcasting."

First newsreader: "What explains the loss of contact in Paris if it isn't zombies?"

Second newsreader: "Rioters. There have been gun battles and a number of explosions. Unfortunately, we have not been able to obtain details. The White House and Pentagon claim that they are in touch with the civil and military forces in France."

Third newsreader: "Do zombies use guns and explosives?"

Second newsreader: "The terrorists are using guns and explosives. Reports are that things are currently quiet in Paris."

First newsreader: "Has the government reestablished control in Paris?"

Second newsreader: "It is daytime in Paris. The streets emptied as soon as the sun came up.

People are not barricading the streets right now; they're barricading their apartment buildings."

Once the Captain finished his third cup of coffee, he felt he could delay no longer and left for work. As he walked up the street to the subway other commuters joined him. He noticed that the number of drivers on the road had increased since yesterday. There were still abandoned cars, some double-parked, some even up on the sidewalk, but in general the roads seemed clearer.

After leaving Old Town, the subway cars began to cross the river. The Captain looked out the window; he could see the regular auto bridge to his left. Many police cars sat on the bridge, their blue lights flashing. A large crowd of people stood on the bridge trying to move past the police officers only to be turned back. The subway cars flashed by, and in just a moment they reached the other side and descended below ground into a tunnel.

A man sitting next to the Captain spoke up, "I wonder what's happening on the bridge."

The Captain ignored him as a fellow passenger answered. "Protesters on the 14th street bridge. They've decided to block the bridge."

"What are they protesting?"

The passenger shrugged his shoulders, "Food, gas, lodging, security, pretty much everything."

The Captain arrived in the RLSO, to discover Lieutenant Junior Grade Gula alone manning the office. A half dozen sailors and dependents also milled about looking for legal assistance.

Gula greeted the Captain anxiously, "All these people have been coming in. You and the XO are the only ones I've seen. Nobody else has come in."

"Have any of the civilians come into work to help?"

Gula rubbed his hands together nervously as he answered, "No one is here. None of the civilians have been in sir. It's Saturday sir."

"Is the XO in his office?" he asked.

"Sir, Commander Invidia has gone to headquarters. You're supposed to go there too. All senior officers are supposed to report to OJAG."

The Captain wondered for a moment why he was only now getting this message about a meeting. Then he paused to consider whether Gula could be safely left in the office alone, whether Gula could even be trusted to answer the phones.

At twenty-eight years of age, Gula was a tall man in figure, but already past his prime in form. His waistline testified of too much food and beer and too little exercise. His blond hair, once thick, was already thinning and receding.

Gula's intellectual abilities matched his physical decline. It was an open secret that he had been unable to pass his state bar exam and had obtained his license by traveling to another state where the success rate was near one hundred percent. The Captain initially limited Gula's legal duties because of suspicion of incompetency. He quickly found his suspicions confirmed.

Assigned to legal assistance, Gula had written numerous letters threatening landlords, contractors, and other people he disliked with investigation and prosecution by the United States Navy. In one instance, Gula threatened a dependent wife with prosecution for fraud and perjury, alleging she had misrepresented her expenses and monthly income during ongoing divorce proceedings with her sailor husband.

Ultimately, the Captain had restricted Gula to administrative tasks unless supervised by a more senior officer. He had also delayed Gula's promotion to full Lieutenant.

Normally, it was unheard of for clients to come in on a Saturday. The office was generally unmanned, and real legal help was unavailable as a practical matter in a world where most administrative offices were closed on weekends.

As the Captain considered what to do, Gula continued talking, panic just below the surface. "Sir, all these people have been coming in. You and the XO are the only ones who came into the office. Nobody else has come back."

When the Captain said nothing in response, Gula shifted about defensively. "They want help with all sorts of things, wills, divorces, child support."

The Captain looked at Gula impatiently, "Sort it out. If it's not a real emergency tell them to make an appointment."

When Gula continued to look shell shocked, the Captain began to call over those in the waiting room, each in turn.

First sailor: "My kids are missing. No reason to keep giving child support to my ex. How do I get it stopped?"

The Captain turned to Gula. "Make him an appointment."

Second Sailor: "My wife's parents were rich. They're missing now. How do I get my share?"

The Captain turned to Gula. "Make him an appointment."

Civilian man: "My husband won't put me on his page two as his dependent. I'm entitled, but I can't even get an ID card. I need to know how I make him do this."

The Captain turned to Gula. "Make him an appointment."

Third Sailor: "My old will left everything to my brother and my nephews. No need now. How do I get a new will?"

The Captain turned to Gula. "Make him an appointment."

The final request for help came from a couple, a sailor and his wife. The wife had a visible black eye. She came up to the counter with her husband but spent her time looking down at the floor. The sailor presented himself as spokesman. "My wife went crazy because of the kids missing. I had to slap her to get her to stop. You understand, because she was hysteric, out of control. My asshole neighbors called the cops after she went outside. You'd think they'd have better things to do right now."

The sailor looked over to his wife and pointed, "She don't want to press charges.... Do ya?"

The wife said nothing. She shook her head slowly back and forth, and then went back to staring at the floor.

The Captain stopped the sailor from saying anything more. He called Gula over and told him to take the wife to his office. "Hear what she has to say and advise her accordingly."

The sailor strenuously objected, but the Captain told him to shut up and sit down. After Gula and the wife stepped out, the Captain explained that the Legal Assistance Office could not help with this matter, but the Defense Service Office could.

The man's wife and Gula returned to the waiting room in less than half an hour. The Captain hoped that Gula had advised the wife on how to get a protective order or a divorce. The confused look on Gula's face told the Captain, no such luck.

The sailor also studied Gula and his wife. The expression on his face changed from panic to surly triumph. "Let's go. These people ain't going to help us." The sailor stood and walked out of the office, his wife, still looking at the floor, followed him out the door trailing several steps behind.

After clearing the office, the Captain turned to go. He was uneasy about leaving Gula in charge, but he had little choice. He would have liked to blame Invidia, but he knew the thought to be unfair. Invidia could not be blamed for OJAG shanghaiing all of his competent junior officers. As he hurried across the Navy Yard, however, he did think it fair to harbor suspicions about the notice for today's meeting. He wondered whether his XO had again failed to pass on a message promptly.

He arrived to find a dozen captains and two dozen commanders already assembled in the conference room. One of the Admiral's aides fooled with a projector. In a moment, a slide showing the emblem of the Judge Advocate of the Navy appeared on the screen. The Captain heard one of his colleagues, sotto voce, "Not another fucking PowerPoint."

The aide continued her briefing in a very matter of fact tone. "Military personnel have been sent to hospitals, power plants, and refineries. Roads, bridges, trains, airports, and transportation hubs are under guard. In some areas, grocery stores and commercial centers are under guard. Additionally, mobile strike forces are being organized to deal with any serious threats. FOB's will be built to provide support in areas lacking necessary infrastructure."

The aide continued to speak as the slides switched to a series of maps marked with colored squares and circles. "Unfortunately, there is a serious shortage of military personnel. Civilians will augment the military. The Army will be responsible for training and equipping them. Certain rural communities and towns have already been identified as too small and isolated to rely on local police forces. Fortified hamlets, in which the community can shelter, particularly at night, are being built at Federal expense. At a minimum, these fortified hamlets will have HESCO barriers, watchtowers, and razor wire.

The aide continued. "In infested areas, the population will be moved, by force if necessary, to the nearest fortified hamlet. At night, areas outside the hamlets will become free-fire zones."

The aide shuffled through a series of slides concerning manpower priorities. "All military departments will identify personnel available for assignment as individual augmentees for security details and quick reaction forces. Available soldiers, sailors, and airmen, currently assigned to administrative tasks, will receive combat and weapons training, and be assigned to such joint task forces as soon as practical."

The Captain became immediately defensive. Security details? Augmentees? He suspected his officers would be among the first to go.

The aide noticed the audience looking uncomfortable. "Don't worry; the lawyers won't be assigned as trigger pullers. They'll be assigned to the joint task forces being formed, but to perform jobs requiring expertise in the law. There will be civil affairs teams to restore order among the civilians, and military commissions to enforce

Federal law, as well as the President's executive orders.

The Captain interrupted, "What do you mean restore order among the civilians?'

The aide responded glibly. "Don't worry sir. We will be covering this in subsequent briefings." With this reassurance, the aide went on with her briefing. "As you know, the President has ordered that military forces at home be reinforced by units presently overseas. Many of these units are actively engaged. They will disengage and return home. Unfortunately, there are limits to our resources. We are currently overextended."

The Captain was having more and more trouble understanding how all this related to the Navy's lawyers. "Overextended?" What did that mean? He did not intend to be particularly loud as he answered his own question, "Abandon our allies."

The aide took up his question as if he had asked it directly, "Not abandoned, sir, but for the foreseeable future, a much lower priority. We simply do not have adequate forces at our disposal."

The aide summarized other details with a series of bullet-point slides. "There will be aggressive quarantine of those bitten. There will be searches of homes where any infection is suspected. Doctors will be on hand to check for any signs of infections. Lethal force has been authorized against those who do not cooperate."

The Captain again interrupted his tone one of alarm, "We're going to shoot civilians who don't cooperate with quarantine?"

"If necessary, absolutely!"

The Captain tried to sit patiently as the training dragged on through the rest of the day. It aggravated him that he had been forced to give up his Saturday for this nonsense. He did not begin to pay attention again until they turned to a new subject, the nature of the enemy.

The aide began to click through a series of slides showing images of men and women in different states of decay. Several slides looked like autopsy photographs. "We also must stop calling the enemy 'zombies,' " she intoned. "It is a mistake to imbue them with characteristics that can mislead or confuse."

The aide then launched to a video. It showed a creature strapped to a table. Its skin looked like heavily tanned leather. Its eyes were completely black. When the bright light shined in its eyes it squirmed as if on fire. It punctuated its speech with hisses and clicks as it cried out, "Why—d-d-doing t-t-t-this?"

The man standing by the table took a scalpel and drew a "Y" shape incision across the creature's shoulders and chest. A thin black line of fluid followed the blade as he sliced through the skin. The creature never flinched as its skin was pulled back. A large pair of green sheers appeared. They looked like something better suited to a garden than a surgery. It took some effort for the surgeon to open the creature's sternum. The shears did not so much cut as crack, and the sound of breaking bone could be heard as the creature's chest was manhandled apart. The creature's heart and lungs were now exposed even as it continued to squirm. It also tried to speak, but only gurgling sounds could be heard. Once the heart and lungs were removed and set aside the thing stop twisting on the table.

The aide aimed a laser pointer at the screen. "As you can see, the enemy is impervious to ordinary pain, but their hearts still pump a kind of blood. Most of their bodily functions continue, just in a modified way. They maintain intelligence, but at a rudimentary level. They are as violent and unpredictable as a rabid dog."

At the end of the day, the Captain left work for another trip on the subway. He walked to his house tired and a little demoralized. The day had been wasted. He operated in a vacuum without purpose or accomplishment.

As he walked home, he carried several bags of groceries for Mrs. Delaney. This one favor for an old woman represented the biggest achievement of his day. His arms felt tired from carrying the weight. Still, he thought, he should be grateful; these cloth bags were easier to carry than the plastic bags everyone used in the old days.

He walked until he came to a crowd of people standing outside a bar. The place was jam-packed, and a portion of the crowd had moved out onto the sidewalk and even onto the street. The Captain repeatedly called out "gangway" as he pushed through. The people in his path paid no attention.

From out on the sidewalk, he could hear a musician inside playing the piano and singing a ballad. The crowd joined in drunkenly on the chorus, "Waltzing Matilda, waltzing Matilda. You'll come a-waltzing Matilda with me. And he sang as he watched and waited 'til his billy boiled, you'll come a-waltzing Matilda with me."

The sound of the music and singing grew fainter as the Captain walked away. He could hear it no longer when he drew closer to the river. There were fewer pedestrians out in this section of town, and even fewer cars on the road. Some effort had been made to clear the streets, and he saw several places where cars had been pushed aside, but the usual level of traffic had not resumed.

When the Captain neared the end of the street, he came to a jewelry store. He had passed the store that morning on his way to the subway and then everything had been in order. Now broken glass covered the walkway leading from the shop to the sidewalk. Large fragments of glass still clung to the store's door frame.

The Captain started past the entranceway of the shop, glass fragments crunching underfoot, but stopped and looked into the store. All of the lights were on, and all of the display cases inside smashed. The Captain could see that the broken glass around the door had been piled up as the door swung through the shards. It appeared the attackers had started to break through the door before realizing it was unlocked. The Captain now pushed open the door and called into the shop. No voice answered him.

The Captain looked back out onto the street. The few persons walking about paid him no attention. He hesitated to go into the shop. He called again and still heard no voice in reply.

He decided that continuing home remained his best course of action. He could report the robbery of the jewelry store to the police by phone. As he started to leave, he noticed a bracelet discarded amongst the fragments of glass. It lay in the debris near the entranceway. He must have stepped over it when he pushed open the door. He put down his bags and bent down to pick up the bracelet. It was composed of dozens and dozens of large diamonds.

The Captain knew little about jewelry, but he knew enough about how much such things cost. He had looked at bracelets such as this several times. He had wanted badly to buy such a bracelet for Anna as a gift. Even with his pay as a Navy captain, he felt he could never afford such a thing; there had always been other bills and other expenses.

He stepped out onto the sidewalk and placed the bracelet across his wrist. The diamonds sparkled in the afternoon sun. He turned it this way and that catching the light. He turned it this way and that looking for the tag or code that would reveal the price. He found none. He was reminded of the joke: "If you have to ask the price you can't afford it."

He could well imagine the bracelet on Anna's wrist. He had never brought her anything so extravagant. He knew how pleased she would be with such a gift.

The Captain looked up and down the sidewalk but could see no one. He took the bracelet and tossed it up; he felt the weight of the thing as it fell back into the palm of his hand. He looked at the bracelet and watched the stones sparkling with the last rays of daylight, hinting at captured rainbows.

It would be a shame to discard the bracelet among the shards of glass. He looked at the ransacked store. He guessed that the owners were gone. They had likely disappeared on the first day; that would explain why the doors remained unlocked, the lights on, no alarms set.

He held the bracelet across his wrist. He stepped out into the street and let the light from day's end glitter amongst the stones.

Entitled, Those Who Rank Themselves In Order; Revealed At Mecca:

We have adorned the lower heaven with the ornament of the stars: and we have placed therein a guard against every rebellious devil; that they may not listen to the discourse of the exalted princes (for they are darted at from every side, to repel them, and a lasting torment is prepared for them); except him who catcheth a word by stealth, and is pursued by a shining flame.

Ask the Meccans, therefore, whether they be stronger by nature, or the angels, whom we have created? We have surely created them of stiff clay.

Thou wonderest at God's power and their obstinacy; but they mock at the arguments urged to convince them: when they are warned, they do not take warning; and when they see any sign, they scoff thereat, and say, This is no other than manifest sorcery: after we shall be dead, and become dust and bones, shall we really be raised to life, and our forefathers also?

Answer, Yea: and ye shall then be despicable There shall be but one blast of the trumpet, and they shall see themselves raised: and they shall say, Alas for us! this is the day of judgment, this is the day of distinction between the righteous and the wicked, which ye rejected as a falsehood.

Gather together those who have acted unjustly, and their comrades, and the idols which they worshipped besides GOD, and direct them in the way to hell; and set them before God's tribunal; for they shall be called to account.

The Koran, Chapter XXXVII Entitled, Those Who Rank Themselves In Order; translated by George Sales, 1734.

CHAPTER-18 – WE'RE NOT MONSTERS, WE'RE A DISEASE

Saturday, Day Six: South of Wheeler Dam, Alabama

The General looked out over the road. He could hear horns, klaxons, and sirens. In the distance, he could see approaching engines. He adjusted his dark spectacles and watched the white, and red, and blue flashing lights as the engines sped past.

The spectacles the Sailor had provided him were superb. At the first hint of light, the General would put them over his eyes. They wrapped around his face and skull, dark and protective.

Many of the scarecrows now had similar protection for their eyes. They gathered dark glasses in the places they raided; some of the others covered their eyes with a kind of blindfold, consisting of a band of wood across their face with just a narrow slit to admit light. Unfortunately, many of the scarecrows still lacked eye protection.

The sunlight was their enemy. When the sun began to brighten the open spaces, they sought protection. The sunlight burned holes into their eyes and heated their leather skin until it felt cracked and shrunken. They could not continue the march once the sun was up.

The General hated these periods of waiting. As much as he desired sleep, he could not rest. He would find a place to lie down and cautiously close his eyes. He would force his mind away from the things that oppressed him. He longed for sleep, a deep sleep that would provide respite for body, mind, and soul. This want bedeviled at him as badly as his hunger and thirst. Whenever he began to sleep the others would let their presence be known. They were always there, just beyond the partition that lay to the other side of dreams.

On other long marches, he had seen men fall to the ground overwhelmed with fatigue, but not the scarecrows. The scarecrows feared sleep as much as him. When they lay down, they tossed and turned like creatures haunted. None of them truly slept. None of them spoke of what lay beyond the partition.

After trying to rest for a few hours, the General reached his limit. He got up and walked among the scarecrows. He asked a question here and there before going back to his place beneath the trees. He returned to studying his maps.

The General wanted to travel close to the Tennessee River, the way he had along the Wolf River, but sparse forest cover and ever denser populations forced him further and further south. Everywhere the land was flooded with light, and the swiftly moving river itself had become bloated lakefront.

"That's the source of all the light," the Sailor explained. "They dammed the river and the dams provide the electricity for all the lights."

"They dammed the river?"

"Not one dam, a half dozen dams for cheap power and flood control."

The General looked again at his maps. That explained the notation of "Wheeler Dam." He wondered if it had something to do with General Joe Wheeler. He dismissed the thought as unlikely. He did not know which the most was amazing, that they had harnessed the power of the river, or that they had turned that power into electric light. He would have liked to approach closer to the river and see the dams, but the amount of light and number of houses made this impossible.

When the sun went down it was time to resume the march. The General merely had to walk, and scarecrows followed. They joined in ones and twos and in a short time they numbered in the hundreds. They walked a path ill-defined and poorly understood bounded by fear and appetite.

The General had never known a group to march so quietly. Always, in his experience, marching men, no matter how fearful or tired, joked with one another to pass the time and to encourage each other. These scarecrows with whom he marched were grim. They could march without food, water, or sleep. They could march without complaint.

From the fringes of the woods, they saw roads, or cleared fields, or an occasional home.

Lights in the windows of these homes were beacons advertising the presence of the living. The light drew the scarecrows, even as the light itself repelled them. Every time the General discovered scarecrows bunching up near such homes he would drive them forward.

He enlisted a group of scarecrows as a provost guard armed with sticks. Each time they approached a lighted house, the General had his provost herd the stragglers back. They struck with their sticks at those who resisted. Once the General had to personally intervene and threaten to shoot several scarecrows to keep them moving forward.

After several hours of walking, the General found what he was looking for, a collection of houses far from the main road. A narrow road ran up to the houses with trees and earthen embankments on both sides.

The General took the Yankee aside, "We will try yah torpedoes hare."

The General held the scarecrows back as the Yankee prepared. The Yankee and his bomb makers dug a hole in the road leading up to the houses. The Yankee planted two small barrels. Wires ran from the barrels back into the woods.

The General watched the houses from a distance. He knew the people in the houses remained awake. Light shone from their windows as bright as daylight. The General could not look directly at the light, but he could see the interruption of the light, the briefest of shadows, as the people inside passed near their windows. The General could not tell how many people occupied the houses or whether they had weapons.

The Yankee and his scarecrows finished their preparations in silence. Finally, the General signaled for the attack to begin.

Scarecrows approached the houses carrying chunks of firewood or stones. They stepped up to the houses and smashed the windows. Those at the front moved blindly and managed to break only a few of the windows, but to the back of the houses, they broke the windows freely. As windows caved in, screaming began. The scarecrows did not enter any house, but they continued to throw chunks of wood or stone at the windows. One of the scarecrows hurled bricks from a walkway. The satisfying crash of glass followed.

The scarecrows in the front of one of the houses, already blind from the shining lights, grew careless. The burst of a shotgun, fired from one of the broken windows, added to the blinding light. Scarecrows hissed and croaked as they fled into the darkness. The shotgun fired again and one of the scarecrows fell to the ground. In a moment it returned to its feet and escaped to the woods in a kind of hopping, skipping motion.

Suddenly, a dog leaped through a broken window and pulled down a running scarecrow. It backed away, barking frantically, as other scarecrows grabbed at it. Whenever a scarecrow approached, the dog rushed forward and flew at its throat. The people inside of the house called to the dog, but it would not give up charging and retreating. The ferocity of the dog kept the scarecrows from approaching. There were fewer shotgun blasts now. The General wondered if the gunners hesitated to fire for fear of hitting the dog, or could it be the darkness hid the scarecrows too well.

Now the General heard the sound of sirens. The soldiers would be here soon.

The General called out to the scarecrows around him, "Remember, those who surrender ... do no harm!"

When he heard the sirens draw near, the General signaled the scarecrows forward to press the attack in earnest. One jumped onto a porch roof as effortlessly as climbing an ordinary step. It carried an ax. In a moment, it stood by the train of wires that entered the house strung from tall poles leading back from the street. It swung the ax in a flurry of sparks. From the sparks came flame flashing down the ax and consuming the scarecrow, but it did not matter. The house went dark. The scarecrows rushed in from all sides to the sound of shotgun blasts. A woman began to scream. He could hear the dog barking, and then the barking stopped.

The second and the third and the fourth house were surrounded in turn. Flashes of light from the shotguns mingled with the flashes of light from the breaking lamps. The farmers fought at their windows and doors. The farmers fired their guns into the darkness as long as they had shells. Then the screams came. Each small citadel fell with a crescendo of pain.

Two engines, lights flashing red and white and blue, came speeding along the road. They turned to go up the drive just as the fourth house went dark. As soon as the engines began to roll towards the houses, a great gout of earth and metal and fire flew up into the night. The lead engine bucked into the air surrounded by flame; then it fell back to earth. The light of the flame disappeared in thick black smoke.

The second engine immediately began to back down the roadway. It spun its wheels so fast that gravel went shooting up into the air. It kept backing down the road until it turned and went out of sight.

The General directed his gunmen to fire on the retreating engine, but the thing moved so fast that only a few shots struck home; certainly not enough to stop it. The torpedo had been impressive, but not enough to ruin both engines. It disappointed the General that one engine had escaped.

The General turned his attention to the wrecked engine. He tried to see into the engine's cab, but it was filled with smoke. The General thought that the occupants must be dead. He stood up and began to walk forward. At this moment one of the doors of the engine flew open. A man rolled out into the gravel of the road, leapt to his feet and began to run.

As soon as he ran, three scarecrows broke from cover in pursuit. Other scarecrows hurried to the wreckage of the engine. In an instant, they yanked open the other door and pulled out the second occupant now blackened from the smoke and fire.

One of the scarecrows fastened its teeth to the soldier's neck. Another bit at the wrist. A third pulled at the soldier's clothing, not merely clothes, but a heavy vest of armor of some sort. With the flesh exposed, the General could see the figure he imagined to be a soldier was, in fact, a woman.

One of the scarecrows reached in to pull at the woman's body, not pulling, cutting, scrapping. It held a piece of glass in its hand. Now the woman began to scream. Her screams only excited the frenzy of the scarecrows. They pushed each other aside in their efforts to reach their victim. They attached themselves to the woman's body like so many leeches.

The scarecrow leading the attack batted at the others fighting to feed. This scarecrow wore a long dress and, unlike all of the others, had hair flowing past its shoulders. Its efforts to keep hair out of its eyes frustrated it. Eventually, it pulled at the hair and a wig fell to the ground; then it began to feed in earnest.

The heavy scent of blood flooded the air and the General paused. He felt the thing awakening in his gut. The hunger threatened to overwhelm him. He wanted to charge in, drive the scarecrows off, and take his fill. The General, his insides turning and twisting, could almost taste the woman's blood, sweet with sorrow, rich with agony.

Other scarecrows began pulling and cutting. They stripped the flesh from the woman's leg down to the bone. The woman soldier no longer screamed as the scarecrows fought and tore at her. Some had knives, some had only their fingernails. They pulled off bits of flesh and pushed away from the others to avoid sharing their captured morsels.

He thought the woman soldier must be dead as he watched the scarecrows consume her. One of the scarecrows regurgitated the flesh that it had eaten. It sucked at the blood and liquefied fat like a spider. He watched another scarecrow break open a leg bone it had made off with to get to the marrow.

The General could not look away. He could not go back. He refused to go forward. He struggled against it. Finally, he gained control of his need and turned to go.

He heard gunshots. Looking out across a field he saw that the scarecrows had caught up with the soldier who had fled the explosion. He fired his weapon as they surrounded him. Suddenly they charged from all directions and he began to scream. A second group of scarecrows headed to the spot where the man fought and struggled. The screaming stopped well before these scarecrows could arrive.

The General approached the first farmhouse as a scarecrow crossed his path. The scarecrow spoke aloud, "I'm sorry, I'm sorry. I didn't mean to. I'm sorry."

The scarecrow walked drunkenly but spoke with clear speech. Blood stained the rags of its shirt and sleeves. Blood dripped down its chin. The General could smell the sweet hungry tang of its feeding.

The General knew that he should be revolted at the scarecrow's appearance, but the smell so overpowered his senses he could only think of the blood. His mouth watered with hunger and desire. The smell of the blood caused a tearing pain in his gut, worse than any wound he had ever suffered.

The General stood and faced the scarecrow, "Shut yah mouth." As he spoke, he realized that his speech was barely intelligible, "Shut up, shut up." His mouth felt full of gravel.

He struck the scarecrow with his fist, and when the scarecrow fell to the ground, he began to kick it. "Shut yah mouth. God damn yah, shut yah mouth."

His victim continued its apology, "I'm sorry, I'm sorry." Finally, it rolled beyond the General's punches and kicks and ran off.

When the General stepped up onto the porch of the farmhouse, he could see a group of scarecrows huddled in a corner. Once again, he could smell the sweetness of blood. He looked for the body they had savaged, but it was not a man, it was the dog.

The dog, a shepherd of some sort, had been so badly torn he could not recognize the breed. As the scarecrows sawed at its flesh with knives and pieces of glass, the dog lifted its head for a moment and looked up at those who held it. It made one last effort to break free and then collapsed.

Blood and pain, blood and pain, and sorrow, the General fled to the next house. As he stepped into the house, he waved his pistol at the scarecrow nearby, "How many prisoners.... How many have yah taken?"

"Two .... Woman and daughter."

The General gestured wildly with the pistol, "Keep 'em safe – or back ta hell."

The General walked into the next house. He could hear the sounds of breaking glass as the scarecrows quickly extinguished the last of the lights, but wonders of wonders, up on a wall in faded grays and greens and reds, a new world, unimagined.

One of the scarecrows almost smashed the screen, but the General stopped it.

He watched the magic lantern mesmerized. The bright light made it hard to look at the screen. The General had to put on his dark glasses so that he could see more clearly. The figures on the screen were blurry with bright light, but he could hear their voices clearly. The people of the magic lantern looked out into the room and spoke calmly.

"—of the so-called 'missing,' are in fact the so-called 'returned.' They are all suffering from the same disorder." The figure pronounced these last words emphatically.

The second figure responded, "Doctor, surely the condition of the 'returned' cannot be attributed to simple illness."

"Why not? I know that the changes in appearance and behavior of the victims have been extreme, but what is extraordinary and unexplainable now, will likely be quite understandable in the future. We are only now beginning to grasp the capacities of the human brain. If we do not fully comprehend the limits of a healthy brain, should we so readily dismiss the possibility that this current calamity is attributable to some sort of illness; hysteria so extreme that it manifests itself as a hitherto unknown dysplasia."

As the General watched the magic lantern he spoke aloud. "Mah God.... Mah God."

Behind him, scarecrows went up the stairs. He could hear their heavy tread in the rooms above. Upstairs he could hear screaming, a woman's scream, followed by the sounds of struggle, but the General could not look away from the people of the magic lantern and the songs of their voices.

The Old Soldier arrived and made his report, "One less engine. Two taken.... We'uns got repeaters, black rifles ... and two pistols. Mo-wah in house."

Now the Yankee arrived and pulled at the General's sleeve to get his attention. The Yankee held up a small screen in the General's face. The bright lights of the screen cascaded writings and diagrams. "It's all 'ere General—need supplies—but can b-b-blow up even them a'mored ca's."

The small screen in front of the General turned to images of young men playing with rockets and bombs, images of boys laughing as bombs detonated. The Yankee scrolled through screens that pulsed with bright lights, a magic lantern show of explosions and burnings.

The General noted the reduction in the Yankee's hiccups and stutter. He could see the scarlet splashed across the Yankee's shirt. He could smell the fresh blood that stained his clothes. The General forced himself to turn back to his magic lantern show.

One of the figures on the screen argued loudly and forcefully. He waved his hands about like a ringmaster engaged in some extraordinary reveal. "—only appears the dead have returned. Throughout the history of the human race, viruses have inserted DNA copies of their genetic material into us. With each successive generation, we have grown less and less human. It was only a matter of time until some trigger caused some new and unexpected mutation. After all, viruses are by nature immortal."

The General turned and called out excitedly to all who could hear him, "Mah God! We air not devils! We air a disease!"

Deck Log - Seventh Day

SHIP TYPE: D A	HULL NUMBER: AS 00	YEAR: 43	MONTH: 09 ZONE: C DAY: 21 E	USS __CYCLOPS__ AT / PASSAGE FROM __NORFOLK VA__ TO __MUSCAT OMAN__

POSITION	ZONE	TIME	POSITION	ZONE	TIME	POSITION	ZONE	TIME	LEGEND
0800 L_____ ; BY ___ A_____ ; BY ___			1200 L_____ ; BY ___ A_____ ; BY ___			2000 L_____ ; BY ___ A_____ ; BY ___			1 - CELESTIAL 2 - ELECTRONIC 3 - VISUAL 4 - D R

TIME	ORDER	CSE	SPEED	DEPTH	RECORD OF EVENTS OF THE DAY
00-04					ASSUMED THE WATCH. STEAMING AS BEFORE. WATCH REPORTS CONDITIONS NORMAL. LIEUTENANT D. M. OVERTON, USN
0350					REPORT OF MURDER OF CREW MEMBER* STOREROOM 3-10-2-A. THROAT SLASHED
04-08					ASSUMED THE WATCH. STEAMING AS BEFORE. LIEUTENANT R.S. MERRIAM, USN
0450					*CREW MEMBER IDENTIFIED AS PS2 GOTTSCHALK

Third Deck - Forward, Crew's Berthing and Storage

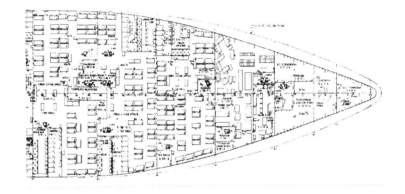

The Book of the Dead, Funerary Hymn:

Those who dwell in the heights and those who dwell in the depths worship thee. Thoth and the goddess Maāt have laid down thy course for thee daily for ever. Thine Enemy the Serpent hath been cast into the fire, the fiend hath fallen down into it headlong. His arms have been bound in chains, and Rā hath hacked off his legs; the Mesu Betshet shall never more rise up.

The Literature of the Ancient Egyptians, by E. A. Wallis Budge, 1914.

CHAPTER- 19 – MURDERED SAILORS AND NEW TACTICS

Sunday, Day Seven: The Red Sea Approaching the Gulf of Aden

When Lieutenant Irawell finished the midwatch, he went straight to his stateroom for a nap. Sundays were supposed to be holiday routine, even at sea. He imagined getting a few hours of sleep, followed by a leisurely brunch, then coffee in the lounge, perhaps while the television played some light entertainment or a movie. Reality quickly intervened. Hardwick came to fetch him before he could even close his stateroom door.

She briefed him as they went below to the third deck. "PS2 Gottschalk. She never made it to berthing. They found her in a storeroom about an hour ago."

"It happened an hour ago?"

"They found her an hour ago, sir."

"I'm only now finding out?"

"Sir, Medical was up first and declared her dead."

"Where's she now?"

"In the storeroom. The space has been sealed off and Porter and Oxford are on guard."

"How was she killed?"

"Throat cut, sir, but you're going to have to see it."

When the Lieutenant arrived, he found Porter and Oxford standing to either side of the storeroom door. He looked in and then told Hardwick to go find Acedian and have him bring his camera.

Gottschalk's corpse had been strung up by her heels and hung from a pipe. Her trachea and portions of her spine were visible as her head lolled on the deck. The Lieutenant could not see a clean cut this time. Her throat had been torn, the wound ragged. Despite the savagery of the attack, there was surprisingly little blood. He looked about the space but saw no signs of struggle. There was no blood splatter, no pooled blood, no blood tracks along the deck. He did see, however, a drip pan resting on the deck stained with blood.

The Lieutenant mastered his breathing before he spoke. "Could she have been killed elsewhere and her body dragged here?"

"It's possible. The attack was definitely different than with Mulvey. Also, her clothing has not been disturbed."

The Lieutenant turned to Acedian. "Photograph everything and close off the space. Get a body bag and store it in the reefers. We'll send another message to NCIS. Maybe this time they'll respond."

The Lieutenant returned to his office and tried to reach the XO by phone. When the call went unanswered, he walked up to the XO's offices. When he did not find him there, he went up to the Captain's offices.

"Sir, we've finished processing the scene of Gottschalk's murder. We've photographed it and picked up anything that looks like it might be evidence. Her body's been transported for storage in one of the reefers."

The XO gave a terse response, "Did you learn anything yet?"

"No sir."

"Then why are you here?"

The Lieutenant did not reply. He turned on his heel and headed down below. Arriving in the wardroom, he poured a cup of coffee. He began to pace alongside the portholes that pierced the bulkheads. He muttered obscenities and various derogatory terms under his breath as he walked back and forth. His imagined confrontation ended only when one of the stewards came over to say that he and the other senior officers had been summoned to the Captain's conference room.

The Lieutenant arrived in time to hear Powers making a recommendation to the XO. "We must keep everyone at general quarters. My folks kin go through ship an' not worry about people moving about."

Crammer offered a suggestion. "Not much we can do about someone breaking lights and battle lanterns, but we can build motion alarms and place alarms on all compartment doors and hatches."

The XO responded with a question, "Do we have parts onboard for that?"

"Yes sir. I think so. Easy enough to build magnetic circuits to check for doors opening and closing. We should have PIRs onboard, or some other kind of infrared sensors, to build motion detectors. If we've got the parts, my guys can build it. Might take some time to wire things and set up silent alarms. If we wire it up, we can find out where they're hiding."

Powers nodded his head enthusiastically, "Clear out the lower decks, except fo-wah security patrols. Set up ambushes fo-wah anything that moves down thaar."

O'Day spoke up next. "Are you sure that will work? If the killer is a reanimated zombie, do the Zs give off enough heat for a PIR motion detector to work?"

Crammer answered, unconcerned by the underlying assumption. "Not to worry, there should be enough thermal difference for the PIRs to work. I'm not sure about the sensitivity of the sensors, but, living or dead, there should be sufficient differences in the heat energy given off from the Zs as compared to the surrounding area."

The Lieutenant heard Lamb speak, just under his breath. "Maybe they should build some sonar sensors while they're at it. Explore the ship's bilge; maybe the Zombies are swimming around down there."

After the meeting, the Lieutenant went up to CIC for the afternoon watch. MM1 Moore was already seated behind the radar operator. "Lieutenant, I'm not sure how many more CIC watches I'll be standing. I'm supposed to start standing engineering soon."

The Lieutenant did not try to hide his disappointment. "Will someone take your place?"

"Nobody knows. Every watch is shorthanded these days."

The Lieutenant considered this for a moment before posing another question. "Is there any way to get this changed?"

"I already told 'em I didn't want to go. Engineering is the last place I want to be right now."

The Lieutenant commiserated, "I expect it is pretty unpleasant down there with the heat."

Moore chuckled to himself. "Lieutenant, you've never stood an engineering watch, have you? I'm not worried about the heat, but the noise, or rather the lack of some types of noise.... It's hard to hear people moving around down there. Not that there are many people. People don't lounge around down there. Most of the time, it's only the watchstanders keeping their logs.

"There's all sorts of hidey holes, if you don't want to be found. There are the bilges and the catacombs and machinery. Those things could be tucked away, coming and going however they please."

The Lieutenant tried to inject a note of optimism, "I heard Commander Powers saying that the military on watch will be issued a sidearm. You'll have a pistol if you need it."

Moore responded, "These things ain't people. Shooting them ain't going to stop them."

The usual affable Moore became morose. After a time he posed a question, "Lieutenant, do you believe in ghosts?"

"I don't believe the killer or killers we have onboard are ghosts if that's what you mean."

"No Lieutenant, I mean real ghosts, the supernatural."

The Lieutenant shook his head as he responded, "I don't believe I do. Even what's happening now, we'll find an explanation and all the doomsayers will look ridiculous."

"I think you're wrong sir. Sometimes there's no explanation." Here Moore paused to make sure he had the Lieutenant's full attention. "When I was a kid my Dad bought an old house. It was nearly two hundred years old. It was built before electricity, before even proper plumbing. Everything had been put together over time. There were copper pipes in the walls for gas lighting. There was old knob and tube for electricity, and the plumbing had been put together by drunken clowns.

"The cellar was basically a square box. No place to hide from view. There was an old coal fire furnace down there, mostly sealed up, side by side with a newer oil furnace. The house's foundation was made up from large fieldstones piled one upon the other and mortared in. There was some brickwork in one portion of the floor, but the far side of the cellar was packed earth.

"Well, my Dad was always having problems with the lights in the cellar."

Here the Lieutenant interrupted conversationally, "I'm not surprised, old knob and tube probably."

"Lieutenant, the problem wasn't keeping the lights on; it was keeping the lights off. Every night he would turn the lights in the cellar off, and every morning he would find them turned on again. He would come down at night to check, only to see light coming from beneath the cellar door.

"He was convinced there was a short in the switch, so he started removing the lightbulbs and laying them on the ground. The next night when he checked, the lights were back on, the bulbs in their sockets.

"Finally, he tried staying up all night, waiting in the kitchen by the cellar door. Sure enough, a few hours after midnight, the lights went on. Not only did the lights come on, he could see movement in the light. Something was moving back and forth and causing the light to blink and fade at the bottom of the door jam.

"The next day, he took some two by fours and long nails and sealed the cellar door to the door frame, so that no light could reach the kitchen, and no one could enter the house from the cellar.

"The next day, he found that the nails had eased out of the wood. Two of the nails had come out of the wood and dropped to the floor."

The Lieutenant waited for Moore to finish the story. After a few minutes, he spoke up exasperated, "So what happened?"

"Nothing happened. He moved us out that day and sold the place. He only told me years later why."

The Lieutenant's frustration must have been evident, "MM1, your stories never seem to have a proper ending. You need a beginning and end." Moore reacted to the criticism by becoming monosyllabic. Any further effort by the Lieutenant to engage in conversation that afternoon proved futile.

Throughout the remainder of the watch the smooth seas and the sunny day seemed to draw sailors up to the bridge. Different crew members stopped by to share gossip. Word came in that two sailors from repair had missed morning quarters and could not be found. Soon word came in of repair parties welding shut manhole covers going down into the double hull. Then word filtered up about bloody footprints found around a manhole cover on the fourth deck.

The Lieutenant posed a question to one of the gossips, "Who's saying the footprints were made with blood?"

"Don't know. Might have been dirty water. Didn't see myself. One thing's for sure though, nobody's going into them bilges."

After watch, the Lieutenant went to the wardroom to get chow. Instead of hotdogs and hamburgers, they had barbeque and coleslaw. The salad bar had reasonably fresh lettuce, pickled vegetables, and cold cuts. The Lieutenant ate heartily. Then he grabbed a soda and stepped into the lounge. The television was playing a Sunday news journal of some sort.

"—soldiers, butchers, and executioners. Certain body parts continue to twitch after decapitation. Doctors have frequently reported instances where the hearts of the deceased have continued to beat long after the patient stopped breathing.

"The Lazarus effect has been known to cause the deceased to sit up, raise their arms, even cross their arms onto their chest. Brain stem cells are known to remain alive for even longer. Living muscle or stem cells have been found in patients declared dead weeks before. Our genes can register activity for longer still.

"We really should not be surprised by this mutation. Life is very resilient. What always existed at the genetic and cellular level has now evolved. Some cells have found an alternative means of function where more complex systems have become impossible."

Ensign Jett had been watching the television quietly. Now he pointed at the screen, raised his voice, and began to curse the television expert. "You don't know shit. That doesn't explain the missing children does it, you fat fuck."

The Lieutenant sipped his drink and waited for the next tirade, but the Ensign grew suddenly self-conscious. The television expert continued without further interruption. "— all share a collective unconsciousness. We see evidence of this in our dreams and art, but also in our myths and folklore. We must reintegrate our collective unconscious. It is not surprising that some have turned to God and scripture. It is part of our survival gear as humans. It is also not surprising that these explanations are completely unsatisfying."

The Lieutenant leaned towards the television expert trying to follow the man's reasoning.

The philosopher continued: "Modern religions have failed, but our yearning to find meaning has not been abandoned. Other creatures do not debate good and evil, meaning or reality, heaven or hell. We have evolved to look for meanings beyond the present moment. It is part of the evolutionary track that resulted in our becoming self-aware. We have become self-aware individually and civilized collectively. But not every experience can fit into an ancient collective unconsciousness."

The newsreader tried to regain control of the interview: "But Doctor, I was asking if there was any legitimate theological explanation for these events."

"Don't you see? That's the very point. We want to believe in the hero's quest. We want to admire courage and sacrifice, the ultimate judgment of heaven or hell. But, to embrace the new truths, we must abandon the old myths."

As the philosopher lectured, followed dutifully by the news journalist and camera crew, he slowly walked through an empty museum. They left the renaissance wing, walked past the impressionist, through a sculpture garden, and finally ended in the modern art wing. The philosopher finished his monologue standing in front of a large canvas, painted in a single color. The Lieutenant thought at first it was one of the museum's painted walls until the philosopher stepped back and an exhibition tag became visible.

"All cultures reach a point where its people wake up to the knowledge that their founding myths are fiction. If they refuse to adapt, they must fail. We are in a new age. New myths are required that embrace our new existence. Old concepts of good and evil must evolve if we are to succeed."

Miller had been stretched out comfortably on one of the couches. Now he pointed at the television and spoke up. "In the old days we didn't have TV onboard, I mean satellite TV. We could see the games when tapped copies arrived. Some of the sports channels complained about copyright, so the tapes were often bootlegged. But I never could really enjoy watching a game on tape, after I knew who'd won for a week or more. News and sports live and direct to the ship. I used to think that was a good thing; TV anytime and anywhere in the world. Now I'm not so sure."

Miller turned away from the television and looked over at the Lieutenant. "Judge, things are pretty fucked up and these jerks aren't making me feel any better."

Jett took the hint and switched to a regular news channel. "–at least one attack on a small hamlet. Those in isolated homes are being urged to relocate to new safe zones at night. A spokesman for the governor states they are in the process of contracting with privately owned hotels to provide for those in need, and that these additional defenses will include the issue of weapons to veterans and first responders. Again, the governor–"

As the news reporter spoke into a microphone, the camera panned back and a cul-de-sac became visible at the end of a narrow road. At least two houses were burned to the ground. Several ambulances and police cars were visible, their lights flashing in a gloomy morning. Policemen could be seen walking through the wreckage, their pistols drawn.

Now it was Miller's turn to curse, "Christ almighty, can't you find something more cheerful."

After dinner, the Lieutenant returned to his office. He arrived to find it empty and assumed that Acedian must still be up in the wardroom eating. The Lieutenant halfheartedly pushed papers around on his desk. When a sailor came by asking for legal assistance he treated it as a timely diversion.

The sailor began by explaining he had been trying to reach his wife and kids, "There's no way she got sucked up to heaven. The kids, sure, but not her. I want to stop my allowances going to her. I want to make sure she can't get at my bank accounts."

"You know, people have been having problems getting in touch with family back home."

"She's just ignoring me. I checked my bank account online. She's bouncing checks. I want to get her arrested and want to make her pay me back."

In the end, the Lieutenant could only advise the sailor to close his checking account. Then he sent the sailor down to admin to talk to dispersing about switching his direct deposit.

The Lieutenant had the evening watch. He had a couple of more hours to kill before going back to CIC and did not feel like spending them in the office. He decided to go up to the wardroom. He took a circuitous route, climbing up to the main deck before walking forward along the weather deck.

Amidships, members of a machine crew sat on sandbags, talking and smoking cigarettes. The Lieutenant walked past and found a place he could lean out over the ship's rail without being disturbed. Further forward, he could see sailors at the fo'c'sle securing lines and chains. On the deck above him, three officers leaned on the ship's rails. He could hear them talking among themselves but could not make out any specifics.

The evening seemed a little hotter than it had been that morning. Even with the sun going down and surrounded by water the air was muggy and humid. The wind direction must have shifted because the air felt still despite the twelve knots the ship was making through a calm sea.

Suddenly, the claxon began to sound. "General quarters, general quarters. This is not a drill. General quarters, general quarters."

The Lieutenant turned to go back the way he came down. He passed Hardwick as he went down the nearest ladder to the main deck. Hardwick continued to the bridge.

When the Lieutenant arrived on the mess decks, he found Acedian waiting. One of the petty officers had already taken muster. They waited for orders, the phone talker at the casualty station kept them apprised of events:

"They found a z in the passageway. There was a gunfight. The patrol says the z fired a shotgun."

"—Main deck to second deck clear.

"—The third deck, berthing areas, bow storage spaces and laundry clear.

"—Aft workshops and storerooms on third deck clear.

"—Fourth deck, first and second platforms, and storages areas, clear.

"—Ship's hold, electric shock injury." This was followed later by an update. "Booby trap in electrical wiring, shock-burn as a result of rewiring."

The end of the day passed slowly with only the tidbits of information from the phone talkers keeping them alert. Finally, word came over the 1MC. "Secure from general quarters."

It soon as he was free, the Lieutenant began the climb to CIC. He had done nothing that evening but stand around on the mess decks, yet he felt exhausted. He had trouble following along as Moore related the daylong search for the zombies.

"It started when a couple of guys from Supply went missing. They sent a team down to look for them armed with shotguns and they went missing. Then word came into search all of the lower decks."

"I was in engineering when word came in that they saw a zombie near one of the escape trunks. We set up to cover all entrance and exit points to the engine rooms. We were armed with batons and Flexi cuffs. Somebody found some trash in the catacombs, some sweatpants, a headphone charger. There was a uniform there also. They said it smelled like somebody had been using it to wipe down a toilet."

Moore paused for a moment considering what next to say. He shook his head and went on with his story. "Nobody could spend any length of time in there; the spaces are very narrow, very tight. The air is bad. There was a red sludge everywhere in the catacombs. It smelled like piss and ammonia."

Here, Moore shook himself as if a chill had run up his spine. "Somebody opened an up the escape tube. He reached up and felt resistance. He claimed he saw a body. He called me over. I looked up and it looked like one of our missing guys, a dead body. That's when I reached up and bumped him with my flashlight. I swear to God, he wasn't dead. He woke up. He looked at me. His eyes were so black. I shined my light at his face, and he began to kick and scream. We backed away and left to get help. When we went back, he was already gone."

Moore paused and looked over at the Lieutenant. After a moment he continued, "He was naked, but he was dripping something from his skin. Stink was worse than anything. Moore paused and looked at his clothes and hands for some invisible contamination. He paused for a moment before continuing. "It looked down at me as I shone my flashlight. It screamed when I put the light in its eyes. I think it was Mulvey."

Joel 2:20-31: KJV:

But I will remove far off from you the northern army, and will drive him into a land barren and desolate, with his face toward the east sea, and his hinder part toward the utmost sea, and his stink shall come up, and his ill savour shall come up, because he hath done great things. And it shall come to pass afterward, that I will pour out my spirit upon all flesh; and your sons and your daughters shall prophesy, your old men shall dream dreams, your young men shall see visions: And also upon the servants and upon the handmaids in those days will I pour out my spirit. And I will shew wonders in the heavens and in the earth, blood, and fire, and pillars of smoke. The sun shall be turned into darkness, and the moon into blood, before the great and terrible day of the Lord come.

CHAPTER-20 – THE NEW SOLDIERS

Sunday, Day Seven: Navy Yard

He looks about carefully. He realizes he is not in his room and not in his house. He is in the cave. He is trapped in a narrow passage, one arm tucked beneath him, the other stretched forward. In his outstretched hand, he holds a flashlight. He shines the light back and forth in the cavern beyond. The walls are made of broken stone. The light reflects into his eyes from the moisture gleaming on the walls. He turns off the flashlight, consciously trying to save the batteries. He lays still and he listens. He can hear a heartbeat, not his. The heartbeat comes from the stone around him. He carefully listens while he waits in the darkness. He can hear the sounds of the ocean, the waves crashing against the cliffs that surrounded the island. He can hear the waves striking against the cliffs and he can feel the vibrations up through the bedrock.

He twists his body this way and that trying to worm his way forward or back. His head is spinning from the effort. He can no longer tell up from down. He cannot free his body. He is trapped in the stone passageway.

He knows that none of this is real, but he begins to pray. He has not prayed for many years.

Now he prays aloud. He hears a voice in response to his prayers. He stops and listens. There is someone else in the cave. They are making a keening, panicky sound; it is the voice of a trapped animal. He turns on the flashlight again.

Captain Pride launched himself forward in an effort to be free. He awoke falling from his chair. He stood up in his darkened room feeling foolish. He did not bother sitting down again. He knew he could not possibly get back to sleep.

The Captain went down to the kitchen. He took a moment to look out the window; then he put on a pot of coffee. As the coffee brewed, he toasted two slices of bread. In a few minutes, he had the coffee ready. He sat and drank his coffee and ate the dry toast. He considered turning on the television but he had grown weary of the news stories. There would be time enough to catch up on the news when he got to work. He sat in his kitchen drinking coffee and waiting for the first light of day. Only when the gray light began to seep through the window did he start to get ready.

It had been a very long time since the Captain had been forced to go to work on a Sunday, but the order of the day required all military to appear at their duty stations. As he set out, he knew his appearance in the office on a weekend would be largely symbolic; his was not an operational billet. Still, all available personnel were being mustered to hunt the crazies, and even office workers must show solidarity.

He walked to the subway station going past the jewelry store. Yesterday, he had picked up the diamonds discarded in the rubbish and placed them in a drawer inside the store. He was tempted to go inside and again look at the bracelet; instead, he turned away and hurried up the street, careless of the glass that crunched beneath his shoes.

After traveling uneventfully through the city, he exited the subway station near the Navy Yard and noticed a long line of cars stretching away from the gate and down the road. Security had been tightened, and it took time for the drivers to clear the gate. The Captain congratulated himself on his easy commute. Being without a car might not be the inconvenience he had expected.

Across the street from the gate, a line of civilians waited their turn to enter the convenience mart. The people seemed orderly and patient. As one or two people left the market carrying groceries, one or two people would enter in turn. Two new Marines stood watch at the door.

As the security guard checked the Captain's ID, he turned to follow the Captain's gaze. The guard spoke as he handed the ID card back, "Okay now. Wait till they run out of food."

Once through the gate, the Captain noticed a great many people coming and going along the Yard's sidewalks, and many more cars moving around the narrow streets than normal for a Sunday.

Approaching the legal service offices, he noticed lines of cars waiting to enter the parking garage. An increase in the base's traffic did not translate to an increase in parking spaces. On a whim, the Captain stepped into the parking garage to check on his reserved parking. Sure enough, someone had taken the space for their own despite it being marked "Reserved, Commanding Officer, Regional Legal Service Office." He turned to go into the office only to realize that the parked car belonged to someone he knew. Not for the first time, the XO had taken the Captain's parking space.

As the Captain entered the office, he noticed several of his legalmen moving about. He did not notice any of his officers. A quick survey showed empty offices, no officers, all lights off. The Captain went to find Invidia.

"What are all these people doing on base?"

Invidia was surprised at the Captain's sudden appearance and his tone of voice but quickly recovered. "Reservist, I think."

The Captain continued in a tone of annoyance, "Where are our folks? Did they finish with this emergency training?"

"Everyone is still in training, but they did say we can keep Gula here. We may get some reservists later in the week, assuming they're not grabbed for the Admiral's pet projects."

"What the hell are you doing in my parking space?"

The reason for the Captain's evident irritation began to dawn on Invidia. "I'm sorry. There was a shortage of parking spaces this morning, and I didn't think you were driving in now."

"Next time ask. How come I seem to be the last to hear about it, whenever OJAG schedules a conference?"

Now Invidia started to become assertive. "Sir, I've been passing on messages as soon as I receive them. Assuming you're here."

"When a message comes in like that, I expect you to find me. In case you don't remember, I also have a cell phone."

Invidia responded with "Yes sir," and nothing more.

The Captain went back to his inner office still irritated with Invidia, but even more irritated with Gula. He complained out loud as he sat down at his desk, "OJAG could only spare Gula? Why not sent me a garden gnome." He felt condemned to a special kind of purgatory.

The Captain could not bring himself to deal with the paperwork scattered across his desk. He had no interest in dealing with any administrative tasks. He logged onto his computer. Not surprisingly, there was minimum message traffic this Sunday and none that required his attention. He turned on his office television to watch the latest reports. The first station tuned in with an expert in mid-sentence.

"—zombie apocalypse. These things don't exist in nature." The speaker seemed cool and detached as he spoke.

The moderator followed up with a question, "What about the theory the zombies are the disappeared now returning?"

The expert responded condescendingly, "Nonsense, you've seen the videos. These things are crawling out of the cemeteries. All I'm saying is they're not 'zombies' as the zealots are claiming. They respond to commands. They can answer questions. They are intelligent. They are clearly not zombies."

The moderator shook his head, "Doctor, does that really answer the question? The videos I have seen show the things are incoherent. Their corpses are completely desiccated. Those held and medically examined have minimal vital signs."

The expert continued in the same condescending tone. "Nonsense. They have some initial impediments. Some may be dangerous, but they are still intelligent."

At this point, a video began to play. It showed a group of figures in a dark corridor trying to force open a metal gate. A body lies on the ground nearby. The figures retreat as soon as the camera lights play on them.

The moderator provided a narrative for the video, "These 'non-zombies' have just killed someone they trapped in an alley and tore apart with their teeth and fingernails. These things are mindless animals."

The expert forcefully interrupted, "You are dismissing all this as some sort of cheap horror show. We have an extraordinary opportunity here.

We cannot let panic decided the outcome. Push your emotions aside just for—"

The Captain turned off the television. He felt the target of his irritation shift from OJAG and Invidia to television talking heads. At least now he could call OJAG, and register a complaint about his missing officers, without growing too angry at the Admiral's staff.

When the Captain got through on the phone, he politely asked to be put through to one of the Admiral's deputies, or if possible, to the Admiral herself. Instead of being put through, some anonymous aide told him that everyone was in conference, but he could leave a message.

The Captain explained that he was calling to discuss the status of his Lieutenants visa vi the ability of the RLSO to continue its current mission, including the real and immediate needs of military families to get their affairs in order, for local commands to sort out the status of their missing personnel, and for service members to deal with actual emergencies, as compared to training for commissions and civil affairs teams not yet stood up.

The Captain spoke very politely, but his voice suggested exasperation. The aide responded politely that she would pass on the message as appropriate. There was no hint in her tone that she heard anything particularly imperative or alarming in his communication.

The Captain spent the rest of the day fielding calls from local commands regarding disciplinary matters. Sailors and civilians, present earlier in the week, had stopped showing up for work. The different commands were proposing different solutions, everything from leaving things alone for the time being, to full-on General Court-martial for desertion in time of war. One command even wanted to threaten civilians with court-martial. Several had heard rumors that the President was considering ordering all civilians to return to work using his emergency powers.

As the Captain prepared to leave the office at day's end, he was pleasantly surprised to find Invidia still at work; his Lieutenants, however, had not returned.

After a short subway ride, the Captain started the walk down King Street. As he walked, he enjoyed a perfect autumn day. More pedestrians were out than the day before, and more people drove down the streets. He thought the area unusually busy for a Sunday afternoon.

He passed the many pubs and restaurants that lined the street. Outside of one bar, the people had flowed out onto the adjacent sidewalk and even onto the road. People inside and outside the bar were singing, but in a manner so jumbled, he could not tell whether they sang in unison or competition. Going past he could hear a strong tenor voice above the rest accompanied by an incongruous electric guitar:

"I counted out his money and it made a pretty penny,

"I put it in my pocket and took it to my Jenny.

"She sighed and she swore that she never should deceive me,

"But the devil take the woman, for they never can be easy.

"Mush-a ring dum-a-do, dum-a-da.

"Whack for my daddy-o, whack for my daddy-o, there's whiskey in the jar."

The people outside swung pints of beer in time with the music. Spilled beer flew in the air adding to the hazards of getting through the crowd. As the Captain worked his way along the sidewalk he called out "gangway, let me through," but the crowd paid no attention. He broke free and continued down the street.

Not far from the waterfront he walked passed the ruined jewelry store. He noticed the glass swept away, the broken windows boarded up.

Before going to his house the Captain stopped by the Delaney's. He intended to drop off some groceries and head home, but Mrs. Delaney had other plans. She asked him to come inside and visit. He declined, assuming that her invitation had been made merely out of politeness. As he turned to leave she asked again, "Please, as a favor to me, can you come in and check on George. We have not been able to leave the house for weeks, and I would be most grateful if you would come in and see him."

He followed her into the house, past the kitchen, and towards a back room. A hospital bed stood in the middle of the sick room. Mr. Delaney lay in the bed. A slight plastic tube dangled from his ears and hung below his nose. The Captain could hear the sounds of a machine humming, the oxygen blowing from the tube in a hiss. Some pill jars and a glass of water sat on a table nearby.

This room held a library with dark shelves built into all of the walls, floor to ceiling. Books crowded every shelf. He could see books stacked in the corners where inadequate space on the shelves required it. Sitting in one corner, precariously balanced on a stack of books, sat a small television set tuned to a news station.

Delaney smiled and reached out his hand as the Captain stepped into the room. The Captain took Delaney's hand and shook it gently. He could feel the bones through the paper-thin skin. Still, Delaney made an effort to return the handshake firmly.

The Captain had met the man once or twice before, but if he had been required to describe the circumstances of their introduction; he would not have been able to do so. Since he had last talked to him, Delaney had most definitely changed. His face and body had grown narrow and thin. His hair had gone completely white. A tinge of blue colored his lips.

Delaney noticed the look that the Captain gave him. "Don't worry; I'm not dying just yet. Just can't get up and down the stairs anymore. We can't thank you enough for helping us. How 'bout a cold beer."

The Captain noticed a cooler near the bed holding a single bottle of beer. "I don't want to take your last beer."

"Not to worry, plenty more where that came from. I've got a friend who owns a bar. Practically giving it away. Says he plans to kill himself when the last bottle's gone."

Delaney made this statement so matter-of-factly that the Captain wondered if he really meant it as a joke. The Captain tried to hide his uncertainty as he responded, "Thanks anyway, but I've got to go."

"Now Captain, I may be an old man, but I'm not a dumb man. Keep me company for a few minutes. Amy hates beer, and I hate to drink alone." The Captain began to demur, but Delaney interjected, "Please, you'd be doing me a favor. We may not have much in the way of groceries, but we've got plenty of beer."

Mrs. Delaney called over from the next room. "George, you not supposed to drink beer with your medicines."

"Amy, from what I've gathered, beer will just make them more effective."

Mrs. Delaney came in a few moments later carrying several bottles of beer which she added to the cooler. She also had a can of light beer and a glass mug for Delaney. Delaney shook his head but said nothing.

Delaney spoke again as the Captain opened his bottle of beer. "I wanted to thank you for your help." Delaney noticed the Captain looking over the oxygen machine and the table full of pills. "Don't worry. The electricity has been a little unreliable, but everything is working now and I'm getting plenty of oxygen."

Whatever his illness Delaney seemed cheerful. The crinkles around his eyes hinted at much past laughter, a certain mellowness in a face now framed by an oxygen tube.

"Don't you have an emergency backup?" the Captain asked.

"Had an oxygen bottle for backup, but it's used up already. I'm not worried though, they'll bring another bottle over soon. But enough about me; how are things with you?"

The Captain just looked at Delaney quizzically.

Delaney continued, "I know Anna's missing, how about your kids?"

"The kids are good. The phones are screwed up, but I've heard from both of them. They're safe."

"Thank God." Delaney's concern seemed so genuine it surprised the Captain.

Delaney went on, "You've got great kids. You're lucky…. I expect that Martha has been mobilized by now."

This statement fully drew the Captain's attention, "Mobilized?"

"Yes, with the other cadets. That's certainly not something I expected to ever happen in my lifetime."

Delaney's remarks about the cadets being mobilized surprised the Captain. He had a moment of disquiet sensing that Delaney knew things he did not.

In the background, Delaney's television continued to play. The newsreaders were discussing a local scandal. "—Authorities say that the group of teenagers, rather than calling 911, or trying to provide assistance themselves, decided to record a desperate man drowning."

The news feed switched to a man struggling in a narrow river. It was dark and the image was grainy, but the sound was clear. On one side of the river, a dozen of the monsters hissed and hooted, calling out to each other in unintelligible speech. They stood at the river's edge reaching for the man in the water; they moved back and forth along the river's bank, but they would not enter the water.

A man thrashed about in the middle of the river. He was tangled in something or weighted down. As he ineffectually struggled to reach the other side, he screamed for help. A group of teenagers appeared on the further bank. The newsreaders remained silent and allowed the video to play out.

The man in the water cries out and a teenager's voice is heard in the background. "I bet you he's going to die."

"How much?" responds a second voice.

"Get out the water, you gonna die," yells another.

A fourth voice calls out, "Ain't nobody going to help you, dumb ass."

As the man disappears under the water, one of the teens says, "Oh, he d.e.d dead." The sound of laughter follows.

The newsreader completed his report. "This video has been uploaded nearly two million times. The teenagers involved have not been identified."

The Captain watched the news report in silence. Delaney must have noticed his discomfort and turned the conversation in a new direction.

"You know, when I worked for one of those alphabet agencies we're not supposed to talk about, my time was dedicated to analyzing conflict. At first, it was the struggle between the United States and the Soviets; next, it was the terrorists; now it's something different but really, it's the same.

"When the Soviet Union collapsed, little wars throughout the world continued. I thought this was just a settling, like throwing a large stone into a pond and seeing dying waves of energy reflecting off the edges. I was wrong. We weren't fighting the last of the class warriors holding on in some rearguard action. Even the war against terror … different groups, different causes, but really the wars were the same. A continuation of the oldest of all wars; the war of the angels, some ascendant, some descendent; the course to victory or defeat well charted."

The Captain considered a response, but Delaney continued. "I'm not worried about myself; my timing has always been excellent. We all have to go, what better way to go then at end. You won't miss anything that way. Amy, though, is not prepared for all this. She's the one I worry about." He looked towards the Captain hopefully.

The Captain said nothing. He continued to drink his beer and watch the television. If Delaney wanted something from him, he would have to ask plainly. The Captain was not cruel, but he had no desire to make promises. He was glad when Delaney did not request the favor.

After finishing his beer, the Captain started for home. Mrs. Delaney walked with him unobtrusively as he left. "I'm really worried about him. He needs his oxygen. The way the electricity has been failing, I'm really worried."

The Captain reassured her that all would be well as he went out the door.

The Captain stepped into his house and immediately began making phone calls. After several attempts, the connection went through, and he heard Martha's voice.

"Martha, has something happened with your status? Have the cadets been mobilized?"

Martha seemed genuinely surprised by his question. "Dad, I'm enlisted. All of the cadets in the state schools are part of the state militia, but it doesn't matter; we all volunteered anyway. The professors have been made officers. The school president is now a Lieutenant General. It's been all over the news."

"Martha, militia's not National Guard. You're not part of the Army."

Martha answered in a manner suggesting that her father had not grasped the main point. "Dad we're on State service right now. Right now, it's just the governor, but they said the president will likely mobilize us soon…. The Army's issuing us state of the art rifles; we're getting infrared sights, laser sights, NVDs."

The Captain could not hide his irritation, "Martha, you're a college kid! Don't play at soldier!"

"Dad, how many deployments did you make when we were growing up? You served. Now it's my time to serve. We're going to defend this place. We're needed here. A group of those things have attacked homes and killed people. Groups of those things have been assembling in the mountains."

"Martha, let the professionals handle this."

"Dad, there's no one else. The National Guard is scattered, a lot of them are missing, or failed to show up. There's not enough military. You know that. There are all sorts of things that need to be done. Roads have to be cleared. Food and fuel need to be distributed. Factories, farms, food processing, gas distilleries, power plants— all are shorthanded or shut down. It's my turn to step up."

The Captain said nothing in reply. He knew it would be useless to argue the point on the phone.

Andrews Chapel to Egypt, Alabama

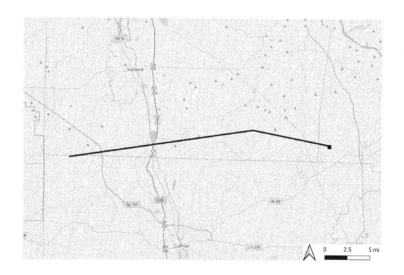

Entitled, The Pilgrimage; Revealed At Mecca:

On the day whereon ye shall see it, every woman who giveth suck shall forget the infant which she suckleth, and every female that is with young shall cast her burden; and thou shalt see men seemingly drunk, yet they shall not be really drunk: but the punishment of GOD will be severe.

There is a man who disputeth concerning GOD without knowledge, and followeth every rebellious devil: against whom it is written, that whoever shall take him for his patron, he shall surely seduce him, and shall lead him into the torment of hell.

O men, if ye be in doubt concerning the resurrection, consider that we first created you of the dust of the ground; afterwards, of seed; afterwards, of a little coagulated blood; afterwards, of a piece of flesh, perfectly formed in part, and in part imperfectly formed; that we might make our power manifest unto you: and we caused that which we please to rest in the wombs, until the appointed time of delivery. Then we bring you forth infants; and afterwards we permit you to attain your age of full strength: and one of you dieth in his youth, and another of you is postponed to a decrepit age, so that he forgetteth whatever he knew. Thou seest the earth sometimes dried up and barren: but when we send down rain thereon, it is put in motion and swelleth, and produceth every kind of luxuriant vegetables.

This showeth that GOD is the truth, and that he raiseth the dead to life, and that he is almighty; and that the hour of judgment will surely come (there is no doubt thereof), and that GOD will raise again those who are in the graves.

The Koran, Chapter XXII, Entitled, The Pilgrimage; Translated by George Sales 1734.

CHAPTER-21 – DOING THE ARITHMETIC

Sunday, Day Seven: South of Decatur

The General was many miles south of the river, but sparse cover allowed for no alternative. The growth of cities along the river and the improvements in the land amazed him, but the risk of crossing the many open fields unsettled him. To the south, dense forest could still be found.

The General remembered traveling these roads long ago. They were back roads even then. He reminisced with the Old Soldier.

"Had good luck hare…. Chased Colonel Streight from Day's Gap ta Cedar Bluff."

The Old Soldier surprised him with his comment. "Was bad luck fo-wah Lieutenant Gould though."

The General grew angry for a moment then paused before responding. "Aah always regretted … killing Gould." He felt compelled to offer further explanation. "He shot me … then aah stabbed him."

The Old Soldier merely shook his head.

They went past Day's Gap always trying to stay close to the cover of the forest. After many hours, the General ordered up the Yankee and his bomb makers. He picked a sunken road that led up to a little hamlet. There was plenty of cover on either side of the road here, and plenty of places to hide.

In the road, the Yankee and his bomb makers struggled to bury the torpedoes. It was difficult to break through the black-tarred surface and dig a pit. Every time they heard an engine approaching along the main road, they scurried to find hiding places among the trees.

Those around the General began to grow anxious as night threatened to turn into day.

The Reverend urged the attack to begin without regard to the Yankee and the bomb makers, but the General waited.

The Sailor urged the attack to begin as Orion began to rise in the night sky, but the General waited.

Green-Black warned that the Army knew where they were, and could attack at any time, still the General waited.

Scarecrows began to disburse in the darkness, fearful of what might happen. If the Army found them now, the hunter would become the hunted. Still, the General waited.

The General kept the scarecrows busy as the night progressed. He ordered trenches dug at the edge of the wood, opposite the place they had buried the torpedo. He sent forward a squad of scarecrows to find places near the houses but ordered them not to be seen and not to draw fire. He told them they would be rewarded, but they must wait.

Fortunately, the people in the hamlet did not venture out. They remained unconscious of what he planned for them. All remained quiet except for the occasional barking of a dog.

Finally, the Yankee had the torpedoes buried, covered, and wired to his satisfaction. As soon as he finished, the General ordered the attack. "Remember, them who surrender, do no harm."

Two scarecrows near the General jumped up and began to hack at the base of a large tree. At the same time word went to the Reverend and those hiding near the houses. The sound of breaking glass could be heard as scarecrows began to smash windows. Immediately the lights come on in the houses followed by the sound of gunfire.

The General spoke to those around him, "Foolish ta use lights…. Better ta shoot inta the dark."

As the Reverend and the scarecrows with him drew the fire of those in the houses, the General waited for the sound of the engines. He watched the farmhouses to his left and the road to his right. Still, there were no engines or sirens. He waited.

The Yankee became inpatient. He checked the place they had buried the explosives. He walked from the torpedo to the tree line kicking fresh dirt over the wires. He sat at the end of a trench, checking the wires and the firing device in his hands. He repeatedly stood, scanned down the road, and then sat down again.

The scarecrows up at the house whooped and yelled. They threw sticks and rocks at the farmhouses. Every few minutes, gunfire erupted from one of the houses. Scarecrows grew bold and raced out of the dark, into the light, and back into the dark. The defenders in the houses fired away when this occurred. The game only stopped when a bullet struck one of the scarecrows. It fell to the ground, got back to its feet, and then shambled off to find cover.

The General could see the scarecrow limping away. "Serves the fool right."

They heard the sound of engines, but not the swift engines with the flashing blue and red lights, something much bigger drove down the road towards them, ironclads of the land.

The General saw boxes of steel and glass slowly moving down the road on giant black wheels. The ironclads rolled along the road, high above the ground. It looked like there was nothing that these machines could not drive around or over. He could see gunners in the top turrets of the ironclads. One gunner smoked a cheroot, relaxed, careless, confident.

The General noted that the men in the turrets wore helmets like knights of old, and had strange goggles covering their eyes. They looked as otherworldly as the elongated scarecrows with their canine teeth that hid among the trees.

The Sailor hurried over to the General. "Armored cars and machine guns.... Should we run?"

"Back ta yah place. We fight."

"Ain't cop cars!"

"Stick ta the plan."

The ironclads came around the curve but stopped for a time as their crews considered their next action. Up at the farmhouses, another burst of gunfire, but now the scarecrows with rifles returned fire. More glass shattered in the houses. Windows went dark as lights failed.

The gunners in the ironclads hunkered down behind their guns. The turrets in the ironclads began to turn left and right looking for targets.

One of the gunners heard the chopping sound coming from the trees. He turned his gun towards the sound. The driver began to back the second ironclad down the road. Even before the tree came down, the gunner began to fire short bursts, "Kirk-kirk-kirk…. Kirk-kirk-kirk." The other gunner began to rake the trees where the General and his scarecrows waited, "Kirk-kirk-kirk-kirk-kirk-kirk…. Kirk-kirk-kirk-kirk-kirk-kirk." The guns filled the woods with smoke and sound.

Despite the shooting, the scarecrows with the axes stayed to their work. They skillfully brought the tree down, just behind the second ironclad, almost landing on it. The Sailor and his wolves in the trenches, armed with rifles, now began to fire down into the armored turrets. They tried to rain bullets down on the ironclad's gunners.

The General watched as his scarecrows worked the bolts of their repeaters and bullets pinged off the ironclads. The General enjoyed the speed of their fire. He enjoyed the concussive sounds of the rifles, fast and loud. Only the smell of the gunpowder bothered him, a strong ammonia smell, an unhealthy kind of stink. At least it burned with little flame and without smoke. "Wonderful weapons," he said aloud.

Despite the bullets striking their turrets, both gunners continued to fire up into the trees. "Kirk-kirk-kirk-kirk-kirk-kirk-kirk-kirk-kirk-kirk-kirk-kirk.... Kirk-kirk-kirk-kirk-kirk-kirk.... Kirk-kirk-kirk-kirk-kirk-kirk."

The General signaled to a second group of scarecrows led by the Old Soldier. They huddled behind a collection of boulders at the top of the hill. They pressed down levers and a great rock began to roll forward. It began to pick up speed and bounced down among the trees. The largest rock never made it onto the road. Some smaller rocks bounced up unto the road and struck the first ironclad. The sound of the rocks striking steel sounded like the hammers of giants working in a forge, but the ironclads remained unaffected. They fired an endless stream of bullets into the tree line, "Kirk-kirk-kirk-kirk-kirk-kirk.... Kirk-kirk-kirk-kirk-kirk-kirk.... Kirk-kirk-kirk-kirk-kirk-kirk.... Kirk-kirk-kirk-kirk-kirk-kirk."

The General and his scarecrows, poised to attack, watched the failure of the rock avalanche with disappointment. The scarecrows that started the avalanched scrambled for cover as the gunners began to fire short bursts into their position. One scarecrow had its head neatly removed from its body; head and body followed the rocks and rolled down the hill.

The ironclads stayed in position, stubbornly refusing to move forward towards the torpedoes.

Both gunners continued to use their guns to rake the woods. The rapid-fire of the big bullets fired into the trees struck like cannonballs. Everywhere dirt and tree branches flew up into the air. The fire came unbelievably fast, "Kirk-kirk-kirk-kirk-kirk-kirk-kirk-kirk.... Kirk-kirk-kirk-kirk-kirk-kirk.... Kirk-kirk-kirk-kirk-kirk-kirk.... Kirk-kirk-kirk-kirk-kirk-kirk.... Kirk-kirk-kirk-kirk-kirk-kirk." There was the briefest of pauses as the gunners scanned for targets and then continued, "Kirk-kirk-kirk-kirk-kirk-kirk.... Kirk-kirk-kirk-kirk-kirk-kirk."

The speed of the fire and the concussive sound was like nothing the General had ever heard. The gunners, hunkered down in their turrets, fired up the hill and into the woods with an infinite stream of bullets. Many of the bullets seemed to catch fire in midair and guided the stream with bright light. Underbrush around the trees began to smolder and burn.

Some of the scarecrows, and even some of the wolves, began to panic. They broke from cover and tried to run up the hill to get away from the ironclads. The gunners directed their fire up the hill in pursuit. The General watched as the great bullets from the cannons ripped those in-flight to pieces.

The Old Soldier came to the rescue. He and two others leaped from the trench carrying flaming bottles. They ran forward and threw the bottles at the ironclads. As the bottles struck the first ironclad, flames covered its entire front.

Despite the flames, the rapid-fire from the ironclad turrets only intensified, "Kirk-kirk-kirk-kirk-kirk-kirk-kirk-kirk-kirk-kirk-kirk-kirk.... Kirk-kirk-kirk-kirk-kirk-kirk-kirk-kirk-kirk-kirk-kirk." Both gunners redirected their guns and began to fire down at the road at the running scarecrows. One of the scarecrows, struck by the rapid-fire cannons, fell onto the road. As he tried to pull himself off the road and towards the protection of a tree, both gunners fired at him and his head and arms and torso flew into the air.

The General called out for the Yankee to prepare to fire the torpedoes, but the Yankee was nowhere in sight.

The General looked around but found most of the scarecrows had fled, evidence of their destruction littered the path of their retreat. The General, waving his pistol in one hand and his knife in the other, called out to those remaining, "Charge!" Running forward he climbed up on a boulder that jutted from the hill. He leaned down as far as he could and began to fire into the open hatch of one of the gunners. In response, the gunner abandoned his turret and dropped down inside his ironclad.

The second gunner rotated his turret and began to fire directly at the General, who jumped back behind a tree. The great bullets of the cannon began to chew up the tree he hid behind. Splinters from the tree and fragments of stone flew into the air; fragments struck the General cutting into the leather of his skin like a knife. It seemed the rapid-firing cannon would soon cut the tree down.

The Yankee called over to him. "Can't win—run!"

"Aah didn't come hare ta do no half-way job of it…. Aah intend ta have 'em all."

As soon as the gunner paused to reload his weapon, the General got to his feet. "Forward! Mix with 'em!" he cried out. "Wa-woo-woohoo! Wa-woo-woohoo!" he yelled as he ran down the hill. He fired at the engine turret as he ran. He heard others screaming as they ran towards the ironclads. Midway down, the General stopped yelling. He was embarrassed to realize his "Rebel Yell" sounded less like a yelling devil, and more like a hooting monkey.

At that moment, the Old Soldier and one of his companions charged forward again with more flaming bottles. One of the bottles broke high against the second ironclad and filled the turret with flame. Now the second gunner dropped down into his vehicle.

The General climbed aboard an ironclad. He could see two men behind large glass windows. He fired point-blank at the windows, but the bullets ricocheted off harmlessly. He scrambled up to the gunner's turret. He tried to force the hatch open, but it was sealed shut. He looked over and saw the Old Soldier on top of the other ironclad, but the men inside had closed up tighter than a bank.

The vehicles began to move back and forth in the enclosed space. The General jumped back down and again fired point-blank at the men behind the windows. His bullets bounced off harmlessly, barely marking the glass. He could see the driver of the ironclad frantically turning the wheel and moving mechanisms inside.

The General turned looking for the Yankee. When he saw him on the ridge above, he called out, "Prepare to fire the torpedo. Ready the torpedo."

The Yankee yelled back in response, "Machine guns—g-g-get the machine guns."

Turning back to the ironclads the General understood. When the gunners had sealed themselves into their vehicles, they left their guns still in the turrets. Several of the scarecrows struggled to carry the guns away as the vehicles moved violently forward and back to shake them off.

The General again pointed his pistol at the driver and began to fire. He knew the bullets would not penetrate the glass, but he hoped the ironclad might still roll forward towards the waiting torpedoes. Instead, the ironclad finished turning in the narrow lane and began to roll forward towards the General. The General ran back up the hill and jumped behind a tree. He assumed that the ironclad would not pursue him off the road and up into the scrub, but his assumption proved wrong. It rolled forward over every obstacle relentless as an elephant. One of the scarecrows, wounded earlier and left on the ground, was caught by the ironclad's giant wheels which rolled slowly, forward and back, mashing it into the ground.

The Old Soldier appeared off to the General's left. He had one of the guns, and another scarecrow had two green tins full of the giant bullets. A third scarecrow ran up behind the General trailing two long coils of brass. The remaining gun had been pulled from the other vehicle by the Sailor and two of his wolves.

The ironclad balanced unsteadily as it slowly continued its pursuit. It seemed so unsteadily that the General rushed back and began to push against its side. It was so top-heavy he hoped it might be rolled over. Several other scarecrows joined him, but they could no more move the thing than they could have moved a mountain. All the while the great black wheels turned and thrashed the surrounding shrub and brush.

Now the farmers, sheltered in the nearby houses, began to fire at the General and those around him. One of the scarecrows went down from a bullet, and before he could be pulled away, the great black wheels of the ironclad rolled over him and crushed him into the ground.

The General retreated up the hill just as the Yankee began to call out again. "Helicopters! Helicopters! Run!"

The General stopped and listened. Over the sounds of the ironclads, he could hear the distant sound of the flying gunships. Scarecrows began to scatter in all directions. Adding to the confusion, the farmers began to filter into the woods. They pursued the scarecrows tree to tree as they fired their rifles and shotguns.

The General called out to those around him, "Attack in all directions!"

Scarecrows ran along the road towards the farmers, driving them back. Other scarecrows threw burning bottles against the ironclads.

Suddenly, a soldier popped back up in a turret armed with a black rifle. He began to fire at the scarecrows, "Tat-tat-tat-tat-tat-tat… Tat-tat-tat-tat-tat-tat." The rifle fired rapidly, easily exceeding the speed of the bolt action repeaters that had so impressed the General only a short time before.

The General emptied his pistol at the soldier in the turret but without effect. As he stopped to reload, he could hear the sound of the flying gunships. He looked up and saw them fast approaching through the air.

The General and his remaining scarecrows ran from tree to tree. The rifle fire of the soldier pursued them, "Tat-tat-tat-tat-tat-tat…. Tat-tat-tat-tat…. Tat-Tat-Tat." A scarecrow near the General was hit, but none stopped. They ran up and over the crest of the hill. They ran for the darkest part of the woods, but now the flying gunships circled overhead.

The firing began in earnest into the woods. The gunships flew back and forth, raining shot and shell, "Brrp-brrp-brrp-brrp-brrp-brrp-brrp-brrp." Trees and brush began to smoke. Scarecrows screamed like wounded animals. The firing never paused, "Brrp-brrp-brrp-brrp-brrp-brrp-brrp-brrp-brrp-brrp-brrp."

The General hid behind a tree trying to make himself small. He watched the gunships send streams of cannon shells into the woods. He could see golden bullets bending into the woods like a stream from a water hose. Back and forth the gunships went. Scarecrows near the General slashed at the ground with their knives, frantically trying to tunnel into the earth. None returned fire and it seemed like the attack would never stop. More flying engines approached overhead. They began to fire cannons and rockets into the woods. The air filled with smoke, with flying splinters, with falling branches. Fire, smoke, and dust obscured everything.

The flying engines dodged in and fly out in low circles. They beat the leaves from the trees with their wings as they came in for an attack. Scarecrows lay on the ground trying to find cover behind the trees. Those hit by a burst of gunfire had limbs ripped from their bodies. The gunfire came from the sky. It proved impossible to find a place of safety.

When the gunships were satisfied, they pulled up into the sky and disappeared.

Many scarecrows had been hit. Those struck in the head or heart lay still and unresponsive. Those with lesser wounds moaned and cried out, not from pain, but fear.

The General looked about at the many casualties scattered throughout the woods. Despite the chaos of the fighting, none of the prisoners had been hit. Somehow, even in the dark of night, the machines could recognize the differences between the scarecrows and the prisoners.

The Yankee, the Sailor, the Reverend, and the Old Soldier gathered around the General for an informal council of war.

The Yankee spoke first. "W-w-we must abandon them, an-and head off with j-j-just a few." He waved towards the scattered scarecrows as he spoke.

The Sailor spoke next. "He has a point. The more of them who follow you, the bigger the target. They can bring in more firepower than just those helicopters. They can blow us to pieces any time they want."

The Reverend spoke as smoothly and fluently as the Sailor. "We are weak and disorganized. We need to reach an armistice if we are going to survive."

The General stood and looked at them each in turn. He did not immediately reply but made them wait. He looked at the smoking battlefield and the many wounded scarecrows. Finally, he turned back to them and spoke. "Yah do not see what's plain…. When they come 'gain… we kin be ready."

Now the General told the Sailor and the Reverend what was needed and sent them out. The Sailor took Brown-Green, and some of his wolves, to the south. The Reverend took Green-Black, and the remaining wolves, to the east.

The General noted, that as the Sailor set out, his friend the Cracker followed along. He trailed just behind the last of the wolves, like a friendly dog anticipating scraps.

After they left the General walked among the wounded. He administered to one scarecrow with a broken back. He administered to a second whose arms had been amputated. He administered to a third without legs.

The General ordered that all of the dead be buried; their severed remains buried with them. No words were spoken as a thin layer of earth covered them. Some scarecrows stood by and watched the burials. Other scarecrows showed no interest at all and simply hurried past.

Deck Log – Eighth Day

OPNAV 3100/99 (Rev 7-84) S/N 0107-LF-031-0498		**SHIP'S DECK LOG SHEET**		IF CLASSIFIED STAMP SECURITY MARKING HERE	

USE BLACK INK TO FILL IN THIS LOG

SHIP TYPE	HULL NUMBER*	YEAR	MONTH	ZONE	DAY
D A	AS 09	43	09	C	22 E

USS __CYCLOPS__
AT / PASSAGE FROM __NORFOLK VA__
TO __MUSCAT OMAN__
CLASS / HANDL

POSITON	ZONE	TIME	POSITON	ZONE	TIME	POSITON	ZONE	TIME	LEGEND
0800 L_____ A_____		BY__ BY__	1200 L_____ A_____		BY__ BY__	2000 L_____ A_____		BY_2_ BY_2_	1 - CELESTIAL 2 - ELECTRONIC 3 - VISUAL 4 - DR

TIME	ORDER	CSE	SPEED	DEPTH	RECORD OF EVENTS OF THE DAY
00-04					ASSUMED THE WATCH. STEAMING AS BEFORE. WATCH REPORTS CONDITIONS NORMAL. LIEUTENANT R.S. MERRIAM, USN
03.30					REPORT OF MURDER OF CREW MEMBER ET2 CARROLL, TOOL ISSUE STOREROOM 4-49-4-A
04-08					ASSUMED THE WATCH. STEAMING AS BEFORE. LIEUTENANT T.J. MCKINLEY, USN

REPORT SYMBOL OPNAV 2100-10   IF CLASSIFIED STAMP REVIEW / DECLASSIFICATION DATE HERE   IF CLASSIFIED STAMP SECURITY MARKING HERE

First Platform/Fifth Deck - Forward, Reefers and Emergency Generator

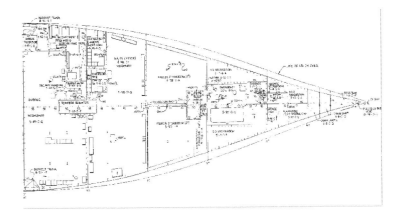

Moral and Philosophical Literature:

The inundation of the Nile cometh, yet no one goeth out to plough. Poor men have gotten costly goods, and the man who was unable to make his own sandals is a possessor of wealth. The hearts of slaves are sad, and the nobles no longer participate in the rejoicings of their people. Men's hearts are violent, there is plague everywhere, blood is in every place, death is common, and the mummy wrappings call to people before they are used. Multitudes are buried in the river, the stream is a tomb, and the place of mummification is a canal. The gentle folk weep, the simple folk are glad, and the people of every town say, 'Come, let us blot out these who have power and possessions among us.' Men resemble the mud-birds, filth is everywhere, and every one is clad in dirty garments. The land spinneth round like the wheel of the potter.

The Literature of the Ancient Egyptians, Leyden, No. 1344, by E. A. Wallis Budge, 1914.

CHAPTER- 22 – SHOOT THEM IN THE HEAD

Monday, Day Eight: Gulf of Aden

Lieutenant Irawell looked forward to the forenoon watch, his favorite watch in many ways. Instead of spending his morning doing paperwork in legal, he would spend it in CIC. He imagined himself stepping out onto one of the bridge wings, looking out over the ocean, and feeling the salt breeze on his face. Letting his paperwork sit unattended in his office seemed a small price to pay. There was only one downside; it gave him plenty of time to attend the morning department head meeting. He was preparing to go to the Captain's conference room when he heard a knock at his door. One of the corpsman told him he was needed again in medical.

Hurrying down the passageway, they met the XO coming from the other direction. The Lieutenant and corpsman braced themselves against the bulkhead. The XO passed by without looking at them or saying anything.

When the Lieutenant reached medical, Crammer and Hardwick were already present. They followed the petty officer to one of the examining rooms. The corpse of ET2 Carroll was laid out on a steel table.

Crammer began to speak, "She belonged to repair. They found her on the third deck. Her berthing space was down there."

The Lieutenant said nothing. He remembered Carroll, an attractive young woman with a soon-to-be ex-husband. The husband preferred drugs and violence to a wife. When she first came to his office for advice on divorce, he wondered how such an attractive and intelligent woman could be connected with such a low-life man. Carroll had bright blue eyes. Now her eyes were dull and dried out.

The Lieutenant turned his attention to Hardwick. "They moved her without calling any of the Master-at-Arms force?"

"They thought it was an emergency. They didn't know what to do, so they carried her to medical."

"Did anyone see what happened?"

The repair officer spoke again, "They found her down there. She never made it to berthing last night."

The Lieutenant stepped forward to the body. He touched her gently on the forehead. The corpse's head rolled to the side. Her throat had been neatly cut.

The corpsman spoke up when she saw the Lieutenant looking at the victim's throat. "The cut was severe enough to go through the trachea."

"Yes, but no tearing, no mauling."

Crammer turned to the corpsman. "Any chance it was an accident or suicide?"

Nowlin responded condescendingly, "Sir, do you think a person could cut their own throat like that? Also, look at the starting cut." The Lieutenant leaned over to examine the wound. He could see what looked like the white bone of the spine. Nowlin continued, "Looks like the cut starts on the right-hand side. I'm pretty sure that Carroll was right-handed."

Hardwick experimentally drew a finger across her throat. "I suppose it's easier to go left to right than right to left. She's also got bruises on her shoulders and arms."

Now Nowlin pulled the sheet down exposing Carroll's breasts and arms. "Somebody held her down while they cut."

The Lieutenant spoke up, "I don't suppose we have the murder weapon?"

Crammer provided the answer. "They looked for a knife or a razor but didn't find anything."

Hardwick added her thoughts, "You don't kill yourself and get rid of the murder weapon. Also, I think the body was moved."

The Lieutenant turned to Hardwick. "Why do you think the body was moved?"

"Not enough blood. There was some blood on her uniform, but there should have been a pool of blood where she bled out. No pool of blood, no knife, no razor."

The Lieutenant was still looking at the corpse when Hardwick asked a question. "What do you want done with the body?"

The Lieutenant took a moment before responding. "Photograph her, take the biometrics and take fingerprints; then take the body down to the reefers and store her with the rest. Seal up the space where the body was found."

The Lieutenant arrived in the Captain's conference room just as the other department heads were finding their places. When the XO was satisfied he had a quorum, he opened the meeting. "Weps, how are we doing with security?"

Powers responded matter-of-factly, "Sir, we've had armed patrols throughout the ship since the day this started. We've searched the ship, every compartment, every storage space. They may be hiding in areas inaccessible ta the rest of us."

The XO's answered incredulously, "What do you mean inaccessible? If they can get there, we can get there."

Powers continued in the same matter of fact tone, "Listening ta the news, these things may have an advantage over us."

"How so?"

"They don't need ta breathe."

Montgomery spoke up, "Sir, I've got a lot of folks who won't go below third deck already."

Powers did not wait for the XO to respond, "Aah think we kin provide security fo-wah the mess cranks when they need ta go below ta break out some hotdogs an' hamburgers." This caused a chuckle to go round the room.

The XO turned to Montgomery. "If we were to close up the hold, how would that affect supply?"

"There are a lot of supplies that we don't need for our day to day operations. I expect we could shift a lot of the stuff we'll need, as long as it's safe for the working parties."

Lamb objected, "That won't work for Engineering."

Powers joined in, "Same for us. We need access ta the hold as well."

The XO nodded his head. "Okay, we can't seal up the hold, but we can certainly seal up a lot of the storage areas and the bilge and ballast areas."

The XO now turned to Crammer, "How is repair doing with setting up motion alarms on the lower decks?"

The Lieutenant could see that Crammer had a spreadsheet with data on specific spaces and alarm types and dates and times. He had readied for a specific question but provided only a general response. "We've got portions of the first and second platforms set up, but for audio alarms only. We are in the process of setting up alarms on Fourth Deck and in the hold."

The XO turned back to Montgomery. "Can we close the berthing area on fourth deck and find places for the crew in berthing on the upper decks?"

"Yes sir, there should be sufficient space."

"Let's do it then."

The XO looked out across the conference table at all of the officers. "We can limit egress below third deck. Have most of the hatches and scuttles below the third deck dogged down and secured; weld 'em shut if you have to. Padlock or seal up any storage areas, lockers, fan rooms, or any other space that we don't need open for regular operations or inspection. Nobody goes below third deck unless they're armed."

Several officers began to protest. The XO ignored them and continued to speak, "We'll have two open hatches, below third deck, one aft and one forward. There will be an armed guard on each ladder."

The XO held up his hand for silence as the protests began, "Yes, I know. Inconvenient, pain in the ass, unworkable. But it is workable. We need to keep the killers off the upper decks and we need to free up manpower for security."

The XO suddenly changed the subject. He held up a few sheets of paper and looked at each of the officers in the conference room. "Big Navy sent out word on how to deal with zombies. Those who die, including natural causes, should be cremated. If cremation is not practical, they should be decapitated, the head stored separately from the body. Alternatively, their hearts should be removed from their body. Those who reanimate can be neutralized by a gunshot to the head."

The XO again paused and looked around the table for dramatic effect. "Don't talk to them, don't negotiate with them, just shoot them in the head."

Powers spoke up, "They're about a day late and a dollar short on that one."

The XO turned and faced the Lieutenant. "I want those bodies in storage taken care of." The XO passed the message to the Lieutenant as he spoke.

The Lieutenant quickly glanced over the message before he responded. "Don't you think ship's security should take care of this?" The Lieutenant realized as soon as the words left his mouth that he sounded whiny.

"You take care of this."

Now the Lieutenant grew angry, "I'll neutralize them, but I'm not decapitating anyone."

"Lieutenant, when I said you to figure it out, I meant for you to figure it out. Get back to me when the job's finished."

Before the Lieutenant could make any reply, the XO turned to Doc Peters. "We are also supposed to quarantine any of our people who are scratched or bitten or wounded by the 'reanimated.' "

"Sir, how long are we supposed to quarantine them?"

"Don't know; it doesn't say."

As the meeting broke up and the officers began to leave, the Lieutenant turned to the admin officer, "Ensign Jett, have we heard from casualty affairs? When can we get the bodies flown off?"

Jett responded with a shrug and by turning his empty hands towards the Lieutenant. "Don't look at me."

After the forenoon watch, the Lieutenant went down to legal, and there was Acedian playing on the computer. He gave him an order as soon as he stepped into the office, "Go to repair and get me six wooden stakes and a hammer."

"You going vampire hunting?"

"Maybe. Get me the stakes immediately. Then meet me back here so that we can go down to the armory."

As soon as Acedian left, the Lieutenant called for Hardwick. She arrived outside of his office in a matter of minutes.

"Lieutenant, we moved the bodies from medical down the reefers like you said."

"Yea, I know. We need to go down there and take care of them."

"But Lieutenant, that's the problem."

The Lieutenant waited for Hardwick to finish. She leaned forward conspiratorially, "We're missing some bodies."

"Okay, were missing some bodies. What does that mean exactly?"

"Sir, I was present when we brought down the two from the fan room and I know exactly where they were stored. I'm not sure where they put the others. This morning we brought Carroll down. I looked around, but I couldn't see where the others were taken."

"Did somebody in supply move them? They didn't like us using their reefers."

"Lieutenant, there should be six bodies down there. Now there's only one."

"Supply must have moved them to one of the other storerooms, or some other chill space."

"Lieutenant, the word is that dead people don't stay dead anymore. Everyone knows.... Everyone knows there are zombies onboard."

As soon as Acedian returned with the wooden stakes, they headed down to the armory on the fourth deck.

The gunner's mate on duty would not issue any weapons. He made a phone call to his boss and Powers arrived shortly thereafter. When the Lieutenant asked to be issued a pistol, Powers looked at him as if he was demanding the surrender of one of his children. After a moment, he stepped inside the armory leaving the Lieutenant, Acedian, and Hardwick standing outside in the passageway.

Powers returned with a holstered pistol. He pulled back the slide to make sure it was not loaded. He wrote down a serial number and then made a quick check of the pistol's functionality by pulling the slide forward and letting it spring back.

Before he handed over the handgun he spoke again, "Yah got yah quals done?"

"No, but I used to own two pistols. I am very familiar with firearms."

"If yah 'ave not got yah quals done, yah of all people already know the answer. Not ta worry though, we're running training up on ta helo deck, then we'll get yah a weapon."

"Okay, so you'll go down into storage and shoot those bodies in the head. If I can't do it, one of your guys will help with that, right?"

The weapons officer said nothing in response. He gestured to one of the gunner's mates. In a moment the petty officer stepped out of the armory space with a semi-automatic pistol and began an abbreviated lecture. "This is an M9. It fires nine-millimeter, Para Bellum." He turned the pistol and pointed towards a switch. "This is the safety." He pulled the slide back and let it slam shut. "This is how you load it. Do not point it at anybody you do not want to shoot, even if you're sure it is unloaded. This is the magazine button. Do not hit it unless you want to drop your magazine." He pushed the pistol, one magazine, and some bullets towards the Lieutenant. "You have ten rounds. The magazine will hold fifteen rounds."

After the gunner's mate handed over the pistol, he read the serial number from the pistol aloud while the Lieutenant checked. He then had the Lieutenant sign a logbook.

The Lieutenant had one last question before he left. "Only ten rounds? Don't I get another magazine and more bullets?"

Powers responded, "Yah have ten bullets. Ho-wah many zombies you 'al plannen on shootin'? As soon as you peg the corpses, aah want the pistol back, understood."

The Lieutenant, Acedian, and Hardwick left the armory and climbed down to the first platform and then forward to the reefers.

Acedian complained as they walked. "We shouldn't be doing this. The weapons department should, or we should just throw the bodies overboard. You should tell the XO we're staff officers and shouldn't be doing this."

The Lieutenant made no response to Acadian's commentary.

Acedian tried a new tack. "XO makes it no secret what he thinks of you."

The Lieutenant merely shrugged his shoulders.

Acedian continued, "I overheard him telling the master chief that you weren't worth a shit."

The Lieutenant stopped and turned on Acedian. He leaned forward and spoke quietly and slowly. "Is there some reason I shouldn't treat your last remark as extremely disrespectful?"

Acedian backed up a step looking from the Lieutenant to Hardwick. "Not me, the XO. No disrespect, I just thought you should know the XO dislikes you."

Lieutenant continued in the same tone of voice. "Because you thought I was too stupid to make that observation on my own."

Acedian began to make apologies, but the Lieutenant ignored him and walked ahead. Acedian only quieted when they came around to the next passageway. Much of this area was dark, lit only by the battle lanterns. There was glass on the deck that crunched underfoot. The Lieutenant gave Acedian a little push towards the reefers just ahead.

Acedian moved forward into the storage area and pulled open one of the refrigerator doors. He began to flip a wall switch up and down, but the space remained dark "Fuck—"

The Lieutenant pushed Acedian aside. He used his watch-standing flashlight to look around the space. The red light played out on shelves and pallets and tables. On the nearest table, he could see a single body bag.

As the Lieutenant continued to point his flashlight around the storage space, Acedian lowered his voice and spoke nervously. "I helped bring Mulvey down here myself. He was right there. He was right on that table in a body bag."

Hardwick now spoke. "That's where we put Carroll. I'm sure this is where Patnaude and Wise were brought. There is only one body bag. There should be six."

"Someone must have moved them. They've got to be in one of the other reefers. We'd smell the stink otherwise."

Acedian backed out into the passageway. "They've gone full zombie."

"What zombie takes his body bag with him? They've moved the bodies, that's all."

Acedian continued to look around. "Maybe they take their body bags the way vampires carry around their coffins. That makes sense. They don't come out except at night. That explains the blood. You can't kill them unless you remove their hearts. If you shoot a zombie in the head, they're dead; if you shoot a vampire in the head they don't care. You kill vampires by destroying their hearts."

Lieutenant continued to point his flashlight around the space. "Maybe we're just in the wrong storage area. The simplest explanation is usually correct."

"Maybe somebody's stealing the bodies."

"Who'd steal a body?"

"Maybe there's a zombie stowaway onboard. He's not only killing them, he's eating them."

"You're telling me a zombie ate those bodies? That's one hell of an appetite."

"I guess you're right. Zombies don't eat the dead. They only attack the living."

"Who says that? You been reading 'The Great Big Book of Zombies?' Maybe the 'Idiot's Guide to Zombieland?' "

Acedian made no response. The Lieutenant began to give directions, "Okay, let's get this over with. You hold the flashlight."

"Maybe we should just leave. They can get a repair party in here and fix the lights. Then they can look for the rest of the bodies."

"Just hold the flashlight."

Acedian stayed behind holding the reefer door open. He shone the flashlight into the darkened space. Even with the light from the flashlight, the Lieutenant stumbled as he moved about. He went up to the table holding the body and unzipped the body bag. As he did so, the head of the corpse fell back exposing a bright red slash across the throat. He could see her eyes half-open, sunken, and recessed. Thankfully, they did not reflect as Acedian played the red light across her face. The bright blue of her eyes was gone.

"It's Carroll."

The Lieutenant raised his pistol. The red light of the flashlight danced about the refrigerated storage space as he readied the weapon. He pulled the slide back and let it slam home loading the first round. He placed the muzzle of his pistol against the left side of Carroll's head and pulled the trigger.

The Lieutenant began to curse, "God damn it. God damn it." He placed his hand to the side of his head and began to shake like a swimmer clearing water from an ear.

Acedian and Hardwick had already backed into the passageway. Acedian had the pinky of his right hand to his ear. "Christ, I didn't know it was going to be that loud." He looked back into the reefer space. "Christ almighty Lieutenant, look at the mess you made."

"How else was I supposed to do it?"

"We should have frozen the body, or better yet taken it out to the fantail."

"We're not done yet. Your turn."

"My turn for what?"

"Hammer one of the stakes through her heart."

Acedian began to shake his head back and forth, "No sir, no sir, not going to do that."

"It's got to be done. You said it yourself, if they're vampires, we have to destroy their hearts."

Acedian just continued to shake his head, "No sir, no, not going to do it."

The Lieutenant looked over at Hardwick. She looked away, showing no inclination to volunteer.

The Lieutenant took the hammer and one of the stakes from Acedian. He stepped back into the storage space. He pulled the body bag open to the corpse's waist. He pulled open her shirt and exposed her breasts. He looked down at her left breast, looking for a place to drive the stake. He stood holding the wooden stake, the hammer in the air. The hammer rose and fell driving the stake down into her heart. He turned and walked back out of the space.

When the Lieutenant stepped out of the reefer, Acedian began to look around at the other storage lockers. He tried opening two different doors. The first door was locked. The other door led into a fan room, unlocked and unoccupied.

The Lieutenant interrupted his search. "We need to get the corpsman down here and find out where they stowed those bodies."

Acedian ignored him and continued to try different doors. Hardwick stopped him with a harsh whisper, "Listen, somebody else is here."

Acedian stopped his movements and looked up and down the passageway. "I don't hear anything except for my ears ringing."

The Lieutenant signaled for Acedian to be quiet. He looked down the passageway but could not see anyone. At the far end of the passageway, the overhead lights had been broken. Even the battle lanterns were dark.

Acedian went to open another door and Hardwick called out preemptively, "Stop doing that ... sir."

Now even Acedian stopped to listen. The Lieutenant held his breath. It was there in the dark, the sound of broken glass being moved by shuffling feet. The Lieutenant whispered for Acedian to shine the flashlight down the passageway. At first, the light could not penetrate the gloom, but then for a split second, it reflected off a face which immediately pulled back into the darkness.

"Who's there? Who the fuck is there?" Acedian called out. The figure had already disappeared.

Now the Lieutenant spoke up, "Is that you Commander? Is that you Commander Alschbach?" The Lieutenant pointed his pistol into the darkness as he spoke. Acedian pushed passed him as he backed up quickly for the nearest ladder. Hardwick stayed with the Lieutenant until he gestured for her to retreat as well. The Lieutenant followed close behind still pointing the pistol down the passageway.

When they finished with the reefers, they returned to the legal office on the second deck. The Lieutenant told Acedian to call the weapons department to make a report. He listened as Acedian talked to someone and provided the basic details of what they had seen near the reefers. Then the Lieutenant took the phone to call up to the XO's office. Happily his phone call went unanswered.

The Lieutenant had the second dog watch as his last duty in a long day. Rather than go back to his office after dinner, he helped himself to a drink from the soda fountain and went into the lounge.

Miller and Unger were sitting in front of the television. They each acknowledged the Lieutenant as he came in with a wave of their hands. The Lieutenant was not surprised to see Acedian also relaxing in the lounge. He acknowledged the Lieutenant with a nod of his head.

Acedian had the television remote and was cycling through channels. A news story came on about an attack on the crew of a container ship anchored at Hampton roads. A video played of a news reporter standing on a dock in the late twilight. He spoke hurriedly into a microphone.

"The Coast guard rescued tonight a sailor forced to jump overboard from his ship after zombies climbed up the anchor chain and attacked the crew. The Coast Guard has boarded the ship and found nine dead bodies onboard."

The Lieutenant spoke aloud as the story played. "Where is the rest of the crew? Those things carry thirty to forty crew members."

Acedian had some prior knowledge of the news story. "They were unloaded. They may have been waiting for a new cargo. If they're waiting for cargo, most of the crew was probably ashore."

The Lieutenant grew immediately suspicious. "More likely the bastard was high on booze or drugs and murdered his shipmates. Easy to blame it on a zombie."

Acedian disagreed. "There could have been a zombie onboard. Those ships are gigantic."

The video had switched to a view of a man standing on a dock. The sailor stood wrapped with a blanket as he tried to explain to the reporter what had occurred.

"The bos'n was the one who brought him onboard. He saw him and still let him come aboard."

"Can you describe who you are talking about?"

"The floater, in the water. He was clinging to the anchor chain. He was like a burn victim."

"He's a burn victim?" the reporter asked.

"Like no burn I've ever seen. It was black and his skin was stretched over the bone. It was enough to make you puke."

The reporter continued to seek clarification, "Was he burned, like some sort of chemical burn?"

"I don't know. Something was really wrong with him, not chemicals. He came up the anchor chain. He waited until we got him up on deck, then he attacked. We couldn't hold him. He was like a rabid dog."

"Was he a sailor from some other ship? If he was dangerous, why did you bring him on the ship?"

The man being interviewed looked surprised by the question. "It wasn't me. Bos'n found him hanging from the anchor chain. He was climbing the anchor chain. When I saw him he was naked. I thought he was dying. He looked like he came out of a concentration camp. When they went to lift him, it was disgusting. He looked drowned."

Here the man being interviewed paused. He looked around and spoke conspiratorially. "He looked like a drowned man, except for the eyes. The eyes looked like drugs to me."

Acedian now turned from the newscast, a tone of disgust in his voice. "He was not a burn victim. He was something else. Something was happening in port and they were stupid enough to let this thing onboard."

When the report came to an end, Acedian looked around the lounge for confirmation. "You see it now don't you?"

The Lieutenant only shook his head. Acedian argued his point forcefully. "It wasn't Mulvey. It was never Mulvey or Asper. One of those things climbed aboard in Port Said."

Isaiah 57:7-14 KJV:

Upon a lofty and high mountain hast thou set thy bed: even thither wentest thou up to offer sacrifice. Behind the doors also and the posts hast thou set up thy remembrance: for thou hast discovered thyself to another than me, and art gone up; thou hast enlarged thy bed, and made thee a covenant with them; thou lovedst their bed where thou sawest it. And thou wentest to the king with ointment, and didst increase thy perfumes, and didst send thy messengers far off, and didst debase thyself even unto hell. Thou art wearied in the greatness of thy way; yet saidst thou not, There is no hope: thou hast found the life of thine hand; therefore thou wast not grieved. And of whom hast thou been afraid or feared, that thou hast lied, and hast not remembered me, nor laid it to thy heart? have not I held my peace even of old, and thou fearest me not? I will declare thy righteousness, and thy works; for they shall not profit thee. When thou criest, let thy companies deliver thee; but the wind shall carry them all away; vanity shall take them: but he that putteth his trust in me shall possess the land, and shall inherit my holy mountain; And shall say, Cast ye up, cast ye up, prepare the way, take up the stumbling block out of the way of my people.

CHAPTER-23 – AVARHOUSE'S GUN

Monday, Day Eight: Navy Yard

He is retreating through the cave. He has broken free, relief washes over him. He looks down and sees he is no longer carrying the flashlight, now there is a pistol is in his hand.

The thing in the further cavern is also free. It follows him through the cave, careful to stay in the darkness. He can see the entrance to the cave, a patch of light showing him the way out. He hurries towards the entrance. He heads to the light. The thing is following but keeps out of sight. It is allowing him to go. He can see the light, brighter now. He turns his back on the thing following him and bolts for the entrance. He dives into the narrow opening, but it is not the entrance to the cave. It is his flashlight shining against the furthest wall.

At first light, Captain Pride reluctantly prepared to meet the day. The pattern of nightmares was costing him sleep, and fatigue was wearing him down. He got ready to go to work in a mechanical way. Everything that he did, he did without thinking.

Leaving his house, he walked up the street in a cold and drizzling rain. Earlier in the week, he thought these walks refreshing, now he discovered a strong dislike of these trips to the subway. He did not look forward to arriving at the office. Mondays always tended to be busy, but he expected this particular Monday to be particularly bad. The many pending tasks guaranteed multiple exercises in frustration. For a start, he needed to call the police yet again to see if they found Anna's car, and he needed to make the necessary appointments to get his car fixed.

The Captain arrived at work and found only Invidia and Gula in the office. None of his other junior officers had arrived. All others remained siphoned off by headquarters. Meanwhile, the phones rang off the hook.

Instead of working the phones, Invidia watched the conference room television. He turned and spoke as the Captain walked in, "They lied when they said all the children are missing. Many may be missing, but a lot are not. They've been interviewing these kids all morning. They found some seven-year-olds. Little bastards can barely form intelligible sentences, but now they're celebrities."

The Captain interrupted to ask his question. "Tell me when we are getting our Lieutenants back?"

"No time soon. Word is that they're going to make some of them federal magistrates. Can you imagine? Most of them are still wet behind the ears. Couldn't tell the difference between a writ of mandamus and a restraining order if it bit them in the ass. Now they're going to be made federal magistrates. And here I am, doing powers of attorney and wills for sailors whose entire worldly estate wouldn't fill a single backpack."

Invidia stopped talking only when the Captain walked away.

The first call that the Captain took that morning came from one of the local commands. Their legal officer called for advice on how to deal with the missing. He particularly wanted to know if they should report them as casualties.

"Are the missing to be listed as MIA, KIA, some other status?"

"I have not seen any official declaration yet. I think we report them as missing in action until word comes down from the Pentagon."

"So, we're supposed to send out a casualty assistance officer to the families and set up benefits?"

"I think that's the safest course of action."

"What if the casualty assistance officer is one of the missing?"

"You assign an officer and follow the regs."

"What if they're a deserter? What about these new regs on deserters?"

"How do you know they aren't one of the missing?"

"He came to work but now won't show up. The message traffic says deserters are going to get rounded up for these punishment battalions. If I write him up for UA, are they going to take him for these punishment battalions? I don't want to lose 'em."

"I'm really not sure what these new regs are. Maybe you should call BuPers."

Later, when the Captain went down to check on Gula in legal assistance, a number of sailors stood by waiting to be helped. Leaving command advice to Invidia, the Captain stepped in to help Gula with the backlog.

The first sailor had a simple question. His landlord was missing. Did he still have to pay rent? The simple answer, yes; he should put the check in the mail. If he was concerned about proof of payments, send it registered mail. Sooner or later, someone would step in and start managing the property and collecting rent, past due, or otherwise.

The next request for help came from a dependent husband whose wife had gone missing.

"How do you know she is among the missing?"

"I called her command and nobody has seen her?"

"Did she ever come home?"

"We haven't been living together for months, but I still want my benefits."

The third client had a similar problem. He had just divorced his 'cheating' wife. He had signed a property settlement agreement as part of the divorce. She got the house and part of his pension. "How do I get a redo?"

The Captain felt obliged to skip lunch as sailors and their dependents continued to come into the office.

In the early afternoon, Invidia came to find him. "That question about the missing casualty affairs officer you passed to me, well they found him and sent him to Quantico for pretrial confinement."

"Pretrial confinement, for a UA? They've started speedy trial. He can't possibly be dangerous."

"They didn't order it. Their Admiral ordered it."

"Why would an Admiral get involved with a UA?"

"It's definite; they're rounding up all the UAs and sending them to Quantico. The rumors about the punishment battalions are true."

"Are they doing that without a trial?"

"I guess it's in lieu of court-martial. Maybe they get to choose."

Throughout the afternoon sailors continued to pile up in the legal assistance waiting room. Finally, the Captain had enough. He went to his office and called OJAG.

"When will my Lieutenants be coming back?" He knew that the tone of his voice was impatient, but he could barely reign in his frustration.

"Not till the present emergency is over, sir."

"Let me talk to the Admiral."

"Sorry Captain, the Admiral's over at the Pentagon. We don't expect her back today."

"My question is real simple, when will my officers be returned? We're swamped here. They're doing no-good hanging around headquarters learning about flying court-martials that may never happen. There's no demonstrated need for such things, certainly no indication that the Navy's going to be policing civilians. There's a need here and now to help the regional commands and to help sailors sort out problems with their families."

As the Captain vented his frustration he could hear a new voice in the background. "Tell him a new age requires new rules."

"Who is that speaking?"

"I'm sorry sir, just someone passing by. I will let the Admiral know of your concerns."

With that, the connection was cut.

The sun was just going down as the Captain headed home. He left the office with tasks unfinished, emails unanswered, and commands with legal questions waiting for follow up; but there were limits to the hours of the day. He also wanted to be on his way before the streets became well and truly dark.

Getting off the subway, the Captain hurried down the street towards home. He could see other pedestrians hurrying along as well. It seemed that people were starting to take the new rules about curfew seriously.

When he approached his house, he could see a police car and ambulance parked outside of the Delaney's. Delaney himself lay on a stretcher waiting.

The Captain went up to the Delaney's door and looked into the home. At the front door, he could see Mrs. Delaney with a policeman. Mrs. Delaney was crying, "We don't have any drugs here."

The policeman held up a plastic prescription bottle, "What's this then?"

"That's my husband's medicine. He had surgery recently."

"Ma'am, this is oxy and a lot of it. Nobody's supposed to have this much oxy."

"My husband's doctor prescribed that. Please, we have to get my husband to the hospital."

The ambulance team stood around on the Delaney's stoop doing nothing. They stood by the stretcher but took no action to move Delaney into the ambulance. They were not taking vital signs. They kept looking to the policeman for directions.

The Captain hurried up to the stoop, "What the hell are you guys doing? Why are you standing around?"

This caused the cop to look up, "Are you family?"

"No, I'm the neighbor."

"What are you doing here?" the policeman asked.

"What's the holdup? If the man needs medical treatment, what are you waiting on?"

"Sir, this is police business. If you are not family, you need to leave."

"I'll leave when you get him in the ambulance."

"Listen, this is police business, don't interfere."

The Captain pushed past and went over to check on Delaney. He spoke to him quietly, "Mr. Delaney? Mr. Delaney?" Delaney gave no sign of recognition; he did not look up; he did not speak. He continued to lean back on the stretcher, his head hanging to one side pressed against his shoulder. He breathed rapidly, a kind of panting.

The Captain turned towards the policeman. "What's the holdup? You can see he's sick."

Mrs. Delaney looked up at the Captain with tears in her eyes, "They think we have drugs. They think we have been taking drugs."

"For God's sake, what is wrong with you people? Get him to the hospital."

The policeman, now with some heat, "Buddy, I'm telling you for the last time, this is police business and you're interfering."

The Captain stood straight up for a moment stepped towards the policeman who jumped back and put his hand on his holster. The Captain leaned all of his bulk slowly forward, his hand to his sides. He spoke slowly and softly, "Get this man on his way to the hospital, or I'll be helping with the wrongful death action against you personally and the city in general. As I'm the only lawyer present, I think it's safe to say, your job won't be worth a shit once the word gets out that you denied an old man medical treatment because you wanted to search for oxy."

Another policeman stepped up and took the first officer aside. At last, the policeman signaled to the ambulance drivers. The drivers quickly moved Mr. Delaney into the ambulance.

Mrs. Delaney made to follow. The first policeman intercepted her. "Lady, I need you to stay. We're not done yet."

The Captain stepped up beside Mrs. Delaney. "Are you arresting her?"

"No, but I need to finish my investigation."

The Captain turned to Mrs. Delaney. "You go in the ambulance. You call me when you need to be picked up." He turned and looked at the policeman, "I'll stay here and help the officers."

As Mrs. Delaney left with the ambulance, the police entered her home. The Captain followed. The two policemen went straight to Delaney's library where the hospital bed and table full of medicines sat.

The first policeman again held up the prescription bottle. "Can't leave this here. Do they have any morphine in the house?"

The Captain kept his voice calm and professional as he responded, "I don't know, but I do know you can't take the man's medicine. He'll need that when he returns home."

"What makes you think he's ever coming back?"

The other officer interjected in a conciliatory way. "We can't leave it here. It will be at the station."

It took the police about an hour to finished looking through the Delaney's cabinets and drawers. They took at least three bottles of prescription pain killers with them. They did not identify the drugs they had seized, nor did they leave any sort of written inventory. In response to the Captain's question, who did the Delaneys need to see to get their medicines back; they provided only the vaguest of answers.

As soon as the police left, the Captain began to look around the house. He found what he was looking for in the kitchen, a set of car keys. Outside, he located the Delaneys' car and drove it to the hospital.

The Captain made his way through an emergency room swarming with medical staff, policemen, and people in pain. One man screamed so loudly, it seemed like his voice would shatter glass. Two policemen and a doctor ran into the space, but the screaming grew only more intense. The Captain moved quickly past the room without looking inside. In a back corner of the ER, he found Mrs. Delaney. She sat in a chair next to her husband's cot. They waited in an exam bay with only a curtain to provide privacy. Delaney lay in the cot still unresponsive. His lips were blue; he struggled for breath.

The Captain gave Mrs. Delaney her car keys and asked what the doctors had to say. She could only shake her head. The doctors had not yet been in to talk to her. The Captain found a chair and sat down next to Mrs. Delaney. He considered saying something comforting but could think of no appropriate remarks. When a nurse came in to say the doctors were still deciding on whether to admit Delaney and transfer him to a room, the Captain took this as an opportunity to make his excuses and leave. He did not want to spend the night in the ER or the hospital.

The Captain stood up to go and offered his hand to Mrs. Delaney. She took his hand and spoke directly, "They won't let me bury him. They say he has to be burned. He has to burn with the others. No wake, no funeral, no honor guard at Arlington." She paused for a moment before continuing, "I suppose it doesn't matter. There's no one left to come to his funeral."

Telling Mrs. Delaney to call him if she needed anything, The Captain left. Privately he hoped she would find no reason to call. He left her alone in the hospital cubical. He did take a moment and ask one of the nurses when the decision would be made on admitting Delaney. The nurses still had no answer. They were too busy rushing about taking care of the living.

The Captain made his way out of the hospital only to become lost in a labyrinth of corridors. Somehow, he got turned around, and instead of going to the front of the building, he ended up in a back parking lot. He had to walk the length of several buildings before he could return to the entranceway. He could smell smoke in the air as he walked. He looked back towards a slight hill that rose behind the hospital. He could see sparks and flames rising into the air at the top of the hill. He could smell burning fuel and something else. The smell reminded him of the burn pits of Afghanistan.

The Captain waited outside of the hospital but saw no taxis. He tried calling a car-sharing service. The software app told him a car would arrive in fifteen minutes; he waited over an hour and the car never showed. His daughters swore by the reliability of these car services. Some reliability, he decided he would never use such a service again.

In the end, he made a call to Avarhouse. When Avarhouse arrived, the Captain could see boxes of MREs in the back seat. The car also stunk of fuel.

"Isaac, what the hell is that smell."

"I've got twenty gallons of diesel in the trunk."

"What are you doing driving around with diesel fuel? This car doesn't use diesel."

Avarhouse answered with a smile, "This stuff is for plan B."

"Plan B? What's plan A?

"You know my place in Winchester?"

The Captain nodded. It had been several years since he had been there. His daughters loved to pick the apples, and they liked Avarhouse. They tried to make a party of it several times, but Anna never felt comfortable with Avarhouse. After the children had grown uninterested in picking apples, Anna had simply refused to go. After several invitations refused over the years, Avarhouse had stopped asking the Prides to visit.

"I've been shifting goods to the farm. I've got all sorts of useful things there, apple trees, cider press, corn, cabbage, lettuce. There's even trout in the stream. I've got a diesel generator. I've got a 500-gallon tank which I'm getting filled. I've even got solar. Soon I'll be able to go completely off the grid.

"And what's plan B."

"This stuff's for plan B. I'm going to store it on the boat. If I need to get out of town and the highways are closed down, the boat's the backup plan."

The Captain seemed unconvinced. "Where do you think you'll get to in the boat? When things hit the fan there won't be any marinas open. There will be nowhere to get gas or food from here to Key West. I hope you really like drifting around eating raw fish."

Avarhouse scuffed at the Captain's objections. "At least those things won't be able to get me."

"You're assuming they don't know how to swim."

"I'll take my chances."

The Captain ended the argument on a conciliatory note, "I guess you've got everything covered."

Avarhouse nodded up and down, pleased to see his sagaciousness was appreciated. "When the shit hits the fan, I'm heading to Winchester. Don't worry though. When everything goes down, you're in; just don't take off with the sailboat without letting me know, just in case."

Avarhouse now pointed to the glove compartment. "Look in there."

The Captain opened the compartment and saw a black leather military holster. He picked up the holster. It held a pistol and a second magazine in a side pocket. He pushed back the leather flap, and then slowly pulled out the pistol.

"Don't hold it up where someone might be able to see it," Avarhouse said with exasperation.

Now the Captain was genuinely interested. "Where did you get it?"

Avarhouse became gleeful, "I got it as a retainer. Look at it. Look closer."

The Captain examined the weapon. He could see matching serial numbers on the barrel and the receiver. He ejected the magazine. The pistol and the magazine shared the same serial number. The magazine was fully loaded. He could feel the pressure of the spring pushing against the bullets. He pointed the pistol towards the bottom of the car and partially pulled back the slide. No round had been chambered.

"Do you see it yet?" asked Avarhouse.

The Captain examined the pistol more thoroughly. He saw the proof marks near the serial numbers. He could make out 1944, and stamps in different places of a bird, its wings spread, not so much the image of an eagle as a vulture. In its talons it held a swastika.

"Do you see it," said Avarhouse gleefully. "Swastikas, that's genuine World War Two, Nazi. That's the real deal. My client's grandpa brought it back from the war. Not even import marks. He brought me a Luger and a Mauser rifle as a retainer, all bring-backs from the war. Look closer, see those lightning bolts? You know what that means don't you?"

The Captain shook his head.

"Those are SS marks, concentration camp," said Avarhouse. "That's where the SS had their weapons made. There's blood on that for sure; museum stuff, mint condition. Anyway, the guy didn't know what he had, but he did know the stuff had never been registered and never licensed. I explained the 'difficulties' of getting a late registration and the criminal implications. The guy walked away from it when he couldn't keep up with his bill."

The Captain held the pistol like it contained an electric charge. He wiped it down with his handkerchief and put it back into the glove compartment. "Isaac, I can't believe you're carrying that around."

"Don't worry, I've got papers. I've got a license. I had to trade the Mauser though. One of the court clerks helped me with my paper work, including the notary block for the registration. Instead of 1944 Luger, the papers say 1914, ipso facto, all registered, all legal in accordance with the new 'curio and relic' rules. Of course, I had to also help him document his brand-new Mauser rifle. Brand new to him that is. He then walked my license up to one of the Judges. He also walked through my concealed carry based on need. That part's actually legit. Seems some folks had been making threats against me."

"Unhappy clients?" asked the Captain.

"Unhappy partners," responded Avarhouse.

Avarhouse continued, "Anyway, I need a pistol on the boat. I would rather not leave it there, but I just don't have a better place right now. You're welcome to keep it in your house if you want."

The Captain shook his head as he responded. "Unlicensed, unregistered, I don't think anyone looking too closely is going to be fooled by your paperwork. No thank you."

"Don't worry. Nobody's going to give a crap about that anymore."

It did not take long to shift the supplies to the boat, but it was still late when Avarhouse left. The Captain sat down in his chair. He thought about turning on the television to watch the news but then thought better of it. He knew he needed to get some sleep or tomorrow would be hell.

He closed his eyes and lay still. He could not keep his mind from wandering, touching on things he did not wish to think about. He concentrated on trying to sleep, but the more he wanted it, the harder it was to find.

He sought a distraction, something to end his restlessness so that he might get to sleep. He thought about Avarhouse's sailboat; rather than relaxing him, he began to wonder if others had seen them loading the supplies. After a time, he got up from his chair and looked out to the dock where the boat was tied up.

With children, college funds, and a mortgage on a waterfront property, the Captain could never have afforded such a boat. Avarhouse had little interest in actually going sailing. He kept the boat as a prestige item, something to show a client or a potential new girlfriend. The Captain, however, rarely missed a chance to get underway.

Depending on the tide, the Captain and his family would sail or motor down the river. It always thrilled him to sail past Mount Vernon, the Ghost Fleet of Mallows Bay, the Great Cross of St. Clement's Island. They sailed to St. Mary's, or St. Michael's, or Annapolis. Arriving at their moorage, they would spend an afternoon exploring some early colonial town. A late dinner followed, often oysters or crabs caught by the local fishermen.

The Captain would lecture his children on the history of the places they passed. Often, he pointed out this or that location where some ancestor lived or came ashore. His daughter Mary could never resist pointing out historic discrepancies in his narratives. His daughter Martha could never resist pointing out that some of their ancestors had come ashore as colonists and some as slaves. Still, they indulged his love of sailing.

Anna too indulged him. He would have forgiven her if she had refused to participate in any more sailing or swimming vacations, but she never opposed his wishes. Once, she had shown a certain humorous acceptance of his nautical hobbies; now she went with him with a kind of grim determination. She was there to keep the children safe.

He could see the dock and knew the boat was secure, but he could not shake a feeling of unease.

He returned to tossing and turning in his chair, but now his mind drifted to Avarhouse's Luger. He wondered if anyone could have seen him hide it in the boat. He tried to remember if he had cleared the pistol. He wondered if he had left on the safety. As he struggled to fall asleep, he kept seeing in his mind's eye the eagles embossed on the pistol's frame, swastikas in their talons. He remembered the feel the pistol in his hand.

Entitled, The Family of Imran; Revealed at Medina:

As for the unbelievers, their wealth shall not profit them at all, neither their children, against GOD: they shall be the companions of hell fire; they shall continue therein forever.

The likeness of that which they lay out in this present life, is as a wind wherein there is a scorching cold: it falleth on the standing corn of those men who have injured their own souls, and destroyeth it. And GOD dealeth not unjustly with them; but they injure their own souls.

The Koran, Chapter III, The Family of Imran; translated by George Sales, 1734.

CHAPTER-24 – MOTHER, DAUGHTER, AND DRONES

Monday, Day Eight: Below Guntersville

The General waited for day's end before resuming the march. An overcast sky had turned to a driving rainstorm that obscured the sun. He considered starting early and walking in the rain and haze but decided it would be better to start later in case they needed the protection of night. Waiting also gave time for his patrols to return. While he waited the General kept the scarecrows busy.

He did not allow them to simply find resting places as before. Instead, he had them dig trenches. He also had one of the rapid-fire guns mounted on an adjacent hilltop, hidden, but with a clear field of fire.

After several hours of waiting in the forest, he heard a disturbance to the rear. The General walked back to see if he could find out why.

The Reverend and his group of wolves had returned with a dozen civilians. The Reverend told him they had walked confidently through the morning. The storm and dark glasses had shielded their eyes; their bodies had been shielded by hostages. The General could see that several of the civilians had been wounded. All appeared to be exhausted trying to keep pace with the wolves through a cold and driving rain.

The Reverend also had discarded his rags and wore a new set of clothes. Unfortunately, he had some difficulty finding a pair of trousers to fit. He looked like an undertaker with a fear of flooding. The General noted the scent of fresh blood on the Reverend and many of the wolves.

Green-Black kept his distance from the Reverend, "I will not go.... with him again."

When the General asked what he meant by this, Green-Black refused to offer anything more.

Within two hours of the Reverend's return, the Sailor and his wolves returned. Best of all, the Sailor pointed to two additional rapid-firing cannons and tins full of bullets.

"We attacked the armory. We could not get in and lost four, but in the yard were two armored cars with machine guns and ammo. Would have gotten the armored cars, but nobody knew how to work them but the soldier, and he got shot first. Tried to get them to start, but it's not like driving a car.

"The men in the armory were waiting for us. They had a wire fence with barbed wire. Some of us cut a way in. That soldier and a couple of others tried climbing. They got hung up in the wire. Men in the armory chewed them up firing with their rifles.

"We got in among the armored cars and took two machine guns. We tried to get the doors open to the armory. There weren't many soldiers there. They kept shooting like they'd never run out of bullets."

As the General heard the Sailor's report, he looked over the rapid-fire guns and the green cans filled with ammunition. He shook the Sailor by the hand, "Whip 'em now ... fo-wah sho-wah."

When they told Green-Black that his companion had been shot attacking the armory, he commented, "Serves him right."

The flying gunships came at noon. They could hear the sound of the engines as they came swooping in towards the forest. The gunships hovered over the treetops.

The storm made it impossible to see clearly into the sky, so the Sailor began to blindly fire the big guns towards the sounds of the engines. The General did not believe they gained any hits, but the enemy kept their distance.

Suddenly, the gunships began to empty their cannons into the woods at an unbelievable rate. Dirt, and leaves, and tree branches flew into the air as the gunships raked the woods, back and forth, back and forth. None could stand against the stream of bullets.

The scarecrows huddled in their holes. Even the Sailor abandoned his guns and dropped down into a hole. One scarecrow's head exploded as he stood to look up, a case of inopportune curiosity.

After firing countless bullets into the woods, the gunships left.

The General waited anxiously the remainder of the day for them to return. He willed the sun to speed its track across the sky. His inability to move, while the enemy could maneuver freely, worried him to distraction.

The General watched a group of stragglers stumbling down the road. They had wrapped cloths around their eyes. They walked down the road sensing, rather than seeing, their path. Their bare feet slapped the wet surface as they walked. When the stragglers drew near, scarecrows called out to them and they happily moved into the darkness of the wood.

The Sailor brought the General's attention to two of the stragglers. "They were shot down during the warehouse gunfight."

"How'd they find us?" the General asked.

"They've been following the looted homesteads."

"How'd they avoid the Army?"

"They didn't. They claim there were more of them at the start."

As soon as the sun went down, the General had the scarecrows on their feet moving east. Even with the coming of darkness, he felt the need to hurry away from their last resting place. As they marched, the Sailor told him there was no need to fear; the airplanes could not see them in the darkness.

It was Green-Black who gave the General pause. "Not true ... They can see at night ... good as day."

The soldier spoke clearly enough, but his words were combined with a series of pauses and hiccups as he struggled with diction. The General made him stand a few paces away. His hard, black, leathery skin had not yet begun to emerge from beneath the pasty surface sloughing away.

"How do they see ... in the dark?"

"Night vision goggle.... They got eyes in the sky.... They can see now.... They can hit ... anytime."

The scarecrows walked facing the driving rain as dumb and mindless as cattle. The General remembered other marches, men huddled around fires, men sleeping beneath thin blankets, hundreds of men coughing, coughing, and dying of fevers.

The Scarecrows hurried east, sometimes on the road, sometimes close to the river and woods. Every few hours something would startle them, and they would scatter into the darkness.

The General urged the scarecrows to hurry. He knew that as soon as the sun rose it would be difficult to continue the march. Many of the scarecrows still lacked the means of shading their eyes from bright sunlight. If required, they could go forward. Shade to light, shade to light, but they would stumble over every tree root or bit of debris, unable to keep a straight line.

Fewer engines traveled the roads at night, but those that did were now mostly in pairs. At one point, engines could be heard approaching and the scarecrows walking on the road sprinted for cover. This caused a large buck deer to spring from the woods and out onto the road. The buck was struck by the lead engine and tossed to the side. The engine continued to head down the road without stopping, despite a clanking noise that indicated the impact had caused some damage. The injured deer lay on the side of the road with the debris from the collision.

The first scarecrows ran up and dug their nails into the wounds of the deer; they licked the blood from their fingers, once, twice, then they turned and walked away. More scarecrows came to the place where the deer lay. They too reached out to touch the deer. They gathered blood in their hands and tasted, but it seemed more a matter of curiosity than desire. They showed none of the wild frenzy at the scent and taste of blood that the General had seen before.

The General now walked over to the dying deer. He could smell the blood in the air, but the tang lacked the sweetness he had noted with the blood of the prisoners. Broken bones protruded from the skin of the deer and rivulets of blood ran to the ground. The General tentatively reached forward and touched the deer. The General tasted the blood that stained his fingertips. For just a moment, it calmed the thing that twisted in his gut. The blood had a bitter taste. There was a wild energy in it, but no sorrow, no mourning, no grief, no sweetness. The General stayed to watch the deer as it died, but he learned nothing.

Marching east, the General made sure that the civilians were kept well mixed among the scarecrows. He could see the greedy, hungry look of the scarecrows. He ordered that no harm come to the civilians and made sure all understood the threat. He resented the need but explained his reasoning. "The Army will blast us from the sky… Keep the civilians safe…. If they air safe, we air safe."

Several times the flying gunships were heard overhead. The scarecrows gathered the civilians tightly to themselves. The gunships left them in peace.

Several times the droning of invisible machines was heard in the sky. The General looked up into the night but could not find the source; it sounded like millions of mosquitoes. Green-Black identified the machines as drones. The scarecrows carefully bunched up with the civilians and no attacks took place.

The General remembered a time in the war when, to clear the roads of torpedoes, the Yankees had marched prisoners ahead of their troops. Troopers had proven reluctant to plant bombs for the Yankees, knowing those most likely killed would be their friends. The General consoled himself that this was no different, a matter of necessity. The civilian shields provided a service for the scarecrows; the scarecrows, in turn, had an incentive to keep the civilians safe.

Certain practical problems became evident with this strategy. The civilians could not march nearly as fast as the scarecrows. They became fatigued much easier than the General's troops. They could not see well in the dark and constantly tripped and fell. The civilians had to be rested, fed, and watered.

Providing for the civilians might have proven impossible, but one of the scarecrows came forward and took charge. The others called her Nurse. She constantly sent out runners to search any houses or stores they passed for food and water for the civilians. She made sure that each civilian had a blanket and other necessities. She also carried a switch made from a tree branch. She used her switch vigorously to keep the civilians moving forward. In her other hand, she carried a club made from a large tree root. If any of the scarecrows came too near her wards, she did not hesitate to strike.

The civilians moved forward like a slave train. Any who fell behind found themselves at first cajoled and then whipped. In addition to Nurse's ministrations with her switch, the civilians had other reasons to keep up.

One civilian, an old man, fell to earth. When he could not be persuaded or whipped back to his feet, Nurse and the other civilians continued to march and passed him by as he lay in the road.

The General halted the march just out of sight of the fallen gentlemen. He had the civilians rest. While they rested, scarecrows scurried back to where the old man had been abandoned.

When the screaming started, the General called out to the crowd of civilians, "That's the last ta be heard … from them that won't keep up."

Walking through the night, they came to a place where four scarecrows had been executed. Their heads had been cut off and shoved on sharpened stakes. The heads formed a barrier across the path in the woods. What was left had been dumped nearby. An effort had been made to burn the remains. The bonfire still smoked and smelled of burned flesh and burned leaves.

The General made sure that the march came close to the barrier. He pointed to the staked heads as his scarecrows passed by, "That's what happens … ta them who don't keep up." He noted with satisfaction less wandering and straggling thereafter.

A mother and daughter, captured during one of the earlier fights, had trouble keeping up with the scarecrows. The mother had been injured, a bite to the arm. When the woman's strength flagged, the daughter begged her to keep walking. She took her mother's good arm and draped it across her shoulders. She helped her mother walk, then she dragged her, and then she almost carried her. She coaxed, first gently, then angrily, then viciously. When her mother continued to fall, the daughter struck at her and cursed at her. She yelled at her to get up.

The General wondered if this was a stratagem, to make her mother so angry that she would find some last reserve. The General had seen such things before with soldiers, but the woman was not a soldier. When her daughter cursed her, she seemed to lose any remnant of strength. Finally, the scarecrows forced the daughter to move on with the others.

Scarecrows who had been marching well, now found excuses to fall back. Soon shrieks and the sound of struggle could be heard. The screaming could be heard for some distance.

It appeared the woman had found some last vestige of strength after all.

The General watched the scarecrows as they returned. Several were bloody. He took a deep breath and called out to the civilians, "Remember … them who don't keep up."

APPENDIX 1

CHAPTER- Notes on Military Terminology:

1MC - 1 Main Circuit, term used for the shipboard public address circuit on United States Navy and United States Coast Guard vessels.

ACU - The Army Combat Uniform is the current combat uniform worn by the United States Army. It is the successor to the Battle Dress Uniform (BDU) and Desert Camouflage Uniform (DCU) worn during the 1980s and 1990s.

ANFO - Ammonium Nitrate and Fuel Oil, a typical explosive mix used in Improvised Explosive Devices (IED).

ATHWARTSHIP - At a right angle to the centerline, a passageway that runs from port to starboard as opposed to fore and aft.

BIG EYES - Oversized ship's binoculars mounted to the deck. Usually located on the signal bridge.

BILGE - The void between the ship's inner and outer hulls, or the lowest point of a ship's inner hull. Also a derogatory term.

BOATSWAIN, BOSUN, BOS'N - Senior rating of the deck department, responsible for the ship's decks and hull.

BOONDOCKERS - Ankle height, steel-toed boots, formerly Navy issued.

BUPERS - Navy Personnel Command, (Bureau of Personnel), administrative leadership, policy planning, and general oversight.

CIC - Combat Information Center. Generally, the electronic brain of a US Navy ship. For a Navy combatant ship, the tactical combat center; for a Navy support ship, a supplemental navigation and communication center assisting operations.

CHOW - Food.

CHILL STORAGE/FREEZER STOREROOM - Refrigerator space on Navy Ship. Responsibility of supply/food services.

CIVMARs - Civilian Mariners, sailors contracted by Military Sea Lift Command (MSC) to supplement naval crew on ships providing logistical support to the fleet.

DECK - Shipboard floors below the main deck are described as "decks" numbered 1, 2, 3, etc.

FANTAIL - The after end of the main deck.

FIRST LIEUTENANT - Officer in charge of the deck department or division.

FLASH - Military message of extreme urgency. FLASH messages are to be handled as fast as possible, ahead of all other messages.

FOB - Forward Operating Base.

FORECASTLE, FO'C'SLE - Forward section of the deck on which the anchor handling equipment is located.

GANGWAY - An opening in the bulwark or lifeline that provides access to a brow or accommodation ladder; when shouted, means to get out of the way.

GEAR LOCKER - A storage room.

HESCO MIL - Modern gabion used for military fortifications. It is made of a collapsible wire mesh container and heavy-duty fabric liner filled with dirt and gravel.

IOTV - Improved Outer Tactical Vest, i.e. bulletproof vest.

JAGMAN - JAG Manual. Navy manual that gives detailed instructions on when and how to prepare incident investigations.

JLTV - Joint Light Tactical Vehicle (JLTV) developed during the Iraq War to defend against improvised explosive devices (IEDs) being used by insurgents.

LEVEL - Shipboard floors above the main deck. Numbered 01, 02, 03, etc.

LIFELINE - Lines erected around the weather decks of a ship to prevent personnel from falling or being washed over the side.

LNCS - Senior Chief Legalman.

LN2 - Legalman Rating, Second Class Petty Officer.

M4, M16 - Standard US/DOD Military Carbine and Military Rifle, both firing caliber 5.56mm NATO round.

M9 - Standard US/DOD Pistol, Beretta, firing 9mm Parabellum round.

MA1 - Master-at-Arms, First Class Petty Officer.

MACM - Master Chief Master-at-Arms.

MAIN DECK - Highest watertight deck running bow to stern on a ship. Shipboard floors below the main deck are described as "decks" numbered 1, 2, 3, etc. Partial shipboard floors below the main deck are described as "platforms." Shipboard floors above the main deck are described as "levels," 01, 02, 03, etc.

MARPAT - Marine Pattern Camouflage uniform.

M-ATV - The M-ATV is a Mine Resistant Ambush Protected (MRAP) All-Terrain Vehicle. It is designed to provide the same levels of protection as the larger and heavier MRAPs but with improved mobility.

MESS DUTY - In the US Navy, a 90-day obligated duty working on the mess decks when first reporting aboard. Sometimes derogatory term, (aka MESS-CRANK'N).

MIDRATS - Midnight Rations, meal served around midnight for those crewmembers going on or off the Midwatch, (The Mid), the watch which begins at 0000 and usually ends at 0400.

MOLLE GEAR - Modular Lightweight Load-Carrying Equipment.

MRAP, (also MAXXPRO) - Vehicles: Mine-Resistant Ambush Protected (MRAP) is a United States military vehicle designed to withstand improvised explosive device (IED) attacks and ambushes. To combat growing numbers of IEDs being used against US forces during the Iraq War and War in Afghanistan, the Department of Defense developed MRAP vehicles, including the M-ATV for use in Afghanistan. While MRAPs offered superior protection from underbody blasts, they were large and heavy and with poor off-road mobility often resulting in vehicular roll-overs.

MRE - Meals Ready to Eat, military field rations, high in calories, and with an extremely long shelf life. Easily carried to and prepared in the field, packages include meals, sides, and snacks, as well as a chemical heater to warm the entrée.

MSC - Military Sealift Command.

NCIS - Naval Criminal Investigation Service, primary law enforcement agency for the US Navy, responsible for investigating all felony criminal matters relevant to the Navy, among other duties.

NON-SKID - On Navy ships, a gray textured paint that provides traction on the weather decks of a ship.

NWU - Navy Working Uniform - Type II & III. Utility Uniform, with multiple pockets on the shirt and trousers, uses a multi-color digital print pattern similar to those introduced by other services.

The NWU has three variants: Type I, predominantly blue with some gray developed for shipboard use; Type II, a desert digital pattern currently used by sailors assigned to Naval Special Warfare Units in desert environments; and Type III, a woodland digital pattern for sailors in expeditionary units.

NVD - Night Vision Device.

OBA - Oxygen Breath Apparatus.

OPREP-3 NAVY BLUE - Messages used to provide the Chief of Naval Operations (CNO), and other naval commanders, notification of incidents that are of high Navy interest.

OOD - Officer of the deck.

OPNAVINST - Operational Naval Instruction.

OJAG - Office of the Judge Advocate General.

PIR - Passive Infrared Receiver.

PLATFORMS - A partial deck below the lowest complete deck, numbered First-Platform, Second-Platform, etc.

POSSE COMITATUS - The Posse Comitatus Act is United States federal law (18 U.S.C. § 1385, original at 20 Stat. 152) signed on June 18, 1878, by President Rutherford B. Hayes. The purpose of the act was to limit the powers of the federal government in using military personnel to act as domestic law enforcement personnel.

QUARTERDECK - The shipboard area, connected by a gangplank to a dock or another ship, where personnel arrive and depart a naval vessel in port. It is where the Officer of the Deck, (OOD) is stationed while at anchor, official visitors received, and ceremonies conducted.

RACK - Bed.

REFRIGERATED STOREROOM - aka Reefers, a refrigerated space on a Navy Ship. Responsibility of supply/food services department.

RLSO - Regional Legal Service Office, provides legal services in a particular region including trial counsel, command services, and legal assistance.

SCBA - Acronym for self-contained breathing apparatus.

SCUTTLE - Round, watertight opening in a hatch.

SCUTTLEBUTT - Rumor or gossip, deriving from the nautical term for open, "scuttled," cask of water, "butt," that became a place for sailors to meet and gossip on a sailing ship.

SEA AND ANCHOR DETAIL - Best qualified sailors to handle Navy ship as she leaves or enters port. Mainly consists of the navigator, quartermasters, helmsman, and line handlers.

SEAL - Acronym for Sea Air and Land. Naval Special Warfare unit trained for unconventional warfare.

SECOND DECK - Next deck below the main deck.

SECURE - (1) - To make fast, as to secure a line to a cleat; (2) - To cease, as to secure from a fire drill.

SICKBAY - Shipboard space used as a hospital or medical center.

SKUNK - Surface contact.

SJA - Staff Judge Advocate.

SOUND-POWERED PHONES - Ship phone system that operates on voice power and requires no batteries or external electrical power source.

SPACE - A room or a compartment onboard ship.

SQUARE AWAY - To put in the proper place, to make things shipshape.

STATEROOM - An officer's room or living quarters onboard a ship.

TOPSIDE - General term referring to a ship's weather deck, i.e. a deck fully exposed to the exterior weather.

TV-DTS - Television Direct-to-Sailors, Armed Forces Radio and Television System programing worldwide via global satellite.

UA - Navy term for "Unauthorized Absence." Less serious than the charge of Desertion. Equivalent to Army "AWOL," absent without leave.

UCMJ - Uniform Code of Military Justice.

UCMJ, ARTICLE 21 ON MILITARY COMMISSIONS - The provisions of this chapter conferring jurisdiction upon courts-martial do not deprive military commissions, provost courts, or other military tribunals of concurrent jurisdiction with respect to offenders or offenses that by statute or by the law of war may be tried by military commissions, provost courts, or other military tribunals.

WATCH STANDING - Traditional, time and type for three-section watch:

    0000 to 0400 Midwatch

    0400 to 0800 Morning watch

    0800 to 1200 Forenoon watch

    1200 to 1600 Afternoon watch

    1600 to 1800 First dog watch

    1800 to 2000 Second dog watch

    2000 to 2400 Evening watch

WEATHER DECK - External portion of a deck exposed to the weather/elements.

XOI - Executive Officer's Inquiry, preliminary to referring a sailor to Captain's Mast/Article 15 of the UCMJ. Personnel embarked on a US Naval vessel have no right to refuse mast.

J.R. Reagan

Common Ratings for Surface Sailors, United States Navy:

Rate	Abbreviation
Boatswain's mate	BM
Damage controlmen	DC
Electrician's mate	EM
Electronics technicians	ET
Enginemen	EN
Fire controlmen	FC
Gas turbine system technician	GS
Gunner's mate	GM
Hospital corpsmen	HM
Hull maintenance technician	HT
Interior communications electrician	IC
Information systems	IT
Legalmen	LN
Logistics specialists	LS
Machinery repairmen	MR
Machinist's mate	MM
Masters-at-arms	MA
Navy counselors	NC
Operations specialist	OS
Personnel specialist	PS
Quartermaster	QM
Religious program specialist	RP
Retail Services Specialist	RS
Yeomen	YN

*Poem: On Passing Deadman's Island, Thomas Moore, 1804

Written On Passing Deadman's Island, In The Gulf Of St. Lawrence, Late In The Evening, September, 1804

    See you, beneath yon cloud so dark,
    Fast gliding along a gloomy bark?
    Her sails are full,--though the wind is still,
    And there blows not a breath her sails to fill!

    Say, what doth that vessel of darkness bear?
    The silent calm of the grave is there,
    Save now and again a death-knell rung,
    And the flap of the sails with night-fog hung.

    There lieth a wreck on the dismal shore
    Of cold and pitiless Labrador;
    Where, under the moon, upon mounts of frost,
    Full many a mariner's bones are tost.

    Yon shadowy bark hath been to that wreck,
    And the dim blue fire, that lights her deck,
    Doth play on as pale and livid a crew,
    As ever yet drank the churchyard dew.

J.R. Reagan

To Deadman's Isle, in the eye of the blast,
To Deadman's Isle, she speeds her fast
By skeleton shapes her sails are furled,
And the hand that steers is not of this world!

Oh! hurry thee on-oh! hurry thee on,
Thou terrible bark, ere the night be gone,
Nor let morning look on so foul a sight
As would blanch for ever her rosy light!

Made in the USA
Middletown, DE
24 August 2020